FIREWORKS

FIREWORKS

ELIZABETH HARTLEY WINTHROP

ALFRED A. KNOPF   NEW YORK   2006

THIS IS A BORZOI BOOK
PUBLISHED BY ALFRED A. KNOPF

Copyright © 2006 by Elizabeth Hartley Winthrop

Published in the United States by Alfred A. Knopf,
a division of Random House, Inc., New York, and in Canada
by Random House of Canada Limited, Toronto.

www.aaknopf.com

Knopf, Borzoi Books, and the colophon are registered
trademarks of Random House, Inc.

Library of Congress Cataloging-in-Publication Data
Winthrop, Elizabeth Hartley, [date].
Fireworks / by Elizabeth Hartley Winthrop.—1st ed.
p. cm.
ISBN 0-307-26295-2 (alk. paper)—ISBN 1-4000-9697-9
(pbk. : alk. paper) 1. Authors—Fiction. 2. Solitude—Fiction.
3. Suburban life—Fiction. 4. Social isolation—Fiction.
5. Loss (Psychology)—Fiction. 6. Rejection (Psychology)—
Fiction. 7. Summer—Fiction. I. Title.
PS3623.I7F57 2006
813'.6—dc22   2005049445

This is a work of fiction. Names, characters, places, and
incidents either are the product of the author's imagination or
are used fictitiously. Any resemblance to actual persons, living
or dead, events, or locales is entirely coincidental.

Manufactured in the United States of America
First Edition

FIREWORKS

1

FIREWORKS

When my grandfather died, I told everyone he'd been killed by aborigines while he was berry-picking in Africa. I told them that I had been there, too. I told this to my friends, and to their parents. I told this to the lifeguard at our neighborhood pool. I told this to the gas station attendants and motel clerks my father and I met on our drive down to Florida for the funeral. I wrote about it in a letter to my mother, who had left us that spring to live in a commune upstate. I was picturing dry, open fields, the occasional crooked tree under which a lion might have lounged or beside which a giraffe might have stood with his neck stretched to reach the topmost leaves. I was picturing jeepfuls of tribal rivals speeding around with shotguns, like what I'd seen in *The Gods Must Be Crazy*, my poor grandfather in the line of fire, myself lying flat in hiding behind a log.

This was during my safari phase. My wife found a picture of me from around this time up in the attic just the other day. She brought it downstairs to show it to me. I was sitting on the porch with a Jack Daniel's, enjoying the sunset. "You were adorable," she said. In the picture, I'm wearing khaki trousers that unzip into shorts around the thigh. I've got a khaki vest on, and a safari hat. There's a stuffed monkey pinned to the back of my pants, and a plastic snake hung around my neck. I'm carrying a small pair of binoculars, and there's chocolate on my face. I got a little chill when my wife showed me the picture, even though it was June. "Mmm," I said. "I'm not so cute."

My name is Hollis. I'm a writer, and I live with my wife in a midsize, coastal New England town. My wife is a teacher. We have no children. We did, but our son, Simon, was killed nearly two years ago by a bunch of kids in a speeding car.

I've been cheating on my wife. My girlfriend, Marissa, is twenty-four, almost fifteen years younger than I am. I met her ten months ago at a bus stop when I was on my way to a meeting with my editor. It was raining, neither of us had an umbrella, and the buses were running late, so instead of waiting we shared a cab, which we quickly redirected from our respective destinations to her apartment. We've spent hours there together every afternoon since then. Some might consider me lucky. But oftentimes, as I'm drifting in and out of sleep in the late afternoon light, I feel lonely. I feel like I'm being rolled around in a huge wave of loneliness. When Marissa asks me what's wrong, I don't say anything about it, because who am I to be lonely? I have Marissa, I have my wife, and I know they both love me. I am never alone.

I went through phases as a kid. I was a fireman for a while. My uncle really was a fireman, so I had the real stuff from him: helmet, gloves, charred bricks from burned-down buildings. I was Robin Hood. I wore the tights only on Halloween, but I carried a bow and arrows around for months. For a while I was a break-dancer. I wore a bandanna and a single black leather glove with the fingers cut off.

"A safari phase," my wife said when she showed me the picture. "I don't think I knew about that one."

"It was brief." I shifted in my chair so I could better see the sunset. I sipped my Jack Daniel's.

My wife stood behind me and ran her fingers through my hair.

Marissa is standing in my wife's kitchen. That's how I think of it when I see Marissa bending to open the cabinets that my wife bends to open, or leaning against the countertops my wife leans against. I watch her in my wife's apron, using my wife's utensils to make us dinner before the fireworks start downtown. She looks up and sees me staring.

"What?" she says.

I shake my head. My wife has gone to spend the Fourth of July with her old college roommate, and so the house is mine alone. This is only the second time Marissa has been here. She seems unbothered by it.

"Is this you?" she asks. My wife has hung the photograph of me in my safari gear on the refrigerator. I nod.

"On my way to Florida, for my grandfather's funeral," I say. "Do you believe I wore that to the actual funeral?"

Marissa smiles and shakes her head. She takes the photograph from the refrigerator door and holds it between the tips of her fingers, just like my wife did.

When my grandfather died, he died suddenly, of a massive stroke. My father decided to drive down to Florida for the funeral, and since he had no one to leave me with, he brought me with him, even though I'd never even met my grandparents.

What I remember most about the drive are the bugs. The farther south we drove, the thicker the clouds of them became, these humming throngs of insects that hovered over the highway and smacked against the windshield as our car plowed through them. And I remember once waking up at a gas station to a sound I couldn't immediately identify. I was in the front seat of the car, alone. Out the side window I could see gas pumps, air pumps, diesel tanks, oil cans. I'd unzipped my safari pants into shorts, and my skin was stuck to the leather of the seat. Ridges of upholstery had set patterns into the backs of my thighs.

The windshield was near opaque with the blood and smear of bugs, and I soon realized that the scratching sound was the sound of a knife against the windshield's glass. As the glass cleared, I could watch my father as he scratched at the glass. His forearms were ridged with muscle, and hairy, and in his hand the knife he used to clear the windshield looked small. I shifted my weight from one side to the other, peeling my skin from where it seemed to have melted into the seat.

"Stroke," I say when Marissa asks me how my grandfather died. "I didn't know him." I shrug. "His wake was the first time I'd ever seen him," I say.

It was the first time I'd met my grandmother, too. When my father and I pulled in to her driveway, it was dusk. We went through the kitchen door and found her sitting at the kitchen table with a rocks glass filled with vodka and milk on ice. There was a slant of evening light coming through the small window above the sink and falling on her hands. I remember staring at the way the light made the webs of skin between her knuckles glow translucent, and I remember the way it glinted in her rings. She wore four rings on one finger, a column of ruby, diamond, emerald, sapphire.

She looked up as we walked through the door. "Mom," my father said.

She lifted her glass to her lips and took a sip. "Who are you?" she said.

I watch Marissa, on tiptoe reaching for a bottle of wine from the rack above the fridge. She is small. Her fingers just reach the nose of a bottle when she really stretches, and she's trying to coax it out one reach at a time so that maybe she can get a good grip on it. I go up behind her and take the bottle down, and she turns so that we are facing each other, very close, her face against my chest. I pause, not because I don't like the feel of Marissa against me, but because this posture was not what I intended. I helped her with the wine so that the bottle wouldn't fall and break, not so that we could be close. Her breath is hot against my chest and she runs her hands down my sides.

It is moments like these that make me feel lonely.

She looks up at me. "What?" she says.

I shake my head and bend to kiss her hair. "Nothing," I say.

"Where would I find a wine opener?" she says.

"Drawer to the left of the sink," I say. She plants a kiss on my chest and steps out from between me and the refrigerator, leaving me face-to-face with myself, safari style.

We were in Florida for ten days. The heat was unlike anything I'd experienced before. My cousins hung off the dock at the lake below my grandparents' house, but I'd seen snakes in that water, so I opted not to join them. I told anyone who asked that I simply was not hot. It would have been a betrayal of my safari persona to admit that snakes could scare me.

I also stayed away from the house, where my aunts helped my grandmother rummage through my grandfather's old things, and where uncles muttered around the kitchen table about what should become of the house, of the property, of my grandmother. My cousin Toby, who was four or five years older than I was and who lived with his mother, my father's only sister, across the street from my grandparents, told me that they wanted to lock my grandmother up, her three sons. He said they thought she was crazy and a drunk. "She's not," he said, slapping a mosquito from his leg with a towel. "I think I would know better than them. I live here, unlike you dumb Yankees." He flung his towel around his neck and ran down to the lake, and I watched him as he cannonballed himself into the water, snakes and all.

I spent a good amount of time in the old storage shed, spinning the wheel of an overturned bicycle and listening to the hum of the spokes when it got going fast.

I spent a good amount of time at work on the tree behind the shed, peeling away the bark and carving words and pictures in the smooth wood beneath.

Then there was my grandmother's car. It was an old car with fins, and it was shiny blue. The seats were green leather and so wide that I could stretch myself out fully on them. My grandmother was in the habit of taking a drive early each morning, maybe because it was the only time she was sober enough to do so, and I guess so she wouldn't lose them she always left the keys in the car. I'd turn them in the ignition partway and listen to the radio for hours at a time. Sometimes, I would lie down and stare at the material drooping from the ceiling as I listened, or up through the window at the sky and trees, all upside down from my angle. Other times, I sat in the backseat and pretended I had a chauffeur. Best, though, was taking the wheel myself and driving through the African brush, dodging killer rhinos and tigers. Best was speeding across the desert plains, kicking up plumes of dust that would hover, then settle and cover my tracks so that the aborigines hunting me down wouldn't know which way I'd gone. Best was hunting for lion and zebra with my loyal dog eagerly peering over my shoulder and sniffing the air as we drove.

My loyal dog was Max, my grandmother's bloodhound. Max was a big, silly dog. His skin had settled in loose rings around his neck, and his jowls drooped an inch below his mouth. His lips slung spit when he turned his head. His ears were like velvet. I liked Max okay. Whenever I drank from my bottle of water, I poured some into my hands for him to drink, too, despite his refusal to play the role of safari hunting dog. He didn't sniff the air or peer over my shoulder when I piled him into the car; he lay drooling in the backseat, his paws hanging over the seat's edge and his eyebrows twitching with dreams. Sometimes I forgot he was even there.

"Such an odd child," my wife said as she stood behind me, stroking my hair. "Although you haven't changed that much with age." She said it fondly, and then she came around and sat on the arm of my chair. "I wonder if your phases ever stopped." The sun was getting red. "Am I just a phase, too, then?" she said, after a minute.

"Don't say that," I said, and I put my arm around her waist.

"No," she said. "No, I don't really mean it."

Marissa and I are buzzed with wine when we finally sit down to dinner.

"We have to eat kind of fast," she says. "The fireworks are in an hour."

I nod and carry our plates outside. She's set the table on the porch so we can watch the sunset as we eat. She brings another bottle of wine out with her.

"Do you know I killed my grandmother's dog?" I say.

Marissa looks up at me. She doesn't look surprised or horrified; just curious. This is one of the reasons I like her. "On purpose?" she says.

"No," I say. "No, I liked Max. That was his name. Max."

"What happened?" she says.

"Locked him in the car," I say. "He was sleeping back there, and I forgot about him. He boiled to death," I say.

"You mean he overheated," Marissa says. She takes a bite of her food.

I shrug. "He overheated." I pour us both more wine. "God, it was pretty awful," I say.

"I can imagine," Marissa says, but she can't. She can't possibly imagine me and my father, early risers, up at the breakfast table the morning we were meant to leave. She can't imagine the look on my grandmother's face as she walked through the kitchen door, terrified, defeated.

"What, forget your keys?" my father said.

She sat down at the table and stared at her hands. They were shaking. "I think I've done something terrible. Oh God!" she moaned, and shut her eyes.

"What is it?" my father said, putting down his fork.

"The car," she said, not opening her eyes.

I followed my father outside to my grandmother's car. She had left the front door open, and I could smell the smell of Max before I could actually see him. He was in the backseat, where I'd left him. His legs were crumpled beneath him, his front paws pointed on their toes. His head was bent back weirdly, so that the whole of his neck was pressed against the material beneath the window, his nose just inches from the nose-smeared glass.

"Shit," my father shook his head. I stared.

"Hey," Marissa says.

I look up at her.

"You okay?"

I nod.

"I ran over a cat once. It was horrible. And the owner saw it happen. She was signaling to me to get me to stop, but I didn't get it, and I kept going. You could hear the crunch of the bones." She shudders and sips her wine. "Let's talk about something else before we lose our appetites. I worked too hard on this goddamn fish not to eat it."

I nod, and I pick up my fork, but I'm not hungry at all. I wasn't really hungry to begin with. I stare at the sun and think about Max dead in the car, the smell of him, the way he must have been pressing his nose against that glass for air until the minute that he died. Losing air must be a painful process until all of it is gone; what air you have left reminds you of the air you don't, of the air you used to have. Maybe losing your mind is like that, too.

My father and I left later than we'd planned that day. I carved my name over and over again into the tree behind the shed while my father buried Max and talked to my uncles about what had happened, and around dinnertime, we left to go.

They sold my grandparents' house soon after that, and my grandmother moved into a home.

"That's cruel," I said. "Toby said she's not nuts, and he would know."

"No," my father said. "This is the best thing for her."

"I don't think she's nuts either," I said. "Anyone would have forgotten about Max, that dumb dog."

My father looked at me strangely. "It wasn't just about what happened to Max," he said. These words were like a life raft. They were like light. They were like air when you've been suffocating. I clung to them.

It's packed down at the fireworks. People are pressed together, arm to arm to back to chest. You can feel the roar of voices. Marissa holds on to my arm. We are drunk.

As soon as the fireworks begin, I know something is wrong. The noise of takeoff is followed not by a brilliant umbrella of color exploding above our heads, but by shrieks and sudden light among us. The fireworks are hitting the pier's huge dangling neon sign that reads "Happy Fourth" and ricocheting back into the crowd. People rush in every direction, grabbing their kids, pushing others out of their way. I grab Marissa and we stand behind a tree near the edge of the emptying square.

"Let's just get out of here," Marissa says.

"We're fine here," I say. "I want to watch." I peer out into the square. There are two people being tended to by paramedics and a few stragglers crossing the square, but otherwise, most people have fled. The explosions are coming more rapidly, now; fuses are catching unleashed fire, and men silhouetted by sparks and smoke are rushing around the firing ground, trying to contain the uncontrolled display. But the fireworks keep coming, rebounding off the sign to dance in wild explosions against the concrete of the sidewalk, one brilliant ball of colored fire after the next. I step out from behind the tree.

"Are you crazy?" Marissa says, trying to pull me back.

I shrug her off. I stagger into the middle of the square and shut my eyes to the spinning world, to Marissa's voice calling my name, to the wail of sirens.

What I want is to walk into the middle of the square and let the fireworks explode around me. I'm hoping for something, some sense of life, something, something. I want to be hit and so cleansed. I want to be spared and so blessed.

I stand with open arms and wait, but nothing happens. The fireworks, I realize, have stopped. It's only me, now, standing opened-armed like Jesus, drunk in an empty square littered with confetti, whistles, soda cans, and candy wrappers. Someone should take a picture, I think, and I start to laugh, and laugh, and there's nothing I can do to stop.

2

FREQUENT FLIERS

Last night, after the fireworks, I called my wife at her college room-mate's house. "I need you to come home," I said. I was drunk. "Can you come home?"

"What is it?" she said.

"I don't know," I said. I heard the toilet flush in the bathroom and I knew that soon Marissa would come out. "I should go," I said, and I hung up the phone.

"You should go," I said to Marissa. "I'm sorry. My wife is com-ing home."

"Is everything okay?" Marissa said. She looked concerned. My wife was not due back for a few more days. "Is she unwell?"

"No," I said. "No, no, everything is fine." And everything was fine, in the way that it is on Christmas Eve when you're a kid and the shapes of the packages under the tree are just right and you only have to wait till morning to open them, or when you're starving in a restaurant and finally see the waiter coming toward your table, his tray stacked high with food. Everything was fine because my wife was coming home.

I met my wife eight years ago, on her doorstep at about three o'clock on a bitter January morning. She was wearing a pair of flannel pajama bottoms and a long-sleeved T-shirt with HEY written in capital letters across the front. Her hair was alive with knots. Her breath streamed from her nostrils, white with cold and dragonlike.

"Yes?" she said.

"I—, I—" I began. "Is everything okay here? Is everything okay?"

I guess if you want to look at it in terms of phases, then this was during my paramedic phase. When I went through phases as a kid, I genuinely wanted to be the thing I was obsessed with: fireman, Robin Hood, break-dancer, safari man. At age thirty, I didn't actually want to *be* a paramedic. I wanted to *write* about paramedics. I had just lost my job as columnist at the city paper; my opinions, the editor told me, were wrong. My novel about astronauts had been a flop. My editor had scrapped all but thirty pages of my fictional account of the life of J. Edgar Hoover. So I'd turned to paramedics. I thought I might well be able to write a TV show on paramedics. People like drama. They like tragedy. They like blood and death and pain, as long as it's not their own. So I started watching first-aid videotapes. I took a CPR class. I sat in on a few pre-med classes at the local college. I rode for a night with my old friend Steve, a paramedic in a town near Bangor, Maine. This was the night I met my wife.

. . .

I have a habit of calling my wife the way a child will call his father in the middle of the night if he is scared or sick, as if by his very presence the father can make demons and headaches go away. After we'd first met and I'd gone back to Massachusetts, I'd call my wife nightly and keep her on the phone for hours. Or I'd call her multiple times in a single night, to keep her updated on my thoughts. I called and called until she finally moved to where I was so we could talk in person. I called her from my father's funeral and asked her to please come and pick me up, because I didn't think I'd make it if I had to drive myself. I called her at her sister's house in Maryland when the dog I was sitting ate a candy bar. I called her from my editor's office when he said he didn't like a chapter that both she and I had considered brilliant. I call her at work all the time, whenever I'm stuck on a sentence, or when I can't concentrate, or when I have a half hour to kill until I'm supposed to meet Marissa. My wife is good to me. When I call her, she answers.

Steve worked a twenty-four-hour shift, and he'd already been working twelve of those hours when he picked me up at the train station. I hadn't seen him in five or six years. We acted glad to see each other, and maybe we were glad.

For a while, we cruised the neighborhood. Steve pointed out local landmarks: high school, library, shopping mall. He drove me by his home, where the windows were dark. He drove us over Suicide Bridge, where he said people jumped at least twice a year. "Usually in winter," he said, shaking his head. "Take a look." I did, but I couldn't make out the features of the rocky gorge he said was two hundred feet below. All I could see was funneling blackness. "Jesus," I said. I stepped away from the railing.

We got take-out burgers and fries and parked on a side street to eat them. As we ate, Steve told me about the first half of his shift.

"Well," he said. "I had a chest pain around ten this morning. That's the usual peak time for cardiacs. And I had a few transports, you know, nursing home to hospital, hospital to nursing home. And my frequent flier called."

"Frequent flier?"

"Yeah. It's funny, there's this group of people scattered throughout the world who feel compelled to call for an ambulance daily, or almost daily. This is for months and years on end. Frequent fliers."

"Hypochondriacs?"

"I don't know if I'd call them that. I think they just might be lonely. After a while, though, you stop taking them seriously. That's always the time when the shoulder pain really is a heart attack."

As soon as Marissa left last night, I sat down at the kitchen table with a bottle of Jack Daniel's and a glass full of ice. I thought about the fireworks, about the noise and the light and the way the sputtering balls of fire had danced across the concrete, chasing the crowd away. I thought about the way I had stepped into the middle of it, hoping either to be hit or not hit, as if stepping into that mess was stepping out of myself, and how it wasn't at all. I thought about the cab ride home, how the whole way, even as I held Marissa's frightened hand, I hoped without real hope that my wife would be at home, waiting for me there. I sat with my Jack Daniel's and I waited for my wife.

We waited on that street for hours, Steve and I. The pavement was glossy with a thin layer of ice, and the street lamps cast tin-colored pools of light beneath them. I watched each infrequent person as he walked down the street, passing quietly in and out of the light of each lamp until he disappeared around the corner. In a house across the street, a man slept. I could see him through his window resting in a blue armchair, his head thrown back with sleep and a magazine tented across his chest.

Four-car pileup, Route 267, seven reported injuries, one pre-sumed fatality, get there. Call from a residence, 49 Backwater, reported stabbing, get there. We have a chest pain, 2800 Cromwell, apartment 5H, get there. Each time a voice came crackling in over the radio, my throat would tighten. The action was what I was sup-posedly there for, but when I thought about it, I didn't want any part of it. I didn't want to see the gorge into which the desperate flung themselves, and I didn't want to see the bloodstains at the intersec-tion where a boy had been squashed by an eighteen-wheeler the day before. I didn't want to see faces contorted by fear and pain. I didn't want to see bodies slack of life. And so when the dispatcher made a call and Steve only shook his head and drummed the steering wheel with his thumbs, I felt relief. "Not my district," he would explain. I stopped paying attention to the dispatcher's voice on the radio after a while, and it was soon after that that Steve suddenly threw the ambulance into gear. "That's us," he said, "let's go," and he turned on the lights and siren and we went wailing across the empty town, warning no one to get out of our way.

The ride is mostly a blur in my memory. I remember fragments. I remember thinking that we must be going very fast, because things as we passed them seemed to leave trails. I remember desperately wanting to ask Steve what the emergency was, but being somehow unable to work my jaw, like in a bad dream when you want to run but you can't. I remember thinking how sirens sound entirely differ-ent from inside an ambulance than they do from the street. I remem-ber soothing myself in the way that I did as a scared kid on a roller coaster, or sick on the bathroom floor, promising myself that it would all be over soon.

We arrived at the house in minutes. Steve sent me up to ring the doorbell and get the door open so it would be ready for the stretcher and gear he was collecting from the back of the ambulance. "Go, go, go!" he ordered. My vision tunneled as I ran up the walkway to the front door of a single-story house. I held the finger of one hand on the doorbell and pounded the door itself with my other hand. I remember gasping and nearly choking on the bitter-cold air. *Open, open, open!* I was thinking to myself. Then my wife opened the door.

There was no emergency. Maybe someone made the call as a prank, or maybe the dispatcher somehow gave the wrong address. Regardless, "Everything's fine," my wife said. "Hey, everything's fine here. Everything's okay." I stared. Steve stood behind me now, his arms full of the things that save lives. My wife's face flashed red and then white as the light atop the ambulance silently spun. She smiled.

"Really?" I said, finally.

"Really," she said. "But thank you."

Her words, like arms, encircled me. I wanted to cry. I wanted to sleep. "Thank you," I repeated.

"Sorry to bother you, ma'am," Steve said, gathering himself and starting back down the walkway.

I stayed where I was. I didn't want to return to the uncertainty of the ambulance, where at any moment I might be called upon to look at something I didn't want to see. I didn't want, quite yet, to leave this haven where I knew that things were okay. "You coming?" Steve called.

"Coming," I said. I took a breath. I was going to say something to my wife, but I didn't know what, really, to say.

I didn't know what to say to my wife this morning, either, as she stood in the kitchen doorway. Outside, she had left the car engine idling, and from where I still sat at the kitchen table I had watched her hurry up the walkway and struggle for a minute with the door before swinging it open, to find herself face-to-face with me, blurred and bleary from a night of waiting.

"What is it?" she said. "What's wrong? My God, you've had me worried!" She stood there in the doorway as if she were afraid to come close. "What?" she said. "What's wrong?"

I stared at her. I didn't know what to say. It was as if I had forgotten what was wrong, or maybe what was wrong was that she was asking me what was wrong, and what I wanted was for her to tell me everything was okay.

I try to explain this to my wife as we stand in the kitchen tonight. I have offered to cook dinner, as if to atone for needlessly summoning her home. The ends of her hair are wet from soaking neck-deep in the bath, like I know she always does. I try to tell her what she did for me that first night we met, and how I am addicted to that, that relief and comfort. It is all I have been able to come up with as an explanation for my actions.

"Do you remember?" I say. "Do you remember how panicked I was that night, standing there on your doorstep? I thought you were dead, or dying, or in trouble. I was terrified."

"You didn't even know me then," she says.

"That's not the point," I say. "You soothed me. You did something. You do something. I love you. I have too much love for you."

"I didn't really do anything at all," she says. "All I did was tell you nothing was wrong. And nothing was. But I don't know if I can tell you that anymore."

She leaves the kitchen and goes to stand on the porch. I watch her through the window as she tightens the bathrobe she is wearing around her and shakes the water out of her hair. She grabs her hair with her fist, and she shakes it, and something about the gesture, how familiar it is, my wife in her bathrobe shaking water out of her hair, pains me with a pain unlike any I've felt before. My impulse is to go to the door and call to her, to go outside and take her in my arms, but I stay where I am. I am almost afraid to call to her, because if I do, and she doesn't answer, if she doesn't turn around, then what will I do with all this love?

3

TENDERS

I fill my time these days with yard work, stories, and the bar. I haven't seen Marissa since the Fourth of July. I haven't seen my wife since then, either—or since two days after. She's gone to spend the rest of the summer with her sister in Maryland, about ten hours south of here. She says we need to be apart, for a while, if we're going to be together. She says she needs to think. I am afraid to think.

I found my father's old chainsaw in the garage a few weeks ago, and it works well to trim the hedge that edges the lawn. I found some old clippers, too, which work well for finishing touches. My wife and I had let the hedge grow tall for the summer so that we'd have more privacy when we sunbathed or grilled out on the lawn, but I figured it didn't matter now if I cut it down a bit. It's something to do. I trim it every three days, and I keep it perfectly square.

The hedge is about waist-high, now, so you can see right over it. I like it that way. I like watching people pass up and down the street in front of the house, and I like being able to look into our neighbors' yard. Our new neighbors have four children, and their yard is better than a playground. They have a swing set, a sandbox, a tree house, a trampoline. I haven't been on a trampoline in years, and oftentimes when I think no one is home I am tempted to go over there and jump awhile. They have go-carts, too. A track has been worn around the perimeter of the yard, which the kids circle endlessly, chasing one another around and around. They never catch up with one another, though, because the carts all travel at the same speed. Their shrieking delight in the pointless, impossible chase fascinates me. There is something about children that fascinates me altogether. When Simon was alive, I could watch him for hours, trying to figure it out. It is the something contained in the pause after a fall, when the child stops for a matter of a second to consider whether he will indulge himself in tears or carry on with whatever game he was playing. It is the thing like a blanket with which the child can shroud himself to find sleep wherever and whenever he needs it—at the dinner table, in the corner of the room at a Christmas party, in the middle of a noisy parade. It's the invisible mask behind which children make their expressions. As I tend to the yard for hours these days, I watch our neighbors' children play out of the corner of my eye and I try to figure out what it is they have that we as adults do not.

I was standing on the lawn yesterday with clippers in my hand, thinking about what had happened at the bar the night before, when I heard my friend Sal calling me from the street. I walked down to the bottom of the yard and faced Sal across the hedge.

"Lawn boy, what's going on?" Sal said.

I shook my head.

"Why so pensive?" he said. "You look all dreamy and lost in thought standing up there with your clippers."

Normally I wouldn't come out and say what's on my mind, but this time I did because Sal had asked what I was thinking about when I was actually thinking about something specific.

"I was thinking about last night," I said. "Down at Pratty's." Pratty's is the name of the bar I go to.

"Find a new woman?" he said.

I glanced at him. "She's gone only till Labor Day," I said. "She's helping her sister with the baby."

"I'm sorry," Sal said. "Bad joke."

There was a shriek from the neighbors' yard. We both looked over there. The neighbors' kids were spitting watermelon seeds and even whole mouthfuls of watermelon at one another.

"So what happened down there, anyway?" Sal said, after a minute.

"I don't know," I said. "It's strange."

"Spit it out," Sal said.

"Well, Crosby was tending bar," I said. "It was a pretty quiet night."

"Yeah, I was going to go down, but Mona didn't want to."

"It was quiet for a while, anyway. Crosby had the hockey team coming in, but not until later, around ten, ten thirty. But it was around nine thirty or so when these two guys came in."

"Guys from the team?"

"No, just two guys. Maybe in their twenties. I'd never seen them before."

I wiped my nose with my sleeve, then took out a cigarette from the case my wife gave me one Christmas, during my smoking phase, which lasted only about a year. I quit when Simon was born. I never really liked smoking anyway, still don't, but the other day at the store I thought I'd get a pack, just to have.

"Light?" Sal said, holding out a lighter toward me.

"Thanks. So first thing these guys do is make fun of Crosby's shirt." Crosby wears short-sleeved Hawaiian shirts every day of the year, even the coldest days. He's a recovering alcoholic who's been off the sauce for fourteen years, but he still works around booze. *It's my job,* he always says. *It's just what I do.* He takes it seriously. He has hundreds of drinks memorized. He knows what you want before you even say it. It's just waiting there on the bar for you. He gets irritable, sometimes, but understandably. I mean, who wouldn't if they were surrounded by stuff they wanted and couldn't have? You have to tread lightly around Crosby.

"Uh-oh," Sal said. "Bad move."

I nodded. "Yeah," I said. "Then these guys take forever deciding what kind of beer they want, and they don't know Crosby, so they're a little—offended, I guess—when Crosby tells them he doesn't have all day. But he didn't. He had the hockey team coming in, right? He had all these black and tans to pour."

"Right."

"So they finally decide what they want and everything's fine. Crosby's setting up the black and tans down at the end of the bar near the door, where the hockey team always sits, you know down there?"

Sal nodded.

"So then all the beers are ready and Crosby goes and gets a plate of nachos from the kitchen and puts it on the bar for the team. So these two guys say they want some nachos, too. And Crosby tells them no. He tells them the kitchen's closed, which it was. See, it shuts at nine, but the cook left the nachos out for the team before he left. So these guys are like, *Well, there's a big plate of nachos fresh out of the oven right there, Adolf.*"

Sal banged his forehead with the heel of his palm. "Bad move," he said again.

"Yeah." Crosby is famous not only for his Hawaiian shirts, but also for his mustache. "I guess Crosby hadn't been all that polite in the way he told them the kitchen was closed, but it's Crosby, you know? And they'd made fun of his shirt."

"So what did he say?"

I tossed the butt of my cigarette over the hedge and onto the sidewalk. "Can you step on that for me?" I asked Sal. I don't want butts on the lawn. "He just said, *Trust me, the kitchen is closed.*"

"What did the guys say?" Sal asked, scraping at the smoldering butt with his toe like an anxious horse, or maybe like a dog burying its shit.

"What could they say? Anyway, it gets to be around ten, and Crosby's doing paperwork or something over near the cash register. I'd noticed one of the guys leave a little bit before, but I hadn't really thought anything of it. Then I saw the other guy get up and get his coat from the rack. Then he looks out the window, then he looks up the bar, then he grabs the whole plate of nachos and runs out the door."

"Did Crosby see him?"

"No. But I did. So I told Crosby what happened, and he goes running out the door, too."

"Did he catch them?"

"No. The first guy who'd left had brought the car around. Like a getaway car. They drove away before Crosby was even outside."

"So what happened? Did he call the cops?"

I shook my head. "So Crosby stands in the doorway for a while. His shirt was sort of flapping in the wind. It was pretty windy. Then after a while he comes back in and just stands there behind his bar, you know, with his hands on it and his head hanging down." I switched the clippers to my other hand and looked from behind my hedge down the block. The clouds were low and dark-bottomed in a way that promised rain. It was still pretty windy. Dust and dry leaves scratched up the street.

Sal glanced up at the sky too, then back at me. "Then what?" he said.

I looked at him. "Nothing," I said. "That's it. I told you it was strange."

"That's your story?"

"I never said it was a story."

"Oh," he said. He seemed disappointed. "Well." He looked at his watch, then up at the sky again. "I should get going," he said. "Mona wants me home to watch some program."

I nodded.

Sal left me how he had found me, standing on the lawn with clippers in my hand. The neighbors' children had gone inside, and it was quiet. I stood there and pictured Crosby standing there like that, and either that or the wind made me shiver. Then I felt a fat drop of rain hit my cheek, and then another hit my hand. The rain was starting, so I dropped my clippers and went inside.

4

FETCHING

I don't often dream, but the dreams that I do have are of the recurring variety. I don't have the same one, two, or three dreams over and over again for years on end, but often as I wander through a dream I am overwhelmed by a sense of familiarity that lets me know that I have been in this place before. It's like watching a movie that you've forgotten you've already seen, or rereading a forgotten book. You sense that things will happen just before they do.

The other night I dreamed a dream I recognized as one I had when I was eight years old, which was the year my mother left us. In the dream, I'm with some friends—a set of twins—and their father. We're in a pinball machine. There are games and pizza stands and ice-cream stands and rides and swarming children everywhere. Popcorn, candy wrappers, and sticky puddles of soda cover the floor. Getting taken to this pinball machine is supposed to be a treat, like getting taken to a carnival or fair, but the roar of voices and the clanging of pinballs and the ballooning faces and the bright pink and blue lights running through their neon tubes completely overwhelm me. Everyone is smiling and shouting and pointing and laughing, but I am drowning in all this fun.

At seven o'clock, the twins leave with their father, and I wait on the sidewalk for my mother to come pick me up. The air outside is just as stale and warm as it was inside the pinball machine, which looms behind me several stories in the air, casting the sidewalk pink with the light shining through its glass walls. I cannot make out anything in the darkness beyond the glow.

This dream has got me thinking about my mother, and it's got me thinking that maybe I'd like to write something about her. It's interesting, because I haven't really thought about my mother for years, since I went to shrinks who'd circle me, eye me, consider me, peel back the layers of my memory, and prod around for an anger or resentment they could never seem to find. *Your mother,* they would say, *yes, let's talk about her.* But I was eight years old when my mother left us and moved to the commune; I was too young to really understand what had happened and so too young to be angry. It's hard to be angry even now, because the only memories I have of my mother are good memories; there are none on which I can dwell to rouse myself to rage. My mother wore a hairnet for a while, and once when she took me sailing it was so windy that her hairnet blew off and caught in the top of the mast and her hair blew wild and I remember thinking she was beautiful. My mother had an old Jeep, and some weekend afternoons she would drive me full speed down the abandoned runway near our house, pretending we were going to take off like a plane. My mother took me for ice cream at an all-night diner once at two o'clock in the morning.

I woke the other night before my mother had fetched me from

the pinball machine, but in the dream I know I had no doubt that she was coming.

In the attic, there is a box of the things my mother left behind at the commune when she disappeared to wherever it was she disappeared to. I helped my father pack it up and fasten it shut thirty years ago, after he'd finally gotten tired of waiting for my mother to come home and we'd driven upstate to bring her home ourselves. The box hasn't been opened since. At first, I knew what was in it, so I had no need to rummage through, and then I sort of forgot that it existed. Then, when my father died and the box moved with the rest of his stuff from his attic to mine, it simply didn't occur to me to open it, even though I'd forgotten what it contained.

Several times this week, ever since the pinball dream, I've stood beneath the attic door and contemplated going up to find the box, but for some reason it's taken until today for me to pull the trap door open and climb the ladder up.

It was the January after our trip to Florida when my father decided it was time to fetch my mother. I'd retired my safari gear shortly after our return north, but I was still wearing daily my Santa hat from Christmas. I remember sitting in the living room watching Saturday morning cartoons when my father appeared in the doorway with a backpack and a cooler. "Let's go for a ride," he said.

"Where?" I said.

"To get your mother," he said. The commune was on the border between New York and Canada, some nine or ten hours away from where we lived just outside New York City. My father and I didn't really discuss our mission as we drove. We listened to Billie Holiday and The Beatles. We ate carrot sticks with peanut butter and we drank the chocolate milk he'd packed in the cooler. We listened to an abridged version of *The Adventures of Tom Sawyer* on tape. My father, I remember, drove fast.

It was cold, and outside on the swollen hills the trees raised their brittle arms up to a blinding, cold white sky.

We arrived at the commune after dark. It was a huge clapboard house that looked more like two or three houses joined awkwardly together. It was in the middle of a flat stretch of land at the end of a rutted road we drove for miles, watching the lump of commune on the horizon slowly grow as we approached the hulking house that finally loomed before us. All the windows were lit, and there was smoke coming from all three chimneys. The porch was one of those that are nearly level with the ground, and as we stood at the door waiting for our knock to be answered I remember noticing a wide porch swing and wanting to sit down on it. I remember there was also a big dog sleeping out on the porch, and I remember how my fingers caught in his nappy fur as I stroked him while my father talked to the man at the door. I was tired.

"Come on," my father said.

I looked up from the dog, then stood and followed my father and the man inside. The man led us down a narrow yellow hall to a small yellow room with a shelf and a sink and a bed.

"This was hers," he said, and he left us there.

My father sat down on the bed, and I sat down next to him because I was tired and I didn't feel like standing.

"Your mother's not here," he said.

"Oh," I said. "Where is she?"

"I don't know," he said, and I remember just the way his back hunched as he held his hand over his eyes.

My wife has rearranged things in the attic. This was how she spent her first weeks of summer. This was what she was doing when she found the picture of me in my safari gear. Boxes are labeled and piled neatly against the walls. Old coats and clothes are hung on a makeshift rack. A table and chair have been set up by the scratched and moldy oval window. On the table, there is an opened can of Diet Coke. It's strange to think that my wife was the last person up here, and that she placed each of these things where they are right now. It makes me not want to move or touch a thing. I can imagine her dragging boxes and stacking them, repackaging old things, breathing in the same thick cedar smell I'm breathing now. I can sense my wife's presence up here. It hovers.

I walk over to the back wall of the attic and read the labels on the boxes stacked against it. OLD CHINA, one label reads. WINTER BLANKETS, reads another, and then the three beside that read INFANT CLOTHES, 1–2 YEARS, and 2–3 YEARS. I find my mother's box beside Simon's two- and three-year-old clothing. I bring it over to the table and set it next to my wife's Diet Coke, where I can see it better by the light coming in through the window. I sit down in the chair and face the box, which is smaller than I remember it being when I packaged it so carefully thirty years ago. For a while as a kid, I took great pride in the organization of things like boxes and suitcases and closets and cabinets. When we went grocery shopping, for instance, our cereal boxes, juice cartons, meats, crackers, and cookies were stacked and ordered in our cart; I would have no random piling. Same thing went for my mother's box, which we packed up after a cold night of sleep on my mother's narrow commune cot.

I woke that morning jammed between my father and the wall. My father lay on his back with his eyes wide open, and when he sensed me stirring, he turned his head to look at me.

"Sleep okay?" he said.

I nodded.

He sat up and ran his fingers through his hair. "I'll be right back," he said, and he left the room.

The mattress was bare, blue-striped and stained. I sat at the window and watched a man outside pulling a tick or a burr from the coat of the dog I'd petted the night before. It was snowing.

My father reappeared with a cardboard box. "I guess we should pack up her things," he said. "I waited for you to do it."

I knelt on the floor beside the box and placed my mother's things, one by one as my father handed them to me, neatly and geometrically inside, putting them together like a puzzle to make optimal use of space and to make sure that nothing would shift in transportation. I paid attention not to *what* went in the box, but to *how* it all went in there. I imagine none of it was too important: a few books, a few shirts, some jewelry or makeup, maybe a photograph or two of me and my father, although maybe she would have taken those with her.

I bring my wife's Diet Coke can to my mouth and press my lips to where her lips have been. Her taste, if ever it was there, is gone now.

The attic is uncomfortably hot. It's as if all summer's heat is trapped up here. I get up from my chair at the table and open the little oval window as far as it goes, and suddenly the muted attic is filled with sounds from outside: passing cars, barking dogs, the kids playing in the yard next door. I sit down again and stare at my mother's box, rolling my wife's Diet Coke can back and forth in between my palms and listening to the children's shrieks, yells, and laughter. I am jealous of them.

They can shriek, yell, and laugh aloud, shamelessly, boldly. They can fight and make up in a minute. Their grudges don't hold. Their decisions are only as hard as choosing what game to play or what color Popsicle to eat. They consider only one day at a time, maybe even only an hour at a time. They can wear things like safari gear for months on end. Some might think of this as ignorance and pity children for it, but I think of it as freedom. I pity instead Crosby, his head hanging over the bar, wiping up the cheese left from the stolen nachos. I pity my father, hunched on my mother's old commune bed, sleepless beside his sleeping child who'd heard only muttering, not words, from the mouth of the man at the commune door.

Maybe this is why I hesitate to open up the box. What will the man now see that as a boy packing the box he did not? Will the now-grown boy hunch like his father did in anger and pain, murmuring *too late, too late,* like a lullaby lulling his son into sleep? I do not want to let our old selves out of there and into this attic, where they all might change into something I can't recognize; I do not want to unpackage what I packed so carefully away.

5

HELLO, GOOD-BYE

always let the phone ring at least three times before I answer it. I live for those seconds between the first ring and the moment I pick up the phone and say, "Hello?" I can imagine in those seconds that my agent is calling to tell me that a prestigious publisher would like to offer me a six-figure advance to write a novel about anything I want to. I can imagine that the CIA is calling to recruit me. I can imagine that someone is calling to say that my long lost mother has died, and in her will she's left me millions. Or I can imagine that my wife is on the line, calling to tell me that she loves me, she's coming home, she's at the airport already and needs me to come pick her up.

Usually it's just a telemarketer calling, and the other day it was Sal, wondering if he could borrow my clippers and my chainsaw. He has become quite jealous of my yard, I think. Sometimes when I pick up, I do or I don't hear a breath, and the line goes dead. When that happens, I listen to the silence for a while. I listen to the blank sound of miles of wires, leading back from my ear through the dark, maze-like tunnels of communication to the ear of another person who realized when they heard my voice that I was actually not the one they wanted to talk to at all.

I've moved my desk so that it's underneath the living room window that looks out on the neighbors' yard. School will start in another month or so, and then colder weather will come, and the neighbors' kids will move their activities indoors and out of my sight. I want to watch them while I can. Watching them in their yard is like watching an ant farm or a beehive or some other chaotically organized system of existence.

I remember the exact configuration of the yard next door when my wife called last Tuesday. One boy was carrying pails of water from the sprinkler to the sandbox, trying to get the sand wet enough, I guess, to make a drip castle. The youngest girl and a visiting friend were running through the sprinkler, back and forth, again and again. The older girl sat on the steps with a Popsicle in her mouth, watching her brother jump on the trampoline. He was jumping hard and high, losing his balance in the air, and he'd just mislanded with one foot between the wire springs when the phone on my desk rang. I waited before answering to see if the girl with the Popsicle would react to her brother's apparent pain. She glanced at him, flipped her hair over her shoulder, and continued to work on her Popsicle, the color from which she was applying to her lips like lipstick.

"Hello?"

"Hi." The sound of my wife's voice caught me entirely off guard. I wished for a second that I hadn't been so preoccupied with the children as the phone rang. I wished that I had let myself imagine that it was she on the line like I've been doing. It would have been somehow more satisfying than startling, then, when I heard her voice. I would have been prepared, better on the phone.

"Hi," I said.

"How are you?" she said.

"Fine, I'm fine," I said.

"Really?" she said.

"Yeah, really," I said. "They might give me a second column at the magazine," I said. "And Andrew's talking to Random House about my burglar stories."

"That's great," she said.

"And I've been thinking about a new set of stories, all about children."

"How appropriate," she said.

We were quiet for a minute. Maybe I'd said too much too fast. I hadn't even asked her how she was. I could hear her breathing, and then I heard a little sigh.

"I miss you," I said.

She didn't say anything.

"So," I said.

"So," she said. "Listen, I just wanted to call to let you know I'm going to Mexico for a week. In case you called and I wasn't here. That's where I'll be."

"Mexico," I said.

"Yes," she said.

There was another pause.

"I've really spruced up the yard," I said. "It looks great. You'll be surprised."

"I should go," she said. "I just wanted to let you know my plans."

"Okay," I said. "I miss you," I said again, and I held my breath.

She paused. "And I miss you," she finally said.

"You do?" I said.

"Hey," she said. "I should go."

I nodded, even though she couldn't see me.

"Bye," she said.

"Bye." I listened to the click on the far end of the line that meant my wife had hung up, but still I sat with the phone to my ear, unwilling to sever the connection between us. I wondered what my wife was doing on the other side of that click. I wondered if she'd simply hung up and moved on to fix something to eat for lunch or to pack her bags for Mexico. But I also let myself wonder if maybe she was still sitting on the bed or in the chair from which she'd called, thinking about me with her hand on the phone and debating whether to pick it up again and to find me waiting there, as she must have known I was.

After a few minutes the phone began to buzz at me, so I hung it up. I looked out the window. Things had changed a bit out there since last I'd looked. The trampoline jumper was rinsing blood from his leg in the sprinkler now. The girls had stopped running back and forth through the water to watch him. The sandbox boy had given up on his drip castle and was in the process of burying himself. The older girl still sat on the steps, chewing the wood of her Popsicle stick. These changes made sense. I sat back to see what would happen next, but it was hard to concentrate. I kept on thinking about what those words might mean: And I miss you.

I've begun to wonder about Mexico. Her sister has three children and a new baby she'd never be able to leave for a week, and as far as I know, my wife doesn't have any other friends who I can imagine she'd want to travel with. Maybe she's in Mexico alone, but the possibility that she's gone with another man seems increasingly real to me.

It's Friday, noon, and it's raining, so the kids next door are inside. I'm sitting at my desk staring at the neighbors' empty yard, sipping Jack Daniel's and waiting for the phone to ring, hoping with a little more hope than I had before that it might be my wife. I am squirming with restlessness. I trimmed the hedge just yesterday, so it doesn't need my attention, although I would give it gladly, even in the rain. I finished the book I was reading last night, and I don't feel like starting a new one. There are no movies I want to see. The phone is sitting on the desk in front of me. I pick it up and dial.

"Hello?" a voice answers.

"Marissa," I say. "It's me."

When I was seven, I had a goldfish phase. I won my first goldfish at the Westchester County Fair by throwing a Ping-Pong ball successfully into one of many small fish bowls containing anywhere between zero and five goldfish. The fishbowl my ball landed in contained one fish, which I carried home in a plastic bag. His name was Jesús. My father found an old aquarium down in the basement of our home that afternoon, which I filled with pebbles from our driveway, Lego palm trees, and the bits of coral my parents had collected for me on their vacation to Bermuda the year before.

It was a big aquarium—too big for only one goldfish, I thought, and so the next day I convinced my father to bring me back to the fair, where I spent hours tossing Ping-Pong balls at fishbowls until I'd won a school.

I loved those fish. I cleaned the tank daily, searched the swamp below our house for weeds and algae to make their habitat more real (I'm not sure how it didn't kill them), fed them only the best fish food, which I judged by the price, and in only the exact measurements called for on the back on the box, flake by flake.

My cat—Clark Kent—loved those fish, too, but as great as either of our love for those fish was, my love for Clark ultimately surpassed my love for the fish. My love for the fish was a phaselike love; it was obsession. My love for Clark was of the deeper, more subtle, and more lasting variety, but it was the kind of love that is so constant you often take it for granted. Clark slept in my room every night; he shit in my bathroom and ate by my desk. And like a true companion, he sat with me for hours staring at the aquarium. He'd sit with his nose to the tank, batting his paws at the glass, and I appreciated his appreciation for my fish. Even if Clark's desire was more to eat the fish than watch them, the tank had a lid, and so the fish were safe.

Until the day I forgot to replace the lid after feeding them. After dinner that night, I returned to my room to find my fish strewn across the carpet, some half chewed, others floating belly-up at the top of the tank.

"Clark!" I yelled. I found the cat right away, cowering under my bed. He knew what he'd done. "You stupid cat!" I yelled, dragging him by his tail out from under my bed, through the house, and out the door. "I hate you!"

We gave those fish a funeral, my parents and I. We stood together solemnly in the bathroom, flushing them one at a time, my fathering muttering a small prayer as I dropped each one in.

I banned Clark from my bedroom that night, and even as I tried to gloat as I listened to him scratching and whining at my door, I found myself wanting to let him in, to take him in my arms and cry into his fat stomach, which often had been salted by my tears.

This night is one of those things I wish I could erase from my memory, but the harder I've tried, the more deeply rooted it's become. Kind of like when I got up for a glass of water one Christmas Eve and saw my father filling up my stocking when I still believed in Santa Claus. I couldn't get rid of that memory, either, although as I got older, that one ceased to matter. But the memory I have of Clark that night is my last; he was, consistent with my general luck, hit by a car the next day, and although he didn't die immediately, the vet saw fit to put him down before I'd had a chance to say good-bye. And so the last thing I ever said to Clark was "I hate you." The last time I touched him, it was harshly, cruelly, by the tail.

After Clark, I developed an intense phobia of parting with anyone on bad terms. I began to fear that each time I saw someone might be the last, and if it should be so I wanted my last memory of that person to be a good one, and wanted to be sure that I had bid him or her a proper good-bye.

I couldn't go to sleep at night if either of my parents was angry with me. If I'd been sent to bed from the dinner table for refusing to eat what my mother had prepared (she was a believer in tofu, wheat germ, grains), I couldn't go to sleep until I'd crept into my parents' room later that night to apologize, to assure them of my love for them, and to be assured of their love for me. When my parents left on an early flight for a vacation, I would get up with them, even at four a.m., and walk them to the door to say good-bye. I required a kiss on the cheek before being dropped off at school; I didn't care who saw it. Who knew, I thought, what could happen at any time? There were the possibilities of heart attacks, fires, car crashes, planes exploding, kidnappings, anything.

This phobia's been lasting, to some extent, but I don't mind that; it's made my catalog of "lasts" mostly good. My last memory of my mother is a good one. She was wearing a purple evening gown stitched through with gold thread. Her hair was in a bun, and she smelled like scallions. "Have some soy nuts with that, love," she said as she handed me the warm milk she often brought me before bed. I ate, and I drank, and then I kissed my mother on the cheek. "I love you," I said, and she told me she loved me, too. When I woke the next morning, she had left for the commune.

My last memory of my father is a good one, too. We'd gone to the golf course that morning to play eighteen holes, but both of us were shitty golfers, so we quit after five and had eggs Benedict and Bloody Marys on the golf-club porch, and after that I put him into his car and said "Drive safe, Dad," and I leaned in and gave him a kiss on the cheek, afraid as always that his heart might kill him before I saw him again, which, this time, finally, it did.

Last time I saw Marissa, though, mars my catalogue of "lasts"; I was crying and terrified and probably terrifying to her as I sobbed my way home before asking her to leave, before telling her, who'd cared for me all night, that who I really wanted was my wife. This is why I need to see Marissa now; I need to make the "last" a good one.

. . .

"A Jack Daniel's, please, with ice," I say. I grab a handful of goldfish from the dish sitting on the bar. I'm supposed to meet Marissa here at three o'clock. It's two o'clock right now.

I take my drink and sit on a stool at one of the high tables by the windows that open into the square. It has stopped raining, finally, and people are slowly beginning to emerge from indoors. More and more of them are wandering from shop to shop, crisscrossing the square, peering over the pier's edge and into the water at the fish who always surface there after a heavy rain. The pretzel men and hot dog vendors have wheeled their carts out of hiding. I haven't been in this square since the night of the fireworks.

I drum my fingers on the table, cross and then recross my legs the other way. I take the pen from my breast pocket and doodle on my cocktail napkin, trace the lines of my palm in blue ink, and tap the beat of "Hey Jude" on the table, giddy with the expectation of company.

I didn't get to say good-bye to Simon. He was four. His birthday had been the month before, and Claire and I had given him a green tricycle. Green was his favorite color. It was a Saturday afternoon, and after a morning of rain the sun had finally come out, so I'd gone outside with Simon to watch him ride his tricycle around the driveway. He pedaled fast on the thing, and I began to chase him, grabbing at him with big, sweeping arms that he pedaled furiously to avoid.

"Here I come!" I yelled in a deep voice, trying to hulk like a giant. He'd pedal up to me cautiously, and I'd make a grab for him as he shrieked, letting him barely escape every time until the last, when I scooped him off the trike and set him down on the back-door stoop.

"How does a Popsicle sound?" I asked him, and he nodded.

"Good," he said.

"Let me guess. You want a red one."

He shook his head.

"Orange?"

He shook is head again.

"Then you must want purple," I said.

"Green!" he exclaimed. "You know I always have the green ones!"

"Oh, of course!" I said. "How silly of me. And what color should I have?"

"You should have green, too," he said.

"All right," I said. "Two green Popsicles coming up."

And I went inside.

Claire was in the kitchen, cutting something up for dinner at the counter, her back to the door. The knife she used clacked loudly against the cutting board; she didn't hear me come in. I tiptoed up behind her and grabbed her around the waist. She startled and let out a cry, then whirled around, laughing as I gathered her up, but shaking her hand, from which small specks of blood began to fly. "Fuck!" she cried, still laughing. "You made me cut myself!"

"Let me see that," I said, holding her hand steady. She'd sliced the tip of her second finger, and it seemed to be bleeding pretty hard. "God," I said, "that doesn't look good. Does it hurt?"

"No," she said, and peered at the wound. "But it doesn't look good, does it?"

"Shit," I said. "I'm sorry, Claire. Wait, sit down, let me get some paper towels. Or maybe you should hold it under water. Come over to the sink."

"No," she said. "That's for a burn. Get some towels, like you said."

"Okay, towels, okay," I muttered, and I brought a handful of paper towels over to where Claire had sat down at the kitchen table. I shuddered as I watched her wrap her finger up. "Now I know better than to scare you when you've got a knife!" I said.

"Yeah, next time I might turn around and take the knife to you!"

"There won't be a next time," I said, leaning over to kiss her, and that's when we heard the squeal of tires, the scrape of metal dragged beneath a car.

Three o'clock comes and goes. I look out the window and play games as I wait for Marissa, guessing that she'll be the third person to approach from the left, and when that proves false that she'll be the fifth person to approach from the right. I listen for the sound of her footsteps. I think about what she might be wearing. My heart races when a taxi slows and stops anywhere nearby, or when a bus pulls into the stop in front of the bar.

At three thirty, I find the pay phone in the back of the bar and dial Marissa's number. I let it ring eight times. Not even an answering machine responds.

At four o'clock, I try calling her again, and again no one answers.

"Another, please," I say, returning to the bar, though I am beginning to wonder at myself. It is my wife I should be waiting for right now. It is that "good-bye" that I should be fixing, though it's not a permanent good-bye.

I was going to cook us dinner that night after the fireworks, after my wife had hurried home, worried, to answer my terrified summons. "What is it?" remember she'd asked, bursting through the door in the early morning to find me drunk and scared at the kitchen table. "What's wrong?"

And I hadn't been able to answer.

"Hollis," she'd said, and she walked over to me and pulled my head against her stomach. "You are not my child," she'd said, even as she ran her fingers through my hair, soothing me out of any real consciousness. I remember as the world faded, though, I could hear the creakings of her insides, the thwumping of her heart.

I woke much later on the living room sofa; I could tell from the way the dust motes glowed in the slant of light coming in long through the sliding door that I'd slept nearly the entire day. I lay there blinking for a while, trying to remember what part of the past day had been a dream, what real, when like a dream herself my wife appeared in the doorway, silhouetted by the sun.

"You're up," she said through the screen.

"Yes," I said. "What have you been doing?"

"Walking," she said, and she slid the door open and stepped inside. "I'm going to take a bath," she said.

I went into the kitchen and filled a pot with water. I pulled scallions and cheese, tomatoes and zucchini from the fridge. I wrapped some bread to heat in foil, opened a bottle of wine.

As I chopped the vegetables up for sauce, I tried to think of what to say to my wife; I knew I owed her an explanation, something. I chopped and I thought and I chopped and I thought and I jumped when I felt my wife's fingers touch my shoulder. I turned to face her. The ends of her hair were wet from soaking neck-deep in the bath, like I know she always does.

We stared at each other for a minute.

"I'm sorry," I said.

She tilted her head just a little to the side.

"I was scared," I said.

"Of what?" she said.

I looked at her for a moment and then I shook my head. I opened my mouth as if to speak, but I said nothing.

"Of what," she said again, more firmly.

"I don't know," I said, because I didn't. She sighed, and began to turn. "Maybe myself," I said, and she turned back.

"The night we first met," I said. "Do you remember? Do you remember how panicked I was that night, standing there on your doorstep? I thought you were dead, or dying, or in trouble. I was terrified."

"You didn't even know me then," she said.

"That's not the point," I said. "You soothed me. You did something. You do something. I love you. I have too much love for you."

"I didn't really do anything at all," she said. "All I did was tell you nothing was wrong. And nothing was. But I don't know if I can tell you that anymore."

She left the kitchen and went to stand on the porch. I watched her through the window as she tightened her bathrobe around her and shook the water out of her hair. She grabbed her hair with her fist, and she shook it, and something about the gesture, how familiar it was, my wife in her bathrobe shaking water out of her hair, pained me with a pain unlike any I'd felt before. My impulse was to go to the door and call to her, to go outside and take her in my arms, but I stayed where I was.

I sat down at the kitchen table and I shut my eyes and let the room, the world, my life, spin and spin around me, dizzying and fast and terrifying—then it steadied, was steadied quite suddenly, by my wife's cool hand on my neck. I opened my eyes and I looked up at her, and she led me silently upstairs.

When I was maybe two or three years old, I fell into the pool of some friends of my parents who were having a barbecue one summer weekend. I didn't even try to swim; I sank like a stone to the bottom of the pool where I sat and let the water waver the hair around my head. I didn't know that anything was wrong; I was not scared. I remember looking up through the water at clouds and trees that rippled like dancers, and shards of sunlight that cut the water like glass, and finally my father, swimming toward me fully clothed with ballooning cheeks and startled eyes and sandaled feet. I remember thinking it was strange that my father was in the water with his sandals on, and then I remember as he snatched me up from the bottom of the pool the light started to grow dim, and as he swam me up and up I was overcome by a powerful need, a need, a need, for what I did not know, until we reached the surface and I took my first gulping breath of air in a sudden reexplosion into life.

This is what it was like to make love to my wife that night, the last night that we spent together. We slept as soon as we had finished, and when I woke early the next morning, it was to my wife's weight settling on the edge of the bed. She was dressed, and there were two duffel bags beside her.

I opened my mouth to speak, but she hushed me. "I'm going to stay with my sister for the rest of the summer. Until Labor Day."

"But—" I began, and she put her finger to my mouth and shook her head.

"We need this," she said. "You need this, and I need this. Otherwise we're not going to make it."

"What do you mean, what do you . . ." I trailed off, silenced by her gaze.

"Hollis," she said. "I'm serious. Until Labor Day."

I stared at her.

"Promise me that," she said, and I knew then there was nothing else I could do.

I nodded.

She stood and took her bags to the bedroom door, and then she turned. "It's because I love you," she said.

And those were her last words to me. I didn't say them back, at least not so she could hear.

I listened to her get into a cab, whose motor I hadn't even noticed until then, and only then I said those words that I wish had been my last: "I love you, too."

At four thirty, I try Marissa one last time.

"Hello?" I hear her voice answer, and I am so startled that I hang up the phone and just stare at it. Then I pick it up again, and again, I dial her number.

"Hello?" she says.

"Marissa," I say.

"Oh," she says.

"Where are you? Are you okay? I was worried. I'm at the bar."

"Look," she says. "I'm not coming, okay?" She says it almost apologetically, I think, maybe with a little pity in her voice.

"You're not?" I say.

"I tried to call you at home, but I guess I missed you. See, I've been thinking, and I know you're going through a rough time, but it's been weeks since I've seen you, and the fact of it is, I've met someone else."

"You have?" I say.

"Yeah," she says. "It's nothing serious, but I want to give it a chance, and— I don't know. I'm sorry."

I pause. "Okay," I say.

"Good-bye," she says.

I go back to my table by the window and look out at the square. A movie has just let out, and the people emerging are shielding their eyes from the daylight after the dark of the theater. A crowd has gathered in one corner of the square around a juggler juggling flaming pins. I watch as he puts them out one by one in his mouth.

At the bus stop in front of the bar, a single person waits to be taken away. He's a businessman, in a dark-blue suit, a tie, and shiny shoes. He carries his trench coat in the crook of his arm and his briefcase in the same arm's hand. In his other hand, he holds an ice cream cone, soft serve, which he bends his head awkwardly to lick every few seconds, catching the drips as they run down the side. His concentration reminds me of the concentration of the neighbors' oldest girl, smearing cherry Popsicle on her lips, making sure to let none of it dribble down the wooden stick and onto her hands.

Then, as I'm watching, before the ice cream has even reached the cone, the man's cell phone rings. He startles, and he drops his cone as he fumbles for his phone. The cone lands top down, splattering a little ice cream on his shoes. I stare at the cone for a second, and at the rapid pool of its melting, and then I look back up from the cone at his feet to the man himself. He has dropped his trench coat, and he has dropped his briefcase, but he has finally found his phone. "Hello?" he's saying. "Hello?" He holds the phone away at arm's length and looks at it, then returns it to his ear. "Hello?" he says. "Hello?" but it's too late. Whoever was there is gone.

6

COMING HOME

wake to the sound of tapping. I sit up suddenly, startled and disoriented, and find myself in the car. I am sweaty and sore; I have spilled my flask of Jack, it seems, or else finished it off; it is empty and open on my lap.

"Sir," a voice is calling through the crack in my window. I smooth out my hair and roll the window down.

"Can I help you?" I ask. "Sergeant Ryan?" I add, reading his nametag.

"This is a residential street," he says. "This is not an appropriate place to be sleeping, and I'm going to have to ask you to move yourself and your vehicle immediately." I consider saying something about how it would be hard to move my vehicle without moving myself, but decide against it.

"I'm so sorry, officer," I say. I look at the clock; it's three in the afternoon. "Three o'clock! I've overslept!" I say. "Good thing you came along and woke me."

"We've had complaints, sir," he says.

"Well I apologize," I say, rolling my seat back up and putting the keys into the ignition. "I'll be out of here right away."

The officer looks at me skeptically. He stands and brushes his hands on his pant legs: mission accomplished. "And you have a nice day!" I call as he heads to his cruiser, which he's parked in front of my car.

I dig the sleep out of the corners of my eyes and then blink wide, trying to bring my surroundings into focus. I'm parked on a side street in the neighborhood where Pratty's is. I'm not sure why I'm here; last I remember I was chatting with a couple from L.A. in the bar in the square—munching on their appetizer, I believe, as I told them how my wife had left me and my girlfriend had stood me up. After that, it's a blur. I suppose I got into my car and lost myself on the way to Pratty's, which is, I guess, a good thing. I probably didn't need any more to drink.

I watch a dog in the alleyway across the street as I try to bring my body into wakefulness. He's skinny and stiff, sniffing the pile of garbage bags stacked against the building across the way. He lifts his leg to pee, but nothing comes out that I can see. He looks over his shoulder at a passing car, and then returns his attention to the garbage, where it seems he's found something to eat. He shoves his nose eagerly into a ripped-open bag for bite after bite. A pigeon struts around near his feet, snatching at fallen crumbs, and watching these creatures eat makes me realize that I am hungry, too; probably the only dinner I got last night was the smoked salmon I filched from that couple's plate. I turn the engine on and slowly drive away in search of a bite to eat.

There is nothing like a cinnamon bun for a hangover. No fancy cinnamon bun, just one of the ones you can get in any gas station or convenience store for less than a dollar, processed and packaged and deliciously unhealthy. My theory is that they're worse for you than too much booze, so your body gets distracted from its hangover and focuses instead on digesting this new, greater poison. I pick up two of these buns and a cup of coffee from the Cheapo gas station just below the highway, and even though I'll be home soon, I decide to check my messages from the pay phone, because this answering machine we've got is relatively new, and to be able to listen to messages from afar hasn't ceased to thrill me.

When I dial in the machine's code, *You have two, new, messages,* the automated voice tells me, which surprises me, because no one's left me messages all summer.

"Hollis," the first one says. "It's Andrew. Listen I know you're going through a rough time, but I need those pages you said you'd have to me last week—" but that is all I listen to before fast forwarding on to the next.

"Um, hi," the next one says. "Hollis, it's Marissa—oh, God, I hope it's okay to be calling, I mean—shit, just call me, okay?" I brighten up at the thought of having a phone call to return, but then I realize that I already have, from the back of the bar, and that her message for me was that she had found someone else, that she didn't want to see me after all. I listen to the message again. She sounds upset; maybe part of her is sad to be without me after all, I think.

I sit in the car with my cinnamon buns and coffee, and before I know it, I have finished them off, so quickly that I didn't even get a chance to enjoy them. I consider getting another, this one to savor, but two were indulgent enough. I pull out of the gas station and wait for the light to change. This light is what my wife and I are sure is the world's longest red light. Two minutes and fourteen seconds it makes you wait; we've timed it. I glance up at the billboard across the street, one I've studied many times as I've been held up at this light. It's been there for years—the first time I saw it was almost three years ago, during a rainy spell that lasted a record-breaking twenty-two days. My wife and I were coming home from a movie.

"Shit," I muttered as the light changed. "Our luck." I watched the windshield wipers flap across the glass.

"Hey, they changed it," my wife said.

"What?"

"The billboard. They changed it." She was peering out the windshield across the street. "It used to be for cigarettes, with that lady on some island."

I squinted across the street. In the left corner of the billboard was a photograph of a girl with curled hair carrying a bouquet of roses; it looked like a photograph that might have been taken before the prom. Underneath the photograph was the girl's name: Ellen Marie Franklin. The rest of the billboard was dominated by large red block letters that spelled out: MISSING. And in fine print underneath were the details of her disappearance: the date and address of where she was last seen, what she was wearing, her intended destination, and the usual statistics—age, height, weight, etc. "Huh," I grunted, acknowledging the change.

"How awful," my wife said. "Those poor parents." She sounded as if she might cry.

I glanced over at her. And she did have tears in her eyes. Alarmed, I reached out for her hand. I wasn't sure what to say. "It's okay," I said. "I mean, they still have hope. They put that sign up, didn't they? She might be out there somewhere."

"That makes it almost worse," she said, wiping her eyes and recomposing her face. "Some sick fuck might be doing awful things to her," she said. The light turned green and I hit the gas. She straightened up. "This world," she said, shaking her head as we drove away.

I pondered Ellen Marie Franklin's fate for months after that, whenever I was held up at that light, staring up at her as she smiled away in the photo. I always felt as if she were looking directly at me, no matter if I were the first, fourth, or tenth car in line, no matter if I'd already taken the left-hand turn and had started driving away from her, and it made me uncomfortable. So I stopped looking. Or I tried, but often, as today, my eyes swept in her direction.

And today, something catches my attention. I look back up at the billboard, and where the red block letters used to spell out MISS-

ING they now spell out REWARD. I try to remember when the last time I saw the billboard was, and I figure it was about a week ago, on my way back from buying my new clippers at the hardware store. So what has happened in this past week that would warrant a change in wording from MISSING to REWARD? Does it mean that Ellen Marie Franklin is dead? Have they found a body? Limbs? Some incontrovertible evidence that the girl is dead? Is the hunt now for her killer, and not the girl herself? Or has the wording changed to intensify the search, so that people who might not care if she is simply "missing" might pay attention more if "any information" will lead to a reward?

The car behind me starts to honk. I shift my focus from Ellen Marie Franklin's face to the afternoon around me. The light has gone green. I pull forward, take the left turn toward home.

I've always hated returning home after a time away. There seems to be an eerie stillness about the house, an empty coldness that makes me shiver, even when it's warm. I'm never sure what to do. I'm not sure whether to wander through the house and switch on the lights in every room to make the place feel lived in, or to let the lights come on in their own time, as the rooms are used. I'm not sure whether to unpack first, or shower, or sort through accumulated mail, or rummage through the fridge for something unspoiled to eat. It always seems an awkward reuniting, like the first moments of a meeting of long-separated friends. I long for the bills to be paid, the refrigerator stocked, the messages returned, the clothes unpacked, the routine returned to, and the house to be familiar, comfortable once again.

I've been gone only a day; yesterday, though, seems so very long ago. I open the kitchen door, which in my haste I left unlocked, and stand there for a minute to imagine it if somehow I were returning now with my wife. We'd have picked up dinner somewhere, maybe a pizza or Chinese, and somehow the awkwardness of return wouldn't matter, wouldn't exist. We'd eat together at the kitchen table and talk about our time apart. I'd tell her how I'd missed her, how she'd haunted me, how I'd trimmed the hedge almost every day and studied the kids next door. I'd tell her about Crosby and the nachos, and my mother's box in the attic. She'd tell me that she loved me, that she'd missed me, that she'd hoped each day she was gone that I would come for her. She'd tell me what she'd done each day, what books she'd read, what movies she'd seen, what food she'd eaten. She'd tell me about Mexico, and we'd have wine, and we'd make love and go to sleep and leave all other worries till tomorrow.

And then I think about the worst homecoming of all, the day that Simon died. We spent only hours in the hospital that day, enough time to talk to police, fill out papers, and so on. It's mostly a blur. Simon, the doctors said, didn't have a chance, was gone before he'd even reached the hospital.

"I'm going to bed," Claire said when we got home.

I nodded, but didn't move from where I stood in the kitchen, my arms hanging apelike at my sides. I listened to her footsteps fade up the stairs. Everything was as we'd left it. A bloodied paper towel sat on the kitchen table. A pile of chopped onions sat on the counter beside the knife Claire had been using to cut them. The microwave door was open. I picked up the bloody paper towel and crossed the room, shutting the microwave door on my way. I lifted the cutting board with the onions and the knife and I threw it all away. I went over to the fridge and pulled out the Popsicles. I pulled out the juice boxes, the string cheese, the Tupperware bin of grapes with the skins peeled off. I pulled all this out and threw it all away.

I grabbed a garbage bag and went into the living room. I swept the jumbo jigsaw puzzle pieces off the coffee table and into the bag. I took apart the train tracks on the floor and dumped the segments in. I pulled the children's books from off the bottom shelf and threw them in there, too. Then I took the entire toy box from the corner of the room and brought it with the bag outside, put it in a pile on the lawn.

On my way back through the kitchen I grabbed the whole box of garbage bags and went upstairs to Simon's room. I bagged his clothes. I bagged his shoes. I bagged his stuffed animals. I bagged his bedding. I bagged his night-light, his E.T. bedside lamp, his walkie-talkies, his little plastic radio. I bagged it all, and I took it all outside. I crossed over to the neighbors' house and rolled the steel drum garbage can they often used for fires from their driveway to my lawn, and I filled it with as many bags as I could. Then I found lighter fluid in the garage, poured it in the can, and set it all ablaze.

As the fire crackled and popped before me, letting up a thick black plume of smoke that funneled upward and forever away, something made me turn and look over my shoulder at the house, and there in our bedroom window I saw Claire's face, pale and blank. I stared up at her, and she stared through me, at something I couldn't see. I still don't know what she was thinking. I don't know what I was thinking, either.

I sigh and flip on the kitchen light. Usually when we go away, we leave things tidy—shoes and clothing put away, the sink empty of dishes, the bed made, the sofa cushions plumped and the cashmere throw draped neatly over the back, magazines closed and stacked on the coffee table. But yesterday, not intending to leave until the moment of departure, I left the place a mess. Dishes are piled in the sink. A pair of rain-soaked sneakers are stinking by the door. Fruit flies hover around the mouth of an uncorked, half-drunk bottle of red wine. Yesterday's sandwich crust sits on its plate on the counter beside a crumpled napkin and a glass sticky with the dregs of orange juice. Several weeks' worth of newspapers cover the kitchen table. Everything's the same as when I left.

I grab a bottle of Jack Daniel's and a glass with ice and bring them with me out to the porch. It's a warm afternoon, and I know if I sit here long enough that over the marshland behind the house the decomposing weeds and creatures will start to let off their eerie hovering light, the ignis fatuus that people once believed was magic.

7

BAYBURY DAY

Our town has a holiday all its own. It's in celebration of a revolutionary battle that never took place here, but that *could* have taken place here, this being an old New England town. In the morning, a band of ragged patriots battles a fully uniformed regiment of British troops in the square in the middle of town. They fight with pitchforks, bats, old rifles, and silver Western handguns that shoot blanks loud into the air. Groups of British lug wheeled cannons behind them, and now and then a whooping Indian darts through the square, wielding a tomahawk, a scalper, or a peace pipe. The combatants shout as they fight; they moan and wail as they die in pools of phony blood, doubling over and grabbing at their wounds, sometimes staggering over the edge of the square where onlookers have gathered with lawn chairs and soda, umbrellas and cameras, and toppling to their deaths into the terrified crowd. After about a half hour of battle, a sudden quiet descends on the square and the smoke lifts to reveal the patriots standing victorious over the strewn and twisted bodies of the red-clad British troops. The crowd bursts out cheering in celebration of the victorious Battle of Baybury, and a parade begins that wanders for an hour and three miles through the town's streets and ends where it begins, in the square where a buffet of burgers, watermelon, pasta salad, and beer has been spread on fold-out tables in the meantime.

I was a British soldier, once, three years ago, contrary to instinct and character. I hate Baybury Day; when I've attended the battle at all it's been out of curiosity. I watch the crowd more than the battle itself and wonder at the way people cheer and gasp and shriek as if what's unfolding before them is real. Because not only is the battle fake, a reenactment, but it's a reenactment of a battle that never actually happened in the first place! It's puzzling to me.

But Simon asked me to.

David's father was going to be a soldier, he said one morning at breakfast.

"Really," I said, sinking down behind the newspaper, afraid of what might be coming.

"Are you a soldier?" he asked.

I took a sip of my coffee. "No, no, I'm not a soldier," I said, clearing my throat.

"Why?"

"I don't like war," I said, peering over the top of the paper. "I don't like guns."

"But they're pretend guns," Simon said.

I didn't know what to say, so I said nothing.

Claire reached over and gently pushed the paper to the table. "Hollis," she said. She looked amused.

I looked at Simon across the table. His face was a painful mixture of hopeful and crestfallen.

"Do you think Daddy would be a good soldier?" she asked.

Simon nodded.

I tried to kick Claire under the table, but she had her legs curled beneath her. She gave me a sideways smirk.

"I think he would be a good soldier, too," she said. "Maybe he will be one if you ask him nicely."

Simon looked at me. "Will you please be a soldier, Daddy?"

I looked back at him, at his pleading little face. I couldn't say no to him. I could never say no to him. I sighed. "Okay," I said.

I've spent most of the morning at my desk, sifting through the past weeks' scribblings for pages to send to Andrew. I've got story notes about the night at Pratty's with the nachos—or story notes about me telling it to Sal, and how he didn't really think it was a story at all. And it's funny, because the way I've got myself, standing behind my hedge, is kind of like how I've got Crosby, standing behind his bar. And remember I felt sorry for Crosby, that night, standing there like that, which made me wonder if maybe Sal felt sorry for me in the same kind of way. But these are drunken story notes, scribbled on a bar napkin that afternoon as I waited for Marissa, and as Sal has said, it's not really a story at all.

I've got notes wondering why animal-rights activists concern themselves so much with cows and pigs and lab rats, and never take into consideration the suffering, say, lobsters go through before they make it to the plate. Or clams. Or crawfish, or snails. Or crabs. They all get boiled or steamed alive. I've thought of writing a little column about it, but Andrew's warned me that the editor's patience over at the magazine is wearing thin with what he calls my "funny business," which he'd probably consider this kind of a topic, even though I'm serious when I ask these questions.

I've got tons of stuff on the kids next door—descriptions of the trampoline, the swing set, the go-carts; descriptions of the kids themselves; accounts of their games, their arguments, their picnics, the sandcastles they've made—but nothing that I've put into any coherent shape. I still need more. I've been waiting here since nine for them to spill into their yard, to take up their toys and play as they have been all summer, but still their yard is empty. I shift in my chair, sip my seventh cup of lukewarm coffee, make sketches of the swing set and the trampoline.

The sudden ringing of the phone breaks what I hadn't even realized was such thick silence. I jump and snatch it off its cradle after only one ring, which I don't normally do, but I don't want to listen to that sound again. "Hello?"

"Hollis? Is that you?"

I recognize Andrew's voice, but I don't want to have to talk to him. What he wants is pages of a novel I've been given the money to write, almost three years ago now, but which for some reason I just can't seem to get to. I stare at the notes scattered across my desk. Half a summer gone, and there's nothing there.

"Hollis?"

Very quietly, I hang the phone up.

A few seconds later, the phone rings again. Again, the noise makes me jump, and I turn the ringer off. After the time it would take for the phone to ring four times, the answering machine clicks into motion and Andrew's voice fills the room. "Look, Hollis, Andrew again." There's a pause. "You there? I know you're there, and I wish you'd answer. Not every time I call is to pester you, you know—I just wanted to let you know that Random House is seriously considering your burglar stories, but there are changes they want made, things we need to discuss. So call me, all right?" He hangs up.

My burglar stories! And he didn't think anything would even come of those! I had a little burglar phase. I didn't do any burgling, although I did sneak around houses to see what kind of locks and security devices a potential burglar would have to deal with so I could more realistically imagine the technicalities on the page. And I did subscribe to five or six local and regional papers, and checked the burglary reports each day, expanding all the good ones into stories.

My burglar stories! I look excitedly around the room, as if for someone to tell the good news to, as if forgetting for a second I'm alone. I pick up the phone and let my fingers dance above the keypad, unsure of whom to call. I so badly want to call my wife! But I know better than that. Marissa? I could call Marissa. I could call her up just to share the news and not even suggest we get together, since she made it quite clear the other day that she doesn't want to see me—though that sadness in her voice on the machine . . . but no. What if her new "someone" answered the phone? What if she got angry at me for calling and our last good-bye was even worse than the one we have now? I sigh. Who else can I call? Sal? I shrug and dial, but an answering machine picks up. I slowly return the phone to its cradle and rest my chin in my palms. I can't really think of anyone else to call. Most of my friends are really my wife's friends, or at least like my wife better than me, which leaves me at the moment both wifeless and friendless.

I flip my yellow pad to a clean page and rummage around my desk for one of the twenty-some odd pens I have but can never seem to find. I settle back in my chair and prop my feet up on my desk. *Dear Claire,* I write, because she's the only one I really want to tell my news, when I think about it. She's the only one who really matters. *I've been sitting here at my desk all morning waiting for the kids next door to come out onto their lawn and play so I can spy on them. Or not spy, exactly, but so I can observe them. That's a better word. I'm trying to work on a new set of stories about children, how they interact, how they're just so different from adults. More free, in a sense. I think I told you about that when you called to tell me you were going to Mexico, but I don't know if you remember. I've moved my desk so I can see right out the window into their yard. They haven't come out yet, today, which is surprising, because the weather is good, so I've just been sitting here and waiting all morning.*

I pause and look up. I realize as I write this that it matters to me that Claire is missing *my* life almost as much as it matters to me that I am missing hers. It bothers me that she doesn't know about all the little things I've seen and done each day, about the books I've read, the movies I've seen, the meals I've eaten, the fact that I've moved my desk, that I'm writing about children, that my burglar stories are going to be published. Because it's the little things that people are made of, really, and little things happen every day.

I keep writing. I tell her about all the things I wished I could tell her all summer. I tell her about the man with the ice cream cone, the fireworks, the nachos, the hedge. I tell her about Sergeant Ryan, and how yesterday I noticed that the billboard has changed.

I look up. The billboard. How could I have forgotten? I hear the faint noise of drumbeats in my head, as if my mind is creating a soundtrack to go along with the suspense, the mystery of it all. *What do you think that means?* I write. *Why* REWARD? *Why* REWARD *instead of* MISSING?

I look up again. The drumbeats are growing noticeably louder, accompanied now by horns. I bang my head with my palm to get it off, this soundtrack-gone-wrong. But it only gets louder and louder, and I realize that the source of the noise is not my mind at all. It can't be. I get up to investigate.

I go out into the front lawn and watch as the Baybury Day Parade approaches from down the street, led by an old-fashioned car with streamers attached. I cross my arms and watch it begin to pass. After the old-fashioned car, in which the oldest man in town is chauffeured—I think he must be 104 or so by now—marches the high school band, blasting from their squeaky horns some patriotic tune that I don't know the words to. Then come the patriots, rugged and ragged and bloody, cheering and shouting as if they've really won a battle. Some wave at me as they pass. I give them a tight-lipped smile. I hate this dumb parade. I hate parades in general.

Next come the British, their heads hung in shame. This year, they seem to be strung like slaves by their ankles along a chain, which strikes me as perverse. Next come a group of westward-bound pioneers in covered wagons, throwing chocolate coins wrapped in gold foil. A few of them land on my lawn. *You wouldn't have the gold till you'd got to California!* I want to shout. *If you don't die of scarlet fever on the way!* I know what's coming next— groups of evangelical preachers, groups of Puritans, groups of Quakers and Shakers, another band or two, baton-twirling girls in little skirts, hay wagons full of kids and old people. I don't know where all the people come from—I've never thought of Baybury as that big of a place—but I know from experience that this parade will be passing for a long while more. I shouldn't have cut the hedge down, after all, I think. I pick up one of the chocolate coins, unwrap it, pop it in my mouth, and head back inside.

I was one of the first British soldiers to die in the Battle of Baybury. I wasn't much up for fighting, that day; plus, my rifle was a model, didn't even shoot blanks. I located Simon and Claire in the crowd and positioned myself as near them as I could, so Simon could see his daddy as a soldier. About five minutes into the battle, after exchanging a number of dodged shots with Sal, I exploded the pouch of stage blood against my chest, gripped my shirt, and staggered screaming in circles. Claire would give me shit for dying so early on, I was sure, but she wouldn't be able to say I hadn't died a good dramatic death. After about a minute, I dropped to my knees and raised my arms to the sky, shut my eyes and let out one last scream, and then keeled over onto my back, my legs twisted beneath me.

The pavement was warm, and it felt good to be lying in the sun, and I thought how I wouldn't even mind it if the battle went on for another hour or more around me.

But next thing I knew, I felt little hands gripping my sleeves. I opened my eyes to Simon's teary face above me, framed by bright blue sky and high and wispy clouds. "Daddy," he was sobbing, "Daddy, Daddy, Daddy," over and over, and even when I sat up and took him in my arms, he clung tight to my shirt and shuddered with tears as shots were fired around us and smoke filled the air.

"Hey, I'm okay!" I said. "It's just pretend. Simon, look, I'm okay!"

Claire was kneeling beside us, now, stroking Simon's back. "Simon," she said. "Simon, Daddy's fine." She stood and helped us up. "Come on," she said, leading us off the square and through the crowd.

We sat on a bench by the harbor, blocks away from the battle. Simon had stopped crying by then, but still he wouldn't let me go. Finally, he lifted his face from my shoulder and looked up at me. "Promise you won't die again," he said.

"Hey," I said. "It's okay, I'm here."

I think I've found the reason why the kids next door aren't playing on their lawn, I write to Claire. *It's Baybury Day, which means I'm going to have to cut this letter short. But think about it, really, why* REWARD? *Love, Hollis.*

I put the pen down and think about it myself: Why reward? What happened to Ellen Marie Franklin? Was she kidnapped? Lost? Killed? Did she elope? Run away? What change has brought about the change in the billboard? I go into the kitchen and survey the piles of papers on the table, two weeks' worth at least. There's got to have been *something* in the paper, *sometime,* so, in the tradition of my burglar research, I start gathering the papers up to bring over to Pratty's. I can't think here with all this noise, and Pratty's wouldn't be a bad place to celebrate the burglar stories, anyway.

I'm almost at the door when I remember that I've forgotten the whole point of my letter to Claire.

I head back to my desk and pick up the pen again. *P.S. I almost forgot! The whole reason I started this letter is because as I was sit-*

ting here waiting for the kids to come out, Andrew called to say that Random House is seriously considering my burglar stories! And you were really the only one I really wanted to tell. Anyway, bye again. I put the pen down, then pick it back up. *XO, I dare,* and then I head to Pratty's.

8

THE SWIMMER

The first time I went to Pratty's was about seven years ago, after one of our nickel drives. That's what we did on rainy days—we went for drives, letting the flip of a coin decide our directions for us. Heads meant left and tails meant right for every fork in the road, and if it was a four-way intersection, we'd flip the coin twice; if each side came up once, it meant go straight ahead.

They were my wife's idea, these nickel drives, though at first we called them penny drives. For a long time I thought she'd made the idea up, that they were something that we, only, ever did, and I remember being strangely disappointed when I learned that she'd gone on penny drives all the time as a kid.

"You did?" I asked. We had followed a dirt road overgrown

with shrubbery and brambles to where it dead-ended at the edge of a swamp.

"Sure," she said, putting the car into reverse. "My father took me all the time while my mom was sick. I don't think he knew what else to do with me on rainy days."

She hooked her arm around the back of her seat, twisted her body up and around to peer out the rear window, and began to maneuver the car backward down the rutted path. I stared at her, and I guess she sensed my gaze, because when she found a place where the brambles thinned enough to turn the car around, she lowered herself back into her seat, put the car into neutral, and turned to face me all in one continuous motion, punctuated with a suspicious "What."

"What do you mean, 'What'?" I said.

She shrugged and raised her eyebrows. "I don't know," she said. "You tell me."

I looked away from her and traced a raindrop rolling down the windshield with my finger.

"Or not," she said, putting the car into gear.

"Okay," I said, turning back to face her. "Do you not know what else to do with me on rainy days?"

"Hollis," she said.

"Well, I don't know," I said. It seemed a valid question; I have a tendency to get antsy when it rains, a tendency to pace and to fidget. It's not necessarily that I want to go outside; it's not necessarily that I *would* go outside if it *weren't* raining. I just don't like the idea that my options are limited. Which I guess they aren't, really. After all, I *could* just go outside and get wet.

Regardless, rainy days make me antsy, and I didn't like the idea that my wife was simply trying to entertain me, like a child. I'd always thought our drives were sort of a romantic way to spend a rainy day. "I thought you liked going on penny drives," I said.

"I do," she said. She looked perplexed.

"You look perplexed," I said.

"I am," she said, and then she started laughing.

"What?" I said.

"Nothing," she said, putting the car back into neutral and laughing harder. "Just you!"

I watched her laugh. I wasn't sure what exactly was so funny.

"I'm sorry," she said, calming down, taking deep breaths.

"Well, I'm glad you find me so amusing," I said, which for some reason made her snort back into laughter.

"Oh, Hollis," she said, sighing, and then she grabbed my jaw and pulled my face close to her own. She looked into my eyes for a second, and then she kissed me. "I'm glad, too," she said. She put the car back into gear, pulled out of the bushes, and started down the narrow road, at the end of which she turned to me for directions. "Well?" she said. "What does the penny dictate?"

I looked at her and licked my lips. I paused, then took a breath. "Is it okay if we start using a nickel?" I asked, at which, again, she melted into laughter.

"Fine," she gasped, unbuckling her seatbelt and opening her door. "But you're going to have to drive!"

I wish I could remember how to make her laugh like that. I wish I could make her laugh like I did on that nickel drive. But then again, I didn't even mean to make her laugh, which makes me wonder if I ever even really knew how to at all.

"What's with the newspapers?" Crosby's asking, nodding toward the foot-high stack beside me on the bar.

"What?" I say.

"The newspapers," he says, "for the third time." He seems annoyed, but I know Crosby better than that. He likes to seem annoyed. It keeps his more rowdy customers in line.

"Oh," I say, "research."

"Ah," Crosby says, curling his top lip upward and itching the bottom of his nose with his prickly little mustache.

Of course, I plan to ask Crosby everything he knows about Ellen Marie Franklin, if he knows anything at all, but I know to take it slow with Crosby. He can be stingy with his knowledge if it seems too eagerly sought.

"How've you been?" I ask, lifting the pint that Crosby has set, unordered and until now unnoticed, in front of me. I raise it at him. "Thanks," I say, taking a sip.

"Not bad," he says. "Haven't seen you in a while," he says.

"Yeah," I say. "I've been busy."

Crosby nods and starts wiping the bar down, re-fanning the piles of white paper cocktail napkins by twisting a pint glass on top of each stack, emptying empty ashtrays, feigning busyness and disinterest in me, his only customer, though I know him better than that. I know by the amount of time he pretends he doesn't that he has something on his mind, some juicy tidbit that he cannot wait to share, so I watch him, and I wait. He scribbles something down on a pad by the cash register and wanders over to me.

"So," he says.

"So," I say, lifting the top paper from my stack as if I'm about to begin reading, though I'm more than curious to know what's on his mind. But two can play his game.

I spread the paper open in front of me and look up at Crosby, waiting for whatever he has to say. But he doesn't say anything, just stares at me, nodding rapidly in that way that he does, from his shoulders, almost, so that his head doesn't bow, so that he can keep his eyes fixed on you all the while. I clear my throat and try again and again to look down at my paper, but again and again my eyes veer up toward Crosby, down and up, down and up, almost in keeping with the rhythm of his nod. I like Crosby, but he's always made me a little uncomfortable, and even though my wife says it's just my being insecure, I think he finds my discomfort amusing.

"So how's Claire?" he says, finally, pulling out a cigarette from the pack in the breast pocket of today's Hawaiian shirt, a blue one with a repeating beach scene printed across it.

I shrug. "Same," I say. Crosby's always liked my wife. Whenever we come in together he gives her all her drinks for free, and sometimes when I come back from the men's room, which I visit on frequent occasion during a night of drinking, I catch them in conversations that always seem to end as soon as I slide onto my stool, the both of them grinning at me. I know better than to even ask to be filled in. If it were anyone but Crosby acting like this with my wife, I'd be jealous, but Crosby's Crosby.

"Still down in Delaware?" he says around his cigarette, which he's paused in his nodding to light. He raises his eyebrow at me.

"Maryland," I say. I spent every day of the first week my wife was gone at Pratty's from five till close; he knows as well as I do that my wife is not in Delaware.

Crosby shrugs, letting a mouthful of smoke out in a messy, undirected cloud instead of, say, blowing it neatly out the corner of his mouth so that it won't get in my face. "Maryland," he says. "So she's still down in Maryland," he says.

"Yeah," I say. I will not fan the smoke away. "Till Labor Day." Which he also knows.

"Too bad," he says, starting to nod again. "A fine woman like that, a fine summer like this."

I busy myself with gulping down the rest of my pint, and as the last sip drains into my mouth, Crosby's nodding head appears ringed in the bottom of the glass. I keep the pint glass raised to my face for a second longer, hiding there and thinking how through it Crosby's face is blurred enough that at least I can't tell he's staring at me with those beady little eyes. And then his face is gone. I set the glass down and open my paper, and just as Crosby's setting a new pint down before me, the bells on the door jangle and we both turn in time to see Larry walker his way through the door.

"Larry!" I call, relieved at the interruption, and I raise my pint glass at him. "Good to see you!"

Larry spends a good ten hours a day in Pratty's, which is easy for him to do since he lives in one of the apartments above it. He says he's a Vietnam vet, but he looks older than that to me. He's got a pretty bad limp (though not necessarily so bad as to warrant a walker—he doesn't always use one and seems to do fine without), very thinning hair, and a sunken mouth that puckers and curls around his toothless gums. His cheeks are sunken, too, and his eyes, and his wrinkles seem delved so deep that all manner of organisms might be living in the folds of his skin. He's a small, skinny man, but he can drink.

Larry squints in my direction, and then his eyes light up. I think one of the reasons I like Larry so much is because he really seems to like me. And because he calls me kid. I like that, too.

"Hey, kid!" he yells. According to Larry, he lost the hearing in his right ear during the war. "Where you been?" he yells, hoisting himself onto his usual stool at the head of the bar. "I been missing you kids!"

Larry calls my wife kid, too. For a second, my heart speeds up as I wait for a questioning look or a look of concern to appear on Larry's face as he realizes that only one "kid" is present. I do not want to talk about my wife anymore, though I'm sure that Crosby would be more than happy to resume the conversation, to fill Larry in on how I've let a fine woman like my wife leave me to spend a fine summer like this down in Delaware. But Larry's focus, at this moment, seems to be on getting himself a beer, which he's eagerly watching Crosby pull from the cooler.

"Crosby!" Larry shouts in greeting.

"How was lunch, Larry?" Crosby asks, setting Larry's big gold can of beer in front of him. I don't think anyone at Pratty's drinks that piss beer except Larry, but he drinks enough of it that they stock it anyway.

Larry waves his hand in front of his face. He's got big knuckles and swollen joints that stretch his skin until it's white. "Ahhhhh, crap," he mumbles. I don't think Larry would eat at all if Crosby didn't send him periodically upstairs for that purpose. "But I hope you're happy, anyway."

"You know I was just thinking about you, Larry!" I call, sliding a few stools down so that Crosby, Larry, and I form an intimate little triangle.

"You were!" he says loudly, and his mouth widens into an oval that I've come to recognize as a smile. Larry's one person I always know how to make smile. I think that's another reason I like him. It's strange; there are a lot of reasons I have for liking Larry, and a lot of people who come into Pratty's don't really like Larry at all.

"I was," I say, although this isn't technically true. But I would have gotten around to thinking about Larry if Crosby hadn't interrupted me to ask about the papers. "I was thinking about the first time I ever came to Pratty's. About seven years ago."

"Seven years!" Larry waves his hand at me. "Seven is nothing. Hell, I been coming here close to fifty! And Crosby, Crosby's been here, what, twenty, thirty, forty, thirty?"

Larry and I both look at Crosby for confirmation. "Twenty-four years and eight months come next week," Crosby says, leaning back and crossing his arms. Like I've said, Crosby's proud of his trade, and even though he can be a little difficult sometimes, he's a good bartender. Like for instance I haven't had to request either of my beers, today, and a little dish of Goldfish has somehow appeared beside me on the bar. I grab a handful as I notice this and nod at Crosby.

"Long time," I say.

"Yes it is," Crosby says.

"Long time," I say again, nodding. I've always thought I'd like to be a bartender, someday, or to own my own bar. I've always thought that would be a pretty good thing. My wife and I could live up above it, and she could paint up there and I could write, and then in the evenings we could come down and hang out in our bar. I've heard Crosby say there's something like a four hundred percent markup on booze. You could probably make a lot.

"Tell the story," Larry commands.

"What story?" I ask.

"The story about me!" he bangs the bar.

"Oh," I say. "Well, it's not exactly a story, per se."

"Just tell it!"

"Okay," I say. I reach for my beer, which has somehow been topped off. Amazing. "It was that fall almost seven years ago when it rained all the time. You remember that? We hadn't lived in this town too long, and we'd never been in this neighborhood before. Or at least we'd never been on this exact street, so we'd never seen Pratty's.

"Anyway, we're driving around, just because it's raining and there's not much else to do, and we end up on this street, stop at the light right on Sherman, you know? Just right there?"

"Course I know that light! Don't I live right down the street from it?" Larry roars. I shrug.

"So we're stopped at that light and then we look over and see Pratty's, see the whole building, you know?"

"Best building on the whole damn street," Larry nods. The street Pratty's is on is on the edge of town, where the crooked old colonials built close against the sidewalk and the narrow streets of downtown give way to uniform rows of cheaper, shutterless three-family homes with fat siding and loose roof shingles, their front steps covered by corrugated tin awnings. Some of these homes are fenced in; some have vicious-looking tethered dogs straining in the lawn; one has a plastic swing set that I've never seen used. Scrawny trees line the sidewalk. For some reason, the street reminds me of late fall, when it's windy and cold and gray and awful. In my mind, when I picture this street, I picture it empty of the summer stoop-sitters and barbecues. I picture the trees bare, dead leaves scudding, the clouds low and fast. It's depressing, until I picture Pratty's.

Pratty's is the only unresidential thing about this street; there aren't any stores or restaurants or anything else like that. The build-ing is the only one that's not entirely wood-sided; the first floor, where Pratty's is, is made of that fake-looking brown brick. A Bud-weiser sign with PRATTY'S scrawled in script beneath extends outward above the doorway, and from the street you can make out through the frosted glass of the front window blurred neon beer signs hanging on the other side. I've always wondered why they bothered to hang neon signs in a frosted window, but I've never asked.

"Anyway," I say. "So we see Pratty's, and we don't say anything, because there isn't really anything to say. We were just driving, and we happened to stop at that light, and we happened to see Pratty's. We didn't point it out to each other, or anything; it wasn't like 'hey look at that!' like you'd do for, I don't know, a bear on the side of the road; we just both noticed it. Maybe we were both thinking somewhere in the back of our heads that it was strange place for a bar, or that it was surprising to see a bar there, but it wasn't really strange or surprising enough to talk about."

"A bear?" Larry says.

"What?" I say.

"When did you see a bear on the road?"

I look at Crosby. He's smoothing down his mustache with his bottom teeth, which he sometimes does when he's trying not to laugh. I've seen him do it again and again when something funny happens. I don't really blame him, though; his laugh, when he does laugh, is a violent little giggle you'd never expect from a guy like Crosby.

"What," I say.

Crosby shrugs and lifts his eyebrows.

"You were telling a story about me," Larry says. "Then you start talking about bears. Where do I fit in?"

I look back at Larry. "I'm getting there," I say. "So we're sitting there in the car in the rain, and we both happen to be looking in the direction of Pratty's when you come out a door. It was pouring, remember, and I was wondering where in the hell you were going without a jacket or anything. Then you just closed your door behind you, opened the door to Pratty's, and went inside, didn't even have to take more than a step."

It was strange; when I saw Larry just duck from his door into Pratty's, that day, I felt some kind of bizarre relief. It was like I'd imagined this whole wet, cold journey for him that made me cold myself, and then he got to just duck into the beery, smoky warmth of Pratty's instead. It made me want to go in, too. I wanted in, out of the rain, off the street. I wanted to hole up in a warm, dark bar and drink away the afternoon, like the man that I'd just seen.

"Then what?" Larry demands.

I shrug. "It was weird. My wife and I just kind of looked at each other to see if the other had seen you, and we both had, and we kind of just decided to park and go inside without really even discussing it." Which is true. It was one of those times when I've felt like there's a preternatural connection between me and my wife, like she understands me without my having to say a thing. Or maybe even like she feels and thinks the same way I do.

"Then what?"

I sigh. "That was just the first time I went to Pratty's."

"Oh," Larry says. He crumples his empty beer can with his fist. "I thought you said you had a story about me."

"Well it is, in a way," I say. Maybe this is one of my problems. In my head, nonstories are better than stories, and nonstories *become* stories in the telling. But I guess most people don't feel that way. Take Sal. He didn't like the nonstory about the nachos. And now Larry. He doesn't seem impressed with the nonstory about him. But I think everything's a nonstory, waiting to be told.

"Well," Larry says. "I gotta take a piss."

The bartop is a wasteland of violated newspaper, none of which, in three hours, has revealed anything that might help me solve the mystery of the billboard. I shove the last paper aside and down the last of my beer.

"Research not going too well?" Crosby's right there, setting a new pint down.

"Jesus," I say. "How do you keep track like that?"

"I know my customers," Crosby says, spreading his hands out on the bar and drumming his fingers. I've been aware of him hovering, circling me as I've been reading, though I've withheld, so far, the purpose of my research, waiting for him to tell me first whatever it is I know he's been dying to say all afternoon. But my resolve has disappeared, weakened by frustration, disappointment, and beer.

"No," I say. "Research is not going well."

Crosby nods.

I tell him about the billboard, and how it's changed. "You know the one I mean?" I ask.

"I do," he says.

"So have you heard anything?"

"Heard anything?"

"Do you know why they've changed it, I mean. I mean, it could be because they've found her body, so she's not technically 'missing' anymore, but instead they know someone killed her and they're offering a 'reward' to find out who. But it could also be that they've given up hope and just assume she's dead. But it could also be that they're trying to *intensify* the search, you know, by making people pay more attention. I mean, a lot of people might pay more attention if they thought they'd get a 'reward' if they found her, whereas 'missing' is sort of less compelling."

"Right," Crosby's nodding slowly, giving me a look.

"So have you heard anything?"

"No," Crosby says.

"Oh," I say. "Well."

"Anything come of your previous research?" Crosby asks, lighting a cigarette.

"Previous research?"

"The gangster stuff." He knows it's burglars. I know he knows it's burglars, like I know he knows my wife is in Maryland, not Delaware, but I don't correct him.

"Yeah," I say. "Actually, yeah. I just found out today. Those stories are going to get published."

"Congrats," Crosby toasts me with his cigarette.

"Thanks," I say.

Then Crosby gestures down the bar to where a couple of guys have just come in, and I nod.

He comes right back as soon as he's served them. "By the way," he says, and I know by the offhand way he's begun that this is what he's been waiting for. "Your little friend was in here looking for you the other day."

I don't have to ask him to know who he means; I can tell by his scornful tone he means Marissa. I made the mistake once of bringing her in here, and Crosby made his dislike for her as clear as he makes his fondness for my wife.

I swallow. "Oh," I say.

Crosby starts his nodding, then heads off down the bar, satisfied with himself, I'm sure.

I think about yesterday, that sadness in her voice that maybe when I think of it was more like desperation. And now I've learned she showed up here, looking for me, which is something she'd never do. She's never been demanding, never been needy. It made her easy to have an affair with, which I liked, but it made me feel expendable, too, which I didn't.

But that she came here? My stomach drops; she must have news for me, bad news, which is the real reason why she didn't want to see me yesterday; she didn't have the heart to break the news right then, but she didn't want to tell me over the phone. The possibilities of whatever news she might have, when I consider them, terrify me. She might be dying, which even though we're not seeing each other anymore would make me sad, because I like Marissa. She might also be sick with something she's given me, and that maybe I've given to my wife. We might all be sick. We might all be dying.

Or she might be pregnant. This possibility fills me with more dread than all the others.

"Crosby!" I call. "I think I'm going to switch over to Jack!"

· · ·

The last time my wife and I went for a nickel drive was in June. That was also the last time my wife and I were at Pratty's together. It was still cold; we didn't really have a spring this year. I'd thought it would be fun to bring sandwiches with us and eat in the car wherever we ended up, which happened to be on a bluff overlooking a long, gray beach maybe forty or fifty miles north of where we live.

My wife was quiet that day; she said she was tired, and now that I think about it, she'd been tired a lot recently.

"Maybe you need a vacation," I suggested.

"Janet did invite me and Inez up to her cabin for the Fourth of July," she said. Janet and Inez were her roommates in college. What I'd meant was a vacation with me.

"You should go," I said, after a minute.

"I don't know," she said.

"Why not?" I said, though the thought of her leaving for a weekend terrified me. I swallowed. "You should."

"Maybe I will," she said.

She stared out the window as she ate, and I followed her gaze to the beach, where a man in a wetsuit was making his way through the rain toward the surf. "He's crazy," I commented, wanting her to know that I was watching what she was watching. "It's freezing."

"I know it," my wife said.

The man didn't slow at all as he neared the water. He walked into it as if it weren't there, letting the waves break into him and over him. He swam out beyond the breakline of the waves, until I could just make out his head bobbing there.

I took a bite of my sandwich, even though I wasn't really hungry anymore. "How's your sandwich?" I asked my wife.

"It's good," she said, holding it in my direction so that I could take a bite. My wife knows I always like to taste whatever it is she's eating. I like to know what she's experiencing, even if I've tasted it a million times before.

"Do you want to try mine?" I asked.

She shook her head. "No thanks," she said. "I know what turkey tastes like."

The whole time she didn't take her eyes from the swimmer, who floated beyond the breakline for some time before heading back in the direction of the beach. I watched him, too, but then, when he got to where the waves break, where the foam is, where one wave breaks in the wreckage of the last, I lost sight of him.

"I don't see him anymore," my wife said, straightening up. "Do you see him?"

"I'm sure he's there somewhere," I said, scanning the water, but the truth was I didn't see him anywhere.

"But I don't see him," my wife said. Her brow was creased with concern.

"No, neither do I," I said. I opened the car door and got out to take a better look. The water was a steely gray. Strong gusts of wind feathered the tops of the waves and sent spray high into the air. Sharp raindrops needled my face.

I got back in the car and pulled the door shut.

"What do you think?" my wife said. "Should we do something? Call someone? I wouldn't want to feel responsible if something happened."

"I'll go down there," I said, though I don't know why I said it. I don't know what I would have done if the swimmer were in real trouble. The water would have been dangerously cold without a wetsuit, and I'm a poor swimmer anyway. I have a tendency to sink, no matter how hard my feet are kicking. But at that moment, I was filled with a sense of purpose, of urgency. "I'll go down there, and you go find a phone."

"Hollis—" I heard her begin, but I leapt from the car before she could say more. I didn't want to give her the chance to dissuade me, to point out that there was nothing I could really do. I started to run down the muddy path of the bluff, and I didn't mind it when I slipped and fell on the way. I didn't mind water sliming the insides of my shoes, raindrops pasting my pants to my thighs, or puddle water climbing from my pant cuffs up my calves. I didn't mind any of that or the cold or the wind at all, because in my mind there was a man down there drowning, and I was somehow going to save him. I wanted to know what that felt like.

I didn't look up until I reached the edge of the beach, and when I did, I saw the swimmer, knee-deep in the water, trudging away from the waves and toward the sand. I stared at him, winded, wet, and suddenly cold. I looked back up at my wife, who had gotten out of the car and now stood at the bluff's edge with her raincoat pulled tight around her. I looked again at the swimmer, and then back at my wife, and then I began the muddy climb back up.

I climbed slowly, suddenly tired, strangely disoriented, hoisting myself upward with fistfuls of grass, conscious of my wife standing above me, watching me, waiting for me in the rain.

"Get in the car!" I called, halfway up. "Stay dry!" But my voice must have been lost in the wind, because my wife stayed where she was.

When I neared the top, my wife reached down and extended her hand to help me the last step up. Her grip was strong, and her hand felt warm over mine. "Thanks," I panted.

"Sure," she said.

We looked at each other. Her hair was plastered to her head, and her face was wet. Her nose was red and runny in the way that it always gets when she's the least bit cold, and it was strange, because I couldn't read her eyes at all. I wasn't sure what she was thinking, just like I wasn't sure what she was thinking as she stood at the window and watched me burn all of Simon's things.

"Now what?" I said.

"I don't know," she said. "We could get a drink," she said.

I nodded. "Okay," I said. "I could use one."

"Yeah," she said. "Me too."

9

A TABLE FOR ONE

I've always found meals alone slightly awkward; aloneness changes mealtime from an activity into a series of chores. First, it's that much harder to decide what to have when you don't have to consider another person's preferences and desires. My wife's a picky eater, so there have always been certain restrictions to our household menu, certain categories of food that are automatically ruled out. I, however, will eat pretty much anything, and the endless options presented on the grocery store shelves overwhelm me when absolutely no restrictions apply. It would be one thing if I were so open to any food that it didn't really matter what I ate, if I could just walk into the supermarket and grab the first thing I saw without thinking about it; instead, I wander through the aisles picking up various

ingredients, pondering all the possibilities, wondering if on this particular night I'd prefer something salty or more on the sweet side,
something more along the lines of meat or starch.

Once that decision has been made comes the second chore—that
of portion size. Meat or fish is fine, in this respect, and chicken, too,
because you can buy a single fillet, if you want to, or a single breast,
or just enough ground beef for a burger. But pasta and rice mixes
come in quantities meant for four or eight people, and enough for
six people comes in the average jar of pasta sauce. Sure, there's no
need to boil all the pasta, but I've always thought that the pasta
from a box that's been left open for anywhere over a week tastes suspiciously chalky, and when you're making a rice mix, like garlic
pesto rice pilaf, you have to make it all at once. And as for pasta
sauce, you're supposed to finish it within five days of opening the
jar, but what if you don't want pasta again that soon? It's a waste.
Same thing if you want a sandwich. You have to buy an entire loaf
of bread, some eighteen or twenty slices, for the sake of a single
sandwich.

Third comes the cooking. I love cooking when I'm cooking with
someone or for someone. When my wife and I cook together, we
have fun. It's an activity we're doing together—it's something we get
to plan, prepare for, execute, and enjoy. Cooking *for* my wife is even
better. I get all secretive and don't let her near the kitchen to see what
I'm doing; I set the table with her mother's old china, crystal glasses,
candles; I make sure everything is perfectly prepared and presented
in the most elaborate, artistic way I can conceive of. I make only
what I know she likes, and I think I can cook pretty well; the best
part of the whole thing is watching her enjoy what I've created.
Cooking alone, though, is another story. The satisfaction just isn't
there.

But the worst part of the whole thing is eating alone. It makes
me self-conscious, and very much aware of my aloneness. I've
always felt bad for people eating alone in fancy restaurants, not only
because they're eating in a fancy restaurant by themselves, but

because if they have to take themselves out to get out for a meal, I imagine that must mean they have to eat alone every night, sitting there at their small tables. It makes me uncomfortable to think of myself as one of them. I'd try to distract myself from my aloneness, but I'm not quite sure how. I don't like TV, so I'd rather not have its company for dinner. I can't read and eat at the same time because each of those activities both requires and deserves more than half of my attention. Either I'll miss my mouth with my fork as I focus on whatever I'm reading, or else I'll focus a little too much on creating the perfect bites and realize that I have no idea what's happened in the past ten pages of my book.

This week I figured out how to overcome the first three obstacles without skipping dinner entirely, which was my initial response to solitude and which I've decided probably isn't the best or most healthy idea, by way of takeout, specifically a little Mexican place downtown called San Miguel. There are several take-out places in Baybury: there's a Thai place, a Chinese place, a pizza place, a falafel place, a sub shop, and this Mexican place. I like all of these, so the only decision I had to make was which take-out place to frequent night after night. When I get tired of burritos, which is San Miguel's specialty, then I'll have to decide on one of the other places, but for now, burritos are fine. I've been walking there and back, too, and it's about two miles round-trip, so I've been getting some exercise, which I figure is probably not bad for me either.

The first night I did takeout, I ate standing at the kitchen counter, but that really took away from my enjoyment of the meal, so for the past two nights I've taken my burrito outside with a bottle of Jack and watched the sun set over the marsh. I don't know if it's the view or the Jack that makes the experience an enjoyable one, but I think I might have finally and fully solved the problem of solitary dining. Which isn't to say that it would ever be my preference; not at all.

The only thing is this dog. Two nights ago, the second night of my new routine, I noticed a scrawny sand-colored dog just sitting there under a tree in the park downtown. The only reason I noticed him is because he looks a lot like Benji, so I probably wouldn't have thought twice when, as I pulled the door shut behind me when I got home, I noticed a dog was standing at the bottom of the driveway, watching as I went inside. But I did think twice, because it was the same Benji dog I'd seen under the tree, which meant that he'd followed me all the way home. And then last night, I saw him under the tree again, and every time I peered over my shoulder on my way home, he was always there, ten yards or so behind me. A few times I stopped and confronted the dog. "Go home!" I commanded, pointing toward town and trying to make my voice gruff, but the dog didn't seem to have any idea what I meant. He followed me all the way home again, but not up the driveway, which I was thankful for. It's not that I don't like dogs; it's just that creatures in general, whether four-legged, upright, or finned, make me nervous. They are too fragile, too susceptible to things like heat, like claws and paws, like the wheels of speeding cars. And I suspect that all this dog is after is my dinner, which likely leaves a pleasant aroma in its wake as I carry it down the street.

This is one reason I'm driving to San Miguel tonight; I'm hoping not to become this dog's habit. The other is because I'd like to take another look at the billboard.

As I drive, I consider the research I've done, which isn't much. There are three Franklins listed in the regional phonebook. There's an R. Franklin, who lives on the very edge of town, on the border between this town and the next. There's a David Franklin, Jr., who lives right in downtown Baybury. And then there's E. and T. S. Franklin, who live, according to the map, on a small, winding backroad that runs inland from the coast following the contours of the marsh. Ellen Marie Franklin could belong to any one of these households, or, I suppose, to none of them, but I think it's likely that her family would be listed now, even if they weren't beforehand, so as to make themselves accessible to any kidnapper who wanted to call and demand a ransom. Just because R. and David are listed singly doesn't mean they don't have spouses and families, and I would guess that E. and T. S. are likely a married couple. It has occurred to me that E. could very well stand for Ellen, and that if this is so, this Ellen could be Ellen Marie's mother and namesake. But I'm jumping to no conclusions.

I pull over at the bottom of the exit ramp and shut the car off. I stare up at Ellen Marie Franklin's round face, her brown curls, her bare shoulders, and her shy smile, and I pull out my notebook and pen to copy down all the essential information, which, once I look it over, isn't really essential at all. She was sixteen when she disappeared, which was three years ago, so she's nineteen now and probably no longer 5'4" and 125 pounds. She's probably no longer wearing the blue jeans or gray sweatshirt she was last seen in, and she's probably nowhere near the north corner of Locust and Wetherley, where she was last seen waiting for the light to change on her way to the pharmacy for her insulin. She is, as a final note at the bottom of the billboard informs, an insulin-dependent diabetic, which doesn't bode well.

But maybe the fact that that piece of information is still on the billboard even after the wording has changed is a good sign. It suggests that she isn't dead, or if she is, that they haven't found her body. If they knew she was dead for a fact, if they'd changed the wording because they'd found her body, wouldn't they have also removed the note about her diabetes from the billboard? The fact that she's a diabetic wouldn't matter anymore, so it would be almost perverse to leave it there.

I nod and write down the last thing I came for—the phone number to call with any information. I look up at Ellen one last time, then I turn on the engine and head for San Miguel.

I head straight for my desk when I get home. It occured to me as I stood at the condiment bar at San Miguel ladling hot sauce and salsa into little take-home condiment containers that the answer to the billboard mystery might be simpler to ascertain than I'd thought. This realization made the ten-minute wait for my burrito nearly unbearable; all I wanted was to get home and to the phone.

I sit down and flip my notebook open to the page with Ellen Marie Franklin's information, pick up the phone, and dial the number I've scrawled at the bottom of the page.

"FBI Boston, Missing Persons," an efficient and mechanical-sounding voice answers.

FBI? This takes me by surprise. I'd expected the line to be dedicated to the Franklin case alone, an Ellen Marie hotline. But the FBI? They must handle thousands of missing-person cases at a time. I bet this voice won't even know who Ellen is, at least not without punching her name into some computer.

"FBI Boston, Missing Persons," the voice repeats.

"Yes, ah, hi, I'm, ah, calling in reference to the Ellen Marie Franklin case?" I say.

"Yes sir, please hold." The voice is nasal, singsongy even if only within a very limited, maybe three-note register. I hear phones ringing in the background, faint voices, then the rustle of the phone being settled, I imagine, between this person's shoulder and ear. A woman, I think, although it's hard to be sure. A black woman. "Okay, sir, you were calling in reference to which case?"

"Ah, Ellen Marie Franklin."

"Franken?"

"Franklin," I say, and I spell it. I hear her punching keys. Just like I thought.

"Okay, sir, go ahead."

"Well, I'd noticed that the billboard announcing Franklin's status as a missing person has been changed. Previously, it said 'missing,' and now it says 'reward.'"

"Uh-huh," the voice intones, both syllables on the same dead note.

I begin to think that maybe I'm taking the wrong approach here, that maybe I shouldn't get into the billboard at all. I clear my throat and try to sound official. "Ah, I'd like to inquire into the status of the Franklin case."

"Inquire into the status?" the voice repeats.

"Yes," I say.

"I'm sorry, sir, I don't quite follow."

Don't follow. What is there to follow? "Um," I say. The official tactic doesn't seem to be working, either. "Frankly, ma'am—" I cringe, praying that the voice is, indeed, a ma'am—"I'd just like to know why the wording of the billboard has changed. I'd like to know if it reflects a change in the status of her case. If there have been any developments."

"I'm sorry, sir, did you have information for me regarding this case?"

"No, I—"

"Okay, sir, well then I'm afraid I can't help you. You have a good night." She says this as if there were no punctuation involved. And she hangs up.

"Right," I say, and hang my own phone up. I do not like being hung up on.

I sigh, feeling what I know is irrationally let down. I'd really convinced myself in the twenty minutes that elapsed from the moment of my epiphany at the condiment bar to the moment the voice answered that it would be that easy to find out the reason for the change. And why shouldn't it be that easy? Why shouldn't I, a concerned citizen, be able to get some simple answers?

I flip to the next page of my notebook and grab a pen. *Dear Claire,* I write. *I've made absolutely no progress in the Ellen Marie Franklin case. I just called the number on the billboard to see if they'd tell me anything, and the voice HUNG UP on me! I'd hope the FBI would be a little more forthcoming with their information, and at least a little more mature than to hang up on a concerned citizen. So anyway, the FBI was a dead end, plus I spent the other afternoon going through the newspapers from the past couple weeks—because I figure it was about a week or so ago that the bill-*

board changed—and I didn't find a goddamn thing. Pratty's, by the way, is not the same without you. Crosby gives me endless shit, even though you'd probably say it's all in my head—but I swear, without you to flirt with, he just picks away at me. I read over what I've written. *Oh, I went through the newspapers at Pratty's, which is why I started talking about Crosby. That was right after I finished my last letter, as a matter of fact.* Which itself is still firmly attached to the spine of this very notebook, a few pages back.

Anyway, a couple of things I've been thinking about: our nickel drives, the first time we went to Pratty's, the difference between a story and a nonstory. I write her about telling the nonstory to Larry, and how it can't really be a nonstory because it's the story of the first time we went to Pratty's, and how, in a way, it's connected to the story, or nonstory, depending how you look at it, of how the penny drive became the nickel drive, *because,* I remind her, *we discovered Pratty's on a nickel drive, remember? And you can't really talk about nickel drives without saying that originally they were penny drives. And don't nonstories become stories in the telling, anyway? I'd think so, but apparently other people—Larry and Sal, for instance—don't.*

I've been thinking that maybe this is my problem. I mean, I haven't written a single page or a complete sentence this entire summer, and Andrew is going to have my head soon. I've got ideas— plenty of ideas, but what he wants are stories, and what I have are nonstories.

I pause, and sigh. My hand aches and my stomach is rumbling. I remember my burrito in the kitchen. *Anyway, I'm starving. I've gotten myself a burrito from San Miguel, which is the best way, I've figured, to tackle dinner. See, mealtime alone is a difficult matter.* I explain to her the hurdles as best I can, and how the same takeout night after night seems the best solution. *Don't you think? Anyway, off to dinner. Love you, Hollis.*

I set my pen down and stand, brushing my hands on my pants, my mouth watering in anticipation of Jack and burrito, and just as

I'm about to head into the kitchen, I notice the light blinking on the message machine. I pause and stare at the thing, trying to remember if it was blinking before I left to pick up dinner.

A message, these days, is an ominous thing. There aren't many people it could be. A month ago I might have let myself consider all sorts of options at the sight of the blinking light—the usual fantasies: it's my mother, it's someone telling me I've won the sweepstakes, it's the CIA and they want to recruit me. A week ago, I'd have entertained the notion that it might be my wife, but I don't really think that's likely, not from Mexico.

Today, I can think of only two real possibilities. It could be Andrew. He could have more information on the burglar stories, which wouldn't be bad news to hear, but he could also be calling to pester, and I'm not in the mood for that right now. It could also be Marissa. I doubt she'd say anything except that I should call her, but there's always the off chance that she might blurt out whatever terrible news I'm afraid she has right on the machine, unable to keep it in anymore. I don't want to hear it. After dinner, I think. I'll enjoy my dinner first, and then I'll listen to whatever whoever it is has to say.

I grab my burrito, a glass with ice, and my bottle of Jack from the kitchen and head in the direction of the back porch. I pause as I pass my desk, my own eyes drawn to the evil blinking eye there. I set my burrito down, for just a second, for just long enough to reach my trembling finger out to the answering machine to press ERASE.

Whenever my father and I returned home in the years after my mother left, my father would drop whatever he was carrying by the door, and without turning on the lights or turning up the heat or putting whatever groceries he might have had away, he went straight into the living room, where, amid a tangle of wires, an oversized, hulking answering machine sat, one of the first of its kind.

We didn't have an answering machine at first. My father was a journalist, and soon after my mother left, he began to work from home instead of commuting into the city to his office at magazine headquarters. He said it would be better for me, this way, and it was, but I think there was more to it than that. I think he was afraid to leave the house, afraid that my mother would call and no one would be there to answer, afraid that she might come home to pick up some belongings and the only way we'd know she'd been there was because her closet was a little emptier than it had been before. Because my father refused to put any of her things away. It was as if she were still living with us—her medicines and creams were still in the bathroom cabinet, her boots still sat on the floor of the hall closet in line with my father's and mine, her jackets still hung beside ours. It wasn't unusual to happen upon an emery board, a bobby pin, a pair of her cheap sunglasses, maybe underneath a cushion on the couch or in a kitchen drawer amid matches, tape, and scissors. I think, for a long while, he really believed that she might come back. Once a weekend walker in the woods behind our house, once a sledder, a wiffle-ball pitcher, an ice cream eater, my father now preferred to spend the weekends reading on the couch, which meant that if I still wanted to do these things I was on my own.

It was the weekend of the Westchester County Fair. This was the highlight of my autumns growing up. This fair had bumper cars and a Ferris wheel, games where you could shoot fake guns or throw Ping-Pong balls into fish tanks (hence the start of my goldfish phase a few years before), fortune-tellers and gypsies, magicians and freaks, cotton candy, caramel-coated apples, and my favorite, fried dough. I didn't necessarily understand as much as tolerate my father's new reluctance to leave the house and join me in our usual outdoor weekend games, but it didn't cross my mind that my father wouldn't take me to the fair. I was up early that Saturday, pacing and fidgeting as I awaited our estimated time of departure. As the hour approached, I periodically checked in on my father as he read there on the couch, jotting down notes with the pencil he kept tucked behind his ear, and to my increasing alarm, he didn't seem to be making the slightest motions toward readying himself. When there were about ten minutes to go and still he'd made no progress, I went into the living room and stood before him. *"Dad,"* I said. "Ten minutes."

He looked at his watch and then looked at me. "Hollis," he said, "this article. I've got to get it done by Monday."

"Dad," I said.

"I spoke to the Grangers yesterday, and they said they'd take you."

"Dad," I said. He liked the fair as much as I did, I was sure of it. He always had. I was the only kid whose father took him both Saturday and Sunday, and I got to stay there for longer than anyone else.

"They should be here in a little while."

"I'm not going to the fair with the Grangers," I said. I went upstairs to my room and watched out the window as the Grangers pulled up in their long, loud, wood-paneled station wagon, their four kids shouting in the back, spitting and punching and pinching, I was sure. I had never liked the Granger kids.

I heard my father knock on my door. "Hollis," he said.

"No," I said.

"Hollis," he repeated, but quietly. He could have opened the door if he'd wanted to; it didn't have a lock. If he'd wanted to, he could have come in and told me I certainly was going to the fair with the Grangers and I was going to damn well like it, and he could have taken me by the collar and led me downstairs and out to the Grangers' car. But my father wasn't like that. A minute later, I saw him out in the driveway, bent down and talking to Mr. Granger through the car's open window. Then he straightened up and waved as they backed out of our driveway and away. He stood there a minute, then he got into our car and drove away himself.

I woke up maybe an hour later to my father shaking me gently. I opened my eyes. "What?" I said.

"Are you ready?" he said.

"Who am I going with now?" I said.

"Me," he said. "If you still want to."

"Why?" I said. "What about your article?"

"It's okay," he said. "I took care of it."

"Can we go tomorrow, too?" I asked suspiciously.

"Course," he said. "Don't we always?"

Downstairs in the living room, the answering machine sat like some strange creature in a wire nest. I paused at the bottom of the stairs to look at it. "What is that?" I asked.

"Answering machine," my father said. "It answers the phone when we're not here, and it plays a tape that whoever's calling can talk into, to tell us they called." He bent down and showed me the tape and the buttons.

"Cool," I said, nodding in appreciation, and I didn't think it strange at all that my father rushed to his new toy whenever we got home, though I didn't really realize until later just what he was waiting for.

My father would have been shocked and horrified, I'm sure, that I just erased a message without first listening to it, and I have to admit that it has made my heart pound some. But the likelihood that it was either my wife or his isn't great, and I feel liberated. Whatever message it was has simply *ceased to exist.* I toast the warm evening air, the marsh, and the setting sun with my Jack Daniel's and start in on my burrito.

The neighbors seem to be having a cookout, tonight, so if you look at our neighborhood as one big room, I'm not really having dinner alone. The back porch is around the corner of the house from the neighbors' yard, so I can't see them from here, but I can hear them clearly, and I can smell the smoke from their barbecue. I hear the *tick-tick-tick* of the sprinkler, and shrieks that I assume are emitted by those whose turn it is to run through the chilly spray. I hear the springs of the trampoline creaking, and by the slow frequency of the jumps, I imagine it must be the oldest boy jumping; his jumps are high and long.

I have watched him jump, and it always makes me nervous—it

makes me nervous when any of them jumps. There is something terrifying about bouncing on a trampoline, I think. You start slow, your legs like rubber bands as you walk from the padded edge to the center, where you begin to jump, gently at first, then higher and higher as you realize you can. All of a sudden you can see a little farther down the street than you ever have before. You can see into the higher branches of the nearby trees, where startled squirrels and birds freeze as an unwinged boy flies by. You can see into the upstairs windows of the neighbors' homes, into their backyards, over the roofs of the houses down the hill. The upturned faces of those on the ground shrink as you rise away like a balloon, higher with each jump, unleashed, free. You jump, and you jump, until suddenly you lose control, your arms flailing as you lose your balance in midair and come crashing down onto your back or onto your head or, worse, through the rusty springs that until now have given you flight.

It seems inevitable, this crash. Whenever I watch my neighbors, it is only the crash that ends one jumper's turn and clears the trampoline for the next jumper up. If there were no crash, why else would a jumper ever stop? Since there is a crash, why would a jumper ever jump? But they do.

"How many hot dogs?" I hear the mother asking. "How many? Harry, are you listening to me? Harry! Stop jumping for a minute and focus! Cathy, Cathy, let your sister go. Who wants a hot dog? Let her go!"

It's strange to be spying on my neighbors by means of a sense other than sight, and in a way it's frustrating, because I'm not entirely sure which voice belongs to which body, and I'm not even sure which kids are in the yard right now; I think only four actually live next door, but I don't know which four they are because there always seem to be at least six or seven kids out playing at a time. Listening to them, rather than watching them, is kind of like hearing a story read aloud; I can never really follow what's going on as well as I can when I'm reading myself. What I'd like to do is take my dinner to my desk, where I'd be able to see them as I eat, but I'm trying to establish a dinner routine, and if I let myself break one rule, I know I'll end up breaking them all and it'll just be Jack for dinner, so I sit tight.

I take a break from my burrito and pour myself another drink, and when I look up from the food in front of me, I see that the dog that's been following me is sitting there in my backyard. He's not too close; he's at the very edge of the yard, where the yard meets the marsh, but he's gazing up at me, watching me eat.

"What do you want?" I say, startled and somewhat unnerved to see him there.

The dog tilts his head and starts to move toward me, then hastily retreats as I leap up and hold my hand out like a cartoon traffic cop and yell in my most menacing voice, "AH AH AH!" The dog whines and circles and settles down again on the edge of the yard, his chin between his front paws.

I sit back down. "You thought you were going to get some of this, huh?" I ask, raising a forkful of burrito in the dog's direction. "You thought you outsmarted me, huh?" The dog lifts his ears and gives his tail a little wag. "Well, no such luck." I shovel the bite into my mouth and chew, holding the dog's gaze with my own.

It's not a bad-looking dog; it's sandy-colored and midsized, a scrawny version of Benji, and even though I'm not a big animal person, like I've said, it has almost human eyes. "Who do you belong to?" I ask. "Huh?" I set my fork down and walk over to the dog, who greets me by turning around in hysterical circles, whining, his tail fiercely wagging. "Hey," I say, reaching out and trying to settle him down. "Hey, hey, whoever you think I am, I'm not, hey." The dog calms down a bit and sits atop my feet, leaning hard against me and looking up, panting hard, his tail still beating. "But who are you?" I ask, reaching under his neck for a collar and tags. But there's nothing there. "No collar, huh?" I say.

I wonder if maybe he's a local dog that I just haven't seen before, so I straighten up and pat my thigh, hoping that this will signal to the dog to follow me. I head in the direction of the neighbors' yard, looking behind me to make sure that the dog is following. I round the corner of the house and look over the hedge into the yard.

Aha. Six kids. Two girls at the sprinkler, just like I suspected. Another little girl in the sandbox, playing with a doll. One boy crouched down and digging a hole beneath a tree, and the older boy, like I thought, bouncing on the trampoline. The last girl is standing to the side, watching him jump with impatiently crossed arms.

"Hey!" I call over the hedge, and immediately, all action stops. Six puzzled faces turn in my direction and watch me as I sidestep through the hedge, which is only about a foot across. I turn and beckon the dog to follow. "Does anyone know who this dog belongs to?" I ask.

The girl waiting for the trampoline turns in the direction of the house. "Maaaaa!" she yells. "A maaaan's heeeere."

The mother appears in the doorway, a baby on her hip. Jesus. It's like the old woman who lived in the shoe. She sees me and comes outside.

"Hi," I say, crossing toward her and extending my hand. "Hollis Clayton, your neighbor." I gesture over my shoulder at our house. These neighbors moved in this spring, but my wife and I haven't been too social in recent years, and I don't think we've ever officially met the Cranes. At least that's the name on their mailbox.

"Hi, Mr. Clayton, Judith Crane. It's nice to finally meet you." She takes my hand and smiles. *Finally,* I think. I wonder if she's hinting at something.

"Yes, I— Ah, my wife and I . . ." I'd like to be able to explain my wife's and my reclusiveness, but I'm not quite sure how. "It's nice to meet you, too."

Judith Crane is, I'd say, in her mid-thirties, and a gentle though somewhat flustered-looking woman—but who can blame her with all these kids around? "I hope we're not being too noisy for you over here—we thought we'd cook out tonight, given the heat we've been having, and Norm—that's my husband—he's away, so he's not here to help me keep them all under control!"

"Oh," I say. "No, no, you're not too noisy at all."

"Good," she says. "I wouldn't want to disturb you. I heard you're a writer?"

"Oh, yes," I say. I'm not big on small talk, and I'm beginning to regret the impulse to come over here. "No, you're not bothering me at all. In fact, I just came over to see if this dog was familiar."

Judith Crane looks surprised. "Dog?" she says, then "Oh!" as she notices the dog at my side. "I didn't even notice him there! How funny!" she laughs, and I smile, trying to be polite. "Oh!" she cries, "the phone!" And indeed, I can hear the phone ringing faintly inside the house. She holds the baby out at me. "Do you mind?" she says, and before I can say anything the baby is in my arms. "Harry, flip the burgers, will you?" she calls as she runs inside. "And the hot dogs could probably come off, too!"

The oldest boy hops off the trampoline and heads over to the grill. His sister (I assume) grabs her chance and takes his place jumping. The other kids have all resumed their activities, leaving me standing with the baby in the middle of the yard.

I look at the baby in my arms. I can't tell if it's a boy or a girl, but it's staring up at me and pinching at my face with its little grabby hands. The feel of a child on my hip is both awkward and familiar. I remember the soft spot on the head, the firmness of a baby's grip, the fleshy rolls around the wrists and ankles. I remember the smell of baby wipes, powder, and diapers, and the ease with which a baby drools. It's awkward, though, because this child is not mine; I do not know its name, or even if it's a boy or a girl. I do not know the right way to hold this baby; it seems to me that most parents are particular about the way their child should be held. I often cringed when I saw others holding Simon without quite enough support to the head, or with one of his legs dangling, or with one of his arms pinned against the holder's chest.

This is, I think, the first child I've held since Simon, and I almost resent having had it thrust into my arms. What if I didn't want to hold it? What if I wanted Simon be the last child my arms ever felt? When Clark Kent died, I vowed I'd never touch another cat again, that Clark would be my last, and I think I held firm to that vow for close to a decade. I didn't make that kind of vow after Simon, but it's still strange to think that the last time my arms were configured this way was around him.

This baby makes a noise and kicks against my side, looking up at me still with its big blue eyes. "Hi," I say, because I'm not sure what else to say. It gurgles and kicks.

I look at the kids playing around me. They seem oblivious to my presence, which is strange, because I feel like some bizarre Virgin Mary statue plunked down in the middle of their yard, a beast at my feet and a babe in my arms. Twenty minutes ago I would have given my eyeteeth to be over here, to be witnessing the play in action, but now what I want more than anything is to be at home.

"Oh! Mr. Clayton," Judith Crane comes rushing through the door. "I'm so sorry to strand you out here—oh look! He likes you!" She smiles as she approaches, stopping two or three yards away from where I stand with the baby and tilting her head as if admiring a work of art. "He doesn't usually take so well to strangers; isn't that nice?" She takes a few steps closer. "Do you have your own children, Mr. Clayton?"

"Hollis," I say.

"I'm sorry?"

"Just Hollis," I say, shifting the baby from one hip to the other and hoping she'll take that as a hint. But she makes no move to take the baby from me.

"Hollis. Right. Well, do you have children of your own, Hollis?"

This is an awkward question to have to answer. If I say no, I feel somehow as if I am denying Simon, or acting as if he never existed. If I say yes, questions will probably ensue that will force me either to lie or reveal that my child is dead, in which case I'm sure Judith Crane will wonder why I didn't just say no, I don't have any children.

"I did," I say.

Judith Crane looks puzzled. "I'm sorry?" she says.

"I did, but he died."

She opens her mouth slightly, pausing before she speaks. "Oh," she says. "I'm sorry."

There are a few seconds of awkward silence. At least I've killed the small talk, if nothing else.

She clears her throat and brushes her hair back. "So," she says. "You were, ah . . ." She looks at me expectantly.

"Oh," I say. I'd almost forgotten the purpose of my visit. "This dog," I say, glancing down. "I was wondering if he was familiar, if you knew who he belongs to."

She looks at the dog and purses her lips. "No," she says. "No, I don't think I've ever seen him." She turns around. "Kids?" she calls. "Hey! Kids!" The kids all glance up from their play. "Does anyone recognize this dog?" They all direct their gazes, briefly, to the dog, and then go back to their play. Judith Crane shrugs. "I guess that means no," she says, apologetically.

"Okay, I just, just wanted to make sure," I say, extending the baby toward her.

"Oh! Silly me," she says, taking the baby from me. "I'm sorry, I should have taken him from you!"

"That's okay," I say, taking a step backward. I want badly to get out of here.

"Can I offer you anything? Cheeseburger? Anything?"

"No," I say, nearly tripping as I take another step back. "I just wanted to check about the dog, but thanks."

"Are you sure? We've got plenty extra, I mean really too much to eat, and . . ."

"No," I say. "My wife's got supper on the stove, so . . ." I shrug and nod and take another step backward. "But thanks for the offer."

"Of course," she says. "It was nice to meet you, Hollis."

"Yes," I say. "You too."

"We should have dinner sometime, or something. You and your wife—what's her name?"

"Claire."

"Claire. It's silly to live next door and not know each other! My goodness! So you and Claire should come over for dinner."

"Yes," I say. I take another step backward and bump the hedge with my back. "That would be fun," I say. "Sometime."

Back in the safety of my own yard, I resettle into my chair and pour myself another drink. The last light is fading above the marsh, so I light the candle on the table and watch the flame grow into life. I sigh and make myself a bite of burrito, which I'd left half-eaten on the table during my unsuccessful excursion next door. I stare at the food on my plate, at the forkload waiting to be lifted to my mouth, and I take a long swallow of my drink. I'm not really hungry anymore.

"Hey," I say to the dog. He's lying on the grass just at the edge of the candlelight. He perks his ears as I set my plate down on the ground at my feet. The dog eyes it, then looks back at me. "Go ahead," I say, pushing it toward him with my foot. "Your half."

10

PRESENCES

I woke the morning after my visit to the neighbors to a male voice I didn't immediately recognize. I was very much aware that I was not at home in my bed, but I waited before opening my eyes to try to figure out exactly where I was so I wouldn't be startled by whatever my surroundings might be. I've always found it terrifying to forget that you're not in your own bed and to open your eyes to what can seem a very strange and awful place, even if moments later you recognize it as your hotel room, or the guestroom of your in-laws.

I seemed to be in a chair. A director's chair, by the feel of it. A breeze and the buzz of hot bugs suggested I was outside, which made me slightly nervous, but the familiar creak of trampoline springs next door eased my worry and enabled me to locate myself in my own director's chair in my own backyard, right where I remembered myself last being, which was a good thing. Now the question that remained was who this voice belonged to.

"Hollis," I heard it say again.

Andrew? I slowly opened my eyes. Andrew stood above me, his hands on his hips.

"Rough night?" he asked.

I straightened up and smoothed my hair down.

"I must have dozed off," I said, glancing at my watch. It was nine a.m.

"Must have," he said, surveying the plate at my feet, the glass and the empty bottle of Jack on the table. "You're a hard one to get ahold of these days," he said.

I gave him a shrug and what I hoped was an apologetic little grin. "Yeah, well, you know."

"Uh huh."

Suddenly the strangeness of seeing my editor from New York standing in my yard in Baybury dawned on me. "Wait a second, what are you doing here?" I asked. Had he come all this way with a million-dollar contract from Random House, or had he come here to collect the nonexistent pages I had long owed him?

"I'm at a conference in Boston this week and have the morning off, so I thought I'd drive up to the shore."

"Oh," I said. "Well." I stood up and brushed my pants off. "Can I offer you anything? Coffee? Tea? There's not much to eat, but if you're hungry—"

"No, thanks," he said. "I had breakfast already. But listen, I need to know if you're going to come to this function or not. I was supposed to let them know last night."

"Function?" I repeated.

"Yes, Hollis, I left you a message about it."

"I didn't—oh. My machine's been acting up, recently, so I didn't really get all the details."

Andrew sighed. "It's part of this conference. It's really just a reception, you know, a cocktail party."

"And?" I said. I'm not big on cocktail parties.

"It's going to be a bunch of editors, a few writers, and lot of people from the publishing world."

"Sounds awful," I said.

"Including Random House."

"What are you saying?"

"I'm saying that they're thinking about the burglar stories, they're thinking hard, and I think it might not be a bad idea if you were to talk to them face-to-face."

"Why?" I said. "I've never had to meet with any publishers before, you've always dealt with that stuff."

Andrew sighed. "Look, Hollis, I know you don't like that whole side of things, but it might not kill you to promote yourself a little. And the burglar stories—they're not a done deal! There are some things they want to go over with you before they commit."

"Like what?" I said.

"I don't know, Hollis, a bunch of nitty-gritty things. That's why you need to go talk to them. Meet them. It's worth it. You're worth it. If I didn't think that I wouldn't have come out here."

I thought about this, that Andrew was saying I was worth it. I sighed. "When is it?" I asked, flatly.

"Friday night. Great. I'll let them know to put your name on the list."

"List?"

"Don't worry about it." He gave me a slip of paper. "Don't lose this," he said. "It's got everything you need to know, time, place, attire, et cetera."

"Attire?"

"So I'll see you Friday?" he said, extending his hand.

"Right," I said. "Friday."

One thing I've never been good at is doing anything when I'm put on the spot. I took piano lessons for a while in high school, until my teacher dropped me because I refused to perform in the concerts she put on once a season to showcase her students. "Why not?" she would say. "You're one of my best students, and you've been playing for less time than any of them!" She didn't understand it when I told her that I didn't like playing for people. I didn't mind if she heard me play, because she was my teacher and lesson time was lesson time, and I didn't mind when my father heard me play, since we did share the same house. I didn't mind being overheard, either—by passersby or whoever my father had on the other end of the phone. But a command performance was simply out of the question. My father gradually learned not to ask me to "play a piece for" anybody, whether my visiting aunt or one of my father's friends, but my teacher persisted in trying to get me to play in her little concerts. I explained to her that I really liked to play only when I felt like it, and preferably when I did not have an audience. She asked me if a tree made a sound when it fell.

"Yes," I said.

"What if a tree falls in a huge forest where there's nobody there to hear it. Does it still make a sound?"

"Yes," I said, and I could tell by her look that that was the wrong answer.

"Wrong," she said. "If no one hears a sound, it's not a sound at all. It's unregistered. A sound unheard is a sound unmade. So if you don't learn to play for an audience, you might as well not play at all. If no one hears you play, your notes vanish into thin air."

"I hear it when I play," I said.

She never knew quite how to argue that point, and eventually she told my father that she simply couldn't teach me any longer because my musical philosophy conflicted so sharply with hers. I didn't really mind. I'd learned all I needed to learn, and though she was a good teacher, I'd never liked her much. She had bad breath, and warts on her fingers that both mesmerized me as they danced over the keys and at the same time disgusted me; I ritually washed the keyboard down after lesson time, afraid that I might catch her case of finger warts.

Honestly, it wasn't that I preferred to play without an audience; the problem was that when asked specifically to play, I could not. I would freeze. I would sit there and look at the keyboard and think about all the notes I had to play to put the piece together, and it overwhelmed me; my fingers simply forgot what to do. I guess that being asked to play made me too aware to play.

And that's what it comes down to in all areas of life, for me: to be too aware of anything is oftentimes debilitating, disorienting, terrifying. The simplest things become unfamiliar and suddenly impossible if you think about them too hard. It's like saying a word aloud over and over again until it sounds like nonsense, or like a word in another language. It's like standing too close to a pointillist painting. It's why I can't take naps; I'm so aware that my purpose in lying down for a nap is to sleep that sleep becomes impossible. Even breathing, that most instinctive of all reflexes, can become hard work if you pay too much attention. I sometimes worry that I think too much about life itself, and I try not to, but the act of trying not to just calls attention to what I'm trying not to do, so I can't help but keep on thinking.

It's the required attire—suit and tie—that's been bothering me about this whole thing. Really, the thing itself is what's bothering me most, but there's nothing I can *do* about *it,* whereas I *can* go up into the attic and rummage through stored suits until I find something adequate to wear. Though I never wear them, I've got some suits from younger days stored away somewhere up there, where my wife has said they will "keep" better than they would stuffed in the back of my closet as they used to be. It will at least give me one less thing to worry about as I worry about Friday.

The attic is as I left it last week. My mother's box is still on the table by the window, alongside my wife's Diet Coke can. Last week I remember thinking it was eerie to be up here because my wife had been up here last and her presence seemed thick in the air, but this week it seems doubly eerie to be up here. My wife's presence still lingers in the neatly stacked and labeled boxes that I know she handled last, in the Diet Coke can on the table. But it seems my presence is up here too, sitting in the chair at the table and staring from soda can to box and back again. I feel like Scrooge visiting Christmas Past. It's strange how a little over a week ago already seems so distinctly "the past."

Most of the boxes with clothing are at the other end of the attic, and I gratefully head over there, leaving my wife, my self, and, though still boxed, my mother having their little party by the window. My wife has labeled all the boxes: WINTER JACKETS, SUMMER CLOTHES, SKI STUFF. There are two boxes labeled SUITS. I pull the topmost suit box from the pile and search around for a loose nail or something to cut through the seal of tape across the box's opening. A long, thick splinter of wood yanked from the ceiling does the trick. I glance guiltily toward the table, knowing that I should have simply gone downstairs and gotten a knife instead of helping the termites in the destruction of the house. Or that's what my wife would have said. I'm not sure what my mother would have said. I feel like you're supposed to know what your mother would say to something like that.

I open the box and survey the suits inside, one at a time. The topmost one looks purple, which leads me to believe that whether kept in a dark box or in the back of a closet, clothing must have a tendency to change color over time. I am certain that I have never owned a purple suit; navy, yes, but purple, certainly not. If my navy suit has gone purple, I fear for the fate of my other suits, and indeed as I lift the purple suit out of the box and inspect the color of the suit beneath, my fears are confirmed. The second suit is an ugly mustard color that I assume must be what my dark brown suit has become. I picture Andrew's expression at the sight of me showing up in purple or puke to this "function" on Friday. It might be a fun evening after all. Better yet, I can use the fate of my suits as an excuse not to attend the function at all. I can simply explain to Andrew that I do not have the appropriate clothes to wear.

I lay the once-navy-now-purple suit out on the floor and stand back to get a good look at it. While I am one hundred percent sure that I have never owned a purple suit, I am five hundred percent sure that I have never owned a suit with flared pant legs. Or a lapel wide enough to store a pistol beneath. And I have *never* worn a kipper tie, which I find neatly folded in the jacket's breast pocket. I pull out the mustard-colored suit and find it to be of a similar design, and suddenly I am flooded with disappointment as I realize that these are not *my* suits, but my father's, which means that my suits are probably in the second box of suits, their colors intact as my wife had said they would be if appropriately stored.

Like my mother's box, this box must have been one of the several that I moved without opening from my father's attic to my own after he died. These suits are the ones my father wore in his twenties. They're the suits he's wearing in the pictures I have of him, my mother, and myself as a baby, though I don't actually remember him wearing them myself. I remember him in whale-ribbed corduroys and flannel shirts, mostly, and the occasional conventional navy suit when the circumstance required. I knew he kept these old suits around, though; rummaging around in the attic for a tent or sleeping bag or something like that once as a teenager I came across this box and asked my father why he bothered keeping those old suits.

He raised his eyebrows. "Those," he said, "are my cancer clothes."

"Your *what?*"

"My cancer clothes. For when I get all old and sick. This stuff's going to hang right off me." He grabbed at the clothes he was wearing. "But that stuff," he directed his eyes atticward, "that stuff'll fit me again."

I had to laugh at that—at the image of my father as an old man hobbling around in flared pants and wide, round collars, and my father laughed, too. I assumed that this was just his cover for nostalgia, though he never admitted as much. So maybe he really did intend to wear these clothes again once the chemo he planned on thinned him out and he figured he had nothing to lose, and when I think about it, why not? Why not relive your youth as you head toward the grave?

I lift the purple- and mustard-colored suits, fold them, and return them as neatly as I can to the box. While I know my wife must have at least opened this box and looked inside to have been able to label it as a box of "suits," I wonder if she actually took the suits out and looked at them. My guess is that she didn't; she had enough boxes to label and things to organize up here that she was probably too busy to do anything but glance at the top suit or two, note that they were indeed suits, close the box up again, and label it. Which means that my father was likely the last one to fold these suits. This realization affects me in the same way as the Diet Coke can on the table, which my wife was the last to drink from, and my mother's box, which hasn't been opened since I packed it up some thirty years ago. I shut the box, glad that I lifted no more suits than the top two from it, glad that there are still suits in this world that he was the last to fold.

It's sad when the distance between times gets so great that there's nothing left from the past to grab onto, when there's nothing tangible left. Clark Kent, for instance, was a big shedder, and his hair clung to couch cushions, carpets, and sweaters for years after he was killed, occasionally even appearing in a forkful of dinner. But his hairs around the house were comforting, and when I couldn't find them anymore, it was sad. It was as if Clark was finally fully gone, entirely immaterial, no longer anything more than a memory.

It's comforting now to have my wife's things still around the house, just as she left them. Some man might lift his absent wife's perfume from the bathroom cabinet to sniff, or sleep with his wife's stockings wrapped around his neck. Some man might gather his wife's clothing in his arms, burrow his face into the folds of her dresses and breathe her in. He might relish the stink of her shoes, or sleep on her side of the bed. But I haven't done any of that, because the more I touch and smell and fondle, the more those things of my wife tranform instead into those things I touch and smell and fondle. I'd like to lift the smelly old sneakers my wife uses for marsh-walking and breath in that smell that, though it stinks, reminds me of her, but I like more knowing that she was the one who touched them last, that she was the one who set them where they're sitting now, just by the sliding door.

When I'm about to open any drawer in the kitchen, it occurs to me that my wife may have been the last to open it, and by opening it myself now I'm erasing one more piece of her. While I was still cooking, I tended only to use one of our many pots and one of our many pans, wanting to leave as much of our cookware as possible last touched by her. There's a glass vase of old sunflowers arranged by my wife down in the kitchen; the water's green and scummed and the flowers brittle and brown, but I cannot bring myself to throw them away. I do not want to touch my wife out of existence in this house, to touch her into memory.

This is maybe the reason I cannot bring myself to open my mother's box on the table. It's less that I'm afraid of what's in there and more that I packed it up when I was eight years old. I like knowing that there's still a piece of me in this world as a child, and if I open the box and go through the contents, I will be touching that child away.

I don't know why it is that it was so very different with Simon. His nonpresent presence was more cruel than a comfort. With Simon, the past couldn't have become the past soon enough.

I seal the box and pull down what I assume is the box of my own suits. I drop it through the trapdoor, and before climbing down myself, I take a breath and bid my wife, my mother, my father, my boy self, my last-week self, and probably the self I'm leaving here now, good-bye.

Sometime during my late twenties, I started suffering from chronic headaches, which went on for about two months before I finally made an appointment at the medical center. Not a huge fan of doctors, I'd have been content to simply continue popping painkillers whenever I felt a headache coming on, except that it had occurred to me that the cause of these headaches might be something like a brain tumor.

My appointment was in late August. The sun was hot on the parking-lot pavement, where I'd spend the next hour until finally deciding it was time to go home. I was just crossing this hot pavement from my car to the clinic doors when I noticed that the doors had been propped open and a steady stream of people was emerging. I paused for a minute, figuring some conference or meeting was letting out and that I'd wait until the flow had subsided before going in instead of fighting my way against the crowd. It was hot in the sun, and so I went over and stood in the shade of a small tree on the edge of the lot, where an old man in tweed was standing. I glanced at my watch anxiously. "I'm going to be late," I muttered, not so much to the old man as to myself.

"Nah," the old man said.

"Huh?" I asked.

"Can't go in there," he said, waving his hand in the direction of the building.

"Why?" I asked.

He shrugged. "Alarm," he said. "Fire."

I looked back over toward the doors of the clinic. The stream of people coming out had thickened and now included, I saw, some in wheelchairs with IV drips in tow, some clad in nothing but those flimsy gowns I hate having to wear, one holding bloody gauze to a half-stitched chin hit by a hockey stick, and another to a finger sliced in the kitchen.

"They can't have a fire drill in a medical center," I said incredulously, and I wandered in the direction of the crowd for someone official-looking to ask about what was going on.

A nurse was directing traffic, sending everybody over to the far corner of the parking lot.

"Excuse me," I said, pushing through the crowd in the wrong direction.

"Sir! Sir!" the nurse called at me, twirling her finger in the air as a signal for me to similarly turn myself around. "We're heading in that direction, sir!"

I paused, then I turned and joined the herd hobbling over to the corner of the parking lot.

It was an interesting crowd assembled there; I sat on the curb and surveyed them all. Worried-looking doctors stalked around with clipboards, surveying the crowd for various patients; a nurse carried tubes of blood in a bucket of ice. There were two women in wheelchairs with all sorts of tubes running from their arms to various packets of fluid hanging from a silver rack on wheels. They laughed and gossiped as if in beach chairs at the beach, their nurses whispering above them. There was a contingency of skinny old ladies huddled in the shade of a canopy of towels held up by anxious-looking nurses. Bursts of laughter occasionally erupted from the knots of orderlies in scrubs, gathered together cocktail-party style. There were many patients who looked like they were there for a routine checkup; they stood around clutching shut the open backs of their little gowns. I was glad the alarm had gone off before I'd gone inside, before I'd had to change into that embarrassing attire.

When I think about that hour, as I sat on the curb and watched the crowd, uncertain of how long it would be before we could all go inside and wondering if a possible brain tumor was really worth sticking around for anyway, it's like a soundless movie reel. There's no sound attached to the memory, and it's almost in slow motion. In front of the crowd—in front of the orderlies, the women in wheelchairs, the skinny old ladies, the worried doctors, and the awkward patients—is the only exception to this soundlessness, a father and son who pace slowly back and forth across my field of vision.

The son is in his early forties, I'd say. He's wearing a suit, so I'd think he's probably taking time off work to bring his father to a doctor's appointment. The father is wearing khakis fastened tight to his wizened frame with a belt, and a long-sleeved plaid shirt unbuttoned to the second button, and his neck skin droops in loose folds from his chin to where it disappears into his shirt. His head is swallowed by a navy baseball cap with a stiff and unbent brim. The two pace back and forth, the father hunched and clinging to his son's elbow, the son sweating and glancing at his watch.

"How long?" the old man asks.

"I don't know, Dad, not too long, now," the son says.

"What's going on?" the old man asks.

"The fire alarm went off," the son says.

"Why?" the old man asks.

"I'm not sure, Dad," the son says.

"How long?" the old man asks.

"I don't know, Dad, not too long, now."

It's like a bad dream, this movie-reel memory, not because it's scary, and not because of its slow-motion quality and selective sound, but because of the horrible, horrible thought that I remember occurred to me nearly every time the father and son passed before me: I hope my father dies before that happens.

I hate that that thought occurred to me, and I hate that since it did, part of me must have meant it. It would bother me less if I thought that I hoped what I hoped for my father's sake. It would bother me less if I thought that I hoped my father would be spared the loss of his mind, the shriveling of his body, the helplessness of old age. But instead I think that I hoped to be spared the pain of watching my father decline, the sense of obligation to take care of him, and the inevitable guilt for sometimes just not wanting to. I think I hoped to be spared having to take on the role of father to my father.

The larger part of me would have rather had my father alive forever, even in a vegetable state, than be without a father in the world. But the awful wish that I made in the parking lot of the medical center had more power than I realized, and my father died of a heart attack a few years later. He never got to wear his cancer clothes. It's always the goddamn wishes I don't mean that come true.

.   .   .

It seems that my own suits are on the verge of becoming cancer clothes; they seem to have gotten smaller during their years in the attic. I can squeeze in there, but it's a tight fit.

Tonight, I was going to forgo the walk to San Miguel and drive instead, just because I'm out of Jack and the liquor store's a hike, but if I'm supposed to wear a suit by the end of the week, I figure I should probably try to shed a few pounds, and walking might help with that, even if it's a longer walk than I'd ordinarily like to take.

Instead of walking around the park on my way home, like I usually do, I walk through it and pause when I reach the dog, who's sitting, as usual, under his tree. I figure another good policy might be to share my dinner nightly with the dog if I'm going to have to wear a suit in a matter of days.

"Hi," I say.

The dog wags his tail.

"Dinner time," I say, and start up again. After a few yards, I pause and turn around. The dog is still sitting under the tree, watching me.

"Come on!" I say, and put one bag down to slap my thigh. But the dog doesn't move. I shrug and walk away, acting as if I don't care whether the dog comes home with me or not. But I did enjoy his company at dinner the other night. I liked that he just showed up at my house even though I hadn't walked for him to be able to follow me. It made me feel as if the dog liked me for some reason, that maybe he'd been following *me,* and not just the scent of my burrito. I glance over my shoulder again after another few yards, as subtly as I can. I don't want to show too much interest, just in case this dog is playing hard to get. And sure enough, the dog's trailing me, interested in me now that I'm no longer showing interest in him. Maybe I am a little more of a dog person than I thought.

11

A DAY IN THE RAINY LIFE

seem to have a new dream to add to my list of recurring ones. In it, I'm in a gym—which is strange because I've never worked out in a gym in my life—and I'm trying to run on the treadmill. I know there are those running dreams in which the dreamer is being chased, but in his panic he can't run fast enough, and keeps on slipping and tripping as the chaser nears. In my dream, it isn't like that. It's not that I can't run fast enough; it's that I can't run at all. My legs simply buckle beneath me. What's terrifying about this dream is how very physical it is. I can *feel* my muscles struggling to support me, to make my legs move, and though I can't feel the force of impact as I hit the moving belt, I can *feel* it as my knees crumple.

I had the dream again last night. I had just fallen, and I was lying on the floor. Beside me, someone was riding a stationary bike, but all I could see from my vantage point was the fan of the front wheel, spinning into a blur as the person pedaled, sounding *tic-tic-tic-tic-tic* as it spun, which *tic-tic-tic-tic-tic* I came to recognize as rain dripping steadily from the gutter as I slowly, gratefully reemerged into this world.

That is something I've always appreciated—a smooth transition from dreams into waking, or the ability to recognize how elements from the dream world correspond with elements from the real world. An air raid alarm in some apocalyptic dream might be just the wail of an ambulance going by. The muttering voice of a worried doctor about to cut me open might just be the hushed voice of my wife on the phone in the next room, or the shriek of an amputating saw might just be the man next door cutting the dead branches off his tree. That's not to say I've necessarily had these dreams, but in my case, this morning, I took pleasure in the transformation of the bike wheel ticking away into the steady sound of rain. I took pleasure that when I stretched my legs and moved them around, they were all there, and did what I willed them to do. I found pleasure, too, in being in the folds of warm white blankets while all around me the world was chilly and wet. I felt good. I had gone to bed early, and aside from my dream, I'd slept well. There's really nothing like a mostly good night's sleep after a long day, a little Jack, and half a burrito, I was thinking, but then I started thinking about the *other* half of my burrito, which was sitting now in the belly of a creature who was certainly not as warm, dry, or comfortable as myself, and about whom, to my annoyance, I suddenly found myself concerned. I got up and peered out the window on the off chance that the dog might still be sitting on the lawn, where I'd bade him good night last night. But, of course, he wasn't there.

As I sit with my coffee at my desk, thumbing through my notes for inspiration, I cannot get this dog off my mind. I can't help but wonder what he does in the rain. I wonder if he toughs it out beneath his tree in the park downtown, taking whatever shelter he can beneath the scant canopy its leaves afford. It isn't a very big tree he lies beneath. I wonder if he has another hangout I don't know about, one that is perhaps a little more cozy and dry.

I come to the last page of my notes, flip it over to the next clean page, and sigh. *Dear Claire,* I write. I tell her about this dog, and about how though I'm willing to share dinner with him, if only for the sake of helping me lose weight, I hesitate to let him inside. *He's not my dog, you know? But today it's raining, and I can't help but wonder what he's doing now. I can't help but wonder if he's wet and cold, though I shouldn't wonder, (a) because he's not my dog, (b) because he's been fine without me, and (c) because he's an animal, and animals don't get cold and wet in the rain like humans, do they? Aren't they somehow equipped for things like weather?* I try to think about other animals, and if I've seen them in the rain. Horses I've seen, and cows, and when I really think about it, they look pretty miserable. They just stand there, their tails flicking now and again, their hooves occasionally stomping the ground, their hair flat against their bodies, their eyes blinking slow. Seagulls I've seen. Seagulls stay low in the rain; they stand in large groups on the sand, behind whatever rock or pile of seaweed will shield them from the wind. And when I think about them, they don't look particularly happy either. *I'm just not sure, Claire. Because when I think about it— about cows, and horses, and gulls—none of them seem any too pleased when it's raining, do they? But it's all part of nature, I guess—animals, weather. And this dog's NOT my dog, and it would be wrong of me to lead him on. And like I've said, he's always been just fine in the rain without me. I bet he even likes the rain. Or if he doesn't necessarily like the rain, I'm sure he has some coping strategy—otherwise, don't you think he'd have thought of me and shown up here in hopes I'd let him in?* I go to each door and look outside, making sure the dog is neither in the backyard nor at the end of the driveway, and then I return to my desk. *And he's not here. So that's that. Anyway, back to work. Love you, Hollis.*

Back to work. I flip again through my notes, then sit back and stare out the window, wishing the rain weren't keeping the neighbors' kids inside so that I could watch them play and feel at least a little productive. Which makes me wonder: What do children do on rainy days? Simon was easy on rainy days; we'd just bring him with us on our nickel drives. In his first couple years, he'd take his nap in the backseat, and then when he got older, we'd sometimes bring a book on tape for him to listen to, or I'd make up a story. All my made-up stories for Simon, in the car or before bed, were about a zookeeper named Grover who knew how to speak the languages of all the animals. Sometimes Simon would take a turn telling a Grover story himself. Simon liked stories, like me.

But other kids, older kids, what do they do? I take the pair of binoculars Claire keeps for bird-watching from the hall closet and return to my desk to see if I can see inside the neighbors' house and perhaps watch the kids inside at play. There are four windows on the side of their house facing ours. The first has frosted glass, so I assume it must be a bathroom. The next two, I think, are the windows to what seems to be the living room. There is a couch with too many pillows on it for anyone to sit down, a glass-topped coffee table with a little basket of what looks like potpourri in the center, and two neat stacks of coffee-table books on either side. There are two old and stiff-looking chairs, the kind with ornately carved wooden arms and legs and a back upholstered in some fine floral print. There are two shelves of glassed-in china against the back wall. I figure this must be the fake living room, the one reserved for entertaining that no one otherwise inhabits. I figure there must be another living room, a *real* living room on the other side of the house, in which the kids are probably gathered now, their toys out on the floor, the sofa stained, the TV in one corner and stereo in another. We have only one living room, but I've known people who have two, and the Cranes' house is certainly large enough that for all I know they might even have three. But of course I can see only the fake one.

Keeping the binoculars to my eyes, I swivel my focus over to the last window. The kitchen. This could be promising. I'm sure if I wait long enough some child is bound to come in for a drink or a snack.

There's a round table in the middle of the room. One wall's lined with cabinets full of what I imagine must be the latest in cereals and snacks for kids, and there's a door that leads outside. Along the other wall is the stove, flanked by counterspace with more cabinets both above and underneath. Along the back wall is the door and the refrigerator. I figure that the sink must be beneath the window, and probably the dishwasher as well.

Suddenly, Judith Crane enters the kitchen. She pulls a container of juice from the refrigerator and a glass from one of the upper cabinets near the stove, and she pours herself a drink, which she downs all at once. She returns the carton to the fridge, and brings the glass to where I have correctly guessed the sink is located, right beneath the window. Though I can't see her hands, from the movements of her shoulders and the downward direction of her gaze I can tell she's washing the glass off. Judith Crane strikes me as the type to double-wash, first by hand, then by dishwasher, though she seems now to be doing a thorough enough job by hand that she could well return the glass directly to the cabinet. I myself would have put it directly into the dishwasher. It's been, I'd say, a good twenty seconds of washing now, and I begin to count, twenty-one, twenty-two, twenty-three, when suddenly, on twenty-four, Judith Crane looks up and directly at me.

I drop the binoculars and sit far back in my chair and out of sight, my heart pounding. I wonder what exactly I should do. Should I stay back and out of sight in the hopes that Judith Crane might think her eyes played a trick on her? Should I return to the window and wave? Should I return to the window, but instead of acknowledging her, fiddle around with the binoculars, as though all I was doing was testing them out, completely unaware of her?

What I'd really like to do is just stay back and pretend nothing ever happened, but if I do that, things might be very awkward next time I see Judith Crane. And I haven't been doing anything wrong.

It's not like I was watching her change her clothing, or even looking into her bedroom, but I realize that by the way I'm acting, it seems as if I *have* done somthing wrong. I bet she thinks it's pretty suspicious, the way I jumped back as soon as she saw me. I bet she thinks I watch her all the time, that I'm some infatuated sicko, and I realize that the best way to dispel this notion is probably to get up, smile, and wave.

I get out of my chair and lean forward over my desk to the window, but Judith Crane is no longer in her own window; in fact, she doesn't seem to be anywhere in her kitchen at all. I hadn't considered this possibility, and I'm not sure what to make of it; I thought she'd have been shocked into place, or else waiting there for me to reappear. Might this mean that she didn't see me at all? Because although I could see Judith Crane quite clearly with the help of the binoculars, without them her kitchen window seems far enough away that it is, I think, quite possible that she may well not have seen me spying. I lift the binoculars from where I've let them fall, intending to compare the view with and without their aid, but when I raise the binoculars to my eyes, I find that in their fall they have broken. No matter how I adjust them, all I can see is blur.

"Shit," I mutter, slouching back into my chair. "Shit, shit, shit."

I pick up my pen. *Dear Claire,* I write, *I just broke your binoculars. Sorry.* I look at my pathetic little message and then scribble it out. *How?* I know she would ask. *Don't tell me you were birdwatching.* No, Claire knows me better than that. She'd know that if I'd been using her binoculars, it was likely for no traditional purpose, and what to me might seem a perfectly legitimate use of binoculars might to her seem crazy. What could I possibly tell her? How could I explain myself?

Coming back from the mini-mall a few exits down the highway, I am, of course, the first car stopped at the long light at the bottom of the Baybury exit ramp, which leaves me face-to-face with Ellen Marie Franklin.

"Ellen!" I say in greeting, peering up at the girl. "And how are you on this rainy day?"

I, myself, am in a much better mood than I had been in when I left the house, having quite possibly embarrassed myself thoroughly in front of Judith Crane and having broken my wife's binoculars in the process. I couldn't explain myself to her, I concluded, and the thought filled me with panic. I needed to get the binoculars fixed, return them to their closet, and say nothing about the incident at all, ever. And I wanted to do it immediately. I wanted to clear this mistake from the slate.

"It shouldn't be a problem," the man behind the repair-shop counter told me, having examined the binoculars. He'd been reading a comic book when I entered the store, and even though the bells attached to the door annouced my entrance, he didn't even look up until he'd reached the bottom of the page. He sat behind a tall counter and in front of rows of shelves with TVs, VCRs, old radios, and other gadgets I couldn't identify, all dangling wires and cables and tagged with colored stickers. At first, I thought he was so engrossed in his comic book that he might not have heard me come in, so I cleared my throat. His eyes remained on his book, but his finger shot into the air, asking for a minute. "Fact," he said, after that minute and a quick survey of the binoculars, "shouldn't take more than a half hour, give or take."

"Great," I said. "Really? Wow, that's great."

The man started filling out a slip. "Sooo," he said, his pen hovering. "You want to pick them up tomorrow? Next day?"

"I can just wait," I said.

"Guess what, bud, got other jobs ahead of yours. Half hour doesn't mean a half hour from now."

"Oh," I said, annoyed and deflated at the prospect of having this blemish stain the day for any longer than necessary. I needed the binoculars fixed today. I was counting on it. "I didn't realize you were so busy." I glanced toward his comic book.

"Lunch break, thank you," he said. "Some people have what, ice cream, candy bar for dessert, I have comics. And you know what, that's a hard thing for me. You know, I had an addiction." The repairman's face reddened, and his veins began to stand out on his forehead.

This was more than I'd bargained for. "An addiction?" I repeated, and I took a step backward.

"That's right," he said. "Sweets. Chocolate especially. You know I had to go to Utah to get it fixed?" He was leaning forward now, his palms on the counter and his neck stretching to the other side, to my side. I wanted to take another step back, but I held my ground, guessing that people, like dogs or horses or bears, can sense when you're afraid and take advantage of it.

"Utah?"

"That's right," he said. "Crazy Russian. Can break any addiction. Cured me. You heard of him?"

"No," I said. "No, I haven't."

"Yeah," he said. "So comics instead. Comics for dessert. Doesn't mean I don't have things to work on."

"No, of course," I said. I eyed Claire's binoculars on the counter, wanting to grab them and run and never return, but wanting more, still, to get them fixed. "I'm sure you've got lots to do." I nodded toward the crammed shelves.

"Yeah," he said. "Yeah, I do. But now that I've *finished* my comics, I can go back to work, and I can start on your binocs after I finish that TV." He gestured toward a TV on a table in the corner, and I nodded.

"Okay," I said.

"Should be finished with the TV in about a half hour. Then I can start on yours."

"So an hour?" I asked. "About?"

" 'Bout that," he said.

"Thanks," I said. "I'll come back then. About an hour. Thanks a lot. That's great."

The repair man stared at me, nodding. He still stood with his arms spread and his palms down on the counter before him, but he'd straightened up, retreated to his side of the counter.

I didn't mind waiting, because as I'd pulled in to the mini-mall, even more thrilling than the sight of the repair shop and the prospect of actually changing the past, of unmaking a mistake, was the sight of a warehouse-sized toy store at one end of the parking lot. I might not have been able to figure out what most kids do on rainy days by spying on the neighbors' kids, but it now occurred to me that there were other ways to figure it out.

I tackled the toy store row by row. The first row had baby toys: little gyms and play mats and rattles, things I was familiar with because of Simon, although they seemed, just a few years later, to be a little more high-tech, a little more vibrant in color, made with better material. There was a stuffed-animal section, and a doll section, and an action-figure section with military figures and superheroes. Some of these guys come equipped with grenades and massive shotguns, some have machetes, and some have explosives strapped around their chests. Some come with tanks, and some with bombers. None of this was new to me, either.

There was another section filled with building sets, blocks, and models, and a "science and discovery" section, which contained things like chemistry sets, crystal-growing kits, butterfly nets, and tadpoles you can grow into frogs. Simon would be nearly six, now, and I bet he'd like this kind of stuff. But it's hard to say that, because I don't know Simon as a six-year-old.

Next, there was a section of board games and puzzles, then a section of outdoor games, like baseball, football, and basketball. I skipped over the aisle of tricycles and such.

The largest section by far was the video game and electronics section, which contained things I'd never seen before. I stood at the glassed-in display of all kinds of handsets and wires and boxes, staring at it and wondering how kids could ever understand how to work it all.

"Can I help you with something, sir?"

I jumped, jolted out of the trancelike state I hadn't even been aware of entering. "Sorry?" I said.

A young man—Bert, his name tag said—was standing beside me. "Is there something I can help you with?"

"Well," I said, wondering if I wanted to get involved with any other salespeople today. But Bert seemed gentle enough. And smaller than me, unlike the chocolate addict. Plus, we were in a toy store. "I guess—could I ask you a question?"

"Of course, sir," he said.

"What do most kids do on rainy days? Blocks? Puzzles? Or—" I gestured at the array of electric wares and video games before me.

"These days, sir? I'd say video games, for sure. On clear days, too. On all days. They're our big sellers, anyway."

"Really," I said.

"Yes, I'd say so, sir."

"I think I'll take one, then," I said.

"You'll take one?"

"Yes," I said.

"Well, sir, did you have any particular system in mind?"

"Oh," I said. System? I shrugged and tried to seem casual. "Whatever you think would be best."

Bert gave me a funny look. "Well, it's really a matter of personal preference," he said.

"I trust your judgment. Whatever you think is good. But probably not overly complicated, if that's a factor."

"Okay, sir," Bert said, still seeming a little bit skeptical. "I should have that ready for you in no time."

And thirty minutes later, here I am at the bottom of the exit ramp, the binoculars safely on the seat beside me, and my console, dual shock controller, cables, and hardware packed away in a large box in the back of the car, asking Ellen Marie how she is on this rainy day, and then immediately wishing I hadn't. Ellen Marie is probably not well at all on this rainy day. She's probably locked in some cellar, or blindfolded, or maybe even decomposing in some ditch or on the bank of some river. She's certainly not playing video games, or spying on her neighbors, or even sitting wet under a tree that at least she can call home.

She smiles down at me. "I'm sorry," I tell her. The car behind me honks to let me know the light's turned green.

I take the long way home, through downtown Baybury and by the park. I look over in the direction of the dog's tree, and sure enough, there he is, lying down with his chin resting on his front paws, his fur wetted into clumps. I pull over and turn the engine off. I draw the hood of my raincoat up over my head and get out of the car.

"Hey!" I call from the edge of the park. The dog lifts his head and looks over at me. "Want to get out of the rain?" I ask. The dog gives the ground a few tentative thwumps of his tail. "Come on!" I call, bending over a bit and patting my thighs like I've seen dog people do. The dog lowers his chin back onto his paws. I straighten up. Maybe the problem is that the dog doesn't recognize me with my jacket and hood. I cross the grass over to him and stoop down, and this time I get the reception I was hoping for. The dog gets up, his tail waving wildly now. "That's right!" I say. "It's me!" It feels good to be greeted like this. "Come on," I say, "let's go." The dog pauses before leaving the shelter of his tree, then follows me to the car. I open the back door for him, and he gladly jumps in, despite all the beach crap cluttering the back. "This is just until the rain clears," I inform the dog before shutting the door behind him.

"Sal!" I say, opening the door for him. "Thank God! I'm up to my ears in these wires and no matter what I attach to what or what I plug in where I can't seem to get this to work!" Sal is a technician, and so, I figure, good with things like setting up video games. I am not. I've spent a good two hours trying to figure it out already.

"Well, what is it?" Sal asks. "No promises, but I'll give it my best shot."

"In here," I say, ushering Sal into the living room, where I've got my "system" and all its various components spread out on the floor in front of the TV. Sal surveys it all.

"Nintendo?" he says.

"Yeah," I say. "Why? Uh-oh, harder than you thought?"

"No," Sal says. "No, not at all. I just . . ." He shrugs. "No, it shouldn't be a problem."

In maybe fifteen minutes, Sal has it all set up.

"You're fast," I say. "You have one of these?"

Sal shakes his head. "No," he says. "My nephews do, though. I helped them set it up last Christmas."

"You played?" I ask.

Sal nods. "Yeah. I wasn't too good, though. I kept on dying. I could see how kids could get into it, though. My sister says the boys sit there for hours playing."

"Should we give it a try?" I ask.

Sal shrugs. "Sure," he says. "Why not?" Then he tilts his head, as if hearing something. "What is that?" he says, and then I hear it, too—whining and scratching coming from inside the bathroom in the hall.

"Shit!" I say. "I completely forgot!" I hurry to the bathroom, where I'd put the dog after he'd gotten tangled up in the wires for the third time as I tried to set things up. I open the door a crack and peer in. The dog looks back at me, panting, his tail wagging. "Sorry," I say, opening the door wide and letting him out.

He goes bounding into the living room ahead of me, and when I get there myself, Sal's crouched down and petting him. "You got a dog?" he asks.

"No," I say. "He's not mine."

"Whose?" Sal asks. "He's sweet."

"I don't know, actually," I say. "I think he pretty much owns himself. He's always hanging out in the park, and I just thought he might want to get in out of the rain."

"Oh," Sal says, straightening up as the dog comes over to see me. "So he's a stray?"

"I guess," I say.

"Oh," Sal says, nodding, looking vaguely skeptical.

"Oh, but don't worry," I say. "He's not rabid, or anything. He's actually nice. We've been having dinner together for the past few nights, so I've kind of gotten to know him, and I'd say he's harmless."

"Dinner?" Sal says. He doesn't seem convinced.

"Yeah, well, you know, he's hungry, I need to lose weight, so, you know," I shrug.

"Right," Sal says.

"So should we play?"

"Yeah," Sal says. "Sure."

Playing a video game is one of the strangest things I've experienced. You're a little man, trying to make your way through a world of fireballs and demons and traps and castles to save a princess somewhere on the other end. You can go down tunnels, or into caves, or up into the clouds, or under the water in search of the girl, picking up money and special powers along the way.

I think I frustrated Sal sometimes, because for me, it wasn't as much about saving the princess as it was about thoroughly exploring the world of the game. I particularly like going up into the clouds.

"You've already done that," Sal would say. "You know there's nothing up there and the thin air's just going to kill you."

"Yeah, but I like it in the clouds," I'd say, and Sal would shake his head as I hopped from cloud to cloud as near as I could to the sun until the air got too thin to breathe and I dropped off the screen to my death.

But that's the thing: You can go into the clouds just for the fun of it even though you know it's going to kill you, because you get to die four or five times over before you're actually dead for good, and if you're lucky and pick up enough coins, you can buy yourself another life or two.

It's probably a good thing that life's not really like that, as much as part of me wishes it were. I'd probably forget which life I was on, and then, when I was down to my last life after I'd squandered the rest of my lives away on things like strict alcohol diets or jumping off tall buildings—not for the sake of dying, but for the sake of flying, of fun—when it really mattered, I might not realize it did, and then I'd die my final death by mistake, before I was really ready.

After I'd died my eighth final death this afternoon and my eyes couldn't focus on the TV anymore, I tossed my controller down and looked at Sal, who himself still had three lives left.

"You're good," I said.

"No I'm not," he said. "I'm just cautious. Except now," and he steered his little man right off a cliff, "I'm ready to die."

Sal killed off all his lives and looked at me. "Well," he said, "not exactly the afternoon I'd bargained for, but it was interesting. Maybe now I'll be good enough to play with my nephews."

"Maybe," I said, standing up. I looked at my watch. "It seems to be happy hour," I said. "Pratty's?"

"God, I'd love to," he said, getting up himself and looking at his watch. "I could use a cold beer." He sighed. "I should get home to Mona, though."

"Swing by and pick her up!" I suggested. Mona likes Pratty's.

"Oh, she can't drink these days."

"Mona can't drink?"

Sal shook his head.

"She okay?" I asked.

"Yeah, yeah," Sal said quickly. "No, she's fine. It's just that," and here he shrugged, almost apologetically, "you know, we're expecting."

"No kidding!" I said. "I didn't know that! Congratulations!"

"Yeah, we just found out ourselves," Sal's eyes kept darting around the room. He was red and seemed on the verge of breaking into a sweat.

"You okay?" I asked.

Sal swallowed. "Yeah!" he said, almost too enthusiastically.

"Hey," I said, wanting to ease his apparent discomfort as best I could.

Sal swallowed again, hard, and looked at the floor. "I'm sorry, Hollis," Sal said.

I've been thinking about that *I'm sorry, Hollis,* ever since I got to Pratty's, alone. I'd thought Sal's problem was that he was nervous about becoming a father, but as I replay the conversation in my head, the more it seems that *I,* and not the fact of Mona's pregnancy, was the source of Sal's discomfort. If he'd answered *Thank you, Hollis,* then I'd think differently, but that my attempt at comfort seemed to make things worse, and that he'd answered it with an apology, makes it clear to me that he was uncomfortable for my sake, that he must have felt something like guilt for expecting a child when he knows I've lost one.

"You look like you could use another," Crosby says, setting a fresh pint down in front of me. I look up at him, jolted out of thought.

"I do?" I say. I hadn't been aware of making any particular expression or looking any way at all, and it unnerves me to think that my face might betray the unsettled feelings I've been experiencing as I replay my parting conversation with Sal.

Crosby shrugs. "Who can't use another, most of the time?" he says.

I nod.

"So," Crosby says, lighting a cigarette. "You coming tomorrow night?"

"Tomorrow night?"

"Yeah. It's Pratty's fiftieth. Open bar, free food. Invite only."

"I didn't know that!" I say, feeling vaguely insulted by the lateness of my invitation. What if I hadn't come in this afternoon? How would I have found out?

Crosby nods. "Nothing fancy," he says. "You know, pizza, burgers, nachos. But not a bad way to spend a Friday night." Friday? Already?

"Shit!" I say. "Is it Thursday already?"

Crosby nods.

"So tomorrow's Friday?"

"I believe that's the order in which the days fall," Crosby says, dragging on his cigarette.

"Shit," I say, suddenly alarmed by the proximity of the current day to Friday, between which I'd been sure there was a buffer of at least another day.

"What's wrong with Friday?" Crosby asks.

"Ah," I say. "I have to go to some goddamn cocktail party in Boston. Some goddamn literary thing."

"Really," Crosby says. "That sounds like tremendous fun." His voice is thick with sarcasm.

"Yeah, tell me about it," I say. "I don't *do* well at cocktail parties. I just don't."

Crosy nods. "I can see that," he says.

"Thanks," I say.

Just then Larry hollers from his usual seat at the end of the bar. "Crosby! I'm empty down here!"

Crosby holds up a finger in Larry's direction as he reaches into the cooler under the counter for one of Larry's beers. "Hollis is too good for our party tomorrow night," he informs Larry as he delivers the beer. I slide my own beer and myself down toward Larry.

"That," I say, "is not true."

"You're not coming?" Larry shouts.

I shake my head. "Can't."

"What's that horseshit?" Larry yells.

"I *want* to, believe me."

"Nope," Crosby says, shaking his head. "Hollis has *another* party to go to. A *literary* party."

Larry gapes. "No!"

"It's for work," I offer lamely. "I have to."

Larry motions to Crosby to come close and whispers something in his ear. Crosby disappears down the bar, and when he returns a minute or so later, he's got four shot glasses of whiskey in each palm.

"Four for me, four for you!" Larry yells. "Then we'll see if you feel like going to any party tomorrow!" He cackles and raises a glass, and what else can I do but raise one in kind? It would be against all rules of drinking etiquette to turn down a drink that's bought for you. And I hardly think that four shots of whiskey will do the damage that Larry thinks it will. He's probably unfamiliar with the quality time I spend nightly with Jack.

"Cheers!" Larry roars, and we gulp the whiskey down.

My wife used to go up to Vermont one weekend a year to ski with her college roommates, and the first year we were married, I decided I'd come along rather than spend a weekend alone, though I ended up spending the weekend mostly alone anyway, since I'm not the best skier and couldn't quite keep up. They'd go off and ski their black diamonds; I'd stick to the greens, the occasional blue, and the lodge, but if I'd had it my way, I would have just ridden the chairlift all day. That, in my opinion, was the best part of whole deal. I loved the fifteen-minute ride to the top, the excuse it afforded to just sit and do nothing at all, or to think about my stories if I wanted to, or to imagine various scenarios in which I was famous or some kind of hero, or even to sing if I felt like it, all while hanging thirty feet in the air on the side of a mountain, the clouds seeming just yards away. Fifteen minutes of total freedom.

Total freedom, that is, as long as I got to ride solo, and so I went out of my way not to share a chair with any chatty stranger who wanted to know where I was from, what my name was, what I did for a living, what I wrote about. "Single?" another solo skier would ask, gesturing for me to join him or her in line. "No," I'd say, "I'm waiting for someone." And as soon as that skier was up and away I'd get in line myself for my own solo journey up the mountain and to wherever my mind might take me in the meantime.

One time, though, there was an older man alone in front of me in line who, when he'd reached the front of the line, let chair after chair go by without boarding, looking instead expectantly at me over his shoulder. I pretended not to notice and busied myself with blowing my nose until the lift operator finally tapped me and asked if I'd please join the gentleman in front of me. "Sure," I grumbled, though I couldn't imagine why it was necessary, and I slid my way up to the man.

"I have a problem," the man said to me the moment our skis had lifted from the snow as we swung away from the ground. Before I could even imagine what kind of problem this man might have (killer, rapist, schizo, acrophobe), he said, "I fall asleep on chairlifts."

I paused. "Oh," I said.

"Narcolepsy," he explained.

"Oh," I said.

"My wife went in for the day and she made me promise not to ride the lift alone. I'd fall asleep in maybe thirty seconds and fall off, see, unless there was someone riding with me."

"Oh," I said. I wasn't sure what was expected of me. "So, should I, I don't know, hold on to you?" I asked.

"Oh no," the man laughed. "Just talk to me."

"Talk to you?"

"Yeah, that's all. Just keep me awake."

"Oh," I said. "Okay."

But then as I went to compile a mental list of questions to ask and topics to discuss, my mind drew a total blank. I simply couldn't come up with anything to say. It was that awareness problem I have, that problem I have of not being able to do anything when put on the spot, the problem that makes me so dread going to this cocktail party tomorrow night in Boston, which dread I'm trying to make clear to Larry and Crosby by giving them the example of the narcoleptic story.

"So you see?" I say. "It's going to be like that."

"How's a party like riding the lift?" Larry says.

"It's not," I say. "What I'm saying is that on the chairlift with the narcoleptic, I *had* to talk, so I *couldn't* talk, and at this cocktail party I'll *have* to talk, so I won't be *able* to talk. I'll be too *aware* to talk."

Larry waves his hand. "Eh," he grunts. "Whatever." He bangs an open palm down loosely on the bartop.

I turn to Crosby. "Do *you* get it?" I ask.

Crosby uncrosses his arms and pulls a cigarette from his breast pocket. "I think I get *it,*" he says. "But I'm not sure I get *you,* Hollis."

"What's that supposed to mean?" I ask.

Crosby shrugs.

"Don't be like that!" I say. I sometimes get sick of Crosby's unwillingness to give a straight answer.

"Like what?" he says.

I shrug back at him. "Like that. What do you mean you get it, but not me?"

"I understand the *it,* and how the *it* makes sense to you, but I think you're the only one the *it* would occur to."

I'm not sure if it's Crosby that's not making sense or the whiskey that's making Crosby not seem to make sense; regardless, there are too many *it*'s in there for me to make sense of. "Right," I say. "Thanks."

"So finish the story," Larry says.

"What?" I ask.

"The story. The guy. So did he fall off?"

"What, the narcoleptic?" I say.

"Yeah," Larry says. "Did he fall off the chairlift?"

"Oh, no," I say. "No, he just kind of had to keep himself awake by asking *me* questions."

Larry looks both disappointed and incredulous. "He didn't fall off?" Larry asks. "Well what kind of story is that?"

I rub my eyes with my palms. "I don't know if I can do this right now, Larry," I say.

"Do what?" he says. "I just want to know what kind of story that is if the guy didn't even fall off."

I sigh. "Two minutes ago, before you knew whether or not the guy fell off, you asked me to finish *the story*, right?"

"Yeah," Larry says.

"So why was it a story then, and it's not a story now?"

"Shitty ending!" Larry bellows. "If the guy's fine, then what's the point?"

"The point is that I was *not* fine," I say. "That was my point in telling the story. Sorry— the nonstory."

"Eh," Larry waves his hand at me, seemingly disgusted.

I shrug. "Hey Crosby," I say. "Time is it?"

Crosby looks at his watch. "Seven thirty."

"Shit," I say. "I've got to get going. It's dinnertime."

"Dinnertime?" Crosby says, his interest suddenly seeming peaked. "Claire home?"

I pause. "No," I say. "No. It's just dinnertime."

I take the dog out before we eat, holding a large umbrella above us both. I was mildly concerned, as I drove home with our burrito, about the interruption rain would have on my dinner routine, as there'd be no sun to watch set and I wouldn't be able to eat outside. But then, as soon as I got home, I remembered the video game, and though I couldn't necessarily play as I ate, I could play in between bites, or eat in between lives.

I take two plates from the cabinet and put half a burrito on each, and the dog follows me eagerly into the living room. "Your half," I say, setting his plate down, "and my half," I say, putting my own plate on my lap where I can protect it in case the dog decides his own half wasn't quite satisfying enough. The dog looks at me expectantly. "Go on," I say, gesturing toward his plate. "Eat! Good boy!" He wags his tail, wolfs his half down, circles, and lies down beside me on the floor. "Can't have mine, though," I say, and I turn the system on, entering back into that world as if into a dream.

12

ABSENCES

t's an hour and a half from Baybury to Boston, and an hour after the function has officially begun, I am still twenty minutes away in traffic that could transform a twenty-minute drive into an hour, easily. I'd decided to arrive at the cocktail party "fashionably late," not so much for the sake of appearing fashionable as to minimize my time at the thing, but I realize now that my late departure from Baybury coupled with this traffic may well make me miss the party entirely. I'd have thought that I'd be delighted at this prospect, but in the end, I'm not, not because my dread has suddenly evaporated, but because I've put so much energy into the dreading that I'd be annoyed if it was all in vain. I've worried new wrinkles into my skin, I'm sure, I've made the effort to go to the attic to dig out old suits,

I've had to exercise and diet to fit into them (which I barely do), and I'm missing free booze and food at Pratty's. And if I miss this party now, I might as well have just said "no" to Andrew from the start and spared myself a week of suffering. Not to mention that if I miss the party now, Andrew will be furious, and of course he'll think I've done it on purpose, which isn't entirely true.

Just as I'd gotten into the car—at five o'clock, exactly on a schedule that would have made me about a half hour late—and turned the blessed air-conditioning on, I realized that the dog was still in the house. I got out of the car and went back inside to find the dog and explain to him that he'd have to leave, now, as I was leaving and wouldn't be around to let him out. I stood in the doorway, ready to call him, but I realized, then, that I didn't know what name to yell. He's just been "the dog." "Um, hey!" I yelled. No answer. "Dog!" I yelled. Nothing. Burrito! I wanted to yell, but I thought that might not be fair, because if indeed the dog has learned what a burrito is, and he came to me from wherever he was expecting one, I'd have nothing to offer. "Hey!" I yelled. Nothing. "Fido!" I tried. Nothing. "Rex! Rover!" I loosened my collar, undid the topmost buttons of my shirt, and took off my jacket and tie before wandering around the house. No dog in the kitchen. No dog in the living room. Upstairs, no dog in the hallway. No dog in the bedroom. The door to Simon's old room was closed; even so, I opened it up quickly and peered inside. Neat guest bed and bureau; no dog. I tried to remember if I'd let the dog out sometime in the middle of the night, and though I didn't recall doing so, I figured there was a good possibility that I might have, too groggy with Jack and sleep to remember. I shrugged, and then before heading back to the car, I decided to pee one last time before hitting the road, a good fifteen minutes behind schedule now.

I went into the downstairs bathroom, and I'd just unzipped my fly when I heard a movement behind the shower curtain. Startled perhaps more easily than I might have been if I hadn't had the party on my mind, I grabbed the plunger with one hand from where it stood beside the toilet and raised it high, and with the other hand I tore back the shower curtain and shouted, "AH!"

The dog lay there in the bathtub looking up at me. He raised an eyebrow and gave his tail a few thumps against the porcelain. "What are you doing?" I said, feeling almost embarrassed. "I was calling you for a reason. It's not my fault if I don't know your name." I pushed the shower curtain all the way open and gestured toward the door with the plunger. "Out," I said. "Come on, out." The dog stood slowly and hopped over the edge of the bathtub. I took a few steps toward the bathroom door, thinking the dog would follow me, but when I turned I saw that he'd paused to take a drink from the toilet. "Don't!" I cried, slamming the seat cover down and almost banging the dog's nose. "I pee in there!" The dog looked at me, and I could tell by the twitching of his tail that he wasn't sure whether to wag or not. I sighed, put down the plunger, and knelt down to pat him. "Go ahead," I said. "Wag." The dog's tail swung into a full-fledged wag as I petted him. "Now," I said, "if you'll excuse me," and I led him through the door before reentering myself. "I'll be right out." I shut the door behind me, which I haven't really had to do at home in years. Claire doesn't care if I pee with the door open, and I've been alone all summer with no one to see me anyway, but somehow, with the dog just outside the door, I felt as if it might be the right thing to do to pee in privacy. Although when I think about it now, maybe I should have let him see me pee into the toilet so that he'd think twice before trying to drink out of it in the future.

I gave the dog a fresh bowl of water to drink before taking him outside and explaining that I'd be back in time for a late dinner, if all went well. And I'm kind of looking forward to getting home to the dog, even though he's made me late. Even though he may well have made me miss this thing, I'm not mad at him. I don't know why, exactly, I'm just not, and I don't think I could be if I tried. I guess what it comes down to is that he's just a dog, which makes me jealous, in a way. I wish I had that same immunity to wrath. I wish that no matter what I did, people couldn't bring themselves to be angry at me, just because I am who I am, like a dog's just a dog. Things would be very different, that way.

Andrew, for instance, wouldn't be cursing under his breath, right now, which I'm sure he is, because I'm late to a function that he's forcing me to go to in the first place, very much against my will. And the asshole in the car behind me wouldn't be honking because I hadn't noticed until this minute that the car in front of me has pulled forward a whole ten feet that I've neglected to fill. And I myself might have already pulled forward those ten feet, because my wife would be here to remind me. Actually, if my wife were here, we probably wouldn't be in this traffic at all because she would have made sure that we left on time.

But. I am not a dog.

The traffic in the lane next to mine starts to move, a bit, and the asshole behind me peels out and into that lane, giving me the finger as he passes by. I smile and wave. I'd switch lanes, too, but I'm sure the second I did, the lane I'd switched into would stop and the one I'm in now would begin to move until I decided to get back into it. So I stay where I am, unmoving, and turn the air-conditioning up full blast, all vents directed directly toward me. Outside, the traffic shimmers in the heat. The man in the car beside me is evidently without air-conditioning; his windows are down and sweat runs wetly down his face; the dog in the back of the pickup a few cars ahead looks equally miserable, his head hung over the tailgate and his dry tongue panting.

As far as I can see through the waves of exhaust and rippling heat, the traffic now seems to be at a standstill, and so to fill the time I take my pen and notebook from the seat beside me, hoping that a change of working venue from desk to car might prove inspirational. I did write my first novel mostly in a car, and whenever we went on long drives with Simon, I'd just open my mouth and a Grover story would be on the tip of my tongue. I flip from my kid notes to my Ellen notes to my Pratty's notes, then flip through them all again, waiting for whatever I'm hoping will grab me to grab, but it doesn't. Finally I flip to the next blank page and start writing what seems to be, these days, the only thing I know how to anymore. *Dear Claire,* I write. *Maybe it's a good thing you're gone this summer, because if you weren't, I wouldn't have you to write to, which would mean I wouldn't be writing anything at all. It's funny, you know, because I'm writing this as I'm driving into Boston for a "literary function," because I'm supposed to be a "writer," because Andrew wants me to talk to the publishers who want to do my burglar stories. What do I tell them I'm working on now? A letter to my wife?*

I set my pen down in frustration.

I've published only one novel in my life.

I wrote it during my fisherman phase, which I entered when I was twenty-eight and newly arrived in Baybury, which has a good-sized fleet of old, rugged fishing vessels tied up down at the piers. I'd wander down there and watch the fishermen rolling up their nets after a day of fishing, unloading catch kept cold in the bowels of this or that boat. I'd watch the larger fish get hauled in cranes from the deck of a boat and up into the back of a waiting truck, and I'd watch the people at work in the dockside fisheries, cutting up bait and gutting, filleting, and scaling the fresh catch. For a while I entertained the notion of becoming a fisherman myself; this was while I was under the impression that fishing was a summer thing only, and so it wasn't till later that could I understand the skeptical looks I got from the fishboat captains when I, a young writer with no experience on the water, asked to join their crews, especially with fall and winter around the corner.

What I noticed as I hung around the docks was that each boat was equipped with a radio, which, when I asked, was described as a sort of CB for boats, with a specific channel designated for the fishing boats coming out of Baybury Harbor. I figured that since I couldn't be *on* a boat myself to experience the real thing, then listening on my own radio to the fisherman talk as they were out at sea would be as close to the real thing as I could get. I got myself a radio at the marina shop downtown, and then religiously I started listening to the men tell one another jokes, brag about the catches they'd just made, or warn others about a fished-out area. I listened to them talk about their destinations and where someday they'd like to go. I listened to them talk shit about previous crew members, drunks or stoners who'd fall overboard and require catching themselves. But after not a long time at all, my purpose in listening to the radio was not so much to eavesdrop on the fishermen as much as it was to listen to the voice.

The voice. The voice was what I considered the switchboard operator of marine radio. The voice answered the calls of fishermen reporting their positions or foul weather. The voice received their calls of distress and dispatched help. The voice listened to their jokes and laughed, tallied up the pounds of fish caught and reported, relayed messages to wives and family. The voice was gentle, but tough; it was grainy, but in a smooth kind of way. It was soothing; it was scolding; it was concerned; it was excited. The voice, it seemed, was the anonymous mother of the sea.

At times I considered pretending to be a fisherman myself, out on my lobster boat alone and lonely. I considered calling in to the voice, reporting lobsters kept or tossed back and the number of empty traps. I wanted to tell the voice a joke, to make the voice laugh. I'd hold my radio in my hand, and I knew that all I had to do was to push the button on the side and speak. I knew how to make a call. I knew to say *niner* for *nine,* and I knew that Charlie stood for *C,* that *Victor* stood for *V,* that *X-ray* stood for *X* and *Alpha* for *A.* I had my marine alphabet down. I knew that *Mayday* meant danger to life, that *Pan pan* meant danger to property, that *Securité* meant danger to safety. I knew to say "over" when I'd finished and "copy that" when I understood what someone else had said. I could have maybe pulled it off, but there was something about pushing that button and breaking into the sometimes dead silence—a silence representing a vast, unseen audience—that terrified me. I was afraid I'd say something wrong, despite my research and attention, and I could imagine other fishermen—real fishermen, the old crusty hands—listening on their own radios and chuckling to themselves: *Will you get a load of this greenhorn? Copy that? Ha, ha, ha . . . Guess who's been watching too much TV!* Worse than being laughed at by that invisible, rugged audience would have been to be laughed at by the voice, so I kept quiet.

I'd listen to the voice as I fell asleep, trying to picture what she looked like. I considered trying to find her—I knew it would be easy enough to find out where the radio channel base was located—but I was almost afraid to. In the end, I liked the voice faceless, because that way she was mine alone. If I'd seen her, I'd have seen what everyone else saw when they saw her, and in that way we'd all be sharing. What I imagined when I imagined her was private, and mine alone. No one else could see what I saw when I imagined her, and in that way I didn't have to share her with anybody.

Anyway, that was my novel, which earned me an advance on another I have yet to produce. I couldn't afford to heat my house as much as I would have liked that winter, so I'd spend each afternoon in the car, listening to the voice and writing the story of a man (not me, but a fisherman, the one I'd like to have been) at sea in love with a voice on the radio, and who, as he listens to her, gets no fishing done at all. He never meets the voice, and they never fall in love, because the voice in the end just disappears, moves on to another job, which is what happened in reality. I guess I'm waiting for something like the voice to happen again, for there to be what people consider a *story* in my life, but these days my life seems to consist only of *nonstories*, which evidently aren't as interesting to other people. I'm looking, though. I know there's a story somewhere in Ellen Marie, somewhere in the kids next door. I'm just waiting to find it.

. . .

I think it's human nature to want to know the cause whenever there's a problem. Take, for instance, a traffic jam. It's far less satisfying, somehow, when traffic that's lasted for miles simply begins to move again than it is when you finally reach the source of the jam, observe it, pass by it, and speed out into the clear and open road ahead. I think it's human nature to want to know exactly *why* you've been sitting for hours in traffic, to want to be able to attribute the jam to something specific, something you can visualize. And I also think it's probably a bit more disappointing, a bit more frustrating, when the cause of the traffic reveals itself as a simple lane closure, or road work. I think most people would rather be rewarded for the delay with the sight of carnage, wreckage on the road.

Today's jam promised a good spectacle, what with the number of emergency vehicles pushing through to the scene, the long wait, and the thick plume of black smoke on the horizon, and I have to say that as I slowly approached, I hoped in the back of my mind that they hadn't cleaned up too much of the mess by the time I got there. I wanted to see smashed glass scattered across the road, twisted metal and the burned-out husk of whatever car had gone up in flames. I wanted to see loaded stretchers, or a driver sitting on the tailgate of an ambulance, answering an officer's questions and tending his head with ice. I wanted to see a drunken driver in handcuffs being shoved into the back of a cop car.

The problem with the scene as I envisioned it was that it included no death. As I envisioned it, the cars involved in the accident were wasted, but the drivers and passengers involved were, while wounded, in good hands and on their way to the safety of the hospital. When I finally reached the scene of the accident, about a half hour before the end of the cocktail party, it was mostly as I imagined: scattered glass, twisted metal, and so on. One car had been loaded up onto the bed of a tow truck, and two others were on the median still, one overturned, one with its hood bent into the shape of an overturned V. If there had been stretchers, they'd already been loaded into ambulances, and there was no one in handcuffs, but there was a mildly shaken-looking man seated on the back of a police car talking to two note-taking officers, just as I'd imagined. The car that had been burning was a blackened, smoking shell, also as I'd imagined, but what I hadn't imagined, and what took me a moment to understand, were the groups of two or three firemen and other emergency workers standing solemnly around the smoldering thing, hands on hips and staring. And it was then that I saw what I would never have allowed myself to imagine, what I would never have allowed myself the desire to see, and what I wish now I hadn't seen, which was the rubbery, black, and smoking form of what was a human being trapped behind the wheel of the burned-out car.

The burned man has made me feel guilty for wanting to see wreckage, even though the accident happened before I found myself hoping for a satisfying scene. I have to keep reminding myself that I hoped to see wreckage, not death. I didn't hope to see death. I would never hope to see death. But I still feel guilty, because that burned man belonged to someone, and there I was wondering if the burned man felt it as he burned, wondering what his burned skin looked like up close, whether he could smell it as his flesh smoldered. If it was my wife burned to death behind that wheel, I'd want to kill some-one like me for rubbernecking, for wondering what she felt as she burned to death. I don't remember much about the minutes after Simon's accident, after Claire and I ran outside to see our son on the pavement, but I do remember vague faces in a gathering crowd, and I remember blinding anger. I don't remember actually lashing out at the crowd, or cursing them, but my wife has alluded to something like this, and I do remember my breath quivering in my throat as Claire held me in the back of a police car and stroked me as the world came slowly back into focus.

I shake my head, trying to get rid of thoughts like these, trying to prep myself for the ten minutes still remaining of this function as I enter into the lobby of the hotel where it's being held. The lobby is mostly empty, except for a man finishing a cigarette by the elevators and a young woman behind what seems to be the concierge desk. Her head is resting in her hands as she reads a magazine or book laid out on the desk below her.

"Excuse me," I say, approaching. She lifts her head slowly and looks at me. "Ah, I'm here for the literary convention cocktail party thing. Can you tell me where that is?"

Without troubling herself to speak, she gestures with her head toward a message board, on which are written the locations of a yacht club members' dinner, a wedding rehearsal dinner, the cocktail party I'm meant to be at, and, at the top of the board, today's date. At the sight of it, my heart begins to pound so loudly I can hear it, and for a moment, my vision fizzles into pixels as it does when you first open your eyes after you've rubbed them hard. Today, this message board has informed me, is my wedding anniversary. How could I have possibly not remembered? How could I have so lost track of time? Our anniversary is something I've always, always remembered; it's the one marker of passing time that I like and look forward to, unlike birthdays, or new years. We don't make a big deal out of it—no gifts, no parties—but we have a routine that I look forward to more than I looked forward to opening my stocking Christmas morning as a kid. Whether or not it's raining, because twice it's rained and we've gone anyway, we take dinner and wine down to the beach at the edge of the marsh and stay there until well past dark. We started doing that on our very first wedding anniversary, after we'd snuck away from a huge party my wife's sister had organized for the occasion. It had been a surprise, and neither of us much likes either parties or surprises, and after an hour everyone was drunk enough anyway that I don't think they even noticed we were gone. I'm wondering now if everyone at this cocktail party is drunk enough that they too won't notice whether or not I show up, and if maybe I should just leave.

"Hollis!" I hear a jumble of voices burst from the hotel bar as the door swings open and Andrew and two other men come out into the lobby. "Impeccable timing, as always!"

Andrew and the other two men cross the room to where I'm still awkwardly standing in front of the message board. I straighten up and clear my throat. "Andrew," I say, all of a sudden feeling nervous, in the way a teenager might coming home late for curfew. "I'm so sorry to be so late. It was . . ." I'd been ready with a full account of the accident, the fire, the traffic, the burned man, but it's gone now. It's my anniversary, and here is the last place I should be. "The traffic . . ." I mutter.

"Don't apologize to me," Andrew says, turning to acknowledge the two men beside him. "Hollis," he says, "Bob Zweigler and Ed Stanton from Random House. Bob, Ed, this is Hollis Clayton."

"It's so nice to meet you," I say. The words sound foreign, unnatural, coming out of my mouth. The *so* that I'd hoped would make me sound genuine and enthusiastic makes me sound either English or snobby, and I regret the addition immediately.

"Likewise," Bob says, sticking out what is a remarkably small hand for me to shake, his fingers like little stumps. He's short and bald.

"So nice," Ed says, and his own *so* makes me wonder for a second if maybe he's English or snobby himself, or if maybe he's mocking me. He dangles a limp hand out. I hesitate for just a second before grabbing it, sensing that Ed is one of those handshakers I hate who simply lay their hand in yours and do no shaking at all. Handshake etiquette is important, if people are going to insist on shaking hands in greeting, which, when I think about it, is a strange ritual. We could just as easily touch toes, or knock heads, or bow, or tap each other on the head or shoulder, and I wonder, as I suffer through Ed's awful handshake, who chose the handshake as a greeting, and why.

"And I'm sorry to be so late," I say again, this time apologizing to Bob and Ed.

"Bob and Ed were hoping to chat with you about the burglar stories and whatnot," Andrew says.

"Oh," I say.

"We were," Bob says. "Terrific stuff, you know. Few things to talk about, though, few reservations."

"Of course," I say.

"Title," Bob says, though I can't quite make him out at first, because he says it with his head down as he rummages through his pockets for what ends up being a handkerchief.

"What?" I say.

"Title," he says, straightening up and dabbing at the beads of sweat that have collected on his scalp.

"Yes," I say. "A title. Yes, it needs one. I've been thinking about that."

"Got one," Bald Bob says, tucking away his handkerchief.

"Oh," I say.

"Lock 'Em Up," he says.

"Sorry?" I say.

"You know, *Lock 'Em Up*. But it goes two ways, you know? Lock up the windows, the car doors, the house, you know, to protect against burglars, but also lock up the burglars, you know, in jail. Could apply to either." Bald Bob looks pleased with himself.

I glance at Andrew. He shrugs. "Yeah," I say. "That could work."

"Hollis," Ed says. "The three of us were just going to drive downtown to get some dinner, and since we didn't get the chance to talk to you, we were hoping you'd join us."

"Oh," I say. "Sure, great." Dinner sounds five times worse than a cocktail party. You can't hide in the bathroom or in the corner at dinner. People can count how many drinks you have. You can't leave early from dinner.

"Shall we make our way to the garage, then?" Andrew says.

"Excellent," Ed says.

The elevator down to the lobby seems to take forever to come, and the four of us stand in awkward silence. I begin to wish I'd gotten here at least in time for one or two drinks.

"This restaurant is meant to be delicious," Andrew says.

"Good," Bald Bob says. "Starving."

I look up at the blinking numbers as the elevator slowly makes its way down to the lobby. Eight, seven, six . . .

"Hollis," Ed says, and I turn toward him. "I'm so curious as to what you're working on these days."

"Oh," I say. This is the question I've been dreading having to answer, especially without the aid of booze, the question to which I'd hoped to have an answer prepared. "Well," I say, "right now I'm actually working on," and I don't know what I'm going to say until I say it, "a children's book." I'm probably as surprised as Andrew, who looks at me with what seems to be mild alarm.

"Really," Ed says. "Very interesting."

"Very," Andrew says.

"A children's book," Bob says.

I look at the three of them, all of them looking at me, wanting me to say more.

"A children's book," I say, and just then the elevator doors open and a family files out. "About a zookeeper who can speak the language of the animals."

"Well," Ed says. "Certainly a topic to be continued at dinner," and we step into the elevator down to our cars.

We're quiet in the elevator, which is stuffy in the way that a bathroom is after a hot shower, and I begin to wonder why we didn't take the stairs the one flight down as I'd taken them up only minutes before. I grind my teeth as the elevator groans its slow way to the basement level, trying not to think about the fact that today is my anniversary and the idea that I should be at home, just in case. I try to focus on the here and now. This dinner is important, I tell myself. This dinner could be important for my career, I tell myself. I tell myself the things I think that Claire would tell me, but then the thought of Claire makes me yearn again to leave here, to go home in case she calls. Finally, the elevator doors creak open, and we emerge into the parking lot.

Bald Bob lets out a big breath and rummages around again for his handkerchief. "Where are we . . . section C, I think, which would be, aha, over this way."

I scan the parking lot for my own car, completely mystified as to where I've left it. I don't see it in the corner of the lot in which I thought I'd left it; nor do I see the purple minivan I parked beside.

"Where are you, Hollis?" Andrew asks.

I think that it might not make the best impression on Bald Bob and Ed if I admit to having temporarily lost my car, so I hold up my finger and pretend to wait for a sneeze as I look around for the door to the staircase. I know where my car is in relation to that; it's having come out of the elevator that's thrown me off.

I spy the door to the stairs across the lot and take a big breath. "Oops, never mind, I guess," I say. Ed looks confused. "Thought I was going to sneeze," I explain, and he nods. "Anyway, I'm over in your direction as well, section C."

We head over to section C, and find our cars, which are only a few spots separated.

"Ed, or Bob, why doesn't one of you ride with Hollis, and I'll ride with the other?"

"Happy to," Ed says. "Mind a passanger, Hollis?"

"No," I say. "Happy to." My mimicking is not intentional. "Glad to have one," I say, trying to cover. "Love the company."

Ed follows me over to my car, which is a much smaller and more rusty ride than Bob and Andrew's. I open the driver's-side door and stick my head in, thinking that I'll just clear away my notes and a couple of newspapers from the passenger seat, which is all I specifically remember being there. I don't specifically remember the numerous empty water bottles, old maps, soda cups, sandwich wrappers, and books that I find; I also don't specifically remember the mildewed towels and beach chairs taking up all of the backseat. I start tossing things from the front seat to the back when the passenger-side door opens and Ed's face appears. "You know what?" he says. "I don't want to put you out," he says. "I'll just ride with the others and see you at the restaurant."

"It's not putting me out at all!" I say. I continue flinging things into the back. "I mean really," I say. "I need to clean this car out anyway. This is a good reminder of why. This is a good start."

Ed puts his hand on my shoulder, and his grip is surprisingly firm in comparison with his handshake. "Really," he says. "Don't bother. We'll talk at the restaurant." He straightens up and shuts the door, hurrying over to Andrew and Bob.

"Okay," I call after him. "I'll see you there!"

As always in Boston, the traffic is terrible, and I've had more than my fill of traffic for the day. I cannot help but think about my wife. I cannot help but to think that she might call. I've done just as she asked me and left her alone, and it seems to me that that might well warrant an anniversary call. Then I begin to worry that she might call while I am gone, or that she might have called already and I've missed it. I ended up unplugging the answering machine the other day because I no longer wanted to have the option of pressing PLAY or ERASE, because in pressing PLAY you hear whatever the message is, and you can't unhear it, and because in pressing ERASE, though you're saved the regret that could potentially result from listening to a message, you're haunted forever by what that message might have been, which is something that you'll never know. I start to wonder if unplugging the machine is better than pressing ERASE. If I got home tonight, for instance, and the machine was still plugged in, I'd risk listening to any messages, in the hopes that one might be from my wife. But now, there will be no way for me to know whether she's called. There will be no way for me to know whether she remembers what today is. And I wonder, if she does remember, and she does call, if that might mean that things are okay again. And if things are okay again, it seems possible that she may even have decided to come home today. It would be like a second wedding, or a restart of our marriage. And the more I think about it, the more appropriate today seems as a date for her return, even if it's still a month till

Labor Day, and the possibility that I might be missing her homecoming makes me feel panicked, desperate.

Of course, the only reasonable course of action seems to be to drive immediately to the beach at the edge of the marsh, to our anniversary spot. I pretend not to notice when Andrew, Bald Bob, and Ed take a left, and I continue on to the highway, which is thankfully free of traffic, and speed homeward. The more I think about it, the more my wife's presence on the beach seems an unquestioned certainty rather than a mere possibility. I can see her there, wearing a T-shirt, flip-flops, and corduroy shorts, waiting for me on the blanket we always bring when we go to the beach. I'll just be able to see her from the parking lot. Maybe then I'll just sit in the car for a while and watch her, which I'd like to have the patience to do, to just watch her exist. But maybe I'll rush from the car and gather her up in my arms. Or maybe I'll walk slowly up to her from behind, so quietly she won't hear me, and simply touch her head. I wonder what will be the first thing that she'll say to me, and what will be the first thing I'll say to her. I wonder if we'll make love, and if we do what that will be like after all this time. My wife, I think. Claire, I think, and I picture the way the red wine will leave little fanglike stains on her lips like it always does, and the way her eyes will water if there is a breeze.

I stop, as usual, at San Miguel, and this time I get two burritos, one for me and one for my wife. I stop at the liquor store and buy a couple bottles of our favorite red, and I head to the beach. I turn the engine off and look in the direction of our spot, on the far end of the beach by the marsh. No one is there. I get out of the car to walk the beach, just to make sure she isn't here, and she's not. I return to the parking lot, angry at myself for letting my imagination get the better of me, for convincing myself so thoroughly that what isn't was, for finding myself suddenly here, leaning against the hood of the car and watching the sky darken, alone. Alone. I am tired of being alone.

I get back into the car and start the engine. I don't feel much like going home, but I don't know where else to go, and there is, if nothing else, Jack waiting for me at home, and though I'm trying hard not to count on it, the dog, who, if he is around, is in luck tonight, dinnerwise.

I drive slowly home, shut off the car, and unlock the kitchen door, quick to turn on the kitchen lights and make the place feel lived in. The dog usually waits at the bottom of the driveway, but I didn't see him there, so I guess tonight it's just me and Jack. I stick the burritos in the refrigerator for tomorrow night, grab Jack and a glass, and head out through the living room toward the sliding door. And then I see through the glass, sitting on the doorstep in the dark gray light of dusk, the figure of a woman, and beside her, the dog.

13

MENDERS

One of our longer nickel drives lasted all of a rainy Memorial Day weekend. We'd planned to go camping up in Maine, so we'd already gotten Simon a sitter, but when we read the forecast, we decided aginst the Maine trip. One night on the drive we ended up in a restaurant in Staunton, Virginia, an old, old town nestled in hills that swell southward into the Appalachians. The restaurant was big, for a town of that size, and crowded as well, and I remember being delighted by all the local beers they had on tap. I remember also the bread, which was some of the best restaurant bread I've ever had. My wife was in the bathroom when they brought out our two steaming little loaves, and I remember my mouth watering as I eyed them, waiting for my wife to return before I dug in. After a minute or so, though, I couldn't resist breaking off a chunk of my personal loaf and buttering it up with the soft butter they'd brought out. And oh my God, that bread. It was so hot, so fresh, so salty and doughy and delicious. I wanted my wife to hurry up and get back from the bathroom, because I wanted her to enjoy her loaf while it was still hot, too, as I was enjoying mine. I was sure that it would lose a little something as it cooled. I reached across the table for my wife's loaf, and I was just wrapping it up in my napkin to keep it as warm as possible when my wife finally returned from the bathroom.

She looked from the partially eaten loaf on my plate to her empty plate to the bundle in my hands, and then she looked at me with her eyebrow raised. I handed the wrapped-up bread to her.

"Trying to keep it warm," I explained.

She unwrapped her loaf and set in on her plate. "Thanks," she said, handing my napkin back to me. She had a funny look on her face.

"What?" I said. "What's that look for?"

"I don't know, exactly," she said. "I just had the strangest experience in the bathroom."

"Tell me," I said. I nodded toward her bread. "Try it. Try it while it's hot. You won't believe it."

She nodded absently and broke off a piece of her loaf, which, I noted to my satisfaction, was still steaming.

"Well," she said, setting the bread back down without taking a bite. "There were two stalls, and I was in one, and someone was in the other. She was in there when I came into the bathroom, and I could hear her crying when I first walked in, and then I could hear her trying not to cry when she realized she wasn't alone."

I glanced from my wife to her bread. I shoved the butter dish toward her. "Butter, in case you want it," I said. "But go on."

"Thanks," she said, picking up the butter knife and loading it with butter. "Anyway, I flushed, and then I washed my hands, and I guess she thought I'd left, because she started sobbing, and I mean real, hard sobs, and normally I wouldn't say anything, but she sounded so miserable I couldn't leave her there without making sure she was okay." My wife looked down at the butter knife, as if noticing it there in her hands for the first time and realizing what she was supposed to do with it. She picked up the chunk of bread she'd ripped off earlier, which was no longer steaming, and held it in her other hand as she continued.

"So," she said, "I asked through the stall door if she was okay, and her crying sort of caught sharply in her throat, because like I said I think she thought she was alone again, and there was silence for a minute, and then the door opened."

I looked from my wife's hand that held the bread to the hand that held the butter knife and willed one toward the other, with no luck.

"And then," she said, "this woman came out, a little younger than me, I guess, and she looked at me for a second, and then she said no, she wasn't okay."

I look up from my wife's hands to her eyes. "And what did you say to that? What was wrong with her?" The story was beginning to draw my attention from the bread.

"Well," my wife said. "I asked her if there was anything I could do. I'm not sure why I asked, because I couldn't have done anything to actually help her problem."

"Which was what?"

"She missed her son," my wife said. "She and her husband recently divorced, and they have shared custody of their son, who's about Simon's age. Almost two. They switch off every two weeks, but she's still not used to it, you know? She's not used to being without him."

"She told you this?"

"Yes, eventually."

"What do you mean, eventually?"

"Well, I'd asked her first if there was anything I could do, remember. And she said yes. And she asked for a hug."

"What did you do?" I asked. I think I'd entirely forgotten about the bread by this point. I was horrified by the thought of a stranger asking my wife for a hug.

"I gave her a hug," my wife said. "What else would I have done?"

I thought about it, but I didn't know. "I don't know," I said. "So then what?"

"Nothing," she said. "That's it. I just gave her a hug." She shrugged. "It was all I could do."

"Huh," I said, trying to imagine what I would have done. I probably would have left the bathroom the minute I heard someone crying, partly to leave him his privacy, partly because it would have made me uncomfortable to hear, and if the crier had come out of his stall, I wouldn't have known what to do.

My wife, finally, though absently, buttered the bread and put it in her mouth. "My God, this is good bread," she said.

"Yeah," I said, even though I knew her bread, by then, was long cold. "It is good, isn't it."

That's one of the qualities I've always admired in my wife—her ability to respond to people as they need her to, even though, like that time in the restaurant, she didn't even know what she was doing. Often I freeze up when confronted with people who *need*; I am not sure how or what to give.

I was not sure how or what to give to Marissa tonight, for instance, after I'd found her bruised and teary on my doorstep. I stood in the living room with my Jack looking at the figure sitting on the steps outside the sliding glass door. Of course, of course at first I didn't so much *think* it was my wife as *hope* it was my wife, but I translated that hope, for the second time tonight, into something concrete, something to believe in, and I set my Jack and my glass down on the coffee table and ran toward the door. I tried to yank it open without first unlocking it, and the figure stood at the noise and turned around, and I found myself, then, not face-to-face with my wife, as I'd hoped, but with Marissa. I wanted to turn around, run out of the house, jump into the car, and drive far away, hoping that when I returned she'd be gone, that she'd leave me alone, that she'd never call again, never look for me at Pratty's again, never show up at my home again.

I unlocked the door and slid it open.

"Hollis," she said, her voice soft, somehow less confident than it has always been.

"Marissa," I said. "What are you doing here?"

"I'm sorry," she said. "I didn't know where else to go."

"Come in," I said. I didn't know what else to say. She followed me inside, through the living room, where I picked up the bottle of Jack and the glass I'd set down, and into the lighted kitchen, where I went immediately to the cabinet to get another glass for Marissa.

"I called before," she said softly behind me. "A few days ago. I don't know if you got the message or not."

I paused at the cabinet with my eyes closed, waiting to confront the moment I'd been avoiding in which Marissa would give me her dreaded news: pregnancy, disease, drugs. I turned around.

"What is it?" I said, and I opened my eyes, able now to see Marissa clearly by the light of the kitchen for the first time tonight. Her left eye was swollen shut and purple, and her lip was cracked. She had the green stain of an older bruise on her right cheek. "Jesus Christ," I said. It was then that I wasn't sure just what to do next; it was then that I yearned for my wife's ability to know what people need.

And so I poured us both a drink. "Jesus Christ," I said again. "What happened?" Marissa looked down and shook her head, seemingly unable to speak. I heard her stifle a sob. I took a chance, then, crossed the kitchen, and put my arms around her. It seemed the only thing I could do, and I thought it was probably what my wife would have done.

I had forgotten how small Marissa is, and how young, only twenty-four. Her bones felt so small that I feared I might break them if I squeezed too tight, and her hair was knotted when I ran my fingers through it as I tried to soothe her.

She seemed to calm after a few minutes, and lifted her head from where she'd buried it in my chest. "I'm sorry," she said, sounding more composed, more like the Marissa I remembered. "I'm just tired. And my fucking face hurts." She made an attempt at a scornful little laugh.

I let her go and went back over to our drinks. "Here," I said. "This always helps me."

"Thanks," she said.

The dog padded into the room and looked at me expectantly. I looked at the dog and then up at Marissa.

"You hungry?" I asked, and she nodded. I got the two burritos from the refrigerator and two plates from the shelf. I put them in the microwave for a reheating and went into the upstairs bathroom to see if I could find some rubbing alcohol, gauze, ointment, or Band-Aids.

I returned to the kitchen and removed the burritos from the microwave, setting one down on the floor in front of the dog and the other down in front of Marissa, who had added ice to her drink and was stirring it with her finger, her chin resting in her other hand. "You eat, okay?" I said. "I'm going to drive down to CVS to get stuff to fix your face up. You be okay for half an hour?"

Marissa looked up. She looked scared, but she nodded. "Yeah, I'll be fine," she said.

I nodded toward the dog. "The dog'll protect you," I said.

We probably could have gotten Marissa's face cleaned up without rubbing alcohol or anything else from CVS, but I thought a few minutes away from the situation would clear my head, or at least allow me to semi-organize everything inside it. I haven't seen Marissa since the night of the fireworks, and it seems as if we've switched roles since then. I remember her coaxing me gently out of the square that night and helping me into a cab, and I remember clutching her hand as we rode home, terrified of I'm still not sure what. I remember her sitting me down at the kitchen table when we got home and fixing me a tall glass of water to go with the Jack that I'd poured for myself. Tonight, it's my turn to help her. It feels good to be the one needed, for once. It makes me feel a little better than myself.

I wander the aisles of CVS looking for what I think might come in handy: maybe some iodine—I think it's iodine—for the cracked lip, an ice pack for the eye, some antiseptic would probably be good, and some ointment. Band-Aids? I can't imagine Marissa wearing a Band-Aid anywhere on her face, so I forgo the Band-Aids, leave the first-aid aisle, and enter instead into the makeup aisle, thinking I'll get her some cover-up or something to hide the purples and greens of her bruises. I'm not sure, though, what kind of stuff to get. The stuff that's called "cover-up" comes in a little tube and looks paintlike and too concentrated to cover a large area, but the powdery stuff that's skin-colored and looks like it might do the trick is called "foundation," and I'm not sure what that's supposed to be used for. My wife doesn't wear makeup, so I'm not familiar with the terms.

I bring both the cover-up and the foundation to the register to ask an employee's professional opinion, and as I'm approaching the counter the woman who's just finished paying turns around and I see the face of Judith Crane. My breath catches in my throat as I remember the binocular incident. For a second I let myself hope that maybe she won't recognize me out of context, or if I don't catch her eye, so I drop my gaze immediately to the floor. I look up only when I see her feet on the floor directly in front of mine.

"Mr. Clayton?" she says. "It *is* you! Judith Crane, your neighbor."

"Of course!" I say. "How are you?"

"I'm doing well," she says. "And yourself?"

"Not bad," I say. "Not bad." I can't tell if her tone is genuinely nice, or if it's falsely nice in the way it might be if you're speaking to someone you think is crazy, or worse, someone you're about to humiliate by confronting them about something like, say, spying. I decide that the latter is very, very possible, and I decide to preempt the confrontation. I clear my throat. "You know," I say. "It's funny we should happen to run into each other, here, because I've been meaning to let you know about something I noticed the other day. Yesterday, as a matter of fact. I had my binoculars out to do a little bird-watching"—and here I inwardly cringe, because what birds can you watch from your living room window on a rainy day?—"because there's this great species of bird that frolics in the rain that I love to watch—"

"Really?" Judith Crane says. "What kind? And you can see them around here?"

"Yes," I say. I'm beginning to wonder whether preemption is going to spare me much humiliation after all. "Oh, God, this is terrible, but I just can't remember their name. It's on the tip of my tongue . . ." I suck in my breath through my teeth. "But I just can't remember it. Isn't that funny."

"So interesting," Judith Crane says, shifting her bag from one hip to the other, almost as if it were a child. "You've got to talk to my husband," she says. "He's an avid bird-watcher, but I'm not sure if he knows about these rain birds."

"Oh yes," I say. "Really beautiful, these birds," I say, eager to get back to the topic I meant to bring up, which was not birds. "Can watch 'em right from home. Which I was doing yesterday, and then I happened to notice, because one landed on your roof—"

"Really!" Judith Crane exclaims.

I nod as I continue. "I happened to notice that your gutters seem to be a little clogged."

"Oh dear," Judith Crane says.

I nod.

"Well that's not good," she says. She looks concerned, now.

"No," I say. "Shouldn't be a problem to fix. I just wanted to let you know, you know, since I happened to see how clogged they were with the help of the binoculars."

"Well I'll have to tell my husband right away," she says. "I swear to God," she says, shifting her bag again. "This house has had nothing but troubles since we moved in."

I begin to have the feeling that I may have gotten myself in a little too deep, in terms of gutters and birds, and probably for no reason, because it doesn't seem that Judith Crane saw me at all yesterday, anyway. If she had, I figure she would have said something like, *Oh yes, I saw you with the binoculars!* But she's shown nothing but enthusiasm (about the birds) and distress (about the gutter). "Isn't it always the way," I say.

"Well, thanks for your sharp eyes," Judith Crane says. "And really, do come over anytime. My husband would love to meet you, I'm sure, and I'd love to meet your wife."

"Yes," I say. "Yes, absolutely."

"Well," Judith Crane says. "I should get back. It was good to see you again. And thanks for letting me know about the gutters!" and she rolls her eyes as if heavenward.

"Good night," I say, lifting the hand with the cover-up to wave good-bye.

She leaves the store and I shut my eyes. Suddenly, I am tired, too tired to decide between cover-up and foundation, so I dump them both along with the first-aid stuff on the counter and buy it all.

There are some people in the world whom I can look at and know that I like them. It can be something in their eyes, their smiles, their expressions; it can be their shoes or the way they're standing; it can be anything, but sometimes I can look at a random person and feel love. I'm not talking about love-at-first-sight love, like I had with my wife; it's more like I can look at that person and know we're the same, that we could probably understand each other. It was like this with Marissa.

I was waiting under a little shelter at a bus stop for a bus to take me to a train that would take me to New York to see Andrew, so understandably I wasn't determined to reach my destination, especially when I saw Marissa duck into the shelter out of the rain. Water dripped from the tip of her freckled nose and glistened in her eyebrows. She was carrying a bag over her shoulder, which when she began to rummage through it I saw was filled with all kinds of things—books, papers, loose money, pens and pencils, a journal, a Walkman, a balled-up shirt, a lighter—and entirely disorganzied. She scooped up a handful of change from the bottom of the bag and began to count it, her nose wrinkled in concentration. She was breathing heavily, from having sprinted through the rain I supposed, and when she'd counted out enough change for the bus fare, she collapsed onto the narrow bench along the back wall, pulled out her journal and a pen, and began to scrawl. She hadn't noticed me standing there, or at least she hadn't acknowledged me, and so I felt a bit more freedom to stare at her as she wrote. She paused for a second in her writing, once, with a look of confusion, or concern, and then an impish grin spread across her face, her tongue came out the corner of her mouth, and she began again to write, messy, sprawling words across the page. It was something about that moment, that grin, the way she was both a woman and a child, beautiful and awkward, that made me know I liked her.

"You a writer?" I asked.

She glanced up from her journal. "Wouldn't I like to think so," she said.

"What does that mean?" I asked.

She finished whatever thought she was working on and shut the journal. "It means," she said, "that I'd like to be a writer. I'd love to be a writer, a rich and famous one who never had to do anything at all but write. Unfortunately, though, I'm a writing waitress. Or a waitressing writer, depending on how you look at it."

"Oh," I said. "What do you write?" I asked.

She shrugged. "Whatever," she said. "Poems, stories, little essays, whatever I feel like."

I hesitated. "I write, too," I said.

"Really," she said. "Are you a writing writer? Or a lawyering writer? Or maybe an accounting writer?"

I paused again. "Well," I said. "I guess I'm a nonwriting writer."

"So you don't write," she said.

"Well," I said. "I was a writing writer, then I was a fathering writer, and then my son died and since then I seem to have been a nonwriting writer."

Her expression changed then from impish to solemn. "I'm sorry," she said.

I shrugged. I wasn't sure what had made me offer that piece of information.

"How'd he die?" she asked.

"Ran over," I said.

"Shit," she said. "How old?"

"Four."

"Shit," she said again. "I'm sorry."

I shrugged again.

"Don't shrug," she said. "It sucks."

I nodded.

We were quiet for a minute or two.

"So what did you write?" Marissa asked.

"Well, I had a novel out," I said. "A bunch of short stories, essays and columns here and there."

She nodded and looked at her watch. "Damn bus," she said.

"I know," I said. "I was waiting here fifteen minutes before you even came."

She shook her head.

"Are you late?" I asked.

"No," she said. "I'm just going home. But I get impatient, sometimes. You late?"

I shrugged. "Not really," I said.

"Where you going?" she asked.

"Why?" I asked, letting myself halfway hope that she was going to ask what she did.

"Well," she said, "if you're headed in my direction and you're not late, maybe we could split a cab, or maybe we could swing by my place and I could show you some of my stuff. It'd be good to see what another writer thinks, even if you're a nonwriting writer."

I nodded, slowly, unsure of what I was getting into. Like I've said, I love my wife. I'd never, never had an affair, but I'd heard these things sometimes helped, sometimes could jolt you out of a rut. There seemed nothing to lose, because in my mind, if I had an affair with Marissa, it wouldn't be something that would make me want to leave my marriage; it would be something that would eventually make our marriage better, because it would make me better. And like I said, I like Marissa. I liked her from the moment I saw her.

We got into a cab and headed to her place. It was September and she'd only just moved here. She'd finished college the year before, having taken two years off after high school to go live somewhere in Cambodia. She had chosen Baybury to live in by shutting her eyes and letting her finger fall onto a map. She was waitressing to support herself, and writing in her free time, and she didn't know anybody here, yet, except for the dog who was always tethered next door, whose name, she explained, was Eleanor, even though he was a male dog.

She lived on the top floor of her building, in a one-room converted attic. "Here we are," she said. The place was spacious, and skylights lined the ceiling.

"Wow," I said. "This place is great."

She shrugged. "Yes and no," she said.

"What's wrong with it?" I asked.

"Well," she said, matter-of-factly, "I live in apartment thirty-six. This is the first address I've ever had that didn't add up to five."

"Oh," I said, confused.

"See," she said, "before, I lived at 31 Canyon Road, which works out, and I grew up first at 403 Fifth, and then at 67 Lombard, and those obviously work out too. But there's no way I can get thirty-six to equal five, and it makes me nervous."

I ran those numbers through my mind. After a second, I decided to risk seeming foolish and I asked exactly how 31, 403, and 67 each equalled 5.

She sighed and brushed her hair out of her face. "Well," she said. "Thirty-one. Three and one is four, four and four are eight, eight and eight are sixteen, six minus one is five. Four-oh-three. Four and zero and three are seven, seven and seven are fourteen, four and one is five. Sixty-seven. Six and seven is thirteen, three and one is four, four and four are eight, eight and eight are sixteen, and six minus one is five. Or sixteen and sixteen is thirty-two and three and two are five. Works out either way. But thirty-six doesn't work. Keeps going back to nine. Three and six are nine, nine and nine are eighteen, eight and one are nine, nine and nine are eighteen, eight and one are nine, et cetera. So that's the trouble with this place. It just doesn't equal five."

I looked at her, still trying to make sense of all the numbers she'd just rattled off.

She shrugged. "It's just the way I've always made sense of my life," she said, and that, for some reason, made it all make sense. We all have bizarre ways, by necessity, of making our lives make sense.

When I get back home, Marissa is asleep at the kitchen table, and the dog is asleep at her feet. I shake her gently.

"Hey," I say.

"Oh," she says. She lifts her head. "I guess I fell asleep."

"I was thinking of something," I say.

"What?" she says.

"The address here. It adds up to five."

"Forty-five?" she says, looking suddenly much more awake. "Impossible. It's one of those niners."

"No, it does work," I say, because I'd worked it out somehow on my way home. "Four and five is nine, nine and nine is eighteen, eight and one is nine. . . . Wait, no, hold on. Four and five is nine, nine and nine is eighteen, one minus eight is negative seven, negative seven times negative seven is forty-nine, four and nine is thirteen, three and one is four, four and four is eight, eight and eight is sixteen, sixteen and sixteen is thirty-two, and three and two is five."

She looks at me, and for the first time tonight she smiles, or she smiles as large a smile as her cracked lip will allow. "No, Hollis. It doesn't work that way."

"Why?" I ask. "I made it come out to five!"

"There are certain rules you have to follow," she says, shaking her head, "which you definitely did not follow."

"Oh, and whose rules?" I ask.

"Mine," she says. "I'm sorry, but this house definitely is not a five."

I sigh. "Fine," I say.

I wait with the dog and Jack outside for Marissa to shower and tend to her face. It is only now, now that I am finally relaxing with my Jack, that I begin to mull over this evening's events—the traffic, the burned man, the dinner that I've skipped, the absence of my wife, our anniversary. It occurs to me that I have no idea what's happened to Marissa, and that in my initial panic, it didn't even occur to me to wonder. Now, though, I want to know who is responsible for her face. I want to know, and I want to avenge. It occurs to me now that, thankfully, it didn't occur to me in my panic that my wife might still be coming home today, because if I'd been thinking that, I might have done something terrible, like throw Marissa out, when I know now that that is not what Marissa needs at this moment, and my wife is not coming home today. It's past ten, now, and our anniversary is nearly over.

I hear Marissa's footsteps behind me. She comes over and sits in the chair next to mine, where a glass is ready with her drink.

"Thanks," she murmurs. I've given her a T-shirt from the bottom of my wife's drawer, and though it makes me cringe to think of her, and not my wife, in it, I feel certain that my wife, under these circumstances, would approve.

"So," I say. "How's the writing?"

"Okay," she says. "I got a few poems published in some little magazine somewhere. Those bee poems that you liked."

"Congrats," I say.

"And you?" she asks.

"Don't ask," I say.

We're quiet for a minute.

"So what happened?" I ask.

She sighs. "Don't ask," she says.

I look at her. "You're not going to tell me what happened to you?" I ask. "Are you kidding?"

She shakes her head. "I can't, Hollis. Not now. I'm sorry. I just . . ." she waves her hand in front of her face and shuts her eyes. "It's embarrassing, you know?" she whispers. She looks at me pleadingly.

Of course, I understand her desire not to talk, not to speak about it. But still, it feels to me like watching a movie when all of a sudden, at the climax, the reel breaks. It feels like reading a book that's only half-written. I want badly to know what happened. I nod my head. "Okay," I say.

We're quiet again, and sip our drinks. "So what's your plan?" I ask.

She sighs. "My mom's driving out here to get me. She left Colorado yesterday sometime, so she should get here I guess tomorrow."

"So you're leaving?" I ask. It's funny, I haven't seen Marissa in a month, but still, it will be a little sad to know she's not around.

She nods. "Guess so," she says. "Didn't go exactly as I'd planned," she said.

"Well, you got some poems out in the world," I offer. "And you met me," I grin.

She rolls her eyes and gives a little laugh through her nose. She finishes her drink, and then she sighs. "I'm tired," she says, and she looks at me.

I gulp, because while I don't want to sleep with her, out of habit, I do.

"I'll set up the pull-out couch," I say.

She nods, though all of a sudden she looks fearful.

"Are you afraid?" I ask.

She shakes her head. "No," she says. "We can lock the doors, right?"

"Of course," I say. "And you can have the dog with you, too. He'll protect you," I say for the second time tonight, though I have no idea whether the dog is capable of such a thing at all.

She strokes the dog. "Where'd he come from anyway?" she asks. "What's his name?"

I shrug. "He came from the park, I guess. I'm not sure what his name is."

Marissa nods as if this is normal. "Well, he certainly likes his burrito," she says.

"He certainly does," I say, and I go inside, set up the pull-out couch, and wander into the kitchen to find something to eat. It makes me nervous to be breaking my dinner routine, but I find a can of black beans to heat up, which, I figure, is as close to Mexican as I'm going to get tonight.

When I return from the kitchen, Marissa is all settled in bed, the dog lying contentedly beside her.

"You lock?" I ask.

"Yeah," she says.

I pause at the bottom of the stairs. "You okay?" I ask.

"Yeah," she says.

"Okay," I say. "Well," and I want to give her another hug, to hold her again, but I figure that to go upstairs is best. "Night," I say.

"Good night," she says.

As I start up the stairs, I hear her call, "Hey, Hollis."

I turn around and poke my head out the stairwell.

"Thanks," she says. I look at her, and pause, and nod, and then I turn and head upstairs to bed.

14

ATLAS SIGHED

Watching people sleep both thrills me and unnerves me. You can stand there and watch their brows furrow and twitch with dreams, and you can imagine what it is they might be dreaming about. You can count the measure of their breathing, and try to match it with your own. People seem to lose their age when they sleep, and if you blur your eyes just enough, you can make out what that person looked like as a child, or what they might look like when they're older. But when I stand over someone sleeping, I can't help but imagine that I am somehow committing an act of violation, because, I figure, that must be what it is to scrutinize someone at their most vulnerable. The thought of being watched sleeping myself makes me shudder with discomfort, but worse is the thought of staring someone into wakefulness and having to explain myself.

It was no different with Marissa this morning. I stood and stared at the purples and greens of her bruised face, the lump that looked to me like a golf ball had been tucked beneath the eyelid of her bad eye, which oozed at the corners, the blood from her lip dried on her chin. The worst of it was that I felt somehow responsible for her wounds. I feel responsible still.

As the kids next door, whom this morning I have to watch from the kitchen instead of my desk, play dodgeball, I am both distracted and increasingly anxious for Marissa to wake up so that I can try to explain myself to her, so that I can apologize, which, I notice, is what Judith Crane next door seems to be instructing her son to do to the crying child he hit in the face with a dodgeball. I wonder what it is about apologies that children seem to so resist. If I had to do it again, I'd get all my apologizing over and done with as a kid, when apologies are for food fights and name-calling.

The phone rings, and I leap to answer it before it rings twice, an old reflex left over from Simon's nap-times when I'm aware that there's a sleeper in the house, a reflex apparently ingrained enough to override my fear of getting into a conversation I'd rather not be in. Before I've said hello, I look at the lifted receiver in my hand, horrified that I've picked it up and must now deal with whoever's on the other end, with whoever's successfully weasled their way into my kitchen uninvited.

"Hello," I say, trying to sound as unfriendly as I can.

"Hollis," Andrew says. I shut my eyes. "So glad you joined us for dinner last night. You really made quite an impression."

"Andrew," I say, quickly skimming through possible excuses I could give: nausea, flat tire, wrong turn.

"I did my best to make you not seem like an asshole," he says.

"Thank you," I say.

Andrew sighs. "I'm afraid it probably didn't make much of a difference what I said. I think you might have blown it on the burglar stories."

I gulp. "Well," I say. "If they really want them, they'll take them even if I didn't get to the dinner. If they don't, they don't. Their loss."

"Or yours, depending on how you look at it."

"The burglar stories are behind me, now," I say. "They were a phase. I don't think I could go back and rework them even if it meant they wouldn't be published."

"A phase," Andrew repeats. "And what's this phase we've moved onto now? What was it, a magical zookeeper?"

"My children's book," I say, brightening up. "My Grover stories. What do you think?"

"I'd need to know a bit more about what you have in mind," he says. "Are you planning a Berenstain Bears–type series? Or are you going to do an epic Grover story, young-adult novel style?"

"Neither," I say. "It's going to be a book of short stories. But they're going to be good, you know, like not just for kids. Like how *Sesame Street* is kind of geared toward adults as well as children, because the writers know that adults a lot of the time are going to be sitting there watching with their kids." I always enjoyed *Sesame Street,* probably as much as Simon did.

"I'd never really considered *Sesame Street* as geared toward adults," Andrew says, but his skepticism doesn't give me the slightest pause.

"When was the last time you watched *Sesame Street*? I mean really watched it."

"Can't say I remember."

"Well, these Grover stories are going to be the same way. They're going to be stories for kids, but they're going to be legitimate short stories, you know, that adults would read."

"*New Yorker* style?" Andrew asks.

"Exactly," I reply, just before I realize that Andrew is making fun of me. "Something like that, anyway," I say. I hear a throat clear behind me, and I turn to see Marissa in the kitchen doorway in her jeans and my wife's T-shirt. I lift a finger.

"Well," Andrew says, and he lets out one of those breaths you let out when you're planning on hanging up soon. "Send pages my way," he says.

"I'll do that," I say, and for once, I mean it.

"Good-bye, Hollis," he says.

I hang up and motion Marissa to come sit down. "Sleep okay?" I ask. It's strange to see her here, strange now to wake with anyone in the house.

She nods as she stretches before slumping into the chair across from me. "Thanks," she says, pushing her long hair behind her shoulders and revealing a small ketchup stain on my wife's T-shirt, the result of, I remember, a french fry fight we'd had in the car years ago. I'd forgotten about the fight, the stain, and the T-shirt itself, since it has, since that day until now, remained stashed in the bottom of my wife's drawer. I am suddenly filled with longing more sharp and desperate and lonely than any longing I have felt for my wife in the weeks she has been gone. It's the type of longing I feel for Simon, the type of longing that acknowledges loss, and it frightens me to feel it for my wife. I do not want to have lost her.

I look from the stain back up to Marissa. "You hungry?" I ask.

"Starving," Marissa says.

I know there are probably some waffles in the freezer, and there's always maple syrup in the cabinet, but I feel uncomfortable with Marissa in the house; I feel a mixture of guilt and nervousness, and I want to get us out. "I don't think there's much to eat here," I say. "But we could go get doughnuts or something."

"Mmm," Marissa says. "That sounds good."

"You ready to go now?"

"Yup," Marissa says. "Let me just get my old shirt and I'm ready to go. I don't think I had anything else with me, did I?"

I shake my head as she disappears into the living room.

Last night after Marissa had gone to bed, I went up to the attic to put away my suit. Or that's what I told myself at first, as I lay in bed staring at the moon shadows of trees against the ceiling. I gathered up the suit that I'd left crumpled on the floor and took a flashlight and a steak knife from the kitchen. In the attic, I turned on the single hanging lightbulb, which shone a circle of light only immediately below it in the middle of the room; I stood there for a minute and watched the lightbulb swing before switching on my flashlight and leaving that circle of light for the shadows by the window where my mother's box still sat out where I'd left it. I set the suit and the flashlight down and pulled the steak knife out; I cut through the tape I'd sealed the box with thirty years before, and before I could decide otherwise, I opened the box.

I don't know what I thought would be in there. I don't know what I was afraid to find. There was a Jimi Hendrix poster, and a poster of Alaska rolled up inside that. There was a broken pair of sandals still marked with the bottoms of her feet. There was a music box that didn't play. There were a few pairs of dangly clip-on earrings, a few barrettes, and several books on things like psychic healing and the afterlife. There was a blue tapestry that I remember hanging on the wall of her commune room, and some faded red curtains that I don't remember.

Maybe what I was afraid to find was the envelope of photographs of me and my father and my mother taken when I was six or seven. We're picnicking somewhere I don't recognize, and judging by our clothing it's summertime. Most of the photographs are of me alone in a too-tight blue-and-white-striped shirt and little brown shorts: in one, I'm up in a tree; in another, I seem to be concentrating very hard as I spread mustard on the slice of bread in front of me. There's a whole series of me doing some kind of a dance, which surprised me, but what surprised me most was the one of me with my face in a huge slice of watermelon. I thought I've always hated watermelon. There are some of me and my mother: the two of us eating our sandwiches side by side, the two of us looking at the camera and smiling, my mother spreading sun stuff on my wrinkled and disgusted face. There are a few of me up on my father's shoulders: in one, I'm reaching up for the tree branch above me as my father smiles at the camera, and another is of the two of us from the back.

Then there's one of my parents together. I must have taken this one. They're sitting side by side at the picnic table. My father's arm is around my mother, and in front of them on the table is a vast and messy spread of soda, beer, cold cuts, chips, Tupperware containers with the organic things my mother liked to eat. They look happy.

Maybe that envelope of photographs was what I was afraid to find because the fact that they are here means that my mother didn't care enough to take them with her.

Jack, in my opinion, is the cure-all drug. I'm not kidding when I say that I think there'd be a lot fewer crazy and unhappy people in this world if we all had a shot of Jack with every meal, or if they just started putting it in the water, like they do fluoride. A couple pulls on the bottle, and I'm good to go, good for doughnuts, coffee, anything.

We waited in line at the doughnut shop, and I was trying hard to decide between cinnamon powdered and chocolate honey-dipped, imagining the taste of each in my mouth and wondering which taste I'd prefer. It always seems to happen that I make the wrong choice when it comes to things like doughnuts, or ice cream flavors, or pizza toppings; I'll have it narrowed down to two or three that I think sound great, choose one, and spend the entire time I'm eating wishing I'd chosen differently, especially when the person I'm with, usually my wife, has chosen that which I did not.

I nudged Marissa.

"Quick," I said, as the woman in front of us received her change. "Chocolate honey-dipped or cinnamon?"

"What?" Marissa said.

"Chocolate honey-dipped or cinnamon?"

"Yuck," she said. "Neither. Jelly."

"I don't like jelly."

"Well then don't get jelly. I'm getting jelly. And glazed. And blueberry."

"Three?" I asked.

"A dozen," she said.

"A dozen?"

Marissa looked at me incredulously. "You don't buy doughnuts singly," she said. "You buy them by the dozen."

"Why?" I asked.

"Think about it," Marissa said. "One doughnut, sixty cents. A dozen doughnuts, three dollars. That's a quarter a doughnut. Why, when I can get a twenty-five-cent doughnut, would I buy a sixty-cent doughnut?"

I nodded, and Marissa stepped up to place our order.

Sometimes I wish I was blessed with other people's logic as well as my own—not all the time, but some of the time. I'm glad that I'm not as concerned as Marissa is about whether or not the numbers in my address add up to five, but I do wish some things would occur to me, like that it's not only more economical to buy twelve doughnuts rather than one, but it also eliminates both the pain of decision making and the anxiety of regret and doubt. Right now, for instance, while I am indeed full from my cinnamon and chocolate honey-dipped doughnuts, I can enjoy that fullness without wondering whether I'd rather be full of the type of doughnut I decided not to get. If I hadn't gotten both of the flavors I was considering, the experience of eating would have been far less pleasureable; it would have been tainted by the possibility that I'd made the wrong decision, that the breakfast I was eating might be that much better had I decided differently. I'm trying to develop that kind of logic, though, the kind of logic that keeps you as far away from crazy as it can—take my burrito dinner strategy, for instance.

"Good call," I say to Marissa. We're sitting quietly in the car in the parking lot outside the doughnut shop. I've finished eating, but Marissa is still at it, starting in on her fourth or fifth doughnut now.

"What?" she says with her mouth full.

"To get a dozen," I say. "I'd have had a hard time choosing between my two."

"Even if I hadn't suggested getting a dozen you still could have gotten two," she says.

I shrug. "I guess," I say. "It was good, anyway."

Marissa puts her doughnut into the box, half eaten. "I've got to stop," she says. "Take them away from me before I eat them all." She closes the box and puts it at her feet. She lets out a loud, full breath. "I don't think my mom is going to get here for a few more hours at least," she says.

"How's she going to find you?" I ask.

"She knows my address," she says, and then she looks at me nervously. "I can't wait for her there, though," she says. "Or I can, I have to, but not inside." She swallows. "And not alone."

"I'll wait with you," I say. "Don't worry." I want to tell her that if I'm going to be as involved as I am in whatever is going on in her life that I deserve to know what exactly it is that's going on, but something about the fear in her eyes as she looks at me, something about the suddenness of it at the thought of waiting alone, keeps me quiet. I swallow my curiosity and sigh. "What do you want to do until then?" I ask.

"I don't know," Marissa says. "It's starting to rain."

I look up at the windshield, which is indeed dotted with the first drops of a storm.

"We could just drive around," she says.

I gulp. "I guess," I say, but I don't know that I can. The rain makes all the difference. The rain would make a day in the car with Marissa a betrayal of my wife, whose sunglasses even now are in the glove compartment, along with salt and pepper she stashes there for drive-thru meals on the road, and whose shirt is beside me, but on the wrong body.

Marissa seems to sense my discomfort, just as I could sense her fear a moment ago. "Or not," she says. She shrugs. "It doesn't matter."

"I have an idea," I say. "I have an idea. There's something I want to show you."

. . .

For my twentieth birthday, my father thought it would be fun for the two of us to go up and rent a little cabin somewhere in New Hampshire or Vermont and spend the weekend, just the two of us, out walking in the woods, fishing the rivers and lakes, sitting out with beers and burgers at night under the stars. This was not exactly the way I'd envisioned spending my twentieth birthday; I was in college, I had friends I wanted to go out with, girls I wanted to pursue. But my love for my father was such that I couldn't say no to him, couldn't bear to think of hurting him that way, and so I ruled out all other birthday ideas and went north with my father. This is the kind of love that I'm talking about; it's love, certainly, but more than that, it's a perhaps irrational desire for another person's happiness. In my mind, my father had planned my birthday weekend for himself as much as for me, and I didn't want to take that away from him. The thought of telling him that I'd rather hang out with my friends on my birthday than spend a weekend with him, doing what he loved to do and what he thought I'd love, too, caused me even more pain than I imagined him feeling if I told him that. And so I went. And it was good. But here things get even more complicated, because even while I was with my father, even while we were having the fun I thought he'd hoped for, I was riddled with guilt that I hadn't wanted to go.

Another memory, same category: It's the first warm day of spring, and Simon and I have taken a picnic lunch to the beach while Claire is teaching. I'm sitting in the sand, and just above me, Simon's up on a small, slippery pile of rocks, peering into a tidepool and munching on pretzels from the Baggie of them dangling from his hand. My mouth is watering for one, so I say, "Hey buddy, can I have a pretzel?"

"Sure!" he says, and I start to stand, because I figure it would be easier for me to mount the rockpile where Simon's standing in a single step than it would for Simon to climb down. But Simon, in his eagerness to share, has already begun the descent, and he slips on his way down. He picks himself up quickly, brushes off his hand.

"You okay?" I ask.

"Yeah, yeah," he says, extending the bag of pretzels to me.

I take a few. "Thanks," I say, and Simon grins and nods and climbs back up to his tidepool.

What's made me think of these things is the feeling they give me, which is the feeling I got when I thought of my wife's belongings in the car, even the dirty napkin tucked in the passenger-side well, the one my wife used to wrap around the ice cream cone she got sometime in June, just a few weeks before she left. The thought of Marissa, and not my wife, sitting in my wife's seat in the car, and the thought of driving around with Marissa, and not my wife, in the rain, aches in the same way as those memories ache.

"You look gloomy," Marissa says from my wife's seat in the car.

I glance over at her and give her a little shrug and smile.

"How come?" she says.

I pull the car over to the side of the road and put it into neutral.

"Huh?" she says. "How come?"

I sigh and shrug. "Just stuff," I say. "Nothing really, though."

Marissa gives me a little sideways smile and squeezes my arm with her small, strong hand.

"Hey," I say. "I'm sorry."

She looks confusedly at me. "Why? What do you have to be sorry about?"

"A lot," I say. "I mean, look at you," I say.

"Hollis," she says, putting her hand again on my arm. "Not everything has to do with you, you know." She smiles impishly and laughs. "Some shit happens without you stirring it up," she says, and she grins and gives me a smack on the arm. She sits back and looks out the window. "So," she says. "Are we here? What did you want to show me?"

"Oh," I say, and I nod through the windshield to where Ellen Marie should be.

Picture this: a huge tent in the middle of a field, blue-and-yellow-striped, three peaks with waving flags. It is nighttime, and the moon is full and grinning. Outside the tent, people stand in line as far as you can see. There are families, groups of teenagers, couples clinging to each other's arms. Men on stilts make their way up and down the line selling their goods: cotton candy, popcorn, programs. All faces are grinning like the moon.

Follow the line from the farthest person you can see to the front; it leads through opened curtains into the tent where more grinning faces and faces are gathered around a crowded circus ring. A clown circles the ring on a unicycle; a juggler juggles eight flaming pins; a lion stands atop a ball, and behind him a man in top hat and tails is standing with a whip. Above them all swing a family of trapeze artists, the father on one swing handing off a child in midair to the mother on another, another child standing with open arms on the platform waiting to assist his father's return.

I sit staring up at the billboard, dumbfounded.

"The Randeville Circus," Marissa says. "Coming to Baybury in October." She looks at me. "So?"

"That's not it," I say. "It changed."

"What changed?"

"Ellen Marie Franklin," I say. "The billboard. It was of a missing girl. Just last week it was. For three years it was."

"Ellen Marie Franklin," Marissa repeats. "Well, what about her?"

I blink my eyes at the billboard, as if the circus is a dust mote in my eye that I can blink away and then once again see clearly.

"Hollis," Marissa says. "What about her?"

"Okay," I say. "It said REWARD, right?"

"Okay," Marissa says.

"As opposed to MISSING."

"Uh-huh."

"Why, do you think?"

"Why REWARD and not MISSING?"

"Exactly," I say.

It doesn't take Marissa long to come up with an answer. "Maybe the parents could afford to offer a reward," she says. "Maybe if they couldn't it would have just said MISSING. I don't know." She shrugs. "Why?"

"She was up there for three years, about," I explain. "And until just the other week, it said MISSING. Then it changed to REWARD. Why, do you think? It gives me a bad feeling. Gave me."

"Huh," Marissa says. "Well maybe they came into money or something. I don't know."

"You think?"

"No," Marissa says. "Not really. I was just trying to support my original theory. But it's not really relevant, anymore, is it? I mean"— she gestures at the billboard with her chin—"she's not up there anymore."

"That gives me a bad feeling, too."

"Well, who is she?"

"Ellen Marie Franklin," I say.

"I understand that, Hollis," Marissa says. "I mean, why do you care?"

I think about that for a minute. "I don't know," I say, because I don't. I look down at my fingers and tug on a hangnail.

Marissa sighs and looks at me with what seems like pity. "Like I said, Hollis, not everything has to do with you," she says, and she pulls my one hand away from where it's picking at the other and holds it for a second in her own.

One of the things my mother took with her when she left us was a painting she'd done of a clown sitting on an overturned milk crate. He was a usual clown: big shoes, red nose, ballooning pants, a hat with a floppy brim and a wilted flower under the band. And he was an unusual clown: he was sad. His mouth was a big red frown. His eyes were sad, too, and a tear had cleared a streak of flesh through the white of his face paint. I hated this painting. It hung in the corner of the kitchen where we ate, behind my father's seat and across from me. It seemed to me that a clown should not be sad. It seemed to me that anyone sad shouldn't be painted, shouldn't be trapped in his unhappiness that way. Or that's what I think now when I remember the painting, how it made me squirm in my seat through dinner.

The summer after my mother left, my father took me to a circus. During intermission, he left me in our seats to get us cotton candy, but only minutes after he'd gone to get in line, I thought I'd rather have popcorn and went after him to let him know. I climbed down from the bleachers and went out to the outer layer of the circus tent where on our way in I'd clearly seen the layout: bathroom, program stand, cotton candy over here, popcorn and hot dogs over there. But we'd arrived at the circus almost late, after everyone was inside and sitting down, and the mostly empty outer tent that I remembered was now peopled into confusion. From within the crowd I could see only hips and arms at eye-level, spilled popcorn and candy-wrappers at my feet, the tent canvas above me rippling in the wind that I knew was blowing hard outside. I tried to push in the direction that I thought was right, but eventually it was all I could do to stay on my feet and I let the crowd push me where it would.

Which was, in the end, at the flap of tent that separated public space from backstage. I stood at the edge of the crowd and tried to catch my breath. I wasn't sure what to do, whether to push back into the crowd and try to find my father, or whether to wait here on the edge of things until the crowd had gone back inside to their seats. I didn't want to be late for the second act, which began with the tightrope walker I'd been eagerly anticipating all night, but the thought of subjecting myself again to the pulsing, sweating push of people among whom I lost all control was terrifying to me. I was standing there trying to pick my father out among all these people before me when a dwarf in a waiter's uniform carrying a tray loaded with sodas came bellowing through the crowd, emerging from the flow where I stood, and at my height. "Coming *through*!" he yelled, this time directly in my face. I blinked. "Yeah!" he shouted. He paused in front of me, looked me up and down, and then lifted his foot with its curled, elfin shoe high and strode backstage through the curtain behind me.

Dumbfounded, I turned and watched him go. He had opened the flap to backstage wide, with a flourish, and it stayed open long enough to give me a quick glimpse of what was back there. I saw a group of ladies in leotards standing in a circle, and I saw an elephant's rear as he disappeared through another curtain. I saw a man spinning a ball on his finger, and a midget with a monkey. And I saw my mother's clown. He was wearing what the clown in my mother's painting was wearing: his shoes were blue, his pants striped red and white, and he had the same hat with the same brim and wilting flower. He was sitting on a milk crate, like my mother's clown, and that awful frown was painted on his face.

And then the curtain closed. I stared. My heart began to pound hard and I began to sweat. What was this clown doing here? What had I just seen? Was my mother's clown a real clown and not just a clown in a painting? Did he know my mother? I took a breath and a step toward the curtain. I pulled it open only enough to peek through. The ladies still stood in their leotards, and the dwarf in the waiter's uniform was delivering them sodas. The man had dropped his spinning ball, and the midget's monkey had climbed atop his head. But my mother's clown was gone.

I told my father I'd gone to the bathroom when I got back to our seats, the tightrope walker's act already underway. He handed me my cotton candy, and I was glad for how effortless it is to eat because I wasn't hungry anymore at all, but I didn't want to hurt his feelings. I wanted to tell my father about my mother's clown, but more than that I wanted him to see the clown himself, so I sat silent and rigid, waiting for the clown to appear in the ring in the flesh.

But he never did. The second act came to a close, and my father leapt up so we could get out before the crowd. I lingered in my seat. "Wait," I said. "It's over?"

"That's it," my father said. "Let's beat the crowd, buddy, come on."

"You sure it's done?" I said.

"Yes," my father said. "What else were you expecting?" he asked.

I paused. "Mom's clown," I finally said. The lights of the tent had come on; we had missed our brief chance to beat the crowd outside. I looked up at my father. His face was blank. "I saw him backstage during intermission. I know I did. I wanted you to see him." My father sat back down on the bleacher beside me and put his hand on my neck. "It was him," I said. "Do you believe me?"

My father's grip tightened around my neck, and it was soothing. He hesitated, and he took a breath. "There are a lot of sad clowns in the world," he said, finally.

I went back to the billboard after waiting with Marissa for her mother. I pulled over, got out of the car, and walked to the base of the billboard. I looked up at the circus scene, which from immediately below took on a nightmarish property that I found appropriate for the billboard of a circus. The ground around the billboard's base was overgrown with weeds and trashed with litter: crushed soda cans, flaps of cardboard, chip bags, Styrofoam, bits of paper that I thought may well have been pieces of Ellen Marie, fallen to the ground here as her picture was scraped away. I picked one of these up and put it in my pocket before copying down the number written along the billboard's frame after the words WANT YOUR AD HERE?

I called the number as soon as I got home, and I asked the man who answered about the Randeville Circus billboard in Baybury.

"What about it?" he asked.

"I was wondering about the placement," I said. "Why that billboard and not another."

"Availability," he said.

"But it wasn't," I said.

"Sorry?"

"Available. There was something there."

"Yeah," he said. "There's always something there. We leave what's up there up until someone else rents the space."

I thought about billboards that I've seen. I have seen movies and television shows still advertised long after their arrival, special holiday rates still advertised in February. "So when did the last thing up there become, ah . . . obsolete?"

"I don't know that offhand," the man said. "I'd have to look that up." He didn't tell me to hold, please, while he did so.

I paused. "Do you mind?" I asked. "I'm from the university," I explained. "We're doing a study on billboards."

I heard him sigh. "Which billboard is it?"

I explained to him again which billboard I was talking about, and I listened to him type the information into a computer.

"Ten months," he said. "Been since November."

"November?"

"Right."

"So the billboard was obsolete from November until now?"

"Yeah, when Randeville rented it."

I thought about this, and I was ready to thank the man and hang up when something occurred to me.

"Well then here's a question," I said. "Here's something you need to explain to me." I cleared my throat. "Why," I said, "was the wording of the old billboard changed about a month or so ago?"

"The wording?"

"It was of a missing girl. For years it said: MISSING, and then this summer they changed it to REWARD. Why, if the advertisement were obsolete, would they have changed the wording?"

"They wouldn't."

"They did."

"They didn't," the man said. "I've got the records right here."

"They didn't," I repeated.

"No," he said. "Like you said, why would they?"

I don't know what to think. I'd like to think it's a conspiracy, that I am being lied to, but I have the nagging feeling that I may have simply been mistaken, that the billboard may have said REWARD all along. It's possible.

The idea makes me uneasy. I think about the time I've spent beneath the billboard this summer, pondering Ellen Marie's fate. I think about the notes I've taken, the theories I've come up with, the newspapers I've searched for clues. I think about how I've worried about this girl, how I've imagined her buried in some field or rolled into a ditch or holed up in some dank cellar or dusty shed. I think about the fact that Ellen Marie's fate was sealed all along, that they'd given up their search in November. I feel like I've been playing a game of hide and seek for longer than anyone else, that I've been trembling in my hiding place in anticipation of being found for long minutes after the game has ended.

Pratty's is empty when I arrive, which is unusual for a Saturday evening. Even Crosby's missing from behind the bar, but only for a minute or two; he emerges through the swinging door to the kitchen with his arms full of a case of beer to restock the cooler.

"Ah," he says when he sees me. "So nice of you to grace us with your presence."

I sigh and shrug, not in the mood for Crosby's shenanigans. "Yeah," I say.

Crosby settles his load atop the bar, and just as he's about to pour me a pint of beer, he eyes me and says, "You look like maybe it's a Jack night."

I shrug again. "How about both," I say.

Crosby nods and pours and sets a pint and rocks glass side by side in front of me. "So," he says. "How was it?"

I take a minute to figure out what he's talking about. How was what? My anniversary? My day with Marissa? Watching unseen through the windshield as Marissa gently approached her mother in the rain, and watching her mother melt with the agony only a parent could feel at the sight of her child's ruined face? "How was . . . ?" I look at him for a hint.

"Your literary obligation." Crosby says it with a mocking tone in his voice.

"Oh," I say. "That." I shrug.

Crosby stands in front of me drumming the bar with his fingers. "Pratty's fiftieth was just fine, thanks."

I'd forgotten about the party here yesterday. "Oh," I say. "I completely forgot. How was it? It was good?"

It's Crosby's turn to shrug now. "Yes and no," he says.

I wait for him to go on, but it's clear after a few seconds of silence that Crosby wants prompting. "Meaning?" I say.

"Well," he says. "It was a good time, but it was too much for Larry."

Now that I think about it, it is strange for Larry not to be at his usual stool at six on a Saturday evening. "What does that mean, too much?" I ask.

"Too much noise, too much booze, too much excitement, too much heat, too much fried food. A little too much of everything, I guess. Keeled right off his stool."

"Jesus," I say. "Where is he? Is he okay?"

Crosby shrugs. "He's alive, if that's what you mean by okay. I think it was his heart. He's at the hospital for another night or two, but I think they're going to let him come home after that."

"You seen him today?"

"Tried," Crosby says. "He's not too keen on visitors, I guess. Not in the hospital, anyway. He told the nurse to tell me that unless I'd brought him a beer I could go home."

I have to laugh at that. "Sounds like Larry to me," I say. "As long as he's still himself."

Crosby nods. "It'd take a lot to kill him," he says. "Hospital's probably doing more harm than good, depriving him of his life-blood." Crosby nods at my own two drinks.

"I guess so," I say.

I sip my beer. I'm glad I wasn't here to see Larry keel off his stool. I think Larry will be glad that I didn't see him, too. I'll be one person who hasn't seen him down and helpless, as I'm sure every other regular now has, which I'm sure pisses Larry off. I'll be one person he can still be his tough old self around, one person who hasn't seen him vulnerable.

But maybe it's more for my own sake than Larry's that I'm glad not to have seen his collapse, because I wouldn't have wanted to see it at all. And who knows whether or not Larry will give a shit whether I or anyone else has seen him down? Maybe Marissa is right; maybe I think I'm more important than I am. Maybe my father had better things to do himself the weekend of my twentieth birthday than go to New Hampshire with me; maybe he'd planned the thing for *me,* and not himself as I'd thought, so that I'd have something to do on my birthday. And maybe Simon *didn't* care that he slipped down the rocks in front of me. Maybe I wasn't as much of an idol, of a figure to impress, as I considered myself to be. Maybe that day was my idea only of a "guys' day out," and his idea simply of a day at the beach. Maybe my wife *wouldn't* care who I went for a drive with in the rain while she's away. And maybe, as Marissa insisted, her face *isn't* my fault.

Maybe. Maybe, maybe, but the thing is, I can't know for sure.

15

ANIMAL KINGDOM

've been back at work on the hedge, but it's slow going, because I'm trying to do some novice topiary shrubbing. I'm trying to shape the hedge into a zoo, with dolphins and penguins and lions and monkeys. I don't know that I've got quite enough hedge to work with, but I think it's worth the effort, and it keeps me in a zoo-like frame of mind, which is good for the Grover stories. I've started thinking about the first. It's going to be a penguin story. Penguins fascinate me, because they're so very gentle and at the same time so very brutal. After the female lays the egg, for instance, the father stands with the egg right on his feet and warms it for months with his low belly. There's something I admire in that, in the willingness to stand for months with an egg on your feet for the sake of a child you don't yet even know. And there's something wonderful about the female's loyalty through all this; she could go off and do her own thing, see other males, but instead she devotedly searches for food and brings it to her spouse. But at the same time, penguins can be pretty awful to one another. When a whole flock of them wants to hunt for food—and they fish for their food—all of the penguins will gang up on a single one whom they'll shove into the water as a sacrificial test. If the penguin comes up fine, they'll all jump safely in; if the penguin gets eaten by a polar bear or some large fish, they'll find other waters to hunt in. It's that capacity for both good and evil, for both love and ruthlessness, for both selfishness and selflessness, that interests me most, because it makes them seem a lot like humans.

"Back at work on the hedge, I see," Sal says from the street. I look up. "What, did you already figure out how to save the princess, or have you given up on it?"

At first, I think Sal is referring to my wife, and his bluntness surprises me. "Did I what?" I ask, holding my clippers half open in midair. I'm about to tackle the penguin's beak.

"The video game. Did you win?"

"Oh," I say. "Oh." The truth is, since last week when I got the thing I still haven't made it past the first level. But then again I've played only late-night, post-Pratty's, post-dinner and Jack. "No," I say. "I'm still working on it." I let my clippers hover above my penguin, but the confused intensity of Sal's gaze on the creature gives me stage fright, and I let the clippers drop. "What?" I say.

"What happened to the hedge, Hollis?"

"What do you mean, what happened?"

Sal shrugs. "I don't know."

"I don't know either."

"Maybe some drunk kid." He shakes his head.

I step back and look at what until now I've been considering my, albeit amateur, handiwork.

"Anyway," Sal says.

"Anyway," I say. "How's Mona?"

"Oh," Sal says. "Mona's good. It was actually her idea to send me over. We're having a big picnic at the beach tomorrow night, friends, family, neighbors, thought maybe you might want to come."

"Oh," I say. My anniversary picnic is one thing, but picnics otherwise put me in mind of bee stings; gritty, sandy food; burned hamburgers; mosquitoes; and, worst, watermelon. Watermelon is stressful. I hate having to eat around the seeds, even though my wife always says you don't *have* to, that the seeds aren't going to kill you. Still, I'd rather not take the chance. And I hate seed-spitting fights. If it were truly just the seeds that were spat, that would be one thing, but on more than one occasion I have had an entire mouthful of watermelon spat at me, seeds and all. "Well . . ."

"Of course if you're busy." Sal shrugs.

"Well," I say, "I'm not really *busy* busy, just, you know, things."

"Course," Sal says. "But if you feel like it, you know where to find us."

"Thanks," I say. "I'll keep that in mind."

"You do that."

I nod. "Thanks," I say. "I will."

I lift my clippers to take another stab at my penguin's beak before heading down to Pratty's for happy hour.

Football season is starting, and at Pratty's they've got a Budweiser football calendar hung up on the wall with a schedule of all the games to be played this year. I used to say that once the Fourth of July has happened, summer is essentially over because of the speed with which it seems to pass after that; but really I think it's the start of football season that marks the true beginning of the end. Usually I'm sad as the Fourth of July comes and goes, and even sadder when the football calendar appears on the wall at Pratty's and football scrimmages increasingly take the place of baseball on the large-screen TV in the corner. But this year things are different. The Fourth of July, if anything, marked the beginning of the summer and the slowing down of time, but now if football season has arrived, then Labor Day is clear on the horizon. I stepped close to the calendar last night, shortly after Sal had left me at the hedge, and counted the boxes separating me from my wife. Not many, anymore. But one of those boxes—tomorrow's box, now—is Simon's birthday.

I've been working on the hedge all afternoon, still trying to get this penguin right, but it's hard to focus. I keep imagining where I was exactly two years ago today, and it's a strange, dreamlike memory, because I remember it not through my own eyes but through the eyes of a spectator. I remember it not from the inside out, as I remember most things that have happened to me, but from the outside in. It makes me feel very separate from myself.

It's the day before Simon's birthday, exactly two years ago today, and I have stopped at Pratty's for a beer on my way home from New Hampshire, where I've driven an hour and a half each way to pick up a collector's-edition model race car for Simon's fourth birthday. I'm the only one in there and can't resist showing Crosby the gift, despite the fact that the car is packaged in all sorts of foam and plastic, boxed, and wrapped. I gently peel back the tape and unwrap the box without making a single tear in the paper; I open the box and slide the car out with all its packaging; carefully, I take it out of its molded Styrofoam cushioning and place it before me on the bar, which I wipe off first with a napkin so as not to sticky the wheels with any beer.

"She's a beauty, huh?" I say, and Crosby nods without much enthusiasm.

I lift the car from the bar and hold it upside down in the palm of my hand. "Look at this," I say. "The wheels are actually attached to miniature axles and"—I turn the steering wheel back and forth—"they actually respond to the wheel."

Crosby nods, wiping down glasses with a dish towel. "Nice," he says.

I set the car back down on the bar and show Crosby how the doors open upward rather than sideways, like a real race car. "This is a model of the actual thing," I say. "Just scaled down, but otherwise, an exact replica."

"Your kid into cars this young?" Crosby asks, and I nod.

"We saw this puppy drive," I say. "Saw the real thing." My wife's cousin is a race car driver, and we'd all gone up to watch him race in the finals of some series in which the driver of the car I'd bought for Simon had broken some big record. Simon had loved it. *Vroom, vroom,* he'd said for weeks after, running his crappy plastic cars around the living room. Now he'd have a real car, a good one.

I leave the car on the bar for a while to admire, showing it off to everyone who comes into the bar. Finally, just as carefully as I'd unwrapped the thing, I repackage it, rebox it, and rewrap it in a process that takes a good ten minutes. I'm about to head home when Larry walks in, and of course I can't leave without showing the car to Larry, and so I go through the whole thing again, unwrapping, unboxing, unpackaging, and so on.

As the memory winds to a close for the fourth or fifth time today, I realize that I have been standing above the hedge with my clippers idly in my hand, that I am having no luck. I look at the sky, waiting for evening to come.

I was thinking earlier as I stood on the lawn how much I love routine, the routine of cocktail hour, burrito time, and after-dinner drink, and when the light finally began to lengthen, I was filled with relief at the thought of surrendering the rest of the day to routine. Until, that is, I'd settled on the lawn with my Jack and seen the number of fish leaping out in the marsh.

There's been a rowboat tethered to a post down on the edge of the marsh for as long as we've lived here. I've always thought it makes the view from our lawn look like a painting. I don't know who the rowboat belongs to, and I've never seen it used before, so I figured that no one would miss it if I took it out for a quick spin.

"How would you feel about some fish for dinner tonight?" I

asked the dog. "It'll be good to have a night off from burritos, don't you think?" At the mention of the word *burritos* the dog started whining and circling. "No," I said, trying to explain, "tonight we're having *fish. Fish. Fish.*" I spoke the word slowly, pointing toward the water. "Come on," I said, downing the last of my third Jack, which most evenings does signal dinnertime. "Let's go find a rod."

The dog refused to go down into the basement with me, but he waited at the top of the stairs while I rummaged around down there through piles of stuff that does not belong to me or my wife. When we moved in, the people who were moving out informed us that they'd left some odds and ends in the basement that they thought we might enjoy; the "odds and ends" turned out to take up the majority of basement space. Claire was livid upon discovering the junk, even though we didn't have anything to fill the basement with ourselves. It was the principle, she said. It was just plain lazy and inconsiderate. I didn't mind, though. I was intrigued by the idea of other peoples' things living in our cellar. I used to go down to the cellar often to rummage through the stuff and see what I could find, and I could always find something good—an old croquet set, a spare ski pole, a worn-out baseball glove, a bike pump, a lawn sprinkler. What I liked better than the things themselves were their histories, which I could only imagine. To whose hand had the baseball glove been molded? What slopes had the ski pole guided its owner down? Where was the other ski pole? What lawns had the sprinkler sprinkled, and what kids had run through its spray? There are ghosts attached to the things downstairs.

I hadn't been down to the basement in months; last time I went I was looking for an extension cord for our Christmas-tree lights, and sure enough I found one. And this evening, too, despite the fact that it's hardly thicker than a pencil and less than three feet long, I did indeed find myself a fishing pole. And so, fishing pole, Jack, and a tin of sardines from the cabinet to use as bait all in hand, the dog and I shoved off in the little rowboat, temporarily disrupting the composition of my view.

I am not the world's most graceful rower. Rowing is a backward sport in every way; you sit facing backward; likewise, you row on whichever side is the opposite side of the direction in which you want to go. Jack probably doesn't simplify things any, coordination-wise, but nonetheless I have managed to row us a good way through the marsh toward the open ocean, trailing my sardine-baited line behind me.

"This is going to be good when it pays off." The dog looks anxiously over the edge of the boat and bats at his reflection in the water. "Here," I say, pulling a sardine from the tin, "have a preview. An appetizer." The dog sniffs at the sardine in my hand. His lips go up. I shrug. "I don't blame you," I say. "I don't much like sardines, either. But fish, fish is good." The dog sighs and settles down in the bottom of the boat. "Here," I say, feeling guilty at the thought of the dog not enjoying himself quite as much as I am, because I *am*. Here I am, on a warm summer evening, out fishing with my man's best friend and Jack. I've got nowhere to be, nothing else to do. I wish I could see myself from the outside in right now; I think I'd be envious of the man in the boat. The thought swells me with pleasure. "Have a little of this," I say, pouring a touch of Jack into my palm and offering it to the dog. He sniffs it and laps it up. "A dog after my own heart," I say, and I "cheers" him and take my own little swig.

The fishing line is floating suspiciously loosely behind the boat, I notice, and so I reel it in to check on the bait, which is gone. It annoys me to think that a fish might have eaten the sardine right off the hook without getting caught. I jam another sardine onto the hook, this time doubling it over and piercing it twice through before casting. I take another swig of Jack, give a little more to the dog, and head oceanward, though all I can see, seated backward as I am, is the receding marsh. The redeeming aspect of rowing's backwardness is that I can keep an eye on my line, which gets me wondering if maybe rowing was designed by fishermen for that exact purpose. That would excuse what otherwise seems an unnecessary complication to the sport. All I need now are some front-view mirrors rigged up in the back of the boat, so I can see the ocean I'm heading toward behind me. Not a bad idea. An idea worthy of real consideration, actually. The other day as Marissa and I waited the afternoon out in the car, we listened to a radio show called *Ideas and Inventions,* to which people called in with ideas just like mine.

One guy called in, for instance, with an idea for prescription mirrors. The mirror is distorted in a way that counteracts its owner's eye deficiency, so that that person can look at himself in the mirror without his glasses on and see himself clearly. This makes sense, because if you must wear glasses to see properly but don't wear contacts, you have no way of seeing what you look like as you actually are. Another guy called in with an idea for caffeinated soap. You get up in the morning, get in the shower, and you're caffeinated before you've even had your coffee. As we listened to the show, I got the idea for a dog umbrella; maybe I was inspired by the raininess of the day. Why should humans get to stand under umbrellas as they walk their dogs and the dogs walk miserably in the rain? I stood under my own umbrella at the pay phone near where we were parked and spent a good half hour trying to get through, but each time I dialed the line was busy. If I ever listen to that show again, I'll be sure to call in with the dog umbrella idea and also now the front-view mirror for rowboats idea.

I stop where the marsh gives way to ocean, nervous to venture farther with sunset fast approaching. I turn the boat around and pause before I start rowing back so I can take a good look at the vast horizon and above it the deepening sky, the lowering sun. I get the dog to sit up as best I can and turn his muzzle in the direction of the view. "Look at that," I say. "How often do you get to see something like that?" The dog whines and slumps back down onto the floor of the boat. I sigh, and start to row. From the look of it, the bait seems to be gone again, but I don't bother hooking another sardine. The fish in here will probably just outsmart me again, and this excursion will have been worthwhile in and of itself, even if I don't catch any fish.

I stare at the sun as I row back in the direction from which I came, wondering unoriginally if the sunset looks the same in Maryland right now, and if Claire is watching it. I look over my shoulder just to make sure I'm headed in the right direction and not into the marsh grass. I've made no progress since I turned around. In fact, I seem to have made negative progress, and realize I am being pulled to sea by the outgoing tide. It is getting darker, and I don't have life jackets on board. I take a deep breath and a little Jack and start rowing with the full force of my body, but even then I'm only stationary, and soon thoroughly exhausted. I drop the oars. "Shit," I mutter. "Fuck it." I sit back with my Jack and put my feet up, surrendering to the drift. I am ready for adventure.

I wish that model race car were still around. I wish I hadn't been quite so thorough in getting rid of Simon's things.

Of course I didn't get everything in my mad sweep of the house. Claire collected what I'd missed—some clothes that had been in the dryer, a ball under the hedge outside, antibiotics in a brown jar with his name and dosage taped to the side. I don't know what she did with those things; I saw her with them in her arms one morning soon after when I came downstairs with a raging headache and my eyes thick with booze.

And then just last spring I found something else I'd missed. Claire and I were attempting a spring cleaning, and the living room, as usual, was my responsibility; Claire thinks I'm a careless cleaner and reserves for herself the more detailed, dirty work of kitchen and bathroom. But I thought this time around I'd try to be more thorough. I moved the furniture piece by piece outside and hit the cushions of the sofa, loveseat, and chairs with a baseball bat to kick up the dust I thought might have settled there. I Windexed the glass-topped coffee table, dusted the wicker basket full of magazines, cleaned the stems of the tall standing lamps. I cleaned the TV and the TV stand. I vaccuumed every inch of carpet, and washed the handprints from the walls. I found what of Simon's I'd missed almost two years before when I went to clean the windowsills. On the sill of the picture window that runs from floor to ceiling, in front of which usually sits the loveseat, amid the dust and grime that had collected there over the years, was a Wacky WallWalker.

For a time, Wacky WallWalkers came in Cheerios boxes—this was before they started putting millennium pennies in there, and after they'd stopped putting stickers inside. Breakfast was Simon's favorite meal because of those cereal prizes. We always let him dig through a new box right away for his prize instead of making him wait until it spilled into his bowl, and he ate more cereal than I'd think a kid his size capable of, the sooner to get a new box. Wacky WallWalkers were our favorite prize, his and mine. They were sticky, octopus-like creatures, and when you threw one against a window, it would cling with its goo to the glass, slowly begin to unpeel leg by leg, and then start to fall until it was suddenly caught, reattached by the goo of another or two of its legs falling too near the glass. Simon and I often stood before the picture window and raced our Wacky WallWalkers down the wall, except I guess it was a backward race, because the slowest WallWalker won.

I wondered, as I stood there with spray and paper towel in hand, whether the WallWalker forgotten on the sill all these years was Simon's or my own; the thought that it was mine, that my hand had tossed it on its final run, was easier to bear. Almost. I bent to pick it up. It had gone gooless and dusty with age, and I wasn't sure what to do with it. I thought I should probably take it immediately to the garbage, because what else would I do with it? Leave it on my desk as a little decoration? Store it away in my underwear drawer? What did I need with a defunct Wacky WallWalker? I took it outside and sat down on the couch, twiddling the thing around between my fingers, which is where Claire found me an hour or so later.

"I'm done with the kitchen," she said. She stood behind me, her hands on my shoulders. I didn't say anything, because I wasn't sure what to say. She paused. "The carpet looks great," she said. Still I said nothing. "Want help getting this stuff back inside?" she said. I was quiet, staring down at the pink rubber in my hands. "Hey," she said, squeezing my shoulders. "Are you not speaking to me?"

I swallowed and lifted the WallWalker up over my head where she could see it. She took it from me, and I don't know, maybe she put it in her pocket, maybe she dropped it on the ground, maybe she tossed it in the bushes, and then without taking her hand from my shoulder, she climbed over the back of the couch and sat down beside me.

"Hollis! Hollis!" I sit upright in the rowboat at the sound of my name. I've floated out the entrance of the marsh and around the corner, and I'm now floating right by the beach where Claire and I have our anniversary picnic. Sal and Mona are at the water's edge, hopping up and down with their pantcuffs rolled, waving their arms and calling my name. Behind them are clusters of people with beer cans, a fire raging in a makeshift pit, a grill, several picnic tables laden with food, kids screaming and zigzagging through it all. Sal and Mona's picnic. I don't know where I thought the tide would take me, but here is not where I would choose to be.

The dog struggles up from the bottom of the boat at the sound of the commotion on the beach and starts to bark in response. "Shh," I say. "It's okay. They're nice." I grab the oars and start rowing toward the shore. I look tentatively over my shoulder at the massive picnic gathered there. "I think," I add.

Sal wades out to meet the boat and pulls it up onto the beach. "Hollis!" he says. "You made it!"

"I'm so glad you decided to come!" Mona says, rushing over. "Sal said he didn't think you could make it!"

"Hi," I say, climbing unsteadily out of the boat. Truth is, I am a little hungry.

"So you thought you'd come by sea!" Mona says. "How clever!"

"Yup," I say. "You know, a little exercise." I stretch and watch as the dog hops out of the boat. He seems shaky, too. "I don't think the dog liked it much, though," I say.

"Don't forget this," Sal says, tossing me my Jack.

I grin. "Booze cruise," I say. "No, I'm kidding, that's for you. For the picnic. I would have brought wine, but . . ." I grin again, looking at the half-empty bottle. "And I was hoping to catch some fish along the way, but . . ." I shrug. "Weren't biting."

"Well that's a good thing!" Mona exclaims. "Because we have more food than we know what to do with! Come, come!" She and Sal usher me up the beach toward the picnic. I shrug, pocket the Jack, and follow them. As we near the crowd, I anxiously wait for everyone to turn silent and stare in my direction; I dread the public introduction I fear will come next—"Everyone, this is Hollis, Hollis, this is everyone!"—but no one seems to notice my arrival. Mona lifts a finger and rushes off to help a crying child with a scraped knee.

"Burger? Chicken? Hot dog?" Sal asks.

"Whatever's easy," I say.

"Well, I was just about to throw on a bunch of burgers—how does that sound?"

I follow Sal over to the grill and watch him lay the raw patties down. I notice a cooler of beer by the table, and Sal notices me noticing and tells me to help myself.

I do.

"So," Sal says. "Lots of people here, so I'm not even going to try with names, but you see those two"—and he gestures toward a pair of boys shaking something in an empty Pringles can—"they're my nephews, the ones with the Nintendo. If you want to talk," he says.

"Okay," I say, but already Sal's calling to them.

"Hey!" he's calling. "Matt, Chris!" They look up from their shaking and Sal waves them over.

"Matt, Chris," Sal says when they've reached the grill. "This is Hollis, a good friend of mine."

"Hey," I say, "nice to meet you." And then "Oh," I say, when I see them sticking out their hands for a shaking, the nicely trained little creatures. I take their hands, one at a time, and give each a good shake. I look curiously at the Pringles can, which sounds as if it's still being shaken, even though Matt's holding it still in his hand. "What's in the can?" I ask.

"Grasshopper!" Chris bursts, and grabs the can from Matt and starts to shake it vigorously.

"Give it here!" Matt calls, and they begin to toss the poor canned hopper back and forth as they make their way away from us and down the beach.

"So that's Matt and Chris if you need Nintendo pointers," Sal says. "But otherwise, everyone else is just family, friends, neighbors, you can introduce yourself. You might have met a few before, I'm sure. Like the Kradblums, over there, you know them." Sal gestures toward Jerry and what's-her-name Kradblum, who used to live a few blocks down from us. I'm pretty sure they moved. I don't think I've seen them in years. The Kradblums catch Sal looking at them, and so Sal waves. They wave back, and since I'm standing there, I wave back, too, even though they probably don't have any idea who I am, anymore.

"Is that—" I hear a voice approaching from behind. "Well it is!" I feel a hand on my shoulder and turn around to face the owner. "Mr. Clayton! I thought that was you! And it's so funny, because we don't know anybody here, but here's my very next-door neighbor! Sal! I didn't know you and Mona knew Mr. Clayton!"

"Hollis," I interrupt.

"Sorry?" Judith Crane looks at me.

"Hollis," I say.

"Hollis," Judith Crane repeats. "Of course. But how do you know Sal and Mona?"

"We go to the same bar," I explain, and then I realize that this might not be the response Sal would have wanted me to offer. "And he lives down the street, and Mona and my wife teach at the same school."

"Really!" Judith Crane exclaims. "Well we just met Sal and

Mona, didn't we?" She nudges Sal, who nods and flips the burgers. He's concentrating hard on scraping off meat that's stuck to the rungs of the grill. "Lamaze," Judith explains to me in a low voice, as if imparting a secret.

"Lamaze?" I repeat.

She nods. "Mona and I are in the same class. Of course, Norm and I have done Lamaze classes many a time, but it's always a good idea to freshen up."

"Oh," I say. "Right, of course." Judith Crane is looking at me proudly, stroking her still-flat stomach with both hands. "Congrats," I say. And then I take advantage of the moment to figure out exactly how many of the kids that frequent her yard are actually hers. "Number . . ."

"Five," she says, and I nod. Just as I'd figured. "Yes, Norm and I . . ." and then she breaks off with a gasp, covering her mouth with both hands. "Norm!" she exclaims. "He's here tonight! Oh, you've got to meet him! I told him about those rain birds, and I know he'd love to talk bird-watching! And he's hardly ever around, you know, business. But he's home for the week!"

"Great," I say. I glance over at Sal, who's looking at me with a puzzled expression.

"I'll go get him," she says. "But wait! Your wife! Is she here? I'd love to finally meet her!"

"Oh," I say, and out of the corner of my eye I see Sal tilt his head. "No," I say. "She couldn't . . . she didn't . . . she's . . . business," I try, shrugging and hoping that Judith Crane won't ask what kind of teacherly business might have called her away in August.

"Don't I know how it is," Judith Crane says, lifting a finger as she starts backing away.

I feel Sal staring at me, and I turn to meet his eyes. "What?" I say.

"All sorts of new hobbies while the wife's on business, huh?" he says. "Video games, bird-watching."

"I haven't actually taken up bird-watching," I say.

"Ah," Sal says. "You can just talk the talk."

I shrug. "Long story," I say.

Sal doesn't push the issue.

"So how's Lamaze?" I ask.

He shrugs. "Weird," he says, scratching his head. "But okay, I guess," he adds, his eyes trained on his burgers.

I shuffle clockwise around the grill, trying to avoid the smoke that has of course been blowing directly in my face. The smoke follows. I watch Sal through the haze, poking at the burgers, lifting each to make sure the underside isn't burning. His Adam's apple is bobbing nervously in his throat. I'm guessing that he's feeling guilty about the Lamaze talk, just like the other week he apologized when he told me that Mona was pregnant. I decide to let him know it's okay by pushing the conversation further.

"Have you got to the *whowhoheeeeeee* breath yet?"

Sal looks up from the burgers. "The what?"

"The *whowhoheeeeeee* breath."

Sal grabs a plate and starts tranferring the burgers to it from the grill. He shrugs. "They all kind of sound the same to me," he says.

"I guess they do," I say. I squat down by the cooler and grab another beer. Things look funny from this height. I'm eye level with a lot of legs, some stationary, some moving, some pairs standing alone and some in groups with two or three other pairs. The flame from the campfire silhouettes several pairs of legs, hands dangling beer cans beside them. I'm eye level with the eyes of Matt and Chris, who seem to have abandoned the Pringles can and have moved on, early, to the watermelon. They're sneaking behind a horseshoe of ladies in beach chairs, dropping watermelon seeds in their hair. Closer to the water, a crew of kids is working on a dribble castle of amazing porportions, and then, just at the water's edge, is the dog, barking ferociously at something in the sand. The dog! I'd forgotten about him. I stand and raise my beer at Sal. "Going to go see what's bothering the dog," I say, and Sal nods.

I wander down to the water's edge to where the dog is circling a pit about two feet in diameter. I take a step closer and peer into the pit, and though it's hard to see in the dusk light, it looks like hundreds of little pebbles have been tossed in there, and what startles me at first, as it's startling the dog, is that the pebbles seem to be moving of their own accord. I get down onto my knees to take a closer look, and only then can I make out the little clawlike legs emerging from what looked from afar like pebbles. The pit is filled with two or three hundred hermit crabs, scrabbling over each other, trying frantically to climb up the side of their prison only to drop back about halfway up when the sides get too steep to ascend. They seem panicked, and while I marvel at a hermit crab's seeming capacity for fear, I marvel too at a child's capacity for cruelty. Although I wonder if cruelty is really what it is. I wonder if it might not be something as simple as curiosity, and doesn't that affect us all?

I stand and brush my hands on my pants. It's fully dark, now, and when I turn and look, the picnic seems all of a sudden far away. Faces glow orange, mouths open to form words I can't make out from here, and the campfire splatters sparks every second or two, causing shrieks of terror and delight from the kids toasting marshmallows on sticks. I look at the rowboat longingly and consider making an escape, but I am hungry, and the cold beer tastes good. I sigh and look at the dog, who's looking up at me. "Shall we?" I say, and we make our way up the beach.

16

MEXICO

It turns out that Norm Crane knew exactly who I was, even though I didn't remember ever having seen him before, from some cocktail party we'd gone to in the very beginning of the summer.

"You were the guy who spilled his drink in the guacamole!" he roared, slamming me on the back. Then he winked. "It made it that much more tasty, bud," he said. I don't remember spilling my drink into any guacamole, but if I was drunk enough to spill like that it makes sense that I wouldn't.

Since we're neighbors, and they were going my way, the Cranes offered to drive me home. I gladly accepted since they were some of the first to leave the picnic, what with four young children who needed their beds.

Imagine this: a Pontiac station wagon, fake wood siding; Norm Crane driving, one large hairy hand draped over the wheel, one on Judith Crane's neck; Judith Crane in the front seat, the youngest of her children—the one I held that evening in her yard—on her lap; the three older children in the backseat, one staring quietly out the window, having been reprimanded for pushing another child at the picnic, the other two engaged in a pinching war that I, curled up in the way-back next to the dog, fear at any moment might dissolve from something good-natured into something brutal. The shocks on the car are loose, and the road is bumpy, and with every bump my head knocks the ceiling. Judith Crane keeps trying to ask me questions, but I can hardly hear her from all the way in the back and over the noise of the kids in front of me.

The oldest Crane child, Harry, steams up the glass of the window with his breath and traces designs with his fingers. He wipes the designs clean, refogs the glass, and writes "fuck you" in slow, careful script. Madeline, age nine, is seated at the opposite window, and as she glances up from her pinching game with her younger sister, Cathy, the letters catch her eye.

"Mom!" she cries. "Mom!"

"You girls can pinch all you want; I'm simply not getting involved," Judith Crane says. "Norm?"

"That's right," Norm says. "You play with fire, you get burned, girls."

"No, Mom, Harry wrote the F word!" Madeline squeals, and at this Harry wipes his hand across the glass, erasing the evidence. He turns to glare at his sister.

"Did not," he says.

"Did so! You just— Mom, he just wiped it away, but I swear!"

"Harry, are you writing profanities on the window?" Judith Crane asks. Harry denies it. "Norm?"

"Harry, I sure hope what your sister said isn't true," Norm says. He's taken his hand from Judith Crane's neck and has both hands now gripping—not draping—the steering wheel.

"It is!" Madeline cries. "I saw it! He wrote it right on the window!"

Judith Crane turns in her seat. "You know the policy on curse words, young man," she says. Then she shifts so she's facing me. I feel caught. I should be staring out the back window, watching the world fade behind us into the night. But here I am, both hands on the seatback, watching this scene like a tennis match or soccer game. "Mr. Clayton," she says.

"Hollis," I say.

"Hollis," she says. "Let's get the final word from you. You've got a pretty good view from back there. Did you happen to notice Harry writing profanities on the window?"

All eyes are on me. I glance from Judith Crane's expectant gaze to Harry's daring one to Madeline's righteous, bratty little stare. The car lurches over a bump and my head hits the ceiling, hard. "No," I say. "I mean, I didn't notice if he did."

"See," Harry says, sneering at his sister.

"No," Madeline sneers back. "He didn't say you didn't, he just said he didn't see it, and I did, and I know you did it." Harry and Madeline both slump back into their seats, and Madeline brushes Cathy off as she tries to reinitiate their pinching war. Judith Crane turns around. I rub my head, feeling for the start of an egg.

"So," Norm Crane says after a few moments of silence, turning around in his seat as he pulls into my driveway. I'm about to say something about such door-to-door service, when he says, "Whaddya say, five-thirty tomorrow morning?"

"Sorry?" I say.

"Five thirty?"

"Five thirty?"

"Bird-watching!" Norm Crane roars. "Haven't found anyone around here to go with, point me out the local birds. We're from Florida, remember, got different species down there. Love to have a guide!"

"Oh," I say.

"Oh do say yes!" Judith Crane turns around in her seat again. "Norm's leaving again the day after tomorrow for what, three weeks this time? Oh, you must while you have the chance!"

"Come on, bud," Norm growls conspiratorily. "Guys' day out?"

"Okay," I say.

"So five thirty?"

"Okay," I say, fiddling with the handle to the tailgate, which won't open. "Sounds good," I say, fiddling some more, without success. "Um, could you let me out?"

"Oh, God! How silly! I forgot that handle's broken!" Judith Crane laughs. "I forgot to tell you, Norm. It broke last week. Harry, will you let Mr. Clayton out?"

Harry swings the door open and lets me out.

"Thanks," I say, and I stand beside the dog, blinded in the beam of their headlights as Norm Crane backs the car down the driveway, smiling and waving into the light until finally they're gone, and it's dark, and it's quiet, and I can see again.

My wife loves to bird-watch. A couple times a month, and more during the summer, she puts on her marsh-walking sneakers, hangs her binoculars around her neck, stuffs her bird guide book in her pocket, and disappears for hours at a time.

Tonight has made me wonder if I might have been missing something good all these years. It was nine o'clock when the Cranes dropped me off, which gave me exactly eight and a half hours to familiarize myself enough with the birds of this region to take Norm Crane bird-watching as if I were an expert. I pulled Claire's bird book from the shelf, poured myself a little Jack for fuel, and headed up to bed to start reading. I wouldn't have known where to begin had Claire not earmarked all the birds that pass through the area, which, I learned, is a major migratory passage route. It turns out that more than 180 species pass through here as summer gives way to fall, but I decided to limit my knowledge to those birds that are most abundant around here, for time's sake if nothing else. Although I can't say that after this bird-watching trip I'll be done reading about birds. This is some of the best reading I've done in years.

Take the great egret, for example. I've always seen them—these large, white, graceful birds stalking slowly through the marsh—but I've never paid them much attention. It turns out they can live for twenty-three years, which means that a lot of the egrets I see each evening have been living on this marsh for longer than I have. And even though there can be up to six eggs in a nest during breeding time, the larger chicks usually kill their siblings, especially when the parents can't provide enough food. This surprises me. I'd think that if there wasn't enough food, the smaller chicks would simply die of starvation or weakness anyway; it seems unnecessary for the sibling to step in and rush the inevitable. It seems like violence for the sake of it. But maybe it's just a bird thing, a bird form of sibling rivalry.

And osprey—there's an interesting bird. I've always noticed their nests up on telephone poles, channel markers, and duck blinds, without knowing what they were. The thing about osprey that gets me is how they get their food. They don't dive into the water head-first for their fish; they plunge in feet first, grab an unsuspecting fish with their talons, and fly it back to their nest. They don't just carry the fish any old way; they rotate their feet out like a ballerina and carry it headfirst through the air, perfectly aerodynamically, to get it back to the nest as quickly as possible while it's still fresh and alive. The thought of what a poor fish can potentially suffer at the claws of an osprey makes me not mind so much that a few fish tonight got free sardines off me. Just imagine swimming along, minding your own business, and suddenly being snatched up out of the water and into the air in the claws of a winged beast, to be pecked alive back at the nest.

My favorite bird so far is the Bonaparte's gull. These birds migrate all the way from Canada to Mexico, passing through here on their way. The male heads south first, and once there he establishes a nice nest for when his family arrives. The female stays up north for a few extra weeks while the child builds his strength for the flight, and then, just before it gets too cold, mother and child fly south and somehow manage to find the exact location of the nest the father's set up down in Mexico. The book offers no good explanation of just how the birds can find one another, which makes me wonder if any bird expert even knows, or if birds have a kind of telepathy that's beyond our understanding. What these birds can do seems to me greater than what any human can do.

But that's only 3 birds I've got fully memorized—weight, wingspan, and all—3 out of a potential 180 I might be called on to identify. I've read up on 20 or so other birds, but the more I read, the less I remember.

I don't know when the birds in the book are replaced by the birds in my dreams, but I awaken with a start from a nightmare of beaks and wings and feathers and talons to the shrill ringing of the phone, and I shoot my hand out to answer before it rings again.

"Hello?" I say.

"Hi."

The world seems to come to a crashing halt around me, and I float suspended in the moment, unable to breathe. The voice is quiet, and very much like my wife's, but I don't want to fool myself. I've had little sleep and plenty to drink, and my mind is full of birds. "Hello?" I say again, carefully.

"Hollis." It is my wife. I sit up and put my feet on the floor.

"Claire," I say.

"Are you awake?"

"Yes. Kind of. Why?" I look at the clock. It's 5:15.

"A hunch," she says.

"A hunch?"

"The day." The day. With little real sleep, today seems a continuation of yesterday. I'd forgotten to notice that Simon's birthday has arrived.

I shut my eyes.

"How are you?" she asks.

"Okay. You?"

"Okay," she says. "I was just awake, so I thought I'd call."

I listen to her breathing, and wonder where she's calling from—if she's sitting at the table in her sister's kitchen, or if she's outside on a cordless phone, or if she's on some street corner calling from a pay phone. Or if she's in bed, as I am.

"How's Maryland?" I ask finally.

I can imagine her shrugging in the pause that follows. "It's Maryland," she says. "Baybury?"

"Baybury," I say. I look at her book, open across my lap, and think of the times she must have held it lying in this very same bed, thumbing through the very pages I'm thumbing through now before her own excursion into the marsh. "I'm going bird-watching today," I say.

"Bird-watching!"

"Yeah," I say.

"I thought you didn't like bird-watching," she says.

"It's a long story."

She doesn't answer right away. "Bird-watching, huh," she says.

"Yeah," I say. "What about you?"

"What about me?"

"I don't know," I say. "I mean, what are you doing today?"

"Oh," she says. "Nothing special. Pat broke her leg last week, so I've got to drive her to the hospital to get her cast changed. I don't know what else."

"Pat broke her leg?"

"She stepped the wrong way off the curb," my wife says.

"Oh."

She sighs. "Anyway," she says. "I should go, I guess."

There are things I want to ask her before she goes. I want to ask her will I see her soon, will I hear from her again, am I allowed to call her, is she going to come back to me. I want to wish her a late happy anniversary. "Okay," I say.

There's a silence, then. I hold my breath, wondering what she's thinking, what she's going to say next. "Hollis," she says, finally. Her tone is different, matter-of-fact, as if she's just thought of something important. "I was just thinking, and if you're really going bird-watching, the male Bonapartes are flying through right now. Read up on them if you haven't. I think you'll like them. There's a platform at the north end of the marsh, near Jackson's Creek, where you can watch them from."

"Bonaparte's gull," I repeat. "I know about those. The ones that go to Mexico. I like those." My wife knows me too well.

"Well, Jackson's Creek, then."

"Jackson's Creek," I repeat.

We hang up.

I sit for a minute on the edge of the bed, replaying the conversation in my head and wondering if I said the right things and left the right things unsaid. I feel suddenly lonely. Yesterday and all yesterday's momentum have hit a wall and launched me forward into a day I haven't prepared for, a day I don't know what to do with on my own. I look at the phone and consider calling Norm Crane to cancel, but just then I hear him pounding on the door downstairs.

"Hollis!" he's calling. "Hollis, let's go!"

I've taken Norm Crane to the platform Claire told me about, up by Jackson's Creek, and it is cozy up here to say the least. And hot. Norm Crane brought over some camouflage for me to wear—pants, jacket, and hat, a special Floridian print that he guarantees works better than the northern stuff he thought I'd have—all of which is at this point drenched in my sweat. The sun's getting hotter and hotter as it rises, and I'm beginning to wish I'd gotten a little more sleep than I did.

I try to point out the birds I've read up on, but they fly so quickly I can't find them through the binoculars, so after the egrets and cormorants, which I knew by sight before today, I don't know which bird is which.

"What's that, what's that?" Norm will say, pointing excitedly at a bird swooping over the marsh.

"Hold on," I'll say, and I'll try to get it in the binoculars so I can make out the markings. "Swallow," I'll say, just to say something, and then I'll recite what I've read about swallows. Norm takes notes, jabbing me in the side with his elbow as he writes. This is how the morning's been going. I feel like a fraud. I'm hot, and tired, and here, I'm sure, is the last place I should be today.

"How about those guys, down there," Norm Crane says, pointing toward the marsh.

"I already told you. Those are egrets," I say.

"Not the egrets, the little guys with the skinny legs." I lift the binoculars, and finally I locate the birds Norm is talking about. "Oh," I say. I peek into the bird book to be sure I'm right, and then I tell him that the birds in question are spotted sandpipers.

Norm writes this down. "That so," he says. "Tell me about them."

"Well," I say. "For one thing, the female will lay eggs for up to four different males at a time. Polygamy of sorts."

"He he," Norm chuckles. "The better system."

"Sorry?" I say.

"Polygamy," he says. "One here, one there, you know."

"Oh," I say.

"Don't you?" Norm says, elbowing me and winking.

"Not really," I say.

"Come *on,*" Norm says. "Nothing shameful about it. I've got three, no, four different ladies myself."

I look Norm in the eye. "You do?" I say.

"Sure," he says. "I'm on business quite a bit, you know."

"So I've gathered," I say.

"I believe you said your wife's on business, no?" he says. "And what kind of business is that?"

I take off my camouflage jacket, despite Norm's earlier protestations when I tried the same thing. But I'm hot, and I don't care if the birds can see us or not. I haven't seen any Bonaparte's gulls anyway.

"I don't think that's any of your business," I say, and my anger surprises me. I'm not sure what is worse: the idea that Norm Crane and I are anything alike in our infidelities, or the idea of my wife cheating on me.

"Hey hey hey, buddy," Norm says, punching my arm and grinning. "I'm just joking around with you."

I'm embarrassed at my outburst, and I try a little grin.

"Anyway," he says, picking up his pen, "where was I? What are those again? Spotted sandpeckers?"

"Pipers," I say.

"What's that?"

"Pipers," I say. "Sand*pipers,* not peckers."

Norm Crane roars. "Shows where my mind is," he mutters as his laughter subsides, shaking his head and writing his notes.

I stare down at the open bird book on my lap.

The function of the teetering motion typical of this species has not been determined. Chicks teeter nearly as soon as they hatch from the egg. The teetering gets faster when the bird is nervous, but stops when the bird is alarmed, aggressive, or courting. The male takes the primary role in parental care, incubating the eggs and taking care of the young. One female may lay eggs for up to four different males at a time. The female may store sperm for up to one month. The eggs she lays for one male may be fathered by a different male in a previous mating.

I turn the page; the next section is devoted to swans. "Swans," I say to Norm Crane. "They mate for life," I say.

"Where?" he says. "I didn't see a swan."

"There wasn't one. I'm just saying," I say.

"Well, maybe so," he says. "They also have enough strength in their necks to strangle a man."

I stare at Norm Crane, who is sweating now more profusely

than I am. He wipes the sweat from his forehead and takes a sip of water from the camel pack he's got strapped to his back. I look back down at the book.

Swans, it says.

It is a popular misconception that mute swans pair for life and that a bird will pine to death when its partner dies. This is far from true, with some birds having as many as four mates in a lifetime, and in some cases actually "divorcing" a mate in favor of a new one. There have even been incestuous relationships reported. However research does show that well-established pairs tend to be more successful at raising their young.

I shake my head and laugh bitterly to myself. I shut the book and pull out the small flask of Jack I've packed along just in case. I'll sit here as long as Norm Crane wants to, but I'm done with birds for the day.

Claire and I once took a trip to Mexico, a couple of months after Simon died. The trip was her idea; it was to "get away." We flew into Ensenada and rented a car, and the first day we spent driving. We went down to La Bufadora, and pushed our way through other tourists and stalls of local food and clothes to a blowhole that sprayed water thirty meters into the air. We drove inland a ways until the dirt and grass gave way to boulders and it was too hot to continue. We listened to voices on the radio speak in a quick Spanish that neither of us understood. Now and then Claire pointed things out—"Look at that truck!" she'd say, or "Feel how hot the glass is," holding her palm against the window. Her voice was strained, falsely cheerful. She was trying; I was silent.

As we drove back into town I stared out the window at the barred, glassless windows of cinder-block buildings and laundry dangling out to dry. I stared at the people sitting at little plastic tables outside makeshift restaurants and bars, and at the stray, skinny dogs pawing the dust beside them, whining for handouts. The cars were many and reckless. Exhaust blurred the air. Limbless beggars in wheelchairs knocked at our windows at each stoplight. I remember I was looking specifically at a woman sweeping the dirt sidewalk outside her shop when Claire cried out. The woman had on a bright red apron, and I remember noting how bright it looked against the green of her storefront and wondering why she'd bother to sweep dirt from dirt.

"Fuck!" Claire cried, and I braced myself as she swerved the car over to the side of the road. "Fuck, fuck, fuck!" She put her head down on the steering wheel. I looked at her from the depths of my stupor. "Is it dead?" she was saying. "Is it dead? Is it dead?"

"Is what dead?" I said.

"Is it dead, Hollis? Is it fucking dead? Did I fucking kill it?"

I turned in my seat and looked out the back window. Some yards behind us, I saw a black pile of dog lying half off the road, motionless. I hadn't even noticed Claire hitting it. I hadn't registered the slightest bump.

"I don't know," I said.

"Well go fucking check!" she said.

I unbuckled my seatbelt and walked back along the hot, cracked road to where the dog lay. The woman I'd been watching had paused in her sweeping to watch, and two little boys with bare feet were venturing shyly closer to the dog. It was one of the many strays that were everywhere you looked; skinny, bald in patches, covered with oozing pink sores. It was dead. It had probably been already half dead when Claire hit it, I thought; she'd probably done it a favor. But I wasn't sure she'd think so.

"You didn't kill it," I said after I'd gotten back into the car.

She lifted her head from the wheel. "I didn't?" she said hopefully. "Oh God, well then help me!" She unbuckled her seat belt and started opening her door.

"What are you doing?" I asked.

"What do you mean, what am I doing? We can't just leave it there!"

"Claire," I said.

"We'll take it to a vet, or something. I don't know," she said.

"Claire," I said. I couldn't tell her that I'd lied, so I followed her back to the dog. She bent down beside it and held her fingers by its nose to feel for a breath. She felt around for a pulse, and found none. Squatting there, she put her head into her hands. I looked up as a rusty carful of teens passed, honking and yelling out the window. The two little boys had stopped about five feet from the dog and stood whispering. The sweeping woman had disappeared.

"Fuck," Claire was saying. "Fuck me."

She took several deep breaths, squatting there, very still. Finally, she stood and thrust the keys toward me.

"What?" I said.

"At least fucking drive, Hollis. At least do that for me. I don't want to fucking hurt anything else."

Later, the only customers, we sat at our hotel bar. We didn't talk; we drank. After a while, an older man came in and sat down at the bar. He called the bartender by name and asked for a margarita and a shot.

"Do I know you?" the bartender asked.

"My wife and I used to come in here every year," he said.

"Ah," the bartender said. "I thought you looked familiar," he said, even though I could tell he didn't remember the man.

"She died this year," the man added after a while.

"I'm sorry to hear that," the bartender said.

"We loved coming here," the man said. He raised his glass in our direction and threw back his shot. I glanced at Claire. She stared into her drink.

"Get them a round, too, on me," the man said, gesturing toward us.

"Thank you," Claire said, looking up.

"You're lovely, the two of you." He raised his glass at us again, and we raised ours and drank.

Soon, a quartet came in with an accordion, a couple guitars, and an upright bass. They lingered at the far end of the bar, chatting with the bartender, and then the man called to them in Spanish. They discussed something, and then the four of them in their suits and hats assembled themselves before me and Claire.

"A serenade," the man said, sending two more shots our way. "On me, to you."

I glanced at Claire. She had a tight smile on her face, and looked at me nervously. The group began to play. "A love song," the old man said over the music. We sat stiffly, giving the quartet the best of our attention. "What," the man said. "Your first serenade?" I nodded. "Ah, amigos, no!" He came over and pulled our hands together, turned our faces with firm, wide fingers so we were face-to-face and looking each other in the eyes. "Yes," he said, "yes, this is how you serenade. Like this. With love. I chose the most beautiful love song for you."

And so we sat there, the two of us, drunk and hot and lost, staring into each other's eyes, holding hands, or gripping them, as if afraid. What were we thinking? I can only imagine: about the dog, about the day, about our son, about ourselves, about this pose we had to maintain, even if only for a song.

17

PARENTHESIS

I wake up just before eight o'clock into something like a dream, into a pocket of time that doesn't seem to belong to the day that has just passed or the day that is to come. The light is low and long, the sun just on the horizon. I lie in bed and try to locate myself, to remember just how I got from the platform in the marsh at noon to my bed at eight o'clock at night. I sit up and consider whether to venture into this parenthesis of time and go to Pratty's or San Miguel or maybe get some writing done, or whether to simply lie back down and fade again into sleep and wait to do anything until tomorrow comes. And then I remember Simon's birthday. I've nearly slept away whatever obligation I have to celebrate, or mourn, or commemorate, or whatever I am supposed to do. I stand up, sure that on this day something is expected of me, but unsure of what that is. Last year, Claire said we had to live the day as we'd live any other, and we did—we went to the grocery store, we painted the lawn furniture, we saw a movie and went out to dinner—but it was different than any other day because we both knew what the day was, and we acknowledged it in looks, with gentle touches of the hand. With Claire, the day had achieved its own sanctity without ceremony, but without Claire, this day could be any other.

What do people do on days like today? My eyes wander toward the bookshelf and the books on grief that Claire has tried without success to get me to read. There may be suggestions in these, I think, but still, I don't want to grieve according to a formula in a book. I look at the phone on the bedside table. This very morning I was sitting in the same exact spot talking on that phone to my wife. If she can call me on this day, can't I call her? Isn't that fair?

I blink at the phone, but I do not reach for it; something, something holds me back. Outside, a car honks and church bells chime the hour: one, two, three, I count—but of course! I stand up suddenly as it occurs to me what I need to do. I need to go to church. My father went to church. He started going after my mother left us, but the only time he ever made me go with him was on Christmas Eve for midnight mass, and it wasn't something that I minded. I remember bitter, snowy nights, and the enveloping warmth of the church. I remember being able to hear the wind howling outside, and imagining the snow collecting thick on the roof and against the windows. The lights would dim as the service began, and cloaked white figures would pass out lighted candles for every parishioner to hold, and then the lights would go out completely. The room flickered in candlelight; deep shadows loomed on the vaulted ceiling. There were no homilies or sermons during midnight mass on Christmas Eve; there was only singing, and I remember watching my father as he sang, his face flashing. He seemed enraptured, absorbed, gone somewhere I wasn't, and I remember being awed and afraid and envious of whatever he was feeling, and wondering whether when I became an adult I would feel the same way.

Still in my dirty bird-watching attire, I pocket away a flask of Jack and hurry to the church nearest my house, the Portuguese fishermen's church at the edge of the park. The main doors are locked shut, but when I try the smaller side door, it opens easily, and I slip inside. The lights are low, but even so I can make out the rose color of the walls and the pale-blue beams that stretch across the ceiling. Columns protrude from the walls, their burdens not the ceiling or the beams, but handmade model boats—fishing boats, schooners, dinghies, each intricately carved and painted. I circle the room, examining each boat individually, astounded by the detail of each, some with pointed bowsprits and spinnakers, some with netting draped across the deck, some with men climbed halfway up the mast on a ladder of netted rope. A ship stands watch over every pew.

I roam toward the altar. Off to the side is a doorway hung with velvet drapes, and a sign above reading WELCOME ALL YE LOST. I stare at the doorway, wondering if that "welcome" applies also to me, an intruder, a stranger. I push the curtains sideways and step inside. "Jesus," I say, not because I find myself face-to-face with a plaster statue of the man, but because of how he looks. He is lit from below and life-size and in color. He is down on one knee, his arms outstretched, his hands bloodied and reaching, his gown stained with dirt and blood. The expression on his face is terrified and terrifying. His mouth is half open, as if he's moaning, his forehead creased, his head thrown back. Blood trickles from the corner of his eye. "Jesus," I say again, shuddering. I want to reach for my Jack, but I am afraid. There is dirt underneath Jesus' toenails, which stick out from beneath his gown. I step backward through the curtain, afraid to turn my back on that hideous statue, as if the thing might lunge at me, grab on to me, keep me with it in that room.

I sit down in the front pew breathing hard, unwilling to let myself be scared out of the church before I've done what I came to do, because sure, I've come to church, but I haven't *done* anything yet. But I'm not sure what to do. I sit there wishing I could pray, wishing I believed in that kind of God. I would pray for Simon. I would pray for my wife to come back to me. I would pray for my father to be happy wherever he is. I would pray for Marissa to be okay. I would pray for Ellen Marie Franklin. I would pray that my mother wonder about me and think about me and maybe come and find me. I would pray that the Grover stories work out. I would pray for the dog. I would pray for forgiveness for whatever I need forgiving for. The more I think about all the things I would pray for, the more I wish I could pray. But you can't just *pray*. You can't ask for things like the things I want to ask for unless you've earned them. I could convert, I think, start coming to church, and then maybe I'd earn a few prayers. But just because you go to church doesn't mean you believe, and what I need is to believe in whomever I'd be praying to.

I approach the altar, take a small candle from a container of them, drop a coin in the coin box beside it, and set it in a holder filled with the stumps of other burned-out candles. I take a match from the matchbook tied to the candleholder, strike it, and hold it above the candle I've set out. It's the only thing I can think to do. "Well," I say, holding the flame to the wick. My voice is loud, and I glance around me nervously. I feel like an impostor. I am an impostor. "Happy birthday," I whisper.

I take a few steps backward, looking at the jumping flame. I pause, unsure of what to do next. I don't want to leave the candle burning unattended, especially with all the ships that would burn if the place went down, but I can't bring myself to blow it out. So I sit back down in the front pew, and I watch it burn.

18

FLIGHT

Maybe it's only because I've had birds on my mind so much lately that I'm noticing all the birds flitting around the yard and calling from the trees, but I'd swear that they're newcomers. I can't imagine having stood out here at the hedge as many mornings as I have this summer and not noticed these little guys hopping around on the sidewalk beyond the hedge in front of me, drinking the water puddled in the curb, pecking at whatever seeds they find in the pavement cracks. I can't imagine having stood here and not listened to their conversations, or wondered what each combination of notes might mean. But maybe I did. Maybe these birds have been hopping around me and singing all goddamn summer, and just because I wasn't thinking about it, just because I didn't know to notice, I didn't. Maybe my own lack of interest and attention made these birds invisible to me. The idea makes me wonder what else I'm missing, what else I'm not noticing because I don't know to notice.

There's one particular bird who's been singing "yoo hoo" so insistently since I've been out here that it's almost all I can hear. I'm beginning to wonder what he wants, this bird, whether he's calling for his mate, or his child, or for help, or if he's just singing away for shits and giggles. "Yoo hoo," he calls. "Yoo hoo, yoo hoo." I scan the branches of nearby trees for the fifth or sixth time today, trying to locate the bird, but the leaves are so thick that I can make out little behind them. "Yoo hoo," he calls.

"Yoo hoo," I whistle back, and I'm surprised by how much like a bird my whistle sounds. "Yoo hoo," I whistle again, and the bird's own whistling stops. I can imagine him frozen up in his tree, his head cocked, wondering who it is that's responding. I wonder if he thinks I'm really a bird, or if he knows better. After a few silent seconds, I whistle again, and then after a pause the bird whistles back.

"Yoo hoo," it calls.

"Yoo hoo," I whistle.

"Yoo hoo."

"Yoo hoo."

I wonder what we're saying to each other.

A door slams over at the Cranes' house. I glance over the side of the hedge that edges their lawn, the unadulterated side of the hedge. Norm and Harry Crane have emerged, Norm with a suitcase in each hand, Harry carrying Norm's briefcase. I crouch down so they can't see me and peer through the branches. Norm Crane opens the back of the car and they load his bags in. Harry dribbles a basketball around their driveway, takes a shot at the hoop mounted above the garage, and misses. Norm Crane gestures to Harry, who tosses the ball at his father. I can't hear them, but I can tell by the gestures that Norm is trying to give Harry pointers. He goes through the motions of making a shot a few times, then finally releases the ball in the direction of the hoop. He misses, too, and maybe it's mean, but I have to chuckle. The ball bounces over onto the lawn and rolls under the trampoline.

"Jude!" Norm Crane has his mouth cupped, bellowing louder than I'd think he needs to. Judith Crane emerges from the house, pushing the door open with her backside, babe in arms. She holds the door as Madeline and Cathy run through, racing each other to the car. Madeline gets there first and buckles herself into a window seat, which must mean that Cathy is stuck with the middle again, since I wouldn't think Harry would stand for anything but the other window seat, the one he sat in the other night, being the oldest and a boy. Cathy stomps her foot, and Norm Crane looks at his watch and ushers his family into the car. They must be delivering him to the airport, I think, and I wonder whether whatever woman he has wherever he's going this time will be there to pick him up. For a second I have the urge to get into my own car and follow them, to watch how they say good-bye. But. I stand up straight again, my clippers at my side, and I watch them as they drive away.

I thought that church was the dream it felt like when I first woke up this morning. I thought that I'd come home from bird-watching, fallen into bed, and slept on through till morning. But as morning wore on, the dream didn't fade, as most do; the details were too precise, too vivid for the memory of anything but something real.

I fell asleep as I sat there with my Jack watching Simon's candle burn, and I woke sometime later to a priest gently shaking my shoulder. I straightened up and tried to discreetly tuck away the flask resting on my thigh, embarrassed to have been discovered with it out and open.

"I'm going to have to ask you to leave, sir," the priest was saying.

"I must have fallen asleep," I said. "I was here to ah, to light a candle for my son," I tried to explain, nodding toward the altar. The candle had burned out. "It's his birthday. Was. Is. It would have been, but . . . I didn't want to leave the candle burning unattended."

"That's fine, sir. But I've finished in the office and I'm going to have to lock the doors for the night."

"Of course," I said, standing up and smoothing my hair. "Of course."

"Do you have somewhere to go?" he asked.

"Sorry?"

"There's a shelter downtown. I don't know if you're familiar with the area. I haven't seen you before."

I paused. I considered my dirty, sweat-stained T-shirt, my cut-off shorts, the flask of Jack. I pulled at my chin and felt the days-old stubble there. I gave a little smile. "Thanks," I said. I didn't want to let him know that I had a home to return to, and a bed to sleep in. There'd be no excuse, then, for my attire, for the flask in my pocket. I wanted badly to get out of there, but the priest stood blocking my pew, gazing at me. I gave him another little smile.

The priest held my gaze for seconds more. "Bless you," he said.

"Bless you, too," I said, though as soon as I said it I wondered whether it was the right response.

The priest laughed. "God be with you," he said, laying his hand atop my head. I cringed inwardly under his touch, sure that were there a God he would curse me doubly for this night. Here I was, an unbeliever faking the motions in order to feel in some way absolved, then letting a priest bless me as somebody else, somebody who deserved a blessing. Finally, he stepped aside, and I slid out from under his hand and into the night.

I've decided to give the hedge a rest, for today. The Cranes' departure broke my hedge concentration, and so I've come inside to do a little writerly work, if it's willing to happen. And maybe it would be, if it weren't for the enticing view of the Cranes' backyard out my window. The swings are swaying gently over there, as if there were a stonger wind than there is. The go-carts are parked in the corner of the yard, by the sandbox. The basketball lies settled against a leg of the trampoline. That trampoline. I've been eyeing it all summer. I look down at my notebook, open to a page of notes I took on the Crane kids in their yard, and a paragraph I wrote on the nature of trampoline jumping. *There is something terrifying about bouncing on a trampoline, I wrote. You start slow, your legs like rubber bands as you walk from the padded edge to the center, where you begin to jump, gently at first, then higher and higher as you realize you can. All of a sudden you can see a little farther down the street than you ever have before. You can see into the higher branches of the nearby trees, where startled squirrels and birds freeze as an unwinged boy flies by. You can see into the upstairs windows of the neighbors' homes, into their backyards, over the roofs of the houses down the hill. The upturned faces of those on the ground shrink as you rise away like a balloon, higher with each jump, unleashed, free. You jump, and you jump, until suddenly you lose control, your arms flailing as you lose your balance in midair and come crashing down onto your back or onto your head or, worse, through the rusty springs that until now have given you flight.*

It seems inevitable, this crash. It is only the crash that ends one jumper's turn and clears the trampoline for the next jumper up. If there were no crash, why else would a jumper ever stop? Since there is a crash, why would a jumper ever jump?

I survey the yard once more and calculate. An hour and a half to the airport, an hour and a half back, and say a half hour seeing Norm Crane off. They've been gone for about an hour, now, so I've still got plenty of time, if I want it. And I do.

Later, I'm set up on the couch with a couple books, a couple years-old *National Geographic*s, my notebook, and some Jack. The dog lies on the chair across the coffee table, staring at me; it makes me a little nervous. I can't get into any of the books, and for a while I've been looking at photographs of Africa and gemstones, but the light is beginning to dim, and I am afraid to reach up to turn on the lamp. I pick up my notebook.

Dear Claire, I write. *I threw my back out this afternoon jumping on the neighbors' trampoline (research) and now I'm stuck on the couch and can hardly move. I found some of your old painkillers upstairs and am taking those, which makes things a little better, but I don't much like this helplessness. But what's worse is the realization that my body has changed. My bones aren't ripe for things like trampolines anymore. Our bodies are always changing, I know, but when did I cross the line from being an able trampoline jumper into someone too brittle for that kind of activity? What other lines might I have crossed? What else can't I do that I still think I can? I want to test myself. As soon as my back heals, I'm going to test myself. I'm going to take an inventory of what I can and cannot do. I'm going to go for a run, just to see if I can. I'm going to see whether I can turn a cartwheel. I'm going to go waterskiing. I'm going to climb a tree. Whatever I can still do, I'm going to start doing every day. I'm not going to let anything else slip away from me.*

What else. Last night a priest thought I was a homeless man. I was in the church by the park—for some reason, I thought I should go there since it was Simon's birthday. I don't know what I was thinking. I don't take it as an insult, don't get me wrong. I don't have anything against homeless people. But it was strange to be thought of as someone other than who I am. It would have been the same if he thought I was a movie star, or a millionaire. What made me feel strange was that he didn't know I was me. But then again, I could be homeless, and if I were homeless, wouldn't I still be me?

The phone begins to ring. The phone is one thing I forgot to bring with me over to the couch. I lift myself and cross the room as quickly and carefully as I can, eager to answer the phone before the machine gets it; I plugged the machine back in yesterday morning in case Claire called again while I was out bird-watching. I'm afraid the machine might scare whoever's calling away, and right now I'm not sure there's anyone I'd mind talking to. The phone rings once, twice, three times, and I've got only one ring left before the machine turns on.

"Hello?" I say, lunging for the phone just as it's ringing for the fourth time, the dog up off his spot on the floor and at my heels. My back tightens in a spasm of exertion. *Fuck.* Hello?" But the machine has clicked on, the old reels slowly groaning into action. "Hello?" I say, jabbing at the machine, trying to turn it off. *You've reached 498-0920,* Claire's voice is saying, and I keep on jabbing at the thing, trying to turn her off. "Hello?" I'm saying, "Hello? Hello?" But Claire's voice keeps going, *We're not here to answer the phone right now, but if you leave your name, number, and a brief message, we'll call you back.* A long beep follows. "Hello?" I say. The machine screeches in the way a microphone does when it's too near its speakers, and so I take a step back. "Hello?" I say, but no one is there. My own voice echoes loudly in the answering machine. "Hellllloooooooooooo," I yodel, listening to myself magnified. The dog whines and runs to the corner of the room. I sigh and hang up.

I bring the phone and phonebook with me back to the couch and try to think of who to call. I could call Sal and Mona and thank them for the picnic, but they know me better than that. I could call Judith Crane and let her know about my back. Maybe she'd bring me some soup, or flowers. Maybe she'd rent me a movie, or make me some tea. I open the phonebook to the C section and run my finger down the list of Cranes. *Crane, Norman.* I tap the listing and get the phone ready for dialing. Then I hear a shout from next door; I arch my neck and peer out the window to see if I can make anything out over there. From the couch, I can see only from the top of the first-floor windows on up to the roof; I can't see the lawn itself, or anyone who might be in it. But someone's there; I hear another shout, and then Harry flies into view, then out of view again, launched high by the same trampoline that's ended me up couchbound. He's shouting something to somebody, but I can't see who.

"Not yet!" I can make out. "In a minute!"

"NO!" I hear Judith Crane bellow. "If you want dinner, the time is NOW!" I wouldn't have thought Judith Crane capable of such sound. I look down at the phone in my hands, my fingers poised over the first digits of the Cranes' number. I look back out the window. Harry is no longer bouncing. A door slams.

I hold the phone out in front of me, reevaluating who to call. I ponder the digits and their corresponding letters. I turn the phone on and dial the digits of my name. H-O-L-L-I-S-C, or 465-5472. I bring the phone to my ear and wait. It rings once, twice, and then those three awful rising notes sound shrill in my ear and that automated voice gives me instructions about dialing beyond my local calling area. Which is interesting. I'd expected a recording that told me that the number I'd dialed isn't in service, but the recording I received instead implies that the number to my name does exist somewhere, just in an area code other than mine. I wonder exactly where my name is someone's number. I wonder if my name is a number to someone's farmhouse set low among sprawling cornfields somewhere in the middle of the country, or whether it's the number to a nightclub in New York, or whether it's the number to a house like my own just a few counties over. I figure there must be a way to find out, and so I dial 0.

"Operator, how may I help you?" a voice answers immediately.

"Hi," I say. "I was wondering if you could help me with something."

"Yes, sir, and how may I help you?"

"Well, I've got this number here that I wrote down the other day, my, ah, sister's number, because she just moved, but I forgot to write down the area code, and I was wondering if you could tell me what area code it belongs to if I read you the seven digits I have."

"Okay, sir, I think I can help you this evening if you just tell me where the number is located."

"Where it's located?"

"Yes, sir."

"Located?"

"Yes, sir, in which state is the number located?"

"Oh," I say. I consider telling her that I'm not sure, that I've got so many sisters I just can't keep straight who lives where, but I doubt if she'd believe that. I take a breath. "If I just read you the number, you can't tell me the area code?"

"Well, sir, I'd come up with a variety of area codes if I based it simply off the number. Numbers are repeated from one area code to the next. And so if you just tell me what state your sister lives in, I can tell you what area code to dial."

"Oh," I say. "California."

"Uh-huh, and the number?"

I tell her the number. There's silence for a few seconds. I can hear the operator punching at a computer.

"I'm sorry, sir," she says. "The number you've provided isn't a number anywhere in California."

"I see," I say. "I must have written it down wrong, I guess."

"Is there anything else I can assist you with this evening, sir?"

"No," I say. "Thanks."

I hang up. I dial C-L-A-I R E-C, and I get another recording, this one telling me that the number I've dialed has been disconnected. I dial Marissa's number. That's been disconnected, too. I dial the numbers of all the places I've lived. My phone number in Westchester is some computer company, closed for the evening. My phone number from college reaches a fax machine. My phone number from the apartment I had before we moved in here is not in service.

I dial Claire's old number in Maine. It rings twice, and then to my surprise a woman's voice answers.

"Hello?" she says.

"Hi," I say, unsure of what to say otherwise.

"Hi," she says.

"How are you?" It seems the next logical thing to say.

"Okay," she says. "Billy's driving me kind of up the wall, and I have a million things to finish before that conference, but otherwise, I'm okay. But how are you?"

"Me?" I say. "Oh, I'm fine."

She hesitates. "You are?" she says. She sounds incredulous.

"Well," I say. "I mean, I threw my back out today, which hurts, but yeah, otherwise I'm fine."

"Who is this?" she demands.

"What?" I say. My heart starts going faster.

"Who is this?"

"Hollis," I say. "This is Hollis."

19

YARD 'N' GARDEN

Our cordless phone hasn't held a charge for more than an hour since the time this winter that I left it outside overnight after I'd left the dinner table drunk to make a phone call to Marissa. It had snowed on and off for the past three days, and the snow lay a foot deep. It was the hard, glistening, crystally kind of snow that seals itself in beneath an icy skin, the kind of snow that grabs the heels of boots and sends the walker forward barefoot and hopping, as it did to me as I stumbled out the sliding door with the phone in one hand and a bottle of Jack in the other.

"Fuck," I remember muttering, balancing on my one booted foot and fishing around behind me with my bare toe for the boot that I'd stepped out of. I found it, finally, though not before having to set my bare foot down in the snow to catch my balance. I stomped my way over to the lawn chairs, which I'd failed to bring indoors before the storm, though Claire had asked me to, and sat down on one of them and its icy, foot high, uncushiony cushion of snow. My ass was wet and cold, and when I tried to lean back, I almost toppled entirely over since there was hardly any chairback to support me above the booster seat of snow. My feet dangled. The light from our bedroom window went on, casting a yellowish glow on things, and I remember wondering if Claire was standing up there in the window, watching me. I wanted badly to turn around and see, but if she was up there, looking out, I didn't want her to see me checking. I would not turn around. I took a deep breath, stood up, and replunked myself down, hard this time, so that I flattened the snow and shaped it as much as I could to my rear. I was settling in.

I unscrewed the cap of the Jack and took a long, warm swig. I remember feeling dramatic, out there, the angry husband out in the snow and cold, and it made my blood rush to think of it that way. I hoped Claire was watching. I hoped she saw me out here, driven to drink, on the phone with someone more comforting than herself. I held the phone out before me, so that if Claire was watching me she'd surely see it. I had to blink several times to shrink the number of phones I saw from four to one, and then I dialed Marissa's number.

"Hello?"

"Hi," I said.

"Hollis," Marissa said.

"S'me," I said.

"I know that." She waited. "Well?"

"Well? Well, what. What do you mean, well?"

"Hollis," she said.

"What, Hollis what?" I said. I felt my anger shift with frightening ease from Claire to Marissa. "What, I can't call you?"

"Hollis," she said. "You shouldn't be calling. You're drunk. And I have people over."

"People? What people? And I'm not drunk," I said. "I can't call you? Who else am I supposed to turn to?" I said.

"Good night, Hollis," she said, and she hung up. I stared at the phone incredulously, and then slammed it into the snow beside me. All of a sudden I felt the deep ache of cold in my bones. All of a sudden I felt empty.

I stared out at the blanketed marsh before me, bluish in the moonlight, and at the black hulk of trees stretching out along the marsh's edge. The marsh ice groaned deep and hollow as it cracked against the pressure of a rising tide, and I shuddered. The light from our bedroom switched off, then, and it was dark.

This was not the way it was supposed to be. I, the angry husband, was supposed to come out here and brave the cold, to prefer it to the warmth of the home behind me. I was supposed to take comfort in my Jack and in my understanding lover, who was supposed to soothe me, to invite me to come over. But my mind was thick with drink, and I was cold, and in spite of myself all I wanted was to go inside, to lie down in a soft tangle of blankets with my wife and sleep. I tried to resummon my anger, but I couldn't even remember why it was I'd come storming out here, or what we'd really argued about at dinner—something, I think, about the pages I wasn't writing, the things I wasn't doing. I'd been drinking for too long, that day, and by dinnertime I'd gotten to the point where I wasn't sure what I was saying, in the way that you don't quite know what you're saying as you awaken from a dream; you speak nonsense, gibberish, but with confidence. Nothing at that moment made sense. I folded myself forward, pressed my forehead against my knees and shut my eyes, and I'm not sure how long later—probably not long at all—I awoke to Claire's voice behind me.

"Hollis," she was saying. "Enough. Come inside."

I sat up and turned around. Claire stood in her nightgown in the sliding door, her body silhouetted by the light from the kitchen. It was too dark to see her face, but her head was tilted to the side in an angle of what seemed to be pity. I tried again to regather my anger, to dwell again on whatever had sent me into my rage, but whatever anger I'd felt earlier was gone, and it had left behind it a terrible void. I was tired. I felt weak and foolish and embarrassed. I recollapsed myself into my knees.

"Hollis," she said.

"I'm sorry," I said. "I don't even know what I said. I don't know what I was saying. I don't even remember why I was angry. I'm out here, trying to be angry, and I don't know why."

"Hollis," she said again. "Come inside. I don't have boots on."

I stood up and turned around to face her. The distance between the doorway and where I stood seemed nearly insurmountable, with the snow and the ice and everything else between us.

"Come on," she said, holding out her arms. I looked at her wearily and slowly started to walk toward her. "Come on," she said. "Come on. It's time for bed."

Needless to say, I didn't remember the phone out on the lawn table in the snow until the following day, when I awoke shamed and groggy alone in bed; Claire had gone off to school. Since then, you've got to keep the phone charging on its cradle almost all of the time; you can't take it with you to the bathroom, or the kitchen, or the couch, like I did last night, for any long period of time because it loses its charge, especially if in intermittent use, like it was last night. It died soon after my conversation with Claire's old number, leaving me alone in the dark. I swallowed Jack and painkillers, haunted by awful images of myself: the self that ran down the bluff that rainy day to save the swimmer, the self that sat at the bar at Pratty's with the model race car, the dirty, drunken self asleep in church, and then the newest—me, a grown man in shorts and a dirty polo shirt, unshaven and giddy, flying through the air, staring at the clouds, bouncing higher and higher and thinking that *this is the life,* trying a one-eighty, then a three-sixty, and then—and this is where it gets really bad—trying to pull off a backflip and landing very, very wrong.

I woke up to the sound of birds. I was starving, and what I wanted was pancakes. Chocolate chip. I went into the kitchen to call the store and have my groceries delivered; I didn't want to put any more stress on my back than I had to by carrying groceries around. I watched the birds flit around in my yard as I ordered. "Do you sell magazines?" I asked.

"Full rack."

I ordered *Bird Explorer* and *Yard 'n' Garden* with the rest of my ingredients.

When the groceries finally arrived, more than an hour after I'd placed my call, I followed the directions on the back of the box of pancake mix, and what I didn't realize until too late was that the recipe made enough to serve eight. By the time I'd cooked all the batter, I had three plates of pancakes each stacked inches high. One plateful consisted of pancakes that spelled out PANCAKES, if you looked carefully. I'd eaten so many chocolate chips in the making that I was too full for more than a single pancake, eaten standing at the kitchen counter. I set a full plate down on the floor in front of the dog; he sniffed it and turned away. I always thought that a dog would eat anything you put in front of him, but this dog is picky.

I stood in the kitchen and surveyed my mess: the batter bowl with batter dripping down its sides and onto the counter; the spoon I'd used to ladle batter onto the griddle lying in its own little batter puddle; the griddle spotted with burned chocolate chips and splattered mix; eggshells, open milk carton, and vegetable oil all out on the table; an empty bag of chocolate chips; three heaping plates of pancakes (one on the floor), an unopened jug of maple syrup standing by. According to my intended plan, the dog and I should have been outside enjoying our pancakes and the morning—at that point early afternoon—and then technically I should have been refreshed and energized and ready to get to work at my desk. But things hadn't gone quite as planned; the groceries came late, I had loads of extra pancakes, I was inside and potentially restless, and—here the bird magazines caught my eye—I had research to do. I'd half told myself that I'd stay in today and recuperate, but there's only one place where I really like to do research, and my back wasn't feeling so bad anymore, and I could hardly remember the last time I'd been to Pratty's anyway, so I wrapped up the pancakes, I packed my bird magazines, Claire's bird book, the painkillers, and my notebook, I let the picky dog out, and I got into the car.

I see the leaves on the trees around my house every day, so I don't notice it as they change day by day; it's been maybe a week since I've seen the trees on the street where Pratty's is, though, and I'm surprised at how much of their summer swell they've lost since I was last here; the leaves are beginning to yellow at the edges and to wilt, a sure sign of an early fall. I pull the car over across the street from Pratty's and stare at the four skinny trees out front. Normally, I'd curse those trees, skinny sicklings succumbing over-early to the dismal barrenness of fall. But not today. Not this year. This year, these trees are more like early Christmas decorations when you're a kid; the sight of them makes my heart race in nervous anticipation. As I stare up at the trees, I notice a curtain draw back in the window upstairs and Larry's wizened face peer out. A wave of guilt washes over me. I'd forgotten about Larry, forgotten about his collapse the other night. I raise my hand in greeting, and the curtain drops.

It takes my eyes a minute to adjust to the dark of Pratty's. It's just past one o'clock, and no customers are inside, but I can hear Crosby rummaging around in the kitchen. I take a seat at the bar, and despite the painkillers it's immediately clear to me that my back will not put up with a slouching posture, and so I move myself and all my things to one of the booths that line the back wall of the bar. The only time I've sat in one of these booths is to play cribbage with Claire, and I can't say I like sitting back here alone.

Crosby emerges from the kitchen with two cases of beer, and he walks right by my booth without acknowledging me, likely as punishment for my absence. He sets the cases down on the bar and begins to unload the bottles into the cooler. When he's finished with that, he squats down behind the bar in front of what I know is a refrigerator. Cartons and cans of juice appear one by one on the bar as Crosby reaches up, and then finally the man himself stands. I'm hoping at this point he'll finally acknowledge me, but instead he begins to transfer the various juices into the plastic easy-pour containers he keeps on ice behind the bar. I tap my fingers on the table in front of me and open *Bird Explorer*. As I've said before, two can play Crosby's game.

But not for that long. Until Crosby acknowledges me, and until I've gotten a drink of some kind—maybe only coffee until later—I can't settle in and really focus on the bird research I want to do, and so, after Crosby's made two more trips to the kitchen for beer, about ten minutes later, I clear my throat. "Pancake?" I ask loudly. Crosby drops the bottle of beer he's putting in the cooler.

"Goddamn it!" he says, looking up and squinting into the shadows of the booth. "What in God's name are you trying to do? Goddamn it!" He looks down at his hand. "I cut myself!" he says. "You happy now?"

Forgetting momentarily about my back, I jump up, at which I, too, cringe in pain—or would like to, but I don't want Crosby knowing about my back. *How?* he'd ask, and I'd never hear the end of it. Ever. Even if I told him I'd hurt it doing something normal, like trimming the hedge. I clench my teeth and go over to the bar, a cling-wrapped stack of pancakes in my hand. "Sorry," I say. "I thought you knew I was back there."

"Why the hell would I think you were back there? You sit at the bar, not in the booths, and I can't see a goddamn thing in this light anyway!" I stand across the bar from him. We both look down at his hand. There's a small sliver of a cut on his palm. "It's small, but it's deep, believe me," he says. He turns on the sink and hold his hand under the stream. "And where the hell have you been?" he asks.

I shrug. "Things have been hectic," I say. I shove the pancakes across the bar at him. "Pancakes?" I ask.

"No," Crosby says. "No, I do not want your pancakes."

"Okay," I say. But I leave the pancakes on the bar anyway. Crosby dries his hand off, inspecting it closely.

"Why the booth anyway?" Crosby asks.

"Research," I say. "I don't want to take up too much space."

"Never stopped you before." Crosby pulls a mop from the behind the bar to clean up the spilled beer.

I watch him clean.

"Saw Larry upstairs, looking out his window," I say, after a minute. "He okay?"

Crosby shrugs. He puts the mop aside and lifts a case of Larry's beer up from the floor. He places it on the bar and slides it toward me. "Bring this up to him and see for yourself. Hasn't been down, much."

I stare at the case of beer. Even though I haven't moved, my back goes into a little spasm, as if in warning. I swallow. "Sure," I say.

Crosby gestures toward the kitchen door with his chin. "Can go up the back way," he says, coming out from behind the bar and heading in that direction himself. "I've got more beer to get behind the bar," he calls, shouldering the door open and passing through. I watch the door swing behind him, back and forth in smaller and smaller swings until it's still. I look again at the case of beer on the bar. I bend my knees slightly, and I slide my fingers underneath the case, wedging it up off the bar. Then I get my forearms all the way underneath the case, until my fingers are curled around the far edge and the corner of the case is resting in the crooks of my elbows, like a forklift. Lift with the legs, not with the back, I tell myself, straightening my knees. I keep my arms in a stiff right angle, and the case lifts with me easily enough. I make my way stiffly to the kitchen door, and just as I'm about to push it open, Crosby emerges from the other side. He's carrying two cases himself, one under each arm. He pauses to assess my awkward posture.

"Little heavy for you?" he asks.

I hesitate and consider what's worse—having an old-man bad

back or being a weakling. I consider admitting to my back after all, but then Crosby would want to know why I hadn't just told him the truth in the first place, and instead of making fun of me for having a bad back, he'd make fun of me for trying to pretend I didn't. "No," I say. "Why, you need me to bring something else up while I'm at it?" I ask.

"No," Crosby says, and resumes his journey over to the bar.

I push through the kitchen door and head up the dark, narrow staircase that leads to Larry's apartment. I've been up here before to deliver dinner, and I always find it depressing. It's a small apartment, a single room with a bed at the far end, by the window, and a sofa, chair, TV, and coffee table at the other end, near the door. There's a cramped kitchenette with a window counter that looks out over the sofa. The walls are bare except for a huge, tattered American flag hung on the wall behind the TV. The bedspread is military-issue green, and the sofa is covered in a similar material.

I can smell the stale cigarette smell from the landing outside the door. It's hot and airless. I give the door a knock in the form of a kick.

"S'open," I hear Larry call.

"Larry," I say through the door. "My hands are full and I can't get the door."

I hear an exaggerated sigh, followed by a bang and a series of clumps and shuffles as Larry makes his way over to the door. He flings the door open and squints out onto the dark landing.

"You!" he says, his wrinkled face breaking into what I consider a smile, his puckered mouth unfolding. "Kid!" And then his smile fades and he gives me a stern look. "Oh, so you're back, are you. How nice to grace us with your presence." He turns around and shuffles back to his couch, leaving me standing in the open doorway. He slumps back and turns on the TV. He flips through his four channels and then turns the thing off again, slamming the clicker down beside him. "Well?" he says, turning toward me. "You just going to stand there all day? Or you coming in?"

"Crosby wanted me to bring you your beer," I say, taking a step into the room. "Where should I put this?"

"Refrigerator."

I nod, and walk into the kitchenette. Very carefully, I squat down in front of the refrigerator, keeping my upper body as still and level as I can. I'm not sure how to get the case off my arms and onto the floor without bending, which I am afraid to do. I try to tip the case forward onto its side so that it's half in my hands, half against the wall. This way, I figure I can lower it down gradually by unbending my arms, using the wall as support. I'm wrong. I tip it forward, and it hits the wall as planned, but my fingers lose their grip and the thing crashes the last six inches to the floor.

"What in God's name is wrong with you?" I hear Larry roar. I look over my shoulder and see him peering over the counter at me.

"Sorry," I say. "I threw my back out yesterday." I open the case and start unloading the beers into the refrigerator, which is otherwise empty except for a couple other beers, a carton of OJ, and a jar of pickles. "At least they're cans," I say, standing, carefully, from the knees.

Larry shakes his head. "Bring us some cold ones," he says, turning around and settling himself back down on the couch and out of sight. I reach into the refrigerator for a couple of the cold beers and take them into the main room.

"So," I say. "How you doing?"

Larry cracks open his beer and gives me a look of disgust.

"Well, what?" I ask. "I haven't seen you in what, two weeks? I'm not allowed to ask?"

Larry's look fades from one of disgust to one of suspicion. "Crosby didn't say anything?" he asks.

"About . . . ," I say.

"Nothing," Larry says, taking a big sip of beer. He licks the residue of foam off his upper lip and grins. "He didn't?" he says.

I shrug and shake my head. "No," I say.

"Heh," Larry says, looking pleased. "I should be the one asking how *you're* doing, kid!" he says loudly, reaching over to thump me on the back. I cringe, waiting for the blow. "Just kidding," Larry says. He cackles. "So what happened?"

I take a sip of my beer. It tastes like piss. I wave my hand in front of my face and swallow the stuff down. "Long story," I say.

"One of those," Larry says. "But," he says, "do you mean long story, or nonstory?"

I sigh. "I can't tell the difference," I say. "We've had this discussion before, remember?"

"The difference is that in a story something happens, and in a nonstory something doesn't. You always tell nonstories. Like that guy who never fell off the chairlift."

"Well," I say. "Then it must be a story."

"You sure?"

"Well, something happened," I say. "I mean, look at my back."

"Okay," Larry says, looking at me expectantly.

"Okay what?" I say.

"Okay, so what's the story? How'd you do it?"

I pause. "Trimming the hedge."

"Nope," Larry says.

"What?"

"Bullshit," Larry says. "If you hurt it trimming the hedge you would have just said 'trimming the hedge' in the first place. You wouldn't have said 'long story.' "

I stare at Larry. He's propped his feet up on the coffee table and looks to be enjoying himself immensely. I feel a bubbling urge to let him know I know all about his heart attack. I take a sip of beer. "Fine," I say. "I was jumping on a trampoline. And I don't want to get into it."

Larry downs the rest of his beer, and then he looks at me, his mouth stretched into the toothless line of a grin. "Whenever you feel like telling that one, I'm all ears," he says. "Long story or non."

I force the rest of my own beer down and stand. "Yeah," I say. "When I feel like it." I cross the room to the door. "There's pancakes downstairs, if you want some," I say as I grab the door handle.

"Hey," Larry calls behind me, "maybe when you tell me how

you fell off that trampoline"—and here he breaks into a chuckle—
"I'll tell you how I fell off my bar stool the other night."

I turn around. Larry's eyes are twinkling, and he gives me a
wink. I shake my head. "Deal," I say.

Yard 'n' Garden has reinspired me to do something with the yard,
even though until now it seems that everything I ever intend for it
goes wrong. I'd planned on turning the yard into something similar
to the Cranes' before Simon died. The swing set he'd picked out on
his birthday arrived mail-order a month later, and too late.

That fall we decided to plant a garden to give us something to
look forward to come spring. It was Claire's idea, really. It was
something she said she wanted to do in memory of Simon. She spent
hours at the nursery, picking out all kinds of bulbs and seed. She
bought a trellis to lean against the house and planted the seeds for
some flowering vine at its foot. She bought two hundred daffodil
bulbs that took us days to plant; Claire trailed after me, carefully
placing a bulb into each of the holes she directed me to dig. It would
have been something, that garden, but the winter was a warm and
wet one, and come spring, the moles were too much to contend
with. Each gray morning, the yard would be crisscrossed with raised
mole tunnels. Claire would sit at the breakfast table and look
mournfully out at the lawn, and just as I promised I would, after
Claire had gone off to school I'd take my coffee outside and stamp
the tunnels down, hoping the moles hadn't uprooted everything
we'd planted. I walked those tunnels like tightropes, placing one
foot directly in front of the other on the soggy, steaming ground, and
it would take an hour at least until the yard was fully flat. But
the next morning, without fail, the tunnels had reappeared on the
ground like raised veins.

"What are we going to do?" Claire said, a few weeks into
spring. It was the sixteenth straight day of rain, the twenty-second of
waking up to a ravaged lawn.

"I don't know," I said, peering out the rain-streaked kitchen window. "I don't know what we *can* do," I said. "I mean, of course I'll keep on stamping them down, but that doesn't seem to do much."

"There must be something," she said. Her voice was hollow, shaky, as if she might at any moment start to cry. I turned around to face her, and sure enough, her eyes were filling with tears. My heart dropped in panic, and I sat down in the chair beside hers.

"Don't cry," I said. "Don't," I begged. Seeing Claire cry unnerves me. "I'll take care of them," I said.

She shut her eyes and took a few large, steady breaths. Then she opened her eyes and looked at me with a little smile. "I'm sorry," she said. "I think I'm overtired," she said. "Crying over moles." She put her hand on my arm. "But do look into it, Hollis," she said.

"I will," I said. I was suddenly filled with excitement at the prospect of having a mission, a project, especially if it was one that I could do for Claire. I wanted to do something for her. I didn't want to see her cry. I'd take care of those moles, I told her. She'd have her garden. I promised.

I went to the library and did research on moles. I went to the garden and hardware store and interviewed the employees. I wandered from lawn to lawn and asked anyone I could find what remedy they used or had heard of to rid their garden of moles. And then one by one, I tried the various remedies out. I poured pickle juice down the mole holes, and castor oil. I collected hair from the barbershop and put that down the holes. I made razor-blade barricades to the entrance of each tunnel. I tried mothballs, rose brambles, and red pepper. I tried to fumigate the tunnels with sulfur. I stuck a hose into a tunnel and tried to flush the critters out. I tried little cherry bombs.

At dinner each evening, I'd tell Claire what I'd done to the tunnels that day, and we'd rise anxiously the next morning to gauge the results. But nothing seemed to work; each morning, the lawn looked increasingly like some rodent battlefield. Finally, Claire came home one afternoon with a trap. I'd been shown the likes of it at the garden and hardware store while I was doing my initial research, but I'd rejected it as an option because it was lethal. It was called the Victor Out O Sight Scissor Trap; you placed it in the tunnel with its jaws held open by a lever attached to a trigger; when the mole bumped the trigger as he made his way through the tunnel, the lever gave way and *pow,* the jaws snapped shut and killed the mole. The instructions boasted that this particular mole trap was better than others because of the power of the jaws; they killed the mole instantly, thus rendering the trap more humane than others on the market.

"Really?" I said. "You want me to use this?"

"I don't know why you didn't set a trap in the first place," Claire said. "The man at the store said it's really the only effective way of getting rid of moles."

"But the trap kills them, Claire," I said.

"But they're killing the garden, Hollis," she said. "Simon's garden." She looked out at the devastated yard and then looked plaintively at me. "Please do this for me, Hollis," she said.

I took the trap from her. "I will," I said. "Tomorrow."

And I did. I set the trap up the following morning, and then I went to my desk to try to write. But I was distracted by the idea of the trap sitting out there, waiting to snap shut on whatever unlucky mole happened the set the trigger off. I went outside every half hour or so to check on the trap, relieved each time to find it empty until that afternoon, when, sure enough, a small, furry little thing lay limp and broken in the trap's jaws. I gulped and pulled the mole out, trap and all. I wondered whether this was a mother mole, or a father mole, or maybe a younger mole, born only this year. I wondered if he was a popular mole, or some kind of traitor mole, or a sex-offender mole, or for I all I knew an accordion-playing mole. I wondered whether there'd been another mole with him to witness his death, and whether other moles had passed by him in fright. I'd never seen a mole in person; it was almost cute. I gently extricated him from the trap's jaws and found a shoebox to bury him in. Was this what I was supposed to do each day? Pull moles one by one from the trap until they were all either dead or scared away? I didn't think I could. Before I put the shoebox into the little grave I'd dug, I lifted the cover and peered in once again at the mole. "I'm sorry," I wanted to say, because I was.

Three weeks later, our yard still a mess and our flowers unbloomed, Claire found the trap in the back of the garage. She said nothing; she simply brought the thing inside and placed it on the table before me. I looked at her, and I wanted to explain, but something in her eyes kept me silent. "I'm sorry, Claire," I wanted to say, because I was, but before I could speak she shook her head and went silently upstairs.

"Hey!" I hear Crosby exclaim. I look up from *Yard 'n' Garden* in my shadowy back booth to see Crosby emerging from the kitchen, the pancakes I'd left on the bar now reheated and steaming on a plate in his hand. "How did you sneak in here?" he says, and only then do I notice that Larry has materialized at his usual seat in the bar.

"Hole behind the refrigerator," Larry says. He leans forward. "When I get wet, I get small enough to fit through a hole the size of my head."

Crosby sets the pancakes down and pulls out one of Larry's beers. "Thought I wouldn't have to stock them down here anymore," he says. "Thought I'd have to send them all up to you," he says, cracking it open and setting it down on the bar.

Larry looks at the beer, and then turns to eye the plate of pancakes beside it. "Actually came down for some of those, too," he says.

"Oh," Crosby says. He reaches beneath the bar for silverware for the two of them.

"Since Hollis offered." Larry stabs at a pancake with his fork and folds the entire thing into his mouth at once. "Where'd he go, anyway?" he says. Bits of pancake spill from his mouth onto the bar as he speaks.

Crosby, not to be outdone, shoves a pancake into his own mouth and gestures toward my booth. "Right there," he says.

Larry pauses, mid-chew, and straightens up to peer in my direction. I raise my hand. "What in the hell are you doing back there?" he shouts.

"Research," Crosby answers for me. "Although I don't know why he's not doing his research at the bar like he normally does. Too good for us these days, I guess."

"Oh ho ho," Larry cackles. "Or is it because of the back?" I take my *Yard 'n' Garden* and make my way as quickly as I can over to the bar, eager to shut Larry up before he gives me away.

"What do you mean, the back?" Crosby asks, turning with his hands on his hips to watch me cross the room.

"Oh, he didn't tell you?" Larry says. "Hollis had a little trampoline accident and threw his back out."

"A trampoline accident?" Crosby says, and he breaks into his maniacal little giggle.

I ease myself gingerly onto the bar stool beside Larry's, relieved at least to be able to cringe openly now at the discomfort. "Thanks, Larry," I say.

"What do you mean, thanks?" he says. "What'd I do? It was a secret?"

"Yeah, it was a secret, Hollis?" Crosby echoes, his eyes twinkling.

"No, no secret," I say. "Never mind." I shoot Larry a look. He shrugs innocently.

"Oopsies," he says. "So what research are you doing now? Still the dead girl?"

I pause. "First of all, she's not necessarily dead," I say. "And second of all, no, this is new research."

"*Yard 'n' Garden,*" Crosby reads, turning my magazine around on the bar. He flips through it, not pausing to look at any one page in particular. "Taking up gardening?" he asks.

"No," I say. "Tried that already, but it didn't work out too well. I'm actually looking to get a birdhouse." I pull the magazine toward me and flip to the back pages, where are advertised all kinds of birdhouses. "I'm just trying to decide which to get." I peruse the selection for the umpteenth time today. I've narrowed it down to two. One is shaped like an igloo. The thing I like about it is that it's translucent, so you can kind of make out what the birds are doing in there. The other is a mini-castle, with turrets and streamers and a plastic moat you can fill with water in which the birds can bathe.

"Lemme look," Larry says, pulling the magazine toward him. He scans the options and then bangs his gnarly finger down hard on one of them. "This one," he says. "This is the one." I look down at the birdhouse Larry's pointing at. It's of military design, which doesn't surprise me; it's a camouflaged bunker.

"You think?" I say.

"This is *the one*," he says. "Crosby," he says. Crosby looks up from the pancakes he's been surreptitiously eating while Larry's been distracted. "Phone," he says, pointing and waving at the phone. "We got an order to place over here," he says.

"Wait," I say. "I'm not sure, yet. I kind of like the igloo one."

Larry waves me silent as Crosby hands him the phone. He dials, and after a minute he clears his throat. "Yes," he says, loudly. "I'd like to place an order. Yah. Yah. *Yard 'n' Garden*. Yeah. I'd like to order ah . . ." and here he runs his finger down the page to locate whatever information they're asking him for, "number three-oh-nine-eight-seven. Bird Bunker. Yeah. Yeah."

"Wait, Larry," I say, but he waves me quiet again.

"Yes I do have another item," he says, and he runs his finger down the page again. "Number three-oh-nine-nine-oh. Coo-Coo Igloo. Yeah. Credit card." I've already pulled my credit card out, but Larry again waves his hand in my face before reaching for his own credit card.

"No," I say. "Larry, please, come on."

"Will you hold on a minute, please?" Larry says into the receiver. He swivels his entire stool to face me. "Would you shut up?" he says.

"But—" I say.

"No," he says. "Don't but me. And write your address down."

He reads his credit card number aloud, and then gives my address, which, at his command, I've written down on a cocktail napkin.

"There," he says, turning off the phone and handing it back to Crosby. "Should get there in two to three business days."

I look at Larry, but Larry's looking straight ahead, his hands clasped around his beer. "What?" he says, still looking straight ahead.

I shake my head, though he can't see me. I don't know what to make of this gesture, what it means, and I'm not sure whether this feeling in my chest is one of happiness, as it should be, or sadness, as it strangely seems. I take a breath and summon my voice, which feels far, far away. "Thanks," I say.

20

THE AVENGER

Marissa called last night. She called to let me know that she had arrived home safely in Colorado, that she had done a lot of thinking on the drive home, and that she wanted to thank me again for taking her in the other night.

"You don't have to thank me," I said. I was sitting at my desk, trying to finish the first draft of the penguin story.

"No, I do," she said. "I was scared. Really scared."

"Still." I looked out the window toward the Cranes' house. Harry Crane was in the kitchen in his pajamas, drinking orange juice out of the container. I thought about the effort I'd put into avoiding Marissa after her first message. I thought about how things might have turned out differently for her had I answered that call, or if she had never met me.

"No, but I mean things had gotten crazy. And it wasn't just Marins, I mean, it was a lot of things."

I straightened up. "Who? Marins?"

"Yeah, Jacob. But it wasn't just him."

Jacob Marins.

I wrote the name down, underlining it three times. This was information I'd not bothered even hoping for. This was information I could use. After we'd hung up, I stared at that name. Jacob Marins. Jacob Marins. Jacob Marins was responsible for Marissa's face. And if Jacob Marins could do that to Marissa, he could do that to anyone. I thought of Ellen Marie Franklin.

I spent most of this morning on the bench outside the coffee shop on the north corner of Locust and Wetherly, which is the spot, according to the old billboard, where Ellen Marie Franklin was last seen.

I tried to picture Ellen Marie in her blue jeans and gray sweatshirt, standing on that corner and waiting to cross the street, but somehow the only way I could conjure her was in the prom dress she's wearing in the billboard picture, her hair curled and roses in her hand. I thought about how the billboard says that this was the place where she was last seen, and how that isn't exactly true. The corner of Locust and Wetherly is *not* the place where she was "last seen," I concluded; it is, instead, the place where she was last *observed,* the place where she was last *noticed.* Unless she was snatched from the corner in broad daylight, which seems unlikely, she moved on from this spot, presumably in the direction of the pharmacy, and she was indeed "seen" again—she was simply not registered. Surely she passed other walkers on the street; surely someone glanced out the window of a passing car, or a restaurant, and saw her making her way down Locust without realizing that what they were seeing mattered. When I think about it now, I may have even seen her after she was "seen" on the corner of Locust and Wetherly, if I was downtown that day, and just because I didn't know to notice her, I didn't—like the birds in my yard who shortly, thanks to Sal, and to Larry, will have not one home, but two.

"Okay," Sal's saying. "So, which goes here? Hollis? Hello?"

"Sorry?" I say. I look down at Sal, who's down on his knees above the hole he's dug for the Bird Bunker's pole.

"This is the spot for the igloo one?"

"Oh," I say. "No, the bunker goes there."

"Okay," he says. "I think this'll be deep enough, don't you?" He stands and prods at the hole with his toe.

"Looks good to me," I say. "And thanks again, Sal," I say. "Stupid back," I say, bracing it with my hands, though really it's not hurting so much anymore.

"You know me," Sal says. "I like doing these kinds of things." He wipes his hands on his shorts. "Plus, Mona's got all these ladies from Lamaze coming over this afternoon and wanted me out of the house anyway."

"Well, stay as long as you want," I say. "I've got some beer inside."

"Sounds good," Sal says, nodding, "soon as we get these up." I watch him set the base of the Bird Bunker's pole near the hole he's dug. "Can you brace the pole with your foot?" he asks, readying himself to raise the bunker on its pole. "Just kind of make sure it gets right into the hole when I lift."

I nod and position my foot against the pole so that it drops directly into the hole as Sal walks it upright. He kicks dirt into the hole around the pole to make it secure. We both stand back and look up at the bunker high atop its perch.

"Perfect," I say.

"That wasn't too hard," Sal says. "Now where do you want the other one?"

"Well," I say, wandering over to the other corner of the yard. "We should leave them their space, you know, not put them too close together, so maybe here?"

Sal goes to get the igloo and its pole, which is leaning against the house, and brings them back over to where I'm standing. "Now," he says, "if you can just hold the pole up a little off the ground, like this, right—can you do that? Is your back okay?" he asks.

"Yeah, it's fine," I say. The bottom end of the pole is resting on the ground, and Sal's placed the top part of the pole, the part to which he must affix the igloo, in my hands as he tries to attach the thing. I watch him work, alternating between the various types of screwdrivers and other tools he's brought over with him. It occurs to me that my own toolbox might not be a bad thing to invest in.

"You ever heard of a Jacob Marins?" I ask.

"Marins?" Sal mutters. "No. Why, should I have?"

"Just curious," I say, shaking my head.

"Shit," Sal says, a second later. "Dropped a screw. Right around here. I felt it bounce off my foot." Sal squints at the ground. "See it anywhere?"

The lawn badly needs cutting, so it's hard to see into the grass, and I don't see the screw, but what I can make out is a snail clinging to the weedy leaf of a dandelion. "Shit," I say. "Hold on. Can I put this down for a second?"

"No, no," Sal says quickly. "Let me just . . ." he takes over my position supporting the pole and I step back. "You okay?" he says.

"Yeah, I just"—and I squat down and pluck the snail from its leaf—"just saw this guy and wanted to get him before I lost him."

"You're going to keep him?" Sal asks, looking confused.

"No," I say. "But I should get him back to the beach."

"The beach?" Sal repeats.

"Yeah. How do you think he got all the way up here anyway?" I wonder aloud. I hold the snail up in front of me and hum at it to see if it'll emerge at the sound like it's meant to.

"It's a garden snail," Sal says. "It's not a periwinkle."

"A what?" I say. Now that he says it—garden snail—the term does sound familiar, but still, I look doubtfully at Sal.

"A garden snail. Not a periwinkle. Not the kind that stick to rocks at the beach."

I stare at Sal, absorbing this information and feeling mildy alarmed at my notion that all snails were rock-clinging sea-lovers. Surely I'd known about garden snails. Hadn't I? Or was my conception of snails one of those misconceptions that most people grow out of before adulthood—unless, that is, they're never corrected? My father, for instance, thought marshmallows were made of apples until my mother informed him otherwise when she came home and found me polishing off an entire bag of them under his watch. *But they're good for him,* my father had protested.

"A garden snail," I say.

"Yeah," Sal says. "They're different from periwinkles—from beach snails. Think of them as slugs with shells."

"Oh," I say, stooping down to return the snail to its leaf. I look up at Sal before I let the snail go. "You sure?" I say.

"Like you said, how would a periwinkle have gotten up here from the beach anyway?"

I can think of a number of ways—in a bird's beak, in a child's pail—but I nod and let the thing go. "Okay," I say. "Back to work."

"While you're down there," Sal says, gesturing with his chin, "I see the screw. To your left. Left a little more. Yeah, you got it. You got it."

I've left Sal out in the yard with the first Grover story and the last beer while I go to the liquor store to pick up a few more. It's the penguin story. I figured the thing out in my head as I worked on the penguin section of the hedge this weekend, and then yesterday afternoon I went inside and wrote it all down. The penguin in the story had been the last left of his flock before he was taken to the zoo. The rest of them had been shoved off icebergs to test the waters before feeding, as penguins do, one at a time, until eventually there were only two penguins left. And when it came down to it, my penguin decided to push rather than be pushed, and then he found himself suddenly alone and lonely, standing on an iceberg in the middle of a vast blue sea of them. Years later, in the zoo, he's still haunted by the decimation of his flock, and by his own culpability.

I was surprised at how easily the story came after these months of writing nothing but notes and ideas and letters to Claire, and I wanted to send the pages off immediately to Andrew, partly to make up for the other night. I think his patience with me is wearing thin. But I've decided to hold on to the story until Labor Day. Claire reads everything I write, and I need and trust her opinion. I'm thinking next of doing something on starlings. I'm going to put starling feed in the igloo birdhouse; then I'll be able to spy on them as they do whatever they'll do in there.

Returning with the beer, I pull up against the curb opposite my house before turning into the driveway to take a look at the hedge from this angle. The penguin is at the far edge of the hedge, and it begs for company. I imagine a starling beside it, and think about how I might tackle that next project. I imagine a giraffe beside that, and then maybe a rhino. My hedge could become famous in this town.

Inside, I put the new case of beer in the refrigerator before heading out back, and then I stand in the sliding doorway to survey the backyard before stepping outside, two beers in hand and my notebook tucked beneath my arm—I want to be able to take notes in case the birds start nesting. The Bird Bunker stands tall in one corner of the backyard, the Coo-Coo Igloo in the other. I notice with satisfaction a bird in a nearby tree who seems to be checking the bunker out. The marsh is starting to take on a fall-like, golden hue, and I notice a couple of egrets standing one-legged in the low-tide mud. In the middle of the yard sits Sal in his lawn chair, the dog at his side. He's got my story in one hand and a beer in the other. I blur my eyes and imagine that Sal is me, sitting out there with his dog and birds and beer, and I am pleased.

I step outside and sit down in the lawn chair opposite Sal's, setting our beers on the table between us.

"So this is a kid's story?" he asks, looking up from the last page.

"Not exclusively," I say.

"And Grover can actually talk to the animals?"

"Take it as you will," I say. "He can communicate. Take it as literal speech or not."

"Huh," he says. He scratches his forehead.

"No good?" I ask.

"No, no, it's good," he says. "Unusual, but good. I'm no reader," he says.

I'd be discouraged if my wife reacted in the way that Sal is to my story, but Sal is not my wife. I pick the story up from off the table where he's set it and flip through the pages. Pages and pages. They feel good in my hands. I flip open my notebook to stick the pages inside so they won't blow away, and then that name catches my eye. Jacob Marins. My ears get hot to think of Jacob Marins out in the world unpunished, myself sitting here feeling all self-content and smug. I've got a responsbility to Marissa. I've got a responsibility to Ellen Marie.

"So you've never heard of any Marins," I say.

"No," Sal says.

I looked up Marins last night in the phone book. There was only one Marins listed—a D. Marins—but I'm not without hope. Jacob could be married; D. could be his wife. Or he could have listed himself under the wrong initial to throw people off his track.

"Why?" Sal asks.

"Curious," I say. I sit back and cross my ankles, trying to relax as Sal seemed to be as I stood in the doorway imagining that he was me. I take a sip of my beer and squint up at the birdhouses, but I can't get my mind to focus on anything but Jacob Marins. I open my notebook again and look at his name, and below it the address I've jotted down from the phone book. It's on a street near Pratty's.

"Hey," I say to Sal. "Want to go get a beer?"

He looks at the beer in his hands, newly opened. "We have beer," he says.

"We don't have darts," I say.

I should have used cribbage as my excuse for wanting to go to Pratty's. I am good at cribbage, but my hand-eye coordination is another story. A couple hours and several beers into it, I have lost to

Sal six times at darts. Crosby has told Sal that if he can beat me ten times straight, he'll clear his month's tab.

I warned Crosby that the bet was a bad idea, but he didn't listen. I warned him that when I aim, I don't aim for specific spots on the dartboard, but for the dartboard in general; more often than not, my darts miss the board entirely and go bouncing to the floor.

"This is sabotage," Crosby's saying. "You're sabotaging me, Hollis."

"I warned you," I say, tossing a dart. It hits the rim of the board and falls to the floor. Larry cackles, as he does every time I throw. "What?" I say, turning to face him. He's set himself up at a table right near the action. He thinks I have bad form. Girl form, he's called it. He shakes his head and shrugs innocently. "Maybe it's your back," he says.

"I had a little more faith in you than this," Crosby says from behind the bar. "I know you're not the best at darts, but six straight losses now? Help me out, here."

"I'm not doing this on purpose," I say to Crosby, tossing another dart. It sticks. "What is that," I say, squinting to see if my dart has landed anywhere that will do me good. "Seventeen!" I say. "I can use that! I hit a seventeen!"

Sal goes up to the dartboard to pull out the darts I've stuck and bends to retrieve the one on the floor. "Eleven," he says.

"What?"

"That was an eleven, not a seventeen."

I squint again. Sal is right. "Fuck," I say. Eleven does me no good at all.

"We could postpone this," Sal says. "Finish another time?"

"That's not in the rules!" Larry bellows.

"There are no rules," I say. I take a seat at the bar, grateful to be off my feet. Hours of darts was more than I bargained for when I suggested we leave the house, but at least I've gotten a glimpse of the Marins house. It's a few blocks east and south of here, on Gilson Street, a street a lot like this one, with cracked sidewalks sprouting weeds, skinny trees, and homes that look the same but for variations in color, fencing, and lawn ornaments. I drove slowly down Gilson on our way here, looking for number 4046.

"What are we doing?" Sal asked.

I pulled over across from 4046 and peered past Sal out the window. 4046 and 4048 Gilson share the same building, which is brown and badly needs repainting; there are two doors at the top of the stoop, and a big hanging plant like a chandelier. There is a doormat outside 4046 with writing that I assume says "WELCOME," or "HOME SWEET HOME"; I couldn't tell from the car. The curtains to the big downstairs window were open, and I could see a lamp on the table beneath it, but nothing inside beyond that. Outside the window, I saw window boxes with withering flowers. There was nothing on the lawn; no grill, no furniture, nothing to suggest that D. Marins has children, and the fencing, compared to the homes around it, seemed relatively new, still unrusted. The carport was empty.

"Where are we?" Sal asked.

"Nowhere," I said. "Just looking." But truly there wasn't that much to see. I wished I had binoculars. I wished it was night, and the glare of the sun didn't prevent me from seeing inside. I wished that I were alone, so that I could sit in the car and wait for whoever might come or go. I'll come back later, I thought. Tonight, after I've dropped Sal off and it's dark enough to see inside. I'll bring my notebook, some Jack, the binoculars, maybe the dog for protection.

I think about this now. I imagine myself in the car with all my gear and the dog, and I imagine Jacob Marins coming home. I imagine a big man, big hands. I imagine a tank top and tattooed arms. I imagine chains around his neck, maybe a cross dangling from one of them. I imagine boots with steel toes. I am no match for a man like that.

"Hey," I say to Sal. He's joined me at the bar and sits rolling a dart back and forth between his fingers. Larry's on his other side. "What would you do if someone hurt Mona?"

"Hurt her?"

"Yeah."

"Depends what you mean."

"Beat her up, say."

"You're asking what I'd do if someone beat Mona up?"

"Yeah," I say.

"Well, if I were there I'd probably hit him back."

I look at Sal and try to imagine this. He's not a big guy, and I've never heard him even raise his voice. "Come on," I say.

Sal shrugs. "What? I couldn't just sit there and let it happen. I'd have to do something."

"I'd fuckin' take 'em out," Larry says, leaning over. "You know how good it feels to take someone out? In the war, man, WHAM, BANG, you know. You don't have to be big, you just need the equipment."

The equipment. "Like what?"

"Like Sal'd get the shit kicked out of him, hand to hand. But give him a bat or something, he's golden."

"This is a fucked-up conversation," Sal says.

"Okay, let's say you weren't there," I say. "That you heard about it after."

"This is a fucked-up conversation," Sal repeats.

"Yeah, but what would you do?"

"Call the cops, call Larry here and let him take care of it, I don't know. It didn't happen." Sal turns to look at me. "What's with you anyway?" he says.

I shake my head. "Curious," I say.

Curious enough that I do return to Gilson Street after I've gone home to the dog for dinner.

We sit out in the yard as usual with our burritos, me with my Jack. It is getting darker earlier these days, and I watch in nervous anticipation of tonight's adventures as the sun drops oblong over the marsh. "What do you think?" I ask the dog. "Are you a protector? Could you save me from Jacob Marins?" I look down at him beside me, his plate licked clean before him. His eyebrows lift as he directs his eyes up at me, but he doesn't lift his head from where it's rested on his paws. "Could you?" I say. The dog lets out a loud, full sigh and tips himself over so he's resting on his side. "Great," I say. I reach down and rub the dog's belly before heading inside to find myself what Larry's called "equipment," and an hour later I'm parked outside 4046 Gilson with a bat, a couple of knives, pepper spray I found in Claire's closet, a tire iron, and a fire poker all assembled in the backseat. Beside me on the front seat are my notebook, Claire's binoculars, a pair of pantyhose to disguise myself if need be, and my Jack.

The windows of 4046 Gilson are all dark, and the carport is still empty. I'd hoped people would be home, that the lights would be on, that I could watch whoever lives inside 4046 Gilson living. I keep glancing over my shoulder at the arsenal I've assembled on the backseat. The collection makes me nervous, and I take a mildewed beach towel from the floor and cover it up. I'm not sure exactly why I've brought these weapons, whether I've brought them as tools of vengeance or defense; I only know that I feel somehow obligated. But if Jacob Marins were to come home right now, if he were to steer whatever big-wheeled geared-up truck I'm sure he drives into the carport, would I leap from the car wielding the bat or a knife or the poker and attack him in Marissa's name? I've never hit anyone before, and it's hard to imagine what it would feel like. I try to imagine the impact of a bat against a skull; would it be a sharp, hard crack like the impact of a bat against a ball, or would it be more like striking a watermelon? Would the skull give and absorb the blow? I try to imagine what it would feel like to stab someone. I wonder how easily the knife would pierce through skin and organs, and if you pulled the knife back out and stabbed again and again whether you'd feel the blade catching on flesh and other things. I shudder; I do not want to know.

Shouldn't I, though? Shouldn't I be itching to lay my hands upon Jacob Marins? I take a swig of Jack and imagine again the big man I've decided Jacob Marins is, with his big hands and his chains and his tattoos and the bandanna tied around his head, and I imagine his truck with its racks and huge tires and his leather vest and all his women, and I imagine the tiny self-storage unit where he's had Ellen Marie tied up all these years, and I imagine one of his big hands against Marissa's face, leaving the bruised green shadow of itself that I tended. I have seen the mark of this man's hand, I think. Shouldn't that be enough?

I wake to the guttural rumbling of a car engine across the street. My head is pounding. I open my eyes; it is morning. I fell asleep with the windows closed, and they are fogged on the inside; on the outside they are wet with dew. I reach across to the passenger door and roll the window down a crack so I can see across the street. Standing in the yard of 4046 Gilson is an old woman in a floral tent dress and a hairnet, a hose held above her head as she reaches up to water the dying flowers in her window boxes. An old brown El Camino idles in the carport, and the woman has turned around to shout something to the driver over the throaty sound of its engine.

I roll the window down halfway for a better view. The door of the El Camino opens, and the driver gets out. He is young, barely in his twenties. His beard is the curly, scraggy type with dime-sized bald spots, likely grown to cover stubborn pimples. He's wearing little silver earrings, a pin through his eyebrow, black pants, and a black T-shirt with something I can't make out scrawled across the front. He jogs toward the house, leaving the engine on and the car door open. He takes the steps of the front stoop two at a time and disappears inside, emerging a few seconds later with a large black backpack covered in silver and white marker and sewn with patches. He gives the woman a kiss on the cheek as he passes by her, gets into the car, and backs it into the street. The woman stands and watches him drive away, the hose lowered now, watering nothing in particular at her feet.

I look at the dashboard clock; it is 6:30. I open the driver's-side window for a little air, and I turn the key in the ignition so I can flip the wipers on to wipe the dew away. The sun hasn't risen high, yet, and the shadows are still long, but already I can feel the day's heat. The street is still and empty except for a few parked cars, this woman standing with her hose, and, at the far end of the street now and out of earshot, the El Camino stopped at a stop sign. The hot bugs buzz.

I rub my eyes. I feel as if I have woken on another planet, or in a different world. Who are these people? Is this woman D. Marins, and this boy her grandson? Is this boy Jacob Marins? I squint down the street after him and just see the El Camino taking a right a few blocks down. I turn my own engine on and follow.

The letters started coming not long after Simon died. Not the condolence letters from friends and family, but the letters of apology from the families of the kids who had hit him, and from the kids themselves. Claire wasn't home to read them; she was meeting with lawyers, sitting in court, listening to testimony. She was dealing with what she called the practical matters, she said that she was doing what needed to be done so that we could move on. I didn't see what difference it made.

I'd say there were ten letters in total. After the first one came, I'd sit at the window like a kid and wait for the mail truck to come down the street, and as soon as it was out of sight again I'd hurry down the driveway for the mail. If Claire happened to be home, I'd tuck away whatever letter of apology had come that day to read later on, in private. These letters were my private collection; I read them over and over again, these things that tried to take the blame for something I felt responsible for, and I tried to let them have it. I wanted to be enraged. I wanted to want to kill these kids, wanted to want them to suffer, wanted to want to do what I'm doing now, sleeping outside their homes and trailing them on their way to wherever they're going at 6:30 in the morning. But somehow the letters only made me feel more guilty. In the end, I was the one had who left Simon out in the driveway unattended, a four-year-old on a new green tricycle.

Even now, as I breathe in the exhaust of this rusted, shuddering El Camino in front of me as we wait at a red light, I cannot summon the anger I'd need for vengeance. I glance back at my towel-draped arsenal on the backseat and laugh to myself. The image of me using these things is as wrong as the image I had of Jacob Marins, this kid with pierced ears and an adolescent beard, if it is him at all. I realize that I do not even know who Jacob Marins is or whether he is responsible for Marissa at all; I realize that this is something I've decided based on very little, and that I seized on his name as an object of blame as I did the letters in the mail. I lower my head onto the steering wheel and shut my eyes and I listen to the faint sounds of gospel coming from my radio until they are drowned out by the sounds of car horns behind me; the light has changed. I lift my head in time to see the glaring face of the passenger in a pickup truck as it swerves around me and through the light, followed by another car, and another, and the fourth car in line I'm sure would also try to pass but for the oncoming car now in the opposite lane. I step on my own gas pedal, but instead of following on in this rushing, angry line of cars, instead of doing what I've set out to do, whatever that might have been, I pull over to the side of the road and let everyone get around me to where they need to go.

21

STUDIES

It's less than a week till Labor Day, now. I've made a list of things to do before then, before Claire gets home, to make things right for her. I need to clean the house. I need to change the sheets, and move my desk back to its spot along the wall. I need to make some headway on the hedge. I hadn't realized that topiary shrubs need daily attention; the penguin has grown hairy with shoots, and without a creature on the hedge's other end, the whole thing looks lopsided. I need to mow the lawn. I need to stock the bunker and igloo with nesting materials to give whatever birds might nest there a head start; so far, none has shown interest. I need to return to Sal the toolbox he left here the other day.

I look up from this list and out at the marsh, one hand rubbing the dog at my side. We've just eaten what I am aware might have been one of our last burritos together. "Might be dog food for you pretty soon," I tell him.

I add this to my list: buy dog food. I'll get the good kind, I tell myself. The junk food of dog food.

I look back out at the marsh. I can tell by the flow of sticks and foam that the tide is headed out, and I trace with my eyes the path the water will take, snaking its way through the yellowing marsh grass out to the sea, the same path I took just the other evening, drunk and giddy and ready to drift in that little rowboat to wherever the tide would take me.

I sit up straight and scan the dimming marsh for the rowboat I've forgotten to get from the beach; of course, it's not there. I add one more item to my list, in capitals and underlined: ROWBOAT.

Sal lives only a few blocks away from me, but I've never been inside his house; he's been mostly a Pratty's friend. His house isn't that different from my own; it's a small, two-floor deal with a front door that's never used and a kitchen door that is, and he's got a hedge out front, like me. From the street, I can't see what the backyard is like, but I know that unlike mine it doesn't face the marsh. Sal lives on an inland block; I live on the edge of town.

Looking at my list as the sun set tonight, I started getting nervous about its length. The longer I studied it, the longer it seemed as I considered all the things I need to do, so I decided to start now, tonight, by bringing Sal his toolbox. I've brought the dog along on a leash I've fashioned out of some rope from the cellar; if I know Claire, the dog is going to have to get used to things like dog food, walks, collars, leashes. Our progress is slow-going; the dog stops to sniff every puddle, every tree, every soiled curb, every stain on the concrete, and it seems somehow rude to yank on his leash and drag him along before he's ready. And I'm in no rush.

It's dark by the time we get to Sal and Mona's, and I hesitate at the bottom of their driveway. I've never had a dog, so I don't know the etiquette, but it occurs to me that to bring my dog inside might be impolite. There's a tree at the edge of the driveway, and I tie the dog to this before pressing on the doorbell. "I'll be right back," I say, looking at him over my shoulder.

I never know how long to stand and wait after I've pressed a doorbell or knocked on a door before either knocking again or leaving. Knocking again seems rude, impatient even if you've let enough time pass. Almost a minute goes by without any answer from inside, and I'm beginning to think that I'll just come back tomorrow when the door opens, a little at first, and then wide as Sal sees that it's me standing there.

"Hollis!" he says, pushing open the screen door so I can step inside. "Come on in!"

The kitchen is flickering in candlelight and smells of scallions and ginger. Mona sits at the kitchen table opposite Sal's vacated chair, sipping on a wineglass filled with milk.

"You're eating," I say.

"No!" Sal says, shutting the door behind me and returning to his seat, pointing to an empty third chair at the table. "Come sit! Can I get you anything? Beer, wine?"

"I don't want to interrupt," I say. I stand in the middle of the room with Sal's big toolbox in my hand. I raise the thing. "I just came by to return this."

"No, no, no," Mona's saying. She's up now, reaching for a plate from the cabinet and then loading it with whatever Asian-smelling thing is on the stove. "I made too much, and it really doesn't keep."

Keep, I think. *Keep* is one of Claire's words. She talks about things keeping, like food and drink and suits in the attic.

"I ate," I say. "I really couldn't."

"Just"—Mona puts the plate into my hands as she passes by me on her way back to the table—"here, eat what you want, come sit down."

I look down at the plate in my hand, vegetables and tofu stir-fried together into a uniform color. It steams. I look up at Sal. "Where should I put this?" I lift the toolbox again.

"Right there's fine."

I set the toolbox down there in the middle of the kitchen and take my seat between Sal and Mona at the table. They have both finished eating, and look at me expectantly. I feel as if I should take a bite to be polite, but Mona hasn't given me a utensil, and I don't want to ask for one as I fear this might make me seem more interested in the food than I am.

"Any birds settle in, yet?" Sal asks.

I shake my head.

"I didn't know you were a bird-lover," Mona says. "Judith says you took Norm out the other morning. Guess he really enjoyed it."

I nod. "We went out for a while," I say. I take it as a good sign that Judith Crane told Mona that Norm enjoyed bird-watching with me.

Sal pours wine into his glass. "Wine?" he asks.

I shake my head. "Thanks," I say. One glass of wine is ten minutes, and one glass of wine might mean two, and what I want is to get out of this dark kitchen and from under Sal's and Mona's gazes. I turn around in my seat to check out the window on the dog outside. He's biting at something on his rump with full concentration. "The dog," I explain. "Tied him up out there."

"I didn't know you got a dog!" Mona says.

"Well, I didn't actually *get* him," I say.

"He's a stray," Sal says, giving Mona a look.

Mona grins and looks at me. "Claire know about this one, yet?" she asks.

I shake my head.

"Speaking of," Sal leans forward, "she'll be back from her sister's next week, no?"

"That's right," I nod. I look toward the window again. The dog out there alone makes me nervous; I'm afraid he might somehow get off his leash and leave, or strangle on it, or that someone might steal him. I wonder if people ever lock their dogs like bikes to things like trees and poles and fences when they have to leave them outside. He's still out there, chewing away at whatever it is.

"How's that been?" Mona's asking as I turn around.

"What?" I say.

"Claire helping out at her sister's."

I wonder if she's asking how that's been for me, or for Claire. "Fine," I say. It seems the best answer.

"GILBERT!" a voice shrieks behind me, and I turn, startled. "GILBERT!" I hadn't noticed the caged bird on the other windowsill until now. He's hopping from one rung to the other of his cage.

Mona laughs. "Don't mind Gilbert," Sal says. "He gets excited sometimes."

I get up out of my seat to take a closer look at the bird. He stops his swinging and hopping and looks right back at me. "This is a starling," I say, surprised to find the wild bird caged in here. I turn around. "I didn't know starlings could speak."

"Gilbert's a special one," Sal says, crossing the room to stand with me at the cage. "Mona's doing, actually. See that feeder? And the bath?" Outside the kitchen window is a tree hung with a large feeder, and below it a large stone bird bath. "Starling feeder. Mona found Gilbert on the ground out there when he was baby."

"I don't know what he was doing there," Mona says from the table. "I mean, he was still bald, like baby bald."

"How long have you had him?"

Sal looks at Mona. "What, three, four years now?"

"Three," Mona says.

"Huh," I say, bending closer to the bird. He tilts his head and blinks at me over and over again, like Crosby. It makes me uncomfortable, so I straighten up. "Big feeder," I say, looking past the bird now and out the window at the feeder directly beyond it.

"We get a lot of them feeding here," Mona says.

It's nighttime, so none are feeding now, but I consider how

strange it must be for Gilbert to be caged on one side of the glass while free and wild starlings feed and bathe on the other. I wonder if they can see one another, and if each thinks the other is a strange sight. I wonder if Gilbert, this talking starling, even knows that he is one of the birds that flit each day outside his window, and if the free starlings recognize this caged creature as one of themselves. This could be a good premise for the next Grover story, which I'd wanted to be a starling story anyway. What must those outer starlings think when they see Gilbert playing on the swings of his cage and speaking his name and listening to the radio Mona's saying now she leaves playing twenty-four hours a day to keep him company?

"Except of course for times like now," Mona's saying, "when Sal and I are in here, at home, having dinner or whatever. Then the radio goes off, but we're here to keep him company."

"Right," I say. I turn away from the window. Sal and Mona are lit from below by the candlelight, both of them looking at me as the shadows play on their faces. "You know, I should get going," I say. Mona's faces wrinkles. Sal looks unsurprised. "See Gilbert here. I'm working on this new book, and, well, I just, Gilbert just gave me an idea, and I want to get started on it before it leaves my head."

"Oh," Sal says. "Sure, of course. That's great."

I escort myself to the door. "Thanks again for your help the other day, Sal," I say.

"Sure," he says, standing now in the doorway and watching as I go to untether the dog. Mona appears behind him, a bemused smile on her face.

"And thanks for the food, Mona," I say, waving and smiling as I walk backward down their driveway.

I wasn't lying when I said I wanted to get home to get started on the starling story, even if my departure was a little abrupt, even if I did want to get out of there enough that I'd have made something up anyway. At home, I push through the kitchen without even bothering to turn on the lights and head straight to my desk to scrawl down my new idea in my notebook, just a few lines before I really get started. But I don't want to really get started until I've moved my desk back to where it used to be, away from the window and over by the wall. I put everything piled on my desk temporarily on the coffee table, and so as not to strain my back, I push my desk back to its rightful spot by leaning against it. It's a less a efficient way of doing things, a little less precise than if I faced forward and pushed with my hands, but after some minutes I've gotten my desk back to where it belongs. I transfer all my stuff from the coffee table to my desk and sit down to work.

Nothing happens. I sit with my pen in my hand, but I don't know how to start. I stare at the blank wall in front of me. In the room's dim light, the white of the wall seems to pixelate into lots of little dancing spots. It makes me dizzy. I blink. I turn around and look out my window at the familiar view of the Cranes' yard. The downstairs lights are out, over there, and I notice a new rope swing hung from the branch of the largest tree. I sigh and turn around again, staring at my notes: *Gilbert, starling in cage by window, outside starling feeder, wild starlings, do they see one another? recognize? what do they think? plans for escape? by Gilbert, or by his outside family?*

A mosquito buzzes by my ear, and I shake my head to shoo him away. A second later, he returns, and no matter how I shake my head or wave my hands around my ears, the buzzing continues until finally I leap up out of my seat, my heart pounding. Across the room, I notice the sliding door is wide open, and I curse myself for having forgotten to close it in my haste to get to Sal's, to get at least one thing off my list. It will be days, I think, before I can work in peace again without damn mosquitoes' buzzing me crazy. I shut the sliding door and return to my desk. The wall facing me swells and bulges in its whiteness. My ears buzz and my ankles itch with imagined bites; mosquitoes hate my blood. There is no way I can work here. Not anymore. I get up again, put all my stuff back onto the coffee table, and push my desk back over to the window. I drag my desk chair over and sit down. The view soothes me: the trampoline, the go-carts, the swing set, the darkened row of windows that I know to be the fake living room, a bathroom, the kitchen. I breathe. Now, I think, now I am ready to work. I gather my things together again, and head into the kitchen to get a little Jack.

I flip the lightswitch on and grab a fifth from the counter by the refrigerator, and then I think twice and decide to get myself a glass. The dog is going to have to eat dog food, and I am going to have to give up drinking from the bottle. I go over to the cabinet and reach up for a glass. I set it down on the counter beside a vase of dead flowers Claire picked and arranged in June. The glass of the vase is opaque with slime, and unlike the sunflowers, which have turned brittle, these flowers hang limply over the edge, their stems turned weak and soft. Standing right above this aged bouquet, I am over-whelmed by its stench and surprised not to have noticed it until now. I wonder if the whole kitchen smells, if Sal smells it when he comes over, if it is a smell that I have lived with without notice all summer. I take the vase over to the trash can, and I pause for just a second before dumping the flowers in. I can do these little things.

I'm on my way back to my desk, a glass in one hand, the bottle in the other, when I notice on the kitchen table a notebook that does not belong to me. All of my old ones are in my desk. Claire's? I won-der. But as far as I know, she doesn't keep a notebook, and if she did, wouldn't she have brought it with her? And wouldn't I have noticed it if it were on my kitchen table all summer long? I transfer my bot-tle into the hand with the glass and pick the notebook up to bring with me into the other room. I settle down at my desk and look at it. It's one of those black and white composition notebooks—the kind I used to use until I got into the kind with a spiral binding at the top—and it's got the initials H. C. written on the front cover, so it must be mine, I think. I open it up to see what I'll find inside. I like finding things like these, things like letters stuck into the folds of books, or money in the pocket of a winter jacket just taken out for the season, things that are your own and familiar but forgotten.

But the writing inside is not my own. It is a child's scrawl, and the pages are complete with lists, schedules, diagrams, maps, and though the handwriting is not familiar, everything else in the notebook is. The drawing on the first page is of my home. There are floorplans of my house, and detailed diagrams of each room. There is one list under the heading of "refrigerator" and dated in mid-July. There is one list under the heading of "closet," and one list lists the books on my personal bookshelf. There are pages that record the hour of my comings and goings on certain days, and whether or not I went on foot or by car, and whether or not I had the dog with me. There is one page dated late July, starred at the top. It records, as most do, my daily activities: *10:30: outside with coffee and paper, 12:00: worked on hedge, 1:30: went inside, 4:45: left on foot, 6:05: came back home, 7:15: MAN COMES OVER WITH DOG!!!!* It is this last thing on that day's schedule that is starred. I remember that day well; it's funny to think that the H. C. of next door was as delighted as this H. C. was when this H. C. stepped into the Cranes' yard that night. We'd been watching each other; we knew each other's habits.

I must have startled Harry tonight. He must have expected me to be later than I was, as I usually am when I go out after dinner. He must have heard me coming up the driveway—I was talking aloud to the dog about how I may well write a Grover story about him, if he's lucky—and ran out through the sliding door, forgetting his notebook in his haste and leaving the slider open. I grin. I look up from the notebook and across the Cranes' yard. Although the downstairs windows are dark, the lights are still on upstairs, and I scan each window carefully, hoping to catch Harry Crane in one and looking out at me, Hollis Clayton, at my desk, reading all about myself. He doesn't know it—in fact, I imagine he's probably terrified by tonight's events—but if I saw him up there, I'd smile, and I'd wave.

22

RECKONING

Harry's notebook accounts for only sections of most of my days, but of course he had other things to do this summer aside from watching me. It's funny the things he noticed: *11:30: Man goes outside with coffee and newspaper. Boxer shorts, T-shirt. Opens up newspaper. Never turns the page. Maybe fell asleep? 12:45: Man goes inside. 1:20: Man leaves in car. Brown shorts, reddish shirt. I think he shaved when he was inside.*

Or from another day: *1:30: Man goes out to hedge. Brown shorts, blue shirt, same as yesterday and the day before. 1:55: Man talks to another man in the street. Looks at the sky a lot, maybe thinks it's going to rain? Keeps switching clippers from hand to hand.*

It is strange to see this version of my summer. I know that the man I was talking to in that last entry was Sal, but I didn't remember what I was wearing, or that I'd worn it for three days, and I probably didn't even realize it at the time. I didn't realize as I spoke to Sal that I was looking often at the sky, or that I was switching the clippers from hand to hand.

I didn't know many things about my summer: that Andrew waited for half an hour at the kitchen door and even stuck a note under the mat before wandering around the house and finding me asleep out back, that Marissa was sitting on the doorstep for three hours before I finally came home from the literary thing in Boston, that Girl Scouts have come by several times with their cookies and rung the broken doorbell of our unused front door. I didn't know that the clippers I've been using are for righties. I am a lefty. I didn't know that there's a bird's nest in my chimney. I didn't know that I hit a skunk with my car coming home one night.

I opened up my notebook last night to compare Harry's entries with my own for certain dates this summer. On Baybury Day he's got me *out in the yard looking mad but eating the chocolate coins anyway*. Baybury Day in my notebook is a letter to Claire. The day I got home from sleeping in the car after being stood up by Marissa, Harry's got me standing in the doorway for eight minutes before going inside. In my notebook is my information on Ellen Marie Franklin. On the day I got Nintendo, Harry was at the window watching me and Sal as we played, and the page is smudged and rippled with rain. In my notebook, that day exists as a letter to Claire philosophizing on how animals feel on rainy days. The day before Simon's birthday in my notebook is a sketch of a Wacky WallWalker. In Harry's notebook, I'm standing at the hedge that I've "messed up" doing no clipping at all, and then, in a rush at the bottom of the page is an account of the Crane family driving me home. My hair was clinging with static to the car ceiling, and Harry felt bad for me when Judith Crane tried to make me "tell on" him.

A large part of me wants to keep this notebook for myself, but

I've told myself that as soon as I've finished my coffee this morning, I will bring it over next door. I sit in the yard going through the notebook one last time, sipping slowly on my coffee and enjoying the idea that Harry is probably watching me right now and terrified to see me with his notebook. I wonder what he thinks of my unconcern, or the leisure with which I am reading through these pages I have read already many times. This last reading is for show.

The last page of Harry's notebook is a copy of the list I've made of things to do before Labor Day. When I reach this final page for the last time, I take a pen, put a check mark by "Sal's toolbox" and add to the bottom of the list "return Harry's notebook," and it is only at this moment that it occurs to me that the only way for this list to be in Harry's notebook is if Harry has gone through my notebook to find it and has seen all the notes on him. I pause, my head bent over Harry's last page. Suddenly I am filled with the anxiety I've been imagining Harry's been feeling since last night, because as much as I've caught Harry Crane, he has caught me. I swallow. The sense of power I've enjoyed sitting out in the open with this notebook and probably in Harry's view evaporates as I realize that I am not the one with the power at all. Harry's not afraid to see me with his notebook, because he's seen mine. I shut the notebook, lick my lips, and stand to cross the hedge. I need to give this notebook back, and now.

It's as if Judith Crane is waiting for me with her hand already on the doorknob; as soon I press the doorbell, she swings the door open. "Mr. Clayton!" she exclaims, a big smile on her face. "What a surprise!"

"Hello," I say.

"What brings you by?"

"I wondered if I could borrow Harry."

Judith Crane looks at me, that smile frozen on her face, but confusion in her eyes. "Sorry?" she says.

"Borrow Harry. Young strength," I explain. "You remember that rowboat I took to the picnic? It's still down at the beach, but

I've thrown my back out and thought maybe Harry could give me a hand rowing it back up the marsh."

"Oh, you poor man," she says. "What happened?"

"What happened?"

"Your back," she says, then "hold on," she says, and she turns and bellows Harry's name up the staircase behind her. "Sorry. You were saying?"

"Nothing," I say. "I wasn't saying anything."

"No, you were, your back."

"Oh," I say. "I was bouncing on your trampoline," I say. Harry knows the truth about my back, so I figure there's no point lying. Judith Crane opens her mouth slightly. "I decided to try to do a backflip, but I guess I'm too old, and," I shrug, "something just snapped."

Judith Crane begins to laugh. "Oh, you are funny!" she says, turning around and shouting Harry's name again up the stairs. Her laughter settles into a smile, and I realize that she doesn't believe the truth. She stands there smiling, and I stare at her smile, counting how long it takes to fade. The fading of anyone's smile fascinates me. It's a private thing that's done in the shadow of a joke when you think no one is looking. It's almost frightening to watch closely as the muscles relax and a face drops, as joy, laughter, or happiness slowly passes out of whomever you're watching. It's an almost ugly thing.

Finally Harry appears beside his mother at the door. "Yeah?" he says, looking down.

"I'd like you to help Mr. Clayton with his canoe," she says.

"Hollis, please," I say. "And it's a rowboat, really."

"I have baseball," Harry Crane says.

"In three hours you have baseball, Harry," Judith Crane says.

"It shouldn't take long," I say. I smile.

" 'Kay," Harry says, and disappears inside for his shoes.

"I almost forgot," Judith Crane says suddenly, digging through the purse she's wearing across her chest as if she's about to go somewhere, which, given her bare feet, doesn't seem likely. She unfolds a piece of paper and thrusts it toward me. "I was in Wiscott the other day and saw this hanging on a telephone pole. I took it to show you in case it was that stray you've had around. I can't remember quite, but I thought it looked a little like him."

I take the flier from her hand. The photograph of the dog at the top of the page is grainy, so it's hard to make out, but it does look a little like my dog. Underneath the photograph, it says, "Missing: Jasper, seven-year-old mutt, beloved pet of the Carmichaels, last seen June 3 tethered in front yard of 86 Stone Street, Wiscott. Will pay reward!"

I fold the flier up and tuck it into my pocket. "Thanks," I say. "I'll look into it."

I didn't like going over to other people's houses when I was young, but after my mother left, there were many afternoons when after school I had no other choice; my father had meetings, errands, work, and I couldn't be left alone.

I minded going to Colton's house the least. He lived in an apartment building, not a house like I did, and I liked taking the elevator up to the fifth floor where he lived. I liked looking out the window of his room across the alleyway and into the windows of the apartment building adjacent to his. He had a table and chairs set up by the window, and Shanty, his housekeeper, would set us up there with glasses of chocolate milk and a bowl of goldfish between us. We invented stories about the people we could see through the few windows that weren't draped with a curtain's gauze or slatted with venetian blinds or translucent with textured glass. Mobsters lived in that building, we said. Kidnappers. We had to be careful not to be seen.

Colton also stole things. He had a stash of candy that took up most of the top drawer of his bureau, all lifted from the deli around the corner from our school. He had penknives with dull blades, and a collection of road maps. I asked him why the road maps. He didn't know. He had a bigger tape collection than anyone our age, all stolen, he said. He had bracelets he was saving for his girlfriend, when he met her. He had odds and ends, things he stole from other people's backpacks at school: key chains, pencil sharpeners, pens with multicolored ink selections, decks of cards, jacks and balls. His stolen goods intrigued me even more than the criminals next door.

Once I stole something from him. It was a little green glass jar, something he'd stolen from Kevin Saunderville's house. There was nothing special about it, no reason for him to have taken it from Kevin or for me to take it from him, but I wanted to know what it felt like to steal. It was on the table with the rest of Colton's stolen goods for the week, and as Colton was looking out the window at the mobster we called Lefty doing dishes, I cupped my hand around the thing and slipped it into my pocket.

I told this story to Harry Crane as we sat parked in my driveway. He had his notebook on his lap.

"Why?" he asked. "Why didn't you take something good, like one of the knives or something?"

I shrugged. "And I threw it out when I got home. At first I put it on my desk, but it made me nervous as I sat there doing homework, so I moved it to my dresser, but it made me nervous there, too, like it was watching me or something. So I threw it out."

Harry kicked the dashboard absently. "So why are you telling me this?"

I blinked. "Don't really know. I guess I just thought we should have a chat. And I guess you kind of reminded me of Colton."

"I don't steal."

"Not that part," I said. I glanced at the notebook on his lap. "The other part. The mobsters next door."

"You going to tell my mom?"

"Are you?" I asked. He shook his head. We were quiet for a minute. "But out of curiosity, why did you do it?" I asked finally. What interested me was what Harry Crane found interesting about me.

"I'm a detective," he said. Then he turned to look at me squarely. "Why'd you do it?"

I thought about this for a minute. "I'm a writer," I said.

Harry nodded and shifted in his seat. I looked at this boy beside me, and then out the front windshield toward the street. A couple glanced up the driveway toward us as they passed on the sidewalk, and I thought they might have thought that we were father and son.

"You know," I said. "I used to have a little boy."

Harry looked at me.

"He'd be younger than you, but I bet if he were around still you might be friends."

"He died?" Harry asked.

I nodded. "Yeah."

"How come?"

I paused. "I don't know," I finally said.

We were silent for a few minutes, and then Harry spoke. "Are we going to go get that canoe thing or what, 'cause I have baseball."

"Nah," I said. "I can do it."

The rowboat, when I get there, is not at the beach. I'd considered the difficulty I might have trying to row the thing back up the marsh alone, and I'd considered the real possibility of being swept out to sea, but that the rowboat might have disappeared entirely had not occurred to me. Somehow, though, I am not at all surprised when I scan the beach and find it empty save for a man searching for probably anything at all with a metal detector. Somehow, it is a familiar feeling.

I turn off the car engine and look out at the beach. It is low tide; on their way out the waves have left behind them layers of stones and shells and weed and glass. It is breezeless, and the air has that deep, rich, low-tide smell to it, rotten and fresh at once. The man with the metal detector walks along the water's edge, waving his machine over the sand in front of him. He's wearing a huge set of headphones attached with wire to the machine's handle, and occasionally he pauses, cocks his head, cups his hand around a head-phone, thinking maybe he's hearing whatever sound might let him know that he has found something. But each time he pauses like this, he shakes his head and moves on.

I pull the flier Judith Crane's given me from my pocket and unfold it. I look closely at the photograph. It's a full-body photo-graph of a dog that does indeed look somewhat like my own, but it's a small photograph, and it's grainy, a photocopy, so it's hard to make out the dog's real features. I bring the flier closer to my face as if this might make things clearer, as if this might allow me to look into the photograph and at the dog himself. Of course, I can see no better this way, so I lower the flier again into my lap and look at it from a distance. *Jasper,* I read again. The dog in the photograph might be a Jasper, but Jasper is no name for the dog I know. He looks nothing like a Jasper. And seven years old? In dog years that's almost fifty, I think, but I've always thought of the dog as closer to my age. The more I look at the photograph, the less it looks to me like my dog. It could be the angle, but the legs look shorter than my dog's legs, and one of his ears is standing up; both of my dog's ears flop over. These inconsistencies fill me with relief. And how would the dog have gotten from his yard in Wiscott to the park in Baybury? It's too far for a dog to walk. How would he have gotten off his tether? Where would his collar have gone? It's coincidence, I con-clude. The similarities are coincidence; the dog in the photograph, this Jasper, is not the dog I have at home.

"Is it?" I asked Sal later. He's the only one aside from Judith Crane who's met the dog, and I was relieved to find him at Pratty's when I got there, just for a quick beer before I dealt with finding a replace-ment rowboat. "I mean look at the legs. And the ears. The right ear especially."

Sal squinted at the photograph. "I don't know," he said. "It's kind of hard to tell. Kind of blurry." He handed the flier back. "But I have to say, it does kind of look like your dog." He shrugged.

"Your dog?" Crosby had materialized above us at the bar. "*Your* dog?" He spread his hands out on the bar and looked at me. "And since when do you have a dog?"

"I guess it's not really mine," I said, though I realized then I had been referring to the dog as mine ever since Judith Crane brought this flier to my attention, ever since my ownership was called into question. "He's just been around."

Crosby set a beer down in front of me and lifted the flier from the bar. "Huh," he said. "*Beloved pet of the Carmichaels,*" he read. He looked at me. "You're holding a beloved pet hostage?" He shook his head.

"I'm not holding anything hostage," I said. "It's not even the same dog, I don't think."

"You don't think," Crosby said.

Larry was down at his end of the bar. He had the newspaper spread out in front of him, which generally means *do not disturb,* but I could tell from his frequent upward glances that his curiosity was getting the better of him. Sure enough, "What's going on down there?" he shouted.

Crosby brought the flier over to him.

Larry looked at it, then looked at us. "So what?" he said.

"Hollis has him," Crosby said.

"I do not," I said. I turned to Sal. "Do I?"

Larry and Crosby looked at Sal expectantly. "It's a bad picture," Sal said, ever diplomatic.

"It says there's a reward," Larry said, looking at the flier again. "Hell, I'm going to call them up then, send 'em over to your house." He thrust the flier in Crosby's direction, and Crosby returned it to me. I looked at the photograph again, trying to summon the conviction I had at the beach that Jasper and my dog are not the same.

"Just remember," Crosby said. "It's *beloved.*"

They made it easy for the beer to be both quick and only one; I began to wish as I sat there that I hadn't shown the flier to anyone, that Judith Crane hadn't shown the flier to me, that Judith Crane hadn't seen the flier to begin with. But instead of leaving Pratty's to deal with the boat, I've come home for a while to collect my thoughts.

I pull into my driveway and turn off the car, and I sit for a minute just to breathe. The hedge looks like hell. The birdhouses are empty. Inside, the dog greets me. I squat down and look at him. "Jasper," I say. "Hey, Jasper." He wags his tail and pants, but this response doesn't change when I try out other names for comparison: Rex, Frankie, Evan, Michael, Spot. No matter what name I use, the dog wags and pants and bats with his paw at my hand whenever I stop stroking him.

At my desk, I add "mini-mall," where I hope to find a replacement rowboat, and "Jasper" to my list. I scan the list; I am unsure what to do next. What are my priorities? Part of me thinks that they should be here, in making things and myself presentable for Claire. They should be starting that other Grover story, proof of my focus; they should be fixing the hedge and getting the birdhouses ready; they should be cleaning the house of the things I've left uncleaned because of her to begin with—things like the bouquet (which I add to my list as I think of it just so I can check it off), or her mud-encrusted sneakers by the door; they should be restocking the refrigerator. But I have responsibilities, obligations that I can't ignore. I can't not replace the rowboat that I've taken and lost, even if I don't know whose it is. And then there's the dog. How can I keep someone's beloved pet? He may well not even be this missing Jasper, but how can I not make sure? To keep him would make me no better than whoever took Ellen Marie Franklin.

I wish Claire knew about these other obligations. If she knew, she'd understand it if she came back to a messy house, an unkempt yard, a bare kitchen, my desk over by the window. But she doesn't know, and the realization of all she doesn't know about my summer makes me suddenly very lonely. The thought of feeling like a stranger to her makes me feel almost like a stranger to myself.

I flip to the next page of my notebook. *Dear Claire,* I write, but I am not sure what to say, or where to begin. I blink at the blank page in front of me, and it occurs to me that even more than I've been missing my wife's actual presence all summer—seeing her across from me at the dinner table, or beside me in bed, or getting out of the shower, or wandering across the marsh with her binoculars—I miss the *fact* of her presence in retrospect and all that her absence has caused her to miss. Her actual presence is recoverable, but this summer can only ever be a blank in our relationship. More than I wish she was here now do I wish that she'd been here all along, even as just a fly on the wall.

What I'd like to do right now is settle in out back with some Jack, call it a day. But. I flip back to my list. I'll shut my eyes and run my finger down it. Wherever I stop is where I'll begin.

23

ALL, NOTHING, NOTHING, ALL

The Outdoor Sports Center is in a huge warehouse in the middle of a secluded lot off the highway outside Baybury. I'd never been until yesterday afternoon, and as soon as I walked through the doors I wished that I had discovered the place earlier, that I was an outdoor sports kind of person. In one section of the store were shelves of sneakers, cleats, hiking boots, rock-climbing shoes, spiked track shoes, moon boots, and snowshoes. Skis, snowboards, toboggans, and plastic saucers lined the back wall. Kayaks hung from the rafters. There was a fishing aisle with high-tech rods for catching tuna and intricately painted, feathered, and hooked little fish to use as bait. In one corner of the store four or five tents of varying size and warmth had been set up. Their flaps were open, and there were sleeping bags inside. A sign mounted against the wall behind the tents invited shoppers to give the tents a try; I lay down inside a small yellow tent and thought that maybe before the weather turned Claire and I should go camping somewhere, maybe Maine, or even Canada. I could get us a tent and a couple sleeping bags, maybe a couple new fishing rods, and a stove to cook whatever fish we caught. I could see us, me, Claire, and the dog, gathered around our campfire roasting marshmallows, Claire laughing in the flickering light as I told how my father thought marshmallows were made of apples.

"Can I help you with the tents, sir?"

I looked down my toes to the entrance of the tent. A salesperson squatted outside, peering in at me expectantly. He was young, but his hair and eyebrows were completely white. He had a wandering eye whose random trajectory I couldn't help but follow with my own eyes.

"Sir?"

I sat up. "Actually," I said. "I'm looking to buy a rowboat." I crawled out of the tent and stood up, smoothing my hair down.

"A rowboat," the salesperson repeated. "This way."

I followed him to the far corner of the store, where a selection of rowboats and canoes leaned against the wall, hull-side up.

"We've got a handful to choose from," he said, slapping the hull of one. "This one," he said, "is going to be your cheapest. And by cheap I simply mean inexpensive; none of these are going to sink on you. . . ."

I tried to pay attention to what he was saying, but his eye kept wandering to the left as if pulled there by some magnetic force. I glanced over my shoulder to see what his left eye seemed to want so desperately to see, and though it could have been anything from the tennis rackets to the golf clubs to the water skis over in that direction, what caught my eye was the swing set just beyond these other things, the same one, as far as I could judge, as the one Simon had picked out for his fourth birthday, the one that had arrived on our doorstep a month too late and now sat still boxed and untouched in the back of the garage. It was a dark pine swing set as opposed to redwood. At one end of the row of swings that hung from the monkey bars—and there were two traditional swings, one trapeze bar, and a horse-shaped swing for two—was a steep, straight, metal slide. At the other end was a good-sized tent-covered platform like a treehouse, with small benches and a table for picnicking. There were three ways to get down and out of this platform: there was a plastic-covered slide, a fireman's pole, and a ladder made of netting. It was a good swing set, deluxe.

It arrived in early October. Claire was at school teaching, and I had gone out for a walk; when I returned, a large box sat outside the kitchen door. I didn't know what it was until I saw that it was addressed to Simon, and then I wasn't sure what to do. I wished I'd remembered to cancel the order. I wished I had been home when it arrived so I could have told them to take it away. But there that cumbersome thing sat, too big to load into the back of the car and take to the post office, too late to do any good. I guess I could have called the company and explained the situation, had them send someone to pick the swing set up and return it to wherever it came from, but I didn't. I couldn't. Instead, I pushed the box into the back corner of the garage, where it's sat now for almost two years.

"So there you have it," the wandering-eyed albino was saying. "What do you think?"

I blinked. "Yeah, that sounds good," I said.

"What sounds good? Which one?"

"That last one," I guessed.

"Excellent choice, sir. You won't regret the extra dollars. This wooden one's a beauty. Comes with custom oars, too, as I said."

"Good," I said. I handed him my credit card, and he gave me a receipt and a slip to hand to the people at the back entrance of the warehouse where all the stock was kept. They mounted the rowboat to the roof of the car, and though I'd planned to row the boat back up the marsh right then, last night, instead I went home and immediately to the garage. The box was, of course, right where I'd left it, though in the past two years clutter had accumulated all around it. I cleared a path to the garage door and slowly worked the heavy thing outside.

It took me almost an hour to get it over to the Cranes'; I couldn't push it through the hedge that separates our lawns, so I had to go down out of my driveway and then back up theirs. I stood sweating on their doorstep, trying to catch my breath. I pressed the doorbell once, then again a minute later; no one was home, so I pulled off the label with Simon's name, put it in my pocket, and left the box on their doorstep. I figured Harry might know where it had come from, but it didn't really matter. Maybe they'd think Norm sent it from wherever he was with whatever woman.

I was looking forward to watching the Cranes set the swing set up, today, and maybe even helping them, but no one seems to be home, still; they must have gone away for the holiday weekend. And even if they were home, it wouldn't matter, because it's raining today. I stand at the sliding door with my coffee in my hand and look out at the marsh. It all looks shades of gray; the water steams. An egret stands on the rowboat's vacant post, its head tucked beneath its wing. I'm a day behind myself; the rowboat should be tethered there by now, should have been last night, but now I'll have to wait for the afternoon when the tide has turned before I can launch it at the beach and ride the current in. If the rain has stopped by then. The dog pads up and stands beside me at the slider, fogging the glass with his muzzle. I squat down beside him and breathe on the glass myself. JASPER, I write through my breath. "Are you?" I ask.

We take the backroads to Wiscott, the curving ones lined thick with shrubbery and trees and houses set far from the road at the ends of muddy, rutted driveways. The leaves seem swollen in the rain, tunneling the road green, the fallen ones pasted wetly to the pavement.

We are the only car I've seen, and I take the middle of the road. I've opened the sunroof for air; the rowboat blocks the rain, and the raindrops hitting the hull thud loudly and sound through the car. The dog sits in the middle of the backseat, looking out the front windshield, attentive and alert, as if he knows where we are going.

Wiscott is a small town, typical New England. I drive us through the downtown streets before trying to find Stone Street; though the town is next to Baybury, I haven't had cause to come here in years. We pass a handful of bakeries, an old movie house, a Laundromat, a coffee shop. Old replica gas lamps and iron benches line the streets, which are mostly empty in the rain. A man with a hooded raincoat stands smoking in a doorway; he watches us pass as if we were the first car to come by in days. In front of the town hall I notice a kiosk with a bulletin board on one side and a map of the town on the other. I pull over and get out. YOU ARE HERE, the map tells me, and I run my finger down the list of street names on the side until I find Stone Street. I look back at the car; it looks small beneath the row boat. The dog is standing in the backseat now, watching me through the window, his nose rubbing against the glass. Nothing is final, I tell myself. Nothing has been decided. We're just here to explore. We're just here so I can look for something, some sign of recognition or excitement on the dog's behalf before I decide anything at all.

I go around to the other side of the kiosk to look at the bulletin board. There are fliers for yoga lessons, handymen, baby-sitters. There is an announcement about the meeting of the town council next Tuesday. There are houses listed for rent, rooms and room-mates sought, cars for sale. There is the same flier that I have in my pocket, searching for Jasper, the beloved dog.

I go back to the car and drive over to Stone Street. I glance over my shoulder to gauge the dog's reaction, but he's busy biting at the bottom of his paw. "Look!" I tell him, pointing at the window. I pull over across from 86 Stone Street. It is a big, Victorian house with a porch that wraps all the way around. It's set back from the street, the front yard fenced in with wooden picket fencing. A huge oak stands in the middle of the yard, a tire swing hanging from the fattest bottom branch. "Look!" The dog looks up at me, not out the window, at stubborn work on his paw all the while. I sigh and open the window a crack; even with the sunroof open, it's stuffy in here, and the vents don't seem to be working. I reach back and open the window a crack for the dog, too; at this he stands, his nose drawn like a magnet to the open air. I roll the window down a little more, so that he can fit his head outside. He does, and then he starts to whine. He paws at the window, as if trying to roll it down some more himself or to climb out of the car entirely, and I feel my heart sink. Is this recognition, or is this just a dog who wants out of the car? There's no way for me to tell. There's no way I can be sure. I could get out of the car myself, ring the doorbell, and ask the Carmichaels straight out whether or not my dog is theirs, but something holds me back. There are too many uncertainties in that—it may have been long enough since they've seen their dog that they, like Judith Crane, might mistake this dog for Jasper, or they might be desperate enough to lie, to take this look-alike dog and pretend it is their own.

"What is it?" I ask the dog. "You need to pee? You want to walk?"

The dog whines, his paw out the window.

"Okay," I tell him. "You want out, then it's out. Just wait one more minute."

I drive us back downtown and find a place to park. I've brought the rope I used the other night for a leash, and this I tie around the dog's neck before letting him out of the car. Immediately, his head goes to the ground and he searches out a place to pee, against the leg of one of the iron benches. "So you did just need to pee," I say, and I am filled with relief. "Now let's go home," I say, opening the car door again, but the dog pulls back. I look at him, and then gently I close the door. The dog looks at me and tilts his head. "Okay," I say. "Let's walk."

The dog is direct in his route; there is no question. He doesn't stop to sniff each thing we pass as he normally does, but pulls taut against the leash and leads me on. I wasn't planning on a walk, so I don't have either an umbrella or a raincoat, and I hunch my shoulders against the rain. I stare at my feet passing over the pavement, over cracks sprouting weeds, over initials carved into the concrete before it dried; I watch wetness spread backward from my toes with every step and finally I see my whole foot drenched as I step into a puddle I don't see until my foot is in it. I let myself be led.

I don't look up until the dog has stopped, hoping somehow that I will find us somewhere other than where I do, which is at the gate of 86 Stone Street. The dog looks up at me, panting, his tail in full wag. "So this is home," I say. The dog jumps up onto his back legs and whines. "Okay," I say. "Okay. I understand." I squat down by the dog and take his face in my hands. His fur is wetted into clumps, and he blinks as water drips past his eyes. "So you're Jasper," I say. I sigh. I know I'm going to have to give this dog back. I know that he is the Carmichaels' beloved pet and, judging by his eagerness to get home, now that he knows how, the Carmichaels are his beloved family, and this his beloved home. How he got to Baybury I don't know, but it doesn't really matter.

I will take him home and dry him off. I'll give his fur a combing through, and tonight, we'll share one last burrito. No, we won't share; we'll each have our own, a special good-bye dinner. I'll let him sleep on the bed, and then, in the morning, I'll call the Carmichaels, and I'll tell them I have found their dog. "Okay?" I'm asking the dog as if I have uttered this plan aloud when I hear the front door of 86 Stone Street groan open and a woman's voice call "Jasper?"

I can imagine how we must have looked to Mrs. Carmichael, man and dog drenched and dripping, crouched side by side in the rain outside her gate. She said she'd been reading by the window when something made her look outside, she wasn't sure what, exactly, and she didn't believe it at first, she said, when she looked out the window and saw us there.

"But then I just knew it was him," Mrs. Carmichael said for the third or fourth time as she returned from the linen closet with a towel. She draped the towel over the dog and knelt down to rub him dry, talking fast about how they'd given up hope, how they'd finally put his dishes and toys away. "Gus wanted to get rid of his things altogether," she was saying—"that's my husband," she laughed— "but I just couldn't bear it, you know? I just knew he was out there, you know? I could feel it." She pounded her chest with her fist. I stood in the doorway, all of a sudden very aware of how wet I was underneath the towel Mrs. Carmichael had tossed me, how my shorts were heavy with rain and my shirt clinging to my skin. Mrs. Carmichael looked up at me. "How did you find him?" she asked.

I looked at her for a second. "He kind of found me," I said. "He'd been hanging out in the park in Baybury. I walk by there every afternoon, and he just started following me home."

"What a sweetheart, huh?" she said, more to the dog than to me. "Yes you are, yes you are," she rubbed him vigorously as she cooed to him through clenched teeth. "Daddy will be so surprised, won't he? Won't he?" She looked back up at me. "My husband went out fishing—today of all days, if you can imagine it—he's just not going to believe it when he gets home."

I tried to smile. "And the kids?"

Mrs. Carmichael's smile faded just a little. "We don't have any," she said.

I nodded.

"Which is why we missed you so much," she turned back to the dog. "You're our baby, aren't you? Aren't you?" The dog wagged his tail as Mrs. Carmichael scratched him behind the ears.

It hurt to watch these two, this reunification, and I wanted badly to get out of there, but I knew that when I left it would be without the dog, and I was not quite ready to say good-bye. So I stood wrapped in my towel in the doorway and I watched them.

"Anyway," Mrs. Carmichael said, finally standing up and releasing the dog, who, I noted and hoped that she did too, came directly over to me. It was my turn to squat down, now, and I went right for the dog's belly, which I know he likes best. He rolled onto his back, his tongue lolling out the side of his mouth. "You'll want to discuss the reward," she said. "We were thinking somewhere around ten thousand, but he's priceless, and you seem to have taken such good care of him . . . look, he really likes you," she said, smiling as she looked down on us.

I looked back up at her. "I know," I said. "I like him, too."

"I'm sure you do," she said. She tilted her head. "Well then, how about fifteen?"

"I don't want a reward," I said. I want visiting rights, I wanted to say. I want partial custody. I want to come back in the middle of the night and steal this dog back.

"Oh, but Mr.—"

"Hollis," I said.

"Mr. Hollis, I insist."

"No," I said. "He's not for sale." Even for fifteen thousand dollars, which I would pay for him, too, if I had it.

"What?"

I dropped my gaze from hers and gave the dog one more rub down. I stood up, then, and cleared my throat. "I should get going," I said. The dog rolled off his back and got onto his feet. He followed me to the door, and I knelt down one last time to look him in the eye.

"You sure, Mr. Hollis?" Mrs. Carmichael was saying, but I was barely aware of her.

"Take care of yourself," I whispered in the dog's ear. "I'll be by with the occasional burrito." I stood up and winked at him, and then I let myself out the door. I was part way down the pathway to the street when I heard the door open again.

"Thank you, Mr. Hollis!" Mrs. Carmichael called from the porch. I lifted my hand in the air, but I didn't turn around. I couldn't.

An hour later, the rain hasn't let up at all; it drums the rowboat's hull as I drive aimlessly around, trying to decide what to do but wanting to do nothing I can think of. I do not want to go to

Pratty's—I don't have the energy for Crosby, or for Larry, and I do not want to talk about the dog, or about Claire, or about Ellen Marie Franklin. I do not want to go home; home without the dog will seem empty, lonely, awful. I cannot work on the hedge in the rain, or stock the birdhouses, or mow the lawn, and cleaning up inside has taken on a whole different meaning now that the dog is gone. I'm not sure I can bring myself to lift his water bowl from the floor and wash it clean, to vaccuum up the hairs he's shed, to scrub his muddy paw prints from the kitchen tiles. Not today, anyway. Which leaves that much more to do tomorrow. I visualize my list, which I have left out for myself on the kitchen table. I have too much to do.

I look at the dashboard clock; it is two o'clock, now, which means the tide has turned. It is pouring; the raindrops smack and blur the windshield even with my wipers on full blast. But I am wet already, and I can think of nothing else to do, so I turn the car in the direction of the beach.

The beach, of course, is empty when I get there. The horizon has vanished in the mist, and the rain tattoos the surface of the water. There is no breeze, and the rain falls straight and hard and warm, I notice when I get out of the car to untie the rowboat and oars from the roof. I toss the ropes into the car and close the sunroof, and then I haul the rowboat down, sliding it over the rear windshield and trunk and finally to the ground. It is wooden, and heavy, and for a moment I worry about my back in this endeavor, but then, *Fuck it,* I think. This needs to be done, and I am wet, and Ellen Marie Franklin is dead, and the dog is gone. What does it matter?

I loop the painter over my shoulder and drag the rowboat slowly down the beach; it sticks in the wet sand and I have to lean hard and pull with all my weight. I stand at the water's edge to catch my breath before embarking. The car parked at the top of the beach looks small, fuzzy with the spray of raindrops, and the path that leads to here from there is awkward, crooked: footprints like paw prints, since all my weight was on my toes, and a zigzagging line left by the rowboat's keel. But here I am, and ready to go. I shove the rowboat into the water, put oars into the locks, and climb in.

I cannot see through the rain more than a few feet around me, but I know that even if I'm rowing in the wrong direction, the tide is stronger than I am and will carry me home in the end, so I row blindly, and hard. Rain pastes my hair to my head, my shirt to my shoulders, my shorts to my thighs. It collects on my lashes and gets in my eyes; it drips off the tip of my nose; raindrops roll down and around my neck. Water collects in the bottom of the boat, but I have nothing to bail with, so I keep rowing. I row past lobster pots tilted with the tide; I row past the point of the beach and into the entrance of the marsh; I row past hunched egrets standing in the mud; I row past the hull of a sunken boat decaying on the marsh grass; I row past a huge blue bird that I don't recognize, one with a gray feathered head and angry eyebrows, long yellow legs and a narrow beak, which opens and lets out a long, loud, awful cry that makes me stop, for a moment, and look.

The bird looks back at me and cries out again, and this time I yell, too. I tilt my head back and open my mouth and let out a loud, long yell of my own. The bird opens its huge wings, then, and labors into the air, and I watch him until he disappears from my sight, swallowed up by mist and rain. I take a breath and I keep on rowing.

I'm not sure how long I've been rowing when I look over my shoulder and see the post where the rowboat belongs appearing through the fog. I row over to it and get out onto the marsh grass. I pull the rowboat up, too, turn it over, and tie it up. Although the tide has done most of the work for me, I am tired and out of breath, and I laugh bitterly to myself when I realize that I could have just launched from the lawn all along. The rain is beginning to let up, I notice, and the far horizon seems to be getting lighter. I brush the hair out of my face and run my fingers beneath my eyes, scooping away the rain collected there, then I turn to make my way toward the house. I've left my shoes in the car, and the marsh grass needles my bare feet, so I walk carefully, my arms out to the sides, choosing my every step as carefully as I can. I don't look up until I see the solid ground of my yard in front of me and I've gratefully set my feet on the soft grass. It's then that I look up. I look up, and when I do, I see Claire standing in the sliding door, watching me. I don't for a moment question that it's her standing there, even though she's two days early. I don't for a minute think that my mind is playing tricks on me, because everything around her is as it should be: the lawn is overgrown, the igloo birdhouse is at a slight tilt, there's a plate from last night's dinner on the outdoor table and an empty fifth of Jack just outside the sliding door. I stop where I am and look at it all, at all these things I have to do, and, finally, I raise my hand and smile.

ACKNOWLEDGMENTS

I am grateful to be able to thank in print many people. Thank you to all my teachers throughout the years. Thank you to Amanda Urban, my agent, and Jordan Pavlin, my editor, and to Emily Molanphy and Jennifer Smith. Thank you to everyone at Irvine who encouraged me and helped to keep the book on track, and thanks a million to Arielle Read.

Thank you to Glenn Schaeffer and the International Institute of Modern Letters, whose generosity enabled me to bring the book to completion.

Thanks goes without saying to my parents, whose support means everything, and to my sisters.

Finally, and of course, thanks and love to Adin.

And Mona.

A NOTE ABOUT THE AUTHOR

Elizabeth Hartley Winthrop was born and raised in New York City. She graduated Phi Beta Kappa and summa cum laude from Harvard University in 2001 with a B.A. in English and American Literature and Language. In 2004 she received her M.F.A. in fiction from the University of California at Irvine, and she was the recipient of the Schaeffer Writing Fellowship for the 2004–5 academic year. She has published stories in *Wind Magazine,* the *Evansville Review,* the *Missouri Review, Red Rock Review,* and the *Indiana Review.* Currently, she is living and writing in Savannah, Georgia. *Fireworks* is her first novel.

A NOTE ABOUT THE TYPE

The text of this book was set in Sabon, a typeface designed by
Jan Tschichold (1902–1974), the well-known German typo-
grapher. Based loosely on the original designs by Claude Gara-
mond (c. 1480–1561), Sabon is unique in that it was explicitly
designed for hotmetal composition on both the Monotype and
Linotype machines as well as for filmsetting. Designed in 1966 in
Frankfurt, Sabon was named for the famous Lyons punch cutter
Jacques Sabon, who is thought to have brought some of Gara-
mond's matrices to Frankfurt.

Composed by Creative Graphics,
Allentown, Pennsylvania

Printed and bound by Berryville Graphics,
Berryville, Virginia

Designed by Soonyoung Kwon